THE INFERIOR

PEADAR Ó GUILÍN

THE
INFERIOR

EMBER

Text copyright © 2007 by Peadar Ó Guilín
Cover design and illustration: henrysteadman.com

All rights reserved. Published in the United States by Ember, an imprint of Random House Children's Books, a division of Random House, Inc., New York. Published in hardcover in the United States by David Fickling Books, an imprint of Random House Children's Books, a division of Random House, Inc., New York, in 2008. Originally published in Great Britain by David Fickling Books, an imprint of Random House Children's Books, a division of the Random House Group Ltd., London, in 2007.

Ember and the colophon are trademarks of Random House, Inc.

Visit us on the Web! randomhouse.com/teens

Educators and librarians, for a variety of teaching tools,
visit us at randomhouse.com/teachers

The Library of Congress has cataloged the hardcover edition of this
work as follows:
Ó Guilín, Peadar.
The inferior / Peadar Ó Guilín.
p.   cm.
Summary: In a brutal world where hunting and cannibalism are necessary for survival, something is going terribly wrong as even the globes on the roof of the world are fighting, but one young man, influenced by a beautiful and mysterious stranger, begins to envision new possibilities.
ISBN 978-0-385-75145-2 (trade) — ISBN 978-0-385-75146-9 (lib. bdg.)
[1. Cannibalism—Fiction. 2. Hunting—Fiction. 3. Stuttering—Fiction.
4. Science fiction.] I. Title.
PZ7.O363Inf 2008
[Fic]—dc22
2007034496

ISBN 978-0-385-73717-3 (pbk.)

RL: 6.0

Printed in the United States of America

10 9 8 7 6 5 4 3 2 1

First Ember Edition 2011

In memory of my father, James Golden

In that people the most natural and honest of virtues and abilities are alive and vigorous; those same virtues that we have warped and adapted to our own twisted tastes.
—Michel de Montaigne: *On Cannibals*

And they said: "Father, it would hurt less if you would eat us: you dressed us in this miserable flesh, take it off."
—Dante Alighieri, *Inferno*, Canto xxxiii, 60

I.
BR⊕THERS

The rule was to keep running – *Don't stop, don't die.* The Tribe needed its strongest to survive. So Stopmouth fled for his life through the streets of Hairbeast territory, while its non-human inhabitants looked on with indifference. Already the cries of his brother were fading behind him.

'Please, Stopmouth!'

The Armourbacks preferred living prey. When they caught Wallbreaker, they'd drive him home with spears to feed their young. The screams of such captives lasted for days, echoing down streets and over rooftops.

Stopmouth tried not to think about it. 'K-keep running,' he told himself. He leaped barrels of flesh and sprinted into an alley narrow enough to give the pursuers some trouble if they were still on his tail.

Stopmouth realized he couldn't hear his brother any more. He skidded to a halt. The hot air of mid-afternoon

1

stank of blood and rang with the booming howls of fighting or mating Hairbeasts. He could feel his heart battering against his ribs and he leaned his tall frame for support against a crumbling wall. *Don't stop. Don't think. Keep running.* He wiped his stinging eyes and whispered the name, 'Wallbreaker.' Humanity might survive without his brother, but Stopmouth knew he could not. Wallbreaker had always been the darling of the Tribe. He'd been a sweet child, grown up to be a great hunter, and people would forgive him anything, even a half-idiot brother. And they had forgiven always, smiling indulgently through the younger boy's stammers in order to please his handsome sibling.

And yet, if Wallbreaker failed to make it back, Mossheart would have to marry somebody else and that would mean . . . Stopmouth pushed the thought away with a shiver of self-disgust. He forced himself to turn round. He tried to spot his brother, but crowds of burly Hairbeasts blocked his way. The creatures filled the market place with the sharp stink of their fur. They bartered for flesh in high gabbling voices and sometimes the larger males would push against each other, chest to chest, until one gave way.

He shoved sweaty brown hair out of his eyes and marched back the way he'd come. The councillors would be angry if they knew what he was doing. 'Suicide!' they'd cry. 'Waste!' He didn't even have a spear to defend himself, having abandoned it in his flight.

He reached the last place he'd heard his brother's voice: an alley flanked by tall buildings where light from the great Roof struggled to penetrate. He found some traces of blood here, but they were old. Stopmouth tiptoed to the far end, his muscles trembling with exhaustion, his body and loincloth dripping with sweat. Here at last he heard the tones of human speech: a whimpering, pleading voice so unlike that of the great hunter Wallbreaker was becoming.

This can't be my brother, Stopmouth thought.

The alley opened onto a small square, where incomprehensible murals covered the walls with swirls of dried blood. A few Hairbeasts watched curiously as Wallbreaker, his fair hair streaked with filth, retreated before the spears of the Armourbacks. He made no effort to take one of his attackers into death with him. Instead, tears flowed freely down his handsome face, shaming him and his family.

Even as his heart swelled with pity, Stopmouth began having second thoughts about a rescue. How could two humans hope to defeat five Armourbacks? The adults reached chest height on a man, but they were broader, and a rock-hard shell made them tough to kill.

Stopmouth gritted his teeth. He wasn't ready to die, but he refused to let these beasts keep his brother. And he still had time – they preferred live prisoners to quick kills.

He swallowed his fear and jogged back to the mouth of the alley. Then he took a quiet lane running parallel to the one the Armourbacks would probably follow to their territory. He'd need to find a place where he could come out ahead of them. And a plan – he'd need one of those too. He'd have to think one up as he ran.

He passed open doorways where lonely Hairbeast females boomed with song. He leaped old drains and clattered over wider stretches of water on metal bridges. All around him the ancient buildings of the city echoed his footfalls or muffled them in carpets of ragged moss.

Far enough, he thought.

A shaky tower stood nearby with a grey-furred Hairbeast snoozing in its doorway. The creatures were larger than humans and he clipped this one slightly as he jumped over it. He pounded up the stairs, ignoring its bellows. He had no idea what it was saying. All he knew was that the creature was unlikely to break treaty to hunt him.

Three floors later he reached the roof. The surface creaked underfoot and cracks snaked all over it. The whole building looked ready to collapse. Maybe that was a good thing – he might be able to turn the bricks and loose lumps of concrete to his advantage.

Stopmouth walked over the rattling roof to the waist-high wall that bordered it and looked down. Almost immediately he saw his brother's blond head. The Armourbacks pushed him in front of them with jabs of their spears. Humans would have surrounded their prey, but

Armourbacks preferred to drive theirs. Perhaps they feared to leave a desperate enemy within striking distance of their backs.

As the pack moved up the street towards his position, Stopmouth carefully pried rocks away from the wall of the tower. He heaved and strained until a few of the larger ones were balanced on the edge. He wiped sweat from his eyes and tried to ignore the thumping of his heart, which had started up again at the sight of the enemy.

'Come on! Come on!' he whispered. He rarely stuttered when talking to himself.

Wallbreaker passed beneath him. Stopmouth held his breath, waiting for the first Armourback. The moments stretched, measured in beads of sweat and a frantic hammering in his ribcage.

Suddenly a flash of light blazed in the sky above him. Heartbeats later a boom followed that shook Stopmouth's tower and rattled the roof beneath his feet.

The Armourbacks lowered their spears and stared up in what might have been astonishment. But they weren't watching Stopmouth – their eyes, and even the eyes of their prisoner, were fixed on the great Roof above. Stopmouth didn't dare follow their gaze. Whatever was happening up there, he wouldn't let it cost him his brother.

He leaned against the largest of his rocks and sent it plummeting towards the Armourbacks. Before it reached its target he grabbed another and flung it after the first. Just as well: the early attempt missed, but the second smashed an Armourback to the ground and snapped the hind legs of another.

'R-run, Wallbreaker!' he shouted. 'R-r-run!' And Wallbreaker did, finding the energy somewhere. Stopmouth had expected the remaining Armourbacks to pursue his brother or tend to their injured. Instead, he saw them dart into an alley flanking his tower. He knew that they were heading for the ground-floor entrance and that they'd reach it before he did. He paced around the roof, looking for a way down, for another building to jump to. Too far! At best he'd end up in an alley with a broken leg, and treaty or no treaty, any Hairbeast would be well within its rights to claim him for the pot. No, he'd have to make a last stand right here. He grabbed stones for his sling while something clattered up the stairwell towards him. Death was coming. He backed away from the doorway, knowing he couldn't hold them there without a spear.

Moments later the creatures burst onto the roof of the tower. They didn't shout as men might have: if the Armourbacks had speech, the human ear couldn't hear it. They advanced through a hail of slingstones with no apparent discomfort and spread out. Stopmouth had never seen living Armourbacks so close. They had flat faces, mostly made of earth-brown shell with gaps for a pair of red eyes.

'C-come on!' he shouted at them, terrified now. 'W-what are you af-fraid of?' He flung another stone and unsheathed his bone knife. If he could get past one of their spears, he might be able to cut an Armourback between the plates of its shell before they killed him.

One of the creatures charged. The spear-tip tore through Stopmouth's loincloth as he dodged to one side. Another spear flew towards his ribcage and drew a red line there before clattering into the wall. Stopmouth lunged after the weapon, but two Armourbacks herded him off as the third retrieved it.

He backed away until he felt the parapet behind him. He could throw himself over: better a Hairbeast should have him than the Armourbacks.

Suddenly a roaring sound filled the air. Something huge and blazing flew over the heads of the combatants and streaked through the sky to crash into some distant part of the city. The ground shook. The wall behind Stopmouth's back groaned and a hole opened in the tower's roof. Two of his opponents disappeared into it, leaving only a rising cloud of dust to show they'd ever existed. Stopmouth and the last Armourback shared a moment of shock and silence. The human recovered first. He screamed and charged his enemy. The creature dropped its spear and ran back the way it had come.

Stopmouth gave chase. Rubble covered the stairs, and

rocks large enough to kill hurtled past with every step. He charged into daylight and found his enemy already dead beneath fallen masonry.

In the distance a column of flame and dust was rising into the air. Stopmouth looked up. There was nothing to be seen but the Roof of the world and the fading light.

2.
THE V⊕LUNTEERS

Stopmouth reached human territory just as Roofglow faded to the weaker light of evening. 'Hey!' Rockface was on guard in the tower, a big hunter with a bigger voice. 'Heard you were dead! Wallbreaker says he saw them get you!'

The young hunter's spirits lifted with the thought that his brother had made it. But why had Wallbreaker said that he was dead? Had he seen the Armourbacks heading for the tower and kept running instead of attempting a rescue?

'That can't be true,' Stopmouth said to himself. 'It can't.'

He was too tired to think about it now. So he hefted the limbs he'd cut from his kill onto his shoulders and stumbled into friendly territory.

But Rockface hadn't finished with him yet: 'You know, Armourback flesh is a lot lighter if you take the shell off.' Stopmouth felt stupid as the older man laughed, but at least he could use the armour as a plate. Nothing would be wasted.

People murmured greetings as he passed into the many criss-crossing streets that made up his home. 'Man-Ways', it was called; or more often just 'the Ways'. Everyone looked surprised to see him, except for a small boy too young to know better and eager to help with the kill. Gratefully Stopmouth passed over an arm crusted at one end with dried blood, and the pair trudged together to Centre Square, where fires burned and voices rose in song.

The wedding, of course. He'd forgotten. The singing died at his approach. Most of the crowd knew Stopmouth and an excited whispering rose among them. However, no one addressed him until his mother burst from their midst and ran towards him.

'Dearest Stopmouth!' she cried. 'Oh, my Stopmouth!'

He dropped the Armourback flesh and put his arms around her thin frame. He pressed his face into her hair as he'd done as a child and felt warm tears against his neck.

'Wallbreaker said they'd killed you,' she said. 'He himself got three of them. Says he crushed them with rocks, but then the others trapped you in a house and he couldn't get to you.'

Uncles and aunties and cousins now felt able to approach. He tried to smile at them, but his eyes caught on

Wallbreaker emerging from the crowd. He broke away from his mother. He'd never felt so betrayed in all his life.

'Y-y-you . . .' he said. His tongue refused to co-operate and Wallbreaker had all the time in the world to step up to him and hug him close as their mother had done. He whispered directly into Stopmouth's ear. 'Later,' he said. 'Please, brother. I told them what I had to.'

Then Wallbreaker turned to the crowd. His blond hair had been cleaned and threaded with carved bones for the wedding. 'My brother is alive! He's alive!'

The celebrations must have been muted until then, but now everybody cheered. Wallbreaker showed the crowd his fine teeth and a pair of dimples. 'Tonight I marry!' He held up one finger to forestall another cheer. He'd always been good at winning hearts. Many thought he'd be chief some-day. But to Stopmouth's eyes, he was sweating more than usual. He saw a slight shake in his brother's arms that had never been there before. Wallbreaker kept talking. 'You won't be seeing me or my wife tomorrow' – laughter – 'or the day after, or the day after that! But from the fourth day on, I will devote what little energy I have left' – more laughter – 'to finding a bride price for dear Stopmouth!'

The cheers were deafening this time, and now every-body surged forward to hug Stopmouth and kiss him. Even Chief Speareye approached and threw heavily tattooed arms around the young hunter. 'Glad you made it,' he said. 'We can't afford to lose the likes of you! Now, for the love of the ancestors, do as your brother says and find a woman to count your days for you!'

His mother took over and sat him down by a fire. She brought him steaming broth in a Flim-skull bowl.

'Your favourite,' she said.

The smell made his head spin and his mouth fill with saliva. He found his strength barely sufficient to lift the bowl high enough to drink, but the first slurp was delicious and he buried himself in it. Afterwards, when his belly was full and warm, his mother came and took his head onto her lap and the whole world seemed to darken around him.

He woke hours later to the sound of drums. Here and there, little drops of Roofsweat plinked onto the ground or fell hissing into the fires. Nobody noticed; it happened every night when the air grew cooler. He felt a frigid droplet rolling off his face and realized it must have woken him. He'd slept through most of the wedding ceremony.

Delicious smells filled the air. Men from nearby streets were dancing and leaping over cook fires and he knew he should have been with them. Beside him, Uncle Flimnose alternated between rubbing his joints and licking Stopmouth's empty bowl. Flimnose's dancing days were over, the scratches on his Tally – one for every day since his naming – almost beyond counting. The younger man shuddered and looked away. Instead, his eyes wandered over to another fire where his new sister-in-law, Mossheart, held court for the last time among the unmarried girls. Their eyes met and she smiled. He smiled back, his heart a stone in his chest.

'How did you get out of the tower?' asked Flimnose.

'The w-w-walls f-f-f—'

'The walls fell,' said Flimnose.

'The fl-fl—'

'Ah! The flash? You saw that? And something crashed to earth! The Tribe talks of nothing else. Somebody said it was a Globe that fell out of the sky.'

Stopmouth stared at his uncle in astonishment, but the old man grinned, as if to say he didn't believe it either.

The drum beat came to an end and men wandered back from the dance, laughing and wiping sweat from their brows. High above, the Roof lay in darkness except for lines of tiny lights that covered it and allowed a man to see maybe fifty steps around him without a torch.

Uncle Flimnose pointed up at them. 'That's where the spirits have their streets,' he said, 'until room is made for them to come down again as a new species.'

Stopmouth nodded politely and clenched his jaw against the stink of his uncle's rotting teeth. Flimnose had helped teach him and Wallbreaker to be men, but lately hunting parties were reluctant to take him on lest he slow them up. Stopmouth felt sorry for him. There was no fate more cruel than to live beyond usefulness without even realizing it. The younger man remembered all those stories of the Traveller's adventurers they used to share after Father had died. Nobody told them like Uncle Flimnose, and who knew how many tales would be lost when he left to join his ancestors? Stopmouth found he had to turn away. He looked over to where married women toured fires with baskets of sizzling flesh. They chanted in time to the music about how the bride would provide many children, how the groom would feed them, how the children would live. Stopmouth buried his face in a hank of Hairbeast pup so he wouldn't have to look at his uncle and think about the man's fate. But Flimnose wouldn't leave him alone. 'Will you chew some of that flesh for me, young man?' he asked. 'Otherwise I'll be sticking to broth and Roofsweat at my own nephew's wedding!' Stopmouth obliged, feeling ashamed for not offering.

When everyone had eaten their fill, the drums took up again. This time it was the turn of the unmarried women to dance. A murmur of anticipation ran through the men, but Stopmouth turned away. He knew his eyes would only be drawn to his new sister-in-law and he didn't want the others to catch him staring.

Instead, he lay back to watch the lights glittering on the Roof. He imagined the lonely spirits there looking back at him, eager to take his place among the living. As he watched, a Globe floated by overhead, its metal shell glittering with lights of its own. Stopmouth wondered idly if it was a living creature and what its flesh might taste like if he could get close enough to crack it open. Men had harboured such vain hopes for all the generations. And yet, if the rumours were true, at least one of them *had* fallen today. If it hadn't . . . He shivered. The miracle had saved his life – balance for the betrayal of a brother who'd not only abandoned him, but had even claimed Stopmouth's kills as his own. He ground his teeth. He'd expected sorrow for the day of Mossheart and Wallbreaker's wedding. He hadn't expected to be so angry.

'Keep it to yourself, son,' said Mother from where she sat nearby, although he hadn't said a word.

He nodded to reassure her. He was nothing without Wallbreaker. Who else would take him seriously with his lazy tongue? No, he'd find his brother soon after the wedding and tell him he wasn't angry, even if it still burned. And so for the rest of the feast he did his best to join in the laughter and the dancing, clapping to the songs he couldn't sing.

At the end of the night Mother handed Wallbreaker's Tally stick over to Mossheart, who would count his days from now on. Then Wallbreaker took his bride's other hand and led her off to bed in the Wedding Tower. Stopmouth tried to cheer with all the rest and forced a smile when other men slapped him on the back and said, 'Your turn next, boy!'

Mother understood. After the festivities she took him home and put him to bed as if he were still a babe.

Stopmouth shielded his eyes and stared out towards the horizon. There was little to see beyond the human streets as morning mists still rose from the trees in the no-man's-land beyond. Then his gaze was drawn to the Roof as eight Globes swept past, for all the world like a hunting party. He heard shouts from others who were watching too. Old-timers couldn't remember such behaviour from their youth, nor from any legend of the Tribe. Globes were supposed to hang in the sky, or to drift slowly by. Their new speed stirred fear into people's hearts like an augury of disaster.

On the ground, life went on much as it always had. Beasts of various kinds who kept treaty with humans walked the streets. Sometimes they hunted each other or traded for flesh and weapons. Wallbreaker said these creatures should be observed, even the friendly ones.

'S-so m-m-many kinds,' Stopmouth had said the first time they'd talked about it. Back then he'd been barely old enough to have a name.

'Yes, little brother, and I can see it's confusing. But you can never know them well enough. Father would have told you that. Friend or foe, their smells, their strengths, their habits. Study them right and they'll all meet your spear in the end.'

So now Stopmouth watched a pod of Clawfolk skitter down the road on bunches of skinny legs while a multi-coloured Flyer surveyed them greedily from a tower, chewing on flaps of its own dry skin.

Human children played at stalking in the bright light of noon. Their mothers looked on, some anxious, some smiling, while others scolded any child too close to supposedly friendly beasts. Women only carried knives, but their ululations of alarm could pass from street to street over the flat roofs of the buildings until hunters came running from every direction.

Stopmouth was relaxing on the roof of his house while Mother scraped moss away from the parapet with an old shoulder-blade. *Scratch, scratch, scratch.* 'It grows so quickly,' she muttered. *Scratch, scratch.* And nobody liked the way it smelled when the juice hadn't been pounded out of it. 'What a nuisance.' She stopped abruptly at the sight of Uncle Flimnose limping by below.

'I heard he hasn't h-hunted in f-fifty days,' said Stopmouth.

'No,' said Mother, her face formed into that mix of affection and sadness she mostly saved for her younger son. 'Even then, he went with a large party and his spear stayed dry. It won't be long now for him.'

As Flimnose's only surviving female relative and marker of his Tally, Mother alone knew exactly how old he was. She rested a hand on Stopmouth's waist. 'When his time comes, I want you to go with him. For the family. Will you do that?'

'W-what about W-Wallbreaker?'

'Wallbreaker won't go.'

'B-but—'

'Hush,' she said.

Stopmouth hadn't seen his brother in a few days. As promised, Wallbreaker had been spending all his time with his new bride. Stopmouth passed his own nights staring at the ceiling, trying his best not to think about that. During the day he distracted himself with foolish efforts to make spear-points from the Armourback shell he'd brought home with him. Mother's visitors laughed at him for this — bone was so plentiful, so easy to shape, that none could understand why he bothered. 'If it's such good material for a spear,' scoffed Uncle Flimnose, 'why don't the Armourbacks themselves make weapons of it?'

Stopmouth had no answer to this. After an entire quarter day he'd succeeded in rubbing a dent no bigger than a finger-joint into a piece of shell. The rock he'd been using came off worse. Still he worked at it, using the rhythm to send himself into a painless trance where Mossheart and Wallbreaker had never married and his brother hadn't abandoned him.

Mother took her gaze from the street and sighed. 'You'll

have to speak to him sooner or later,' she said, and Stopmouth knew she didn't mean Uncle Flimnose.

He looked into her pale eyes and saw how the skin crinkled with worry at the corners. She must have hated to see her sons at odds. How old was she now? How long before he and Wallbreaker must lose her for ever? He could deny her nothing.

He nodded and left her alone on the roof. He collected a spear and his old bone knife and set out for the rooms Wallbreaker and his bride had taken after they'd left the Wedding Tower. On his way across Centre Square he smelled the sharp stink of Hairbeasts, like a mix of metal and human sweat. Five of the creatures strode by, dressed in what might have passed for finery among them: coloured shells, necklaces of human bones (in honour of their visit?) and their clawed hands dyed red. He knew what it meant and felt a moment's fear for his mother, although she still had many days left, being useful and healthy.

Chief Speareye had turned up to meet the Hairbeast delegation. In spite of the heat radiating from the Roof he wore a fur mantle made from a patchwork of the hides of every creature humans hunted. Four wives accompanied him. *See what a provider I am!* he seemed to say. *I can feed them all and their children too!*

The Tribe's fiercest hunters guarded the chief's party. Wallbreaker stood with them, as did the brute, Crunchfist.

Rockface waited nearby, healed of the wound that had kept him on guard duty. A crowd was gathering to witness the trade and Stopmouth tried to edge through it to the front.

The head of the Hairbeast delegation boomed something at Chief Speareye. Humans couldn't speak Hairbeast, or any language other than their own. Every generation or so, somebody would try to learn some non-human tongue, but of all the ancestors only poor Treatymaker had ever succeeded. However, one word of Hairbeast understood by all was the coughing grunt that signified 'flesh'.

The Hairbeasts made that sound now, one after another. Then their leader placed ten human fingerbones on the ground before Speareye.

'Ten!' shouted Speareye. 'They'll give us ten pups!'

'Yes, and they'll take ten of us in exchange!' yelled a woman in the crowd.

Speareye glared in her direction. 'Anybody who doesn't like to eat can say so now.' He waited, but nobody else objected.

'Do we agree?' shouted Speareye. 'Do we agree to ten?'

The people muttered in assent, even the woman who'd complained. Ten was an unusually large number for the Hairbeasts to ask. Stopmouth wondered if they'd begun a war with one of the species that bordered them – the Armourbacks perhaps. Absurd rumours were flying around that Armourbacks and Hoppers had been seen hunting together. Stopmouth shook his head. Of course that couldn't happen. Creatures would need a common language to co-operate in something as complex as a hunt.

The chief accepted the ten fingerbones, and the Hairbeast delegation turned round and left immediately. The crowd began to disperse, muttering in excitement and fear.

Stopmouth took his chance. 'Wallbreaker!'

'Stopmouth!' His brother seemed uncomfortable. He kept scratching his ribs as if they itched terribly. 'It's good to see you. Don't think I've been avoiding you – you'll know what I mean when you're wed yourself someday!' He winked, but the lie hurt anyway. Besides, what Wallbreaker and Mossheart got up to was the last thing Stopmouth wanted to think about.

'We need to talk.'

'You're angry at me,' said Wallbreaker. He was still keeping the palm of his left hand over his ribs. 'You forget to stutter when you want to kill me.'

'I d-don't!'

'Look' – Wallbreaker gripped him by the arm – 'I really thought you were dead, all right?' At last, the truth. 'I saw them follow you into the tower and I hadn't a scrap of strength left in me. I'd have been worse than useless to you. But I've big plans to make it up to you, all right?'

'N-no n-need! I f-forgive—'

21

Just at that moment a careless group of people departing the gathering bumped into the brothers. They knocked Wallbreaker's left hand away from his ribs, revealing the new tattoo that had been placed there. Only the chief could award tattoos, and only for outstanding bravery. This one showed three Armourbacks being crushed by a rock. Wallbreaker caught Stopmouth staring and folded his arms again to cover the tattoo.

'I'll make it up to you,' he whispered. Quickly he turned away, and Stopmouth saw scars from Armourback spear-points dotted around his spine. He was headed for the chief's house, where the tattooed warriors would be holding the flesh meeting. They'd never let Stopmouth in. So he wandered home, angry all over again, and set to work at more mindless rubbing of the Armourback shell. He kept working after dark, unable to sleep, with only the cook fire for company. But his hands were tired now, even if his mind was not. The shell slipped from his fingers and into the flames. He cursed and poked it out again with a stick. But his cursing changed to laughter as soon as he got back to work. He laughed so loudly he woke his mother with it. 'What's wrong, son?' she asked. 'I see you smile for the first time in days!'

'F-fire!' he said. He held up a piece of brown shell as large as his hand. One end of it had been worn away to a perfect point.

Most people got nervous on the night of a flesh meeting. They tossed in their sleep and in waking hours regretted enmities made with the tattooed hunters who could vote. Stopmouth was no different. He worried for Mother in spite of her obvious vigour. He'd heard from some of the women who'd seen her Tally stick that she wasn't that old. But youth was never sufficient protection. All must be able to serve the Tribe, either in life or death. So, knowing he wouldn't sleep anyway, he decided to keep working on his new spear-tips. He finally had the knack of it and made good progress.

By now, frequent handling of the blades had cut a grid of streets into his palms. He cursed as the larger piece of shell caught him again and again. However, eventually he succeeded in melting the tips onto a pair of straight shafts that Wallbreaker had given him for his first hunt. He still didn't understand why the Armourbacks wouldn't use their own shell for tools. But they were known for a fear of fire, so perhaps it wasn't so strange after all.

At last Stopmouth fell asleep gazing at the finished product, overcome by the beauty of the leaf-shaped blades. All thoughts of the flesh meeting, his fears for his mother, sank with him into the darkness.

Thousands of charcoal drawings blackened the houses on Centre Square in the spaces between skulls and other trophies. And there was soot too, from the fires where people came to cook and tell the stories of the Tribe. These twelve buildings, three-storeyed and spacious, had seen John Spearmaker lift the first weapon. The sounds of the Traveller's farewell speech had passed through their curtained doorways, soaking into the very walls that yet other Heroes had given their lives to defend. The Tribe, whose heart this place was, had come again to fill it with life. Children watched from every rooftop or squabbled for a spot on the ancient fountain at the very centre.

Chief Speareye's wives had spread word of a Choosing. Extra guards manned the towers, but almost all the rest of the Tribe – perhaps as many as three thousand human beings – had turned up. Some people wouldn't come, of course; would prefer to bring shame on their families by hiding. Sweat beaded many a brow, and tense speculations passed from mouth to mouth. People jostled and hugged their families close. Speareye climbed onto a platform made of hide and bones that had been set up outside his home. He swept back the patched mantle to reveal a torso of wild tattoos. Each represented an act of greatness in the story of his life. Speareye still hunted better than any of his rivals, but men whispered that his arm was slowing. They said he was grooming his son Waterjumper to take over. The boy, born a few hundred days before Stopmouth, stood awkwardly at his father's side. He had yet to make a first kill, but his frame was filling out and already he had begun to take on the look of his father.

Nearby, tattooed hunters waited in case of need, all standing close to the platform. As Stopmouth pressed forward, he spotted Wallbreaker among them as well as the frightening Crunchfist, who was said to love Choosings and looked forward to them eagerly.

'My people,' cried Speareye. He recited the meaningless ritual, as every chief had before him, winning instant silence. 'I need ten of you to come forward now so that the rest of us can make it Home. Who will act to spare the Tribe?'

'I will.' Stopmouth knew the speaker. Everyone had said Bonefire would volunteer this time. She no longer had a husband and her last son had disappeared during a recent hunt. Her daughter's man had been feeding her, but with another baby on the way . . . People applauded and here and there muttered the formula: 'How brave! She still had a thousand days in her!'

Bonefire stepped through the crowd and climbed onto the platform. She accepted Speareye's kiss and the kisses of others who would miss her. Two more widows followed her into honour, along with a hunter whose broken leg had never healed properly. His young wife tried to stop him, screaming all the while. But the man limped onwards while others kept her back until she lapsed into helpless sobs.

'We need six more, my people!' shouted the chief. No one offered themselves. He seemed disappointed. The crowd grew restless. Some people looked around, others kept their heads down. Here and there, little groups hissed and argued. Stopmouth saw one frail woman being pulled in two directions by a family tug-of-war which ended with her staying put. Finally Speareye snapped his fingers. Hunters pushed into the crowd and grabbed several people. All were old or injured and all had been chosen at the flesh meeting the evening before.

'I can still hunt!' screamed one old man. It was Uncle Flimnose. Tears poured down his face, shaming the whole family. Stopmouth winced. The old man shouldn't be crying, he should have known; Mother would have told him. The Tribe didn't care how old a hunter was so long as his spear drank often. But the women who counted a man's days knew by his Tally when his arms would start to weaken. It was their duty to help him leave the world with dignity and honour.

Some of those who knew Flimnose patted him in sympathy, but most looked away in disgust. Crunchfist barged through the crowd, a big smile on his face. He grabbed the wailing Flimnose by the hair and dragged him to the front.

Now there were ten 'volunteers' whose Tally sticks would be stored in the House of Honour.

'Let's pick the escort,' cried Speareye.

It was an easy mission, though a grave one: a simple exchange of loved ones for food. Stopmouth stepped forward as his mother had asked. Four other hunters joined him: Waterjumper, son of the chief and not much older than himself; Linebrow and Burnthouse, two men of middle age and experience; and Rockface, who would lead.

The volunteers and escorts ate a meal together of dried Clawfolk flesh. Stopmouth offered to chew Uncle Flimnose's for him but the old man refused to eat. Then, with those who could walk supporting the others, they set out for the Hairbeast district while the rest of the Tribe looked on in relieved, respectful silence.

Stopmouth spotted his mother at the edge of the crowd. He cut his thumb and carefully flicked a drop of blood towards her. She smiled. 'Your blood has come back to me,' she said, her face proud, 'and so will you.' People nearby nodded approvingly at the old ritual.

The first leg of the journey took the party to the perimeter of Man-Ways. They trudged down one of the four great streets leading from the square, past crumbling houses that leaned one against the other for support. Most were empty, their only visitors patrols and naughty children searching for ancient spearheads and scraps of rotted hides.

When the group passed the towers, guards peered down to see who'd volunteered.

And others were watching too. In many areas of the city the streets were made of water – Wetlanes, people called them. Blurred shapes waited beneath the surface, shapes that lived in a world every bit as competitive as the one above, and would pull a human under, given the chance. Beyond a metal bridge lay no-man's-land. This was a wilderness between territories. Roads and knee-high walls slept here under blankets of thick moss, while fast-growing saplings defied human efforts to keep the area free of cover for hungry enemies.

Stopmouth's heart beat faster. He'd come back this way less than ten days before when the Armourbacks had almost caught him. He had to work hard to control his terror, wondering if more experienced hunters ever felt the same or were just better at covering it.

Soon, red and purple branches arched overhead to block the light and a thousand tiny mossbeasts buzzed around every member of the party.

As they approached the Hairbeast district, Uncle Flimnose began to wail again and tried to hang back. Rockface frowned and shook his big head.

'P-p-please, Uncle!' Stopmouth whispered.

'You just pray to the ancestors you never get old! So

proud with your Armourback spear. Just you wait! I held you on my knee, I fed you and—'

'Oh, hush!' said Bonefire, the first volunteer. She was a tall, spindly woman and didn't have much flesh on her. But the Hairbeasts wouldn't mind: they prized human marrow above all other delicacies and would swap pups to get it. Sometimes they would even trade the flesh of rare and distant beasts that humans had never seen living.

'That boy can't be more than five thousand days old,' Bonefire continued. 'We had our chance. Let the young have theirs.'

The party stopped within sight of the first Hairbeast guard tower. 'Strange,' said Rockface. He shielded his eyes with one heavily tattooed hand. 'I don't see any sentinels.'

They advanced more cautiously. No Hairbeast walked in the first laneways of the district, but in the distance, great booming cries could be heard.

'Never seen this before,' said Linebrow, one of the other hunters. He was perhaps two thousand days older than Stopmouth. He had few tattoos, but a scar ran the length of his face, driving a wedge across the bridge of his nose. Rockface waved his spear at Stopmouth and Waterjumper, the youngest members of the party. 'You two, move to the front! Use those sharp eyes of yours, hey? Waterjumper, if you see anything, call out. Stopmouth can't always get his voice working.'

The streets stayed empty and the party's nervousness grew. Everywhere, barrels lay overturned; pots of blood waited under half-finished murals. In one house they spotted a few mewling pups, without adults to look after them. The younger ones lacked fur entirely and still walked on all fours.

'We should take those pups now and run for it,' said Waterjumper.

Rockface laughed at him. 'And what if one of the Hairbeasts saw us, Little Chief? Are you going to put the treaty back together when nobody can even speak to them?' The hunter with the scarred nose sniggered too. Waterjumper blushed.

The booming sounds of Hairbeasts drew closer. Two large males ran past them. One of the creatures had blood streaming from its fur. They ignored the humans completely.

A few minutes later the hunters entered one side of a small square at about the same time as four brown-shelled Armourbacks entered the other, their red eyes glittering. Both parties came to a halt. Five human warriors versus four Armourbacks put the odds only slightly in the beasts' favour. Normally two well-matched groups would leave each other alone. Better to hunt weaker prey than risk heavy casualties, only to end up with more flesh than they could carry home.

However, something strange was happening in the Hairbeast district that day, and all the hunters knew it.

Fear grew in Stopmouth's belly. Only luck had saved him in his last encounter with these creatures and he didn't want to fight them again. But it shouldn't come to that. The Armourbacks probably wouldn't recognize the volunteers as non-combatants and would think themselves heavily out-numbered. They might run away. But, to Stopmouth's dismay, Rockface lacked the ability to see things from a beast's point of view.

'Volunteers!' he said. 'Stay back, hey? Go into the laneway we just left. Stopmouth and Waterjumper, take the edges. Linebrow, Burnthouse, keep with me. Aim for the joints. If you get behind one, strike at the base of the neck. They hate that.'

The hunters formed themselves into a line and stepped across to the middle of the square, where their longer reach could be used to best advantage. The four beasts got their backs to a wall, but instead of edging away, as Stopmouth had hoped, they gripped their spears and charged, con-centrating their attack on the centre of the human formation.

Linebrow's spear snapped against Armourback shell. He had no such defence of his own and he cried out in terror and then pain, folding onto the ground like a dropped blanket. Rockface's weapon broke too, but he swayed aside at the last moment and used his knife to slice his attacker's throat.

At the edges of the line Stopmouth and Waterjumper escaped the charge by leaping away and keeping their distance. But when the three surviving enemies pulled back, Linebrow was beyond help and Burnthouse's right arm dangled at his side. He fell onto his behind, staring at his useless limb.

Rockface patted him on the back and took his spear for himself. 'We can win, boys,' he said. He had a manic grin on his face. He knelt next to the Armourback he'd killed and popped an eyeball free. He waved it at the enemy before eating it. 'I'll eat you too!' he shouted, and to Stopmouth's amazement, he laughed. The pause in the fighting had given the young man's terror a chance to grow. His palms sweated on the shaft of his spear. He knew that if they stayed here, they'd die, and that he himself could escape only if he ran.

Too late. The Armourbacks were charging again. Stopmouth braced his spear against the ground and tried to aim the tip towards the neck joint of his attacker. His weapon hit armour instead. To his surprise, it crunched straight through the beast's shell and stopped it dead. The creature's arms twitched so fast they seemed to blur. And then it dropped, taking his spear with it. He tried to pull it free and panicked when the shaft came loose without the tip. But the other beasts seemed to have forgotten about him. Nearby, Waterjumper sat with bloody hands over his stomach and a look of surprise on his face. Only Rockface was still fighting. The two remaining Armourbacks had backed him into a corner and jabbed at him almost playfully.

With shaking hands, Stopmouth unhooked his sling and grabbed a few stones. He aimed for the base of the neck. *Crack!* A perfect hit! One of the creatures dropped soundlessly. His next missile hit shell instead, but now the last Armourback knew he was there, and when it half turned towards him, Rockface shoved a dagger deep into its neck.

'Good boy!' he shouted. 'They hate someone at their backs! They hate it!' Then he saw the first Armourback, which Stopmouth had killed by punching straight through its armour.

'How?' he asked.

'Th-the s-spear-p-p-point. Sh-sh-shell.'

'Speak plainly, boy.'

'Ar-Armourback sh-shell. I m-made it f-f-from—'

'Never mind,' said Rockface. 'You can tell me later.'

Rockface walked over to the wall where Waterjumper and Burnthouse sat side by side in the dust. Waterjumper groaned and held his hands over his belly.

'Let's have a look there, Little Chief,' said Rockface. He tried to pry Waterjumper's hands away from the wound. The boy resisted but had no strength. 'It's not as bad as you think, Little Chief. Don't look at it, hey? I want you to watch the Roof while I bind it. Tell us if you see any Globes.'

Without warning Rockface plunged his knife into Waterjumper's left eye. The boy twitched once and relaxed.

'I don't need any help like that,' said Burnthouse weakly. He'd pulled moss from the wall of the building behind him to stem the bleeding in his arm.

'You'll hunt again, Burnthouse. Your wife will keep marking your Tally so long as we can get you home. What are you doing, Stopmouth? Get over here, boy.'

'A m-minute.' Stopmouth had been slicing fragments of shell from dead Armourbacks. He wrapped all he could carry in Linebrow's loincloth. The poor man wouldn't be needing it now.

Just then the hunters heard sounds of running feet. Before they could react, a dozen Hairbeasts loped into the square. They carried clubs with rocks tied to the ends – a good weapon for fighting Armourbacks if you were as large as they. Blood matted their fur. They boomed and hooted at the humans. One of them approached Rockface, bellowing their word for flesh. It butted him out of the way with its chest. Then it threw Waterjumper's body over its shoulder

34

and loped off. Others stepped forward to claim Linebrow and, shockingly, the Armourback corpses too. Then they were gone again, running down the alleyway from which the humans had emerged.

'It seems,' said Burnthouse, 'the Hairbeasts are no longer at peace with the Armourbacks.'

'Or with us,' said Rockface. 'They took our kills too. Let's get out of here.'

'Wait,' said Burnthouse as Stopmouth helped him to his feet. 'We need to know what's going on. The Hairbeasts didn't seem too worried about the treaty. That's not like them.'

'S-scared,' said Stopmouth.

'What are you scared of, boy?' asked Rockface. 'We won, didn't we?'

'N-n-no, th-th—'

'He means the Hairbeasts,' said Burnthouse. His arm seemed to be causing him great pain. 'Those big hairies were terrified. And so am I! I've changed my mind about finding the cause. Just get me home.'

They went back to the alleyway where they'd left the volunteers, but found only blood and signs of a struggle. They could easily have tracked the trail leading away from the scene but knew that it was too late for the volunteers now anyway. The Tribe had to be told what was going on.

In the distance the men could hear a roar, as if giant

hunting parties were clashing with each other. They ran until they came to a crossroads less than five hundred paces from the empty zone between human and Hairbeast territory. At the end of one of the roads they saw a group of Armourbacks and grey-furred Hoppers surround some Hairbeasts and spear them to death. The three men had heard rumours of this. But who could believe such a thing? It was as if two distinct races, Armourbacks and Hoppers, had found a way to talk to one another and had planned an invasion of the district together. Impossible and shocking.

The humans hurried on, hoping they hadn't been seen. They reached no-man's-land near the crossing over the Wetlane. A guard waved frantically at them from the first tower. Stopmouth turned to look. Two hundred paces behind them, a troop of Hoppers burst from between buildings and approached at great speed. Powerful hind legs drove the creatures forward at twice the length of a man with every leap. Grey fur streamed behind them and long arms were constantly moving to keep them balanced. They were not strong, these beasts, but no faster creature lived in the city and few were more dangerous on open ground. Frantically Stopmouth and Rockface reached for weapons while the injured Burnthouse stumbled on alone. 'Sling first!' said Rockface over the high, excited cries of their enemies. 'We'll get a shot in!' And they did, both stones finding their mark on the lead Hopper, which fell back. Its fall tripped two others while the rest leaped over the pile-up and came on at speed. Their human-like hands held short stabbing spears; their little eyes glinted.

Stopmouth heard a horn blowing back at the guard tower. Shouts told him his people were coming. Too late, too late! Rockface flung his spear when the Hoppers were no more than twenty paces away. He wounded one and knocked another off balance so that its next hop took it into the Wetlane. It screamed in a high voice as the water around it thrashed and turned red. Another Hopper leaped at Stopmouth. He managed to push its spear aside with one hand while the creature's momentum carried it onto his dagger. The impact knocked him from his feet and pinned him under his enemy. He felt its hot breath wet against his face and heard thuds as more of its companions landed on the bridge.

I'm dead, thought Stopmouth. This time I'm dead. Nearby he heard laughter, then shouts and running feet.

The Hopper's corpse was lifted away. He blinked up at the face of Chief Speareye.

'Where's Waterjumper?' said the chief. 'Where's my son?'

3.

MOSSHEART

Stopmouth's tattoo itched at him even now, five days later. It was well drawn, though, everybody said so. It showed his spear punching through the front of an Armourback and out the other side.

'You'll have a dozen soon enough!' said Rockface, slapping him hard across the shoulders. Privately Stopmouth would have traded any tattoo to avoid the terror he'd been through. Even so, for the first time in his life boys his age showed him honour while Brighttooth, Treeneck and Cleareye all smiled at him without mockery. His tongue got in the way of his half-hearted flirting, but no matter; the woman he really wanted lived in his brother's house now.

Rockface had emerged from the battle with his knife plastered in gore and Hopper blood dripping from his teeth. Stopmouth had even heard him laughing during the fight. He laughed more when the girls admired his tattoos. 'I'll be hunting again soon,' he said.

'Already?' asked one.

'For another wife!' he shouted, and to everyone's delight grabbed her up in a hug.

Stopmouth slipped away.

Three tenths later, as Rooflight was dimming, he carried a hunk of Hopper liver up onto the roof of the house he shared with his mother. The air was beginning to cool and the streets were quiet apart from a few Flyers perched on a deserted building. They squawked and tore dried-out flaps of brightly coloured skin from each other's backs, huge dark eyes blinking quickly. Sometimes one would snap its long snout at another, hissing between a thousand pin-like teeth before settling back to the never-ending business of mutual grooming.

Stopmouth had noticed a lot of the creatures about lately. But he wasn't too worried as they kept treaty with humans, who prized their moulted skin for decoration. Still, he watched them closely, remembering Wallbreaker's advice to study beasts at every opportunity. For a while one of the creatures gazed back, studying him in return perhaps.

Mother poked her greying head up through the skylight.

'Stopmouth?' she said. 'We have . . . you have a visitor. It's Mossheart.' She fixed him with a worried gaze, but he waved to show he'd be OK. She nodded, trusting him to keep his feelings to himself.

Mossheart came up quietly and didn't hug him as she used to. When Stopmouth bit off a piece of liver for her, she refused it with a sad smile. 'You know I'm married, Stopmouth.'

He knew it. But she didn't seem to know it herself. Her round face looked drawn and her gaze lacked the sparkle that had thrilled him, even as a child. He pushed the piece of liver towards her again. 'F-family,' he said.

'You're right.' She sounded relieved. 'We're family now.' She took the flesh with trembling hands and ate it quickly. When he offered her more, she took that too until the whole liver was gone, leaving Stopmouth to lick the juice from his fingers. His heart ached as he watched her. How often had he imagined those slender hands entwined with his own? And her lips . . . He knew they were soft. He still cherished the day she'd grown overly excited about something and kissed him on the cheek. He'd never forgotten it.

'Thank you, Stopmouth,' she said. 'Thank you so much. I think . . . I think I am with child.'

Stopmouth nodded and kept his eyes on the horizon. He should congratulate her. He hoped she'd think his stutter prevented him from doing so, but she knew him too well. She bowed her head and for a moment there was silence between them, each looking out over the city. Around them the Ways was settling down for the night. Buildings cooled, walls audibly creaking like the groans of a

40

wounded hunter settling to the ground. Cook fires danced shadows along the four main streets that met at Centre Square, while delicious aromas hunted for noses through windows and up stairwells. Stopmouth's tummy rumbled. Yet he felt no hunger.

'You're so like him,' Mossheart said at last. 'Only he talks more, of course. Always nattering about this or that. If he were here now – you know how he goes on! He'd be talking about the lights in the Roof or even this house. "Who made this city for us?" he'd say. "How did we come to live here?" '

Stopmouth smiled despite himself. His brother had asked those very questions many times and had invented any number of fantastical explanations. It was part of the reason he loved Wallbreaker so fiercely. It was why the Tribe needed him.

Mossheart tugged at her lovely hair, tied back now that she was a woman.

'I wanted to ask you a favour,' she said. 'My husband . . . Well, I don't know if he's always been like this. I thought you might tell me . . . But he doesn't sleep much now. Always pacing. Or if he does sleep, he wakes covered in sweat and he stares at me as if . . . as if he doesn't know me.'

She began to cry. Stopmouth put his arm around her, but she shrugged him off like any other married woman would have done. And then, as the nearby Flyers finished their squabble and took off into the sky, she told him the terrible thing.

'He hasn't . . . Wallbreaker hasn't hunted since our wedding.'

Stopmouth had guessed as much, but having Mossheart put words to his fears shook him badly. He worked it out. *Twenty days.* Hunting parties were needed all the time to keep the people fed. Tattoo or no tattoo, if Wallbreaker left it any longer, he'd be volunteered to the next beast delegation that came trading for flesh. His child – Mossheart's child – would be an orphan and might even end up the same way as its father. Unless, of course, Mossheart were to remarry. For a moment Stopmouth gave in to the temptation of that thought. But he pulled himself out of it by smacking his fist into the parapet. Wallbreaker would be dead. In spite of the recent betrayal, Stopmouth couldn't bear that. He knew Wallbreaker hadn't done it to hurt him. All his life his brother had protected him from the bullies who'd mocked his speech. He'd kept Stopmouth alive through his first hunt, and when their father had volunteered to feed the Clawfolk, it was Wallbreaker who'd explained why it was such an honour for the family before bursting into tears himself.

'I w-will take him h-hunting,' said Stopmouth.

Mossheart smiled at last and wiped her tears away. 'Thank you, dear Stopmouth. I know you cannot take him to the Hairbeast district with all the strange goings-on there. But a hunting party is setting out for Clawfolk territory the day after tomorrow. They would be glad to have two heroes join them.'

Stopmouth blushed.

'It would do you no harm either to start building up a bride price for yourself.'

He bit his lip.

'No, listen, Stopmouth. You can't stay a boy for ever. I had a friend when I was unmarried. Brighttooth. You know Brighttooth, don't you?'

Stopmouth knew her and she wasn't Mossheart. He shook his head and guided Mossheart firmly to the stairway. He assured her before she left that he'd take Wallbreaker hunting with the others in two days' time.

Afterwards he paced around the roof for an hour. Then he took out some Armourback shell and set to work replacing the spear he'd left behind in Hairbeast-Ways.

Stopmouth went to watch some of the tattooed men – some of the *other* tattooed men! – sparring in Centre Square. Their feet shuffled clouds of dust into the air which plastered itself to their sweaty skin. He saw Wallbreaker twirling his spear twice before tapping Roughnose – a man with seven tattoos – on the leg. As he skipped free, he caught his opponent again on the neck. Roughnose laughed and Stopmouth found himself smiling too. No one ever got near his brother. No one ever had. He had muscles faster than slingstones and a mind agile enough to use them. People said he'd finish his life with so many tattoos they'd need to put some on his tongue to find room.

In thirty hunts, no creature had so much as scratched him. Not until the Armourbacks caught him that day in the Hairbeast district.

The men punched shoulders after their bout. Both smiled, but Wallbreaker's joy died on seeing Stopmouth. He approached anyway.

'Come to my house, brother.'

They walked in silence down a mossy path between buildings where Clawfolk chittered as they finished off a wounded Flyer. Normally the men would have stayed to watch. Instead, they stepped into a sturdy little house jammed between larger buildings. Wallbreaker and his wife had it all to themselves.

'Mossheart's off pounding moss with the other married women,' said Wallbreaker.

He didn't offer Stopmouth any refreshment, nor did he invite him onto the roof. Instead, he kicked a few Flim hides into the far corner of the room beside a pair of Tally sticks. One of them must have been Wallbreaker's own, where his age was marked for him every day by a faithful and loving wife. Trophies of every kind – skulls, bones, shells – stared down from the walls. Best of all was the complete head of a Bloodskin dipped in berry juice to preserve it. Wallbreaker had won all these himself, but none recently. When he turned to face Stopmouth, his eyes were hard.

'Mossheart confessed.'

'C-con—?'

'We don't need your charity, Stopmouth. You're supposed to take care of Mother now.'

'I c-can t-take—'

'And you need to start raising a bride price so you can get a wife.' He paused to look Stopmouth in the eye. 'Your own wife.'

Stopmouth felt his mouth go dry. The two brothers, who discussed everything, had never argued over Mossheart. They both wanted her, but knew there could only ever be one winner and who that winner must be. Wallbreaker had never been triumphalist about it before now, or cruel. So it took a dozen heartbeats for his words to sink in. Then Stopmouth nodded and turned to go.

'Wait!'

Stopmouth felt hands on his shoulders. He tried to shrug them off, but Wallbreaker was stronger and he pulled Stopmouth into an embrace.

'I'm sorry. So sorry, brother.' The embrace grew firmer. 'I don't know why I left you that day. All I could think of was their spears in my back – the thought of their beaks in my skin, tearing me apart while I lived.' Stopmouth felt his brother shudder. 'I fled. I didn't see they'd chased you and . . . I'm sorry – I didn't care; I – I wasn't *able* to care. I just ran and didn't stop shaking for two tenths after I got home. I'd never abandon you, Stopmouth. Never. I swear it.'

Stopmouth felt the hug grow tighter and eventually he let his body grow limp. He knew he had his brother back and the world made sense again. When he could trust himself to speak, he said, 'You n-need to h-hunt.'

Wallbreaker took a deep breath. 'We'll discuss this next time, brother.' He no longer seemed so keen to keep Stopmouth from leaving, but the younger brother wouldn't be put off.

'D-day after t-t-tomorrow. W-we're g-going.'

'We'll see,' said Wallbreaker.

Stopmouth shook his head. 'D-day after tomorrow or v-v-volunteer.'

Wallbreaker stared at Stopmouth as if the thought had never occurred to him that the great Wallbreaker, future hero of the Tribe, could be asked to volunteer. Finally he nodded, but the terror in his eyes was unmistakable.

4.

THE BLⵙⵙDSKIN RAID

The mist of morning had just started to clear. People were gathering in Centre Square to hear talk of the strange and sinister happenings in Hairbeast-Ways. Mothers dandled children in the shade of skull-covered buildings while young men – making sure the unmarried girls could see them – jostled each other and pushed forward through the blackened sticks and bones of old fires towards the platform. More experienced hunters with families chafed at being kept away from the never-ending quest for prey. Still, they too were worried. Their task had become even harder now that a whole territory seemed closed to them.

Chief Speareye projected an air of calm. He smiled at his people and waved them silent. But just as he opened his mouth to speak, a great *whoosh* filled the air. Under the Roof, two formations of Globes swept towards each other from opposite ends of the world. Fire and beams of light leaped between them and the crowd cried out in surprise and no little worry at the ferocity of the hunt. Stopmouth felt his jaw go slack – this must have happened the day he'd saved Wallbreaker from the Armourbacks. A sight such as this had distracted his enemies.

One of the Globes suddenly spun higher and exploded. A heartbeat later the watching humans heard the sound of it and saw a huge, perfectly square section of the sky turn black. Beams of light licked out from the other Globes until more of them burst into flames and fragments hurtled down upon the world. Nobody moved until a piece of metal the size of a head landed on a boy in the middle of the crowd, and suddenly everyone was screaming and running for shelter even as the earth rocked with further impacts. More pieces rained down on the Ways, rattling against the roofs of houses, bringing wails from terrified children. A fragment the size of five men plunged into a Wetlane and sent clouds of steam over the tops of the guard towers.

Finally one of the Globe formations fled towards a far section of the Roof. The other followed and soon the air was free of them again. Only one human had died, but it was a full tenth before any of them crept out from their shelters.

Night fell and grids of tiny tracklights on the Roof cast the world into shadow. Fires of moss and bone flickered all over Centre Square and hissed under drops of Roofsweat. On the largest roasted the body of the boy who'd died when the Globes fought. Relatives and friends of the family sat around the other fires in sombre mood while the smell filled their eyes with tears and their mouths with saliva.

For once Wallbreaker wasn't talking much. He'd found a piece of metal from the battle as big as two hands. He poked at it with slivers of bone and bashed at it with rocks. Nobody else wanted the stuff, except for one of Speareye's wives, who'd wound fragments of it into her hair to catch the firelight. Stopmouth expected others to follow her lead within days.

Wallbreaker kept pounding at his prize until a finger-sized piece came away to reveal a dozen strands of metal hair underneath. He didn't notice that Mossheart seemed to be losing patience with his investigations. She caught Stopmouth's eye.

Stopmouth nodded back. He knew what she wanted.

'Wallbreaker?'

'Yes, Stopmouth.' *Clunk!*

'R-r-remember, tomorrow w-we h-hunt?'

Wallbreaker was still pounding at the metal and mightn't have heard. Stopmouth opened his mouth to speak again, but just then the hunter, Roofhead, approached their fire with a shell-plate full of steaming meat. The man kept his composure as he offered the food around. Each person whispered a word of condolence before taking a token sliver of the dead boy's flesh. Most would be left for what remained of the family.

Roofhead thanked them and moved on.

Stopmouth tried again: 'W-Wallbreaker?'

At that moment Wallbreaker gasped. 'Look! Mossheart, Stopmouth, look!' He held the metal he'd been working on up to the firelight.

'I don't see anything special,' said Mossheart.

'Oh, but it *is* special!' said Wallbreaker. 'Watch this. Watch it carefully.'

He hit the metal with a rock. A small piece came away but remained attached to the rest by a few delicate, silver hairs. Wallbreaker pushed the fragment back into its original position. 'Look now!' he said. They did. Stopmouth stared and stared, but saw no difference.

'Nothing happened,' said Mother, though she smiled fondly as she spoke.

'Nothing?' asked Wallbreaker. He turned the piece of metal upside down and shook it for all he was worth. 'Where is it then? Where's the piece I broke off?'

Sure enough, the fragment had moulded itself back into its original position with no sign of a break. 'I-it h-healed itself,' said Stopmouth. 'Just like a broken bone did sometimes, but quick and clean!' The whole family laughed together as they hadn't done in tens of days. They all scrabbled around for pieces of metal of their own, stopping only when Speareye's youngest wife, Housear, stood up to perform the funeral ceremony.

She was pregnant, of course: pregnant women carried out all the Tribe's sacred rituals. When other women pounded moss for clothing, they were the ones to lead the time-keeping chants. When a man needed luck, a gift to a pregnant woman might persuade her to draw charcoal pictures of Armourbacks or Flims with his spear in their bellies, or, in extreme cases, she might call on one of the great ancestors to possess the hunter in his hour of need. Mossheart would be able to do the same when she started to show. She would also be one of those who confirmed the names of children old enough to have acquired them. The child's mother would then have to keep track of its age on a new Tally stick.

Housear cleared her throat and opened her mouth to speak. But no words emerged. Instead, her eyes widened. Everybody turned to see a large group of Hairbeasts shuffling into Centre Square. Stopmouth counted fifteen adults walking upright and as many pups on all fours. The adults carried clubs and sacks of what must have been flesh. Some of them limped or had arms in slings.

Muttering arose among the humans. Fearful talk. Speareye stood and approached the creatures. 'Flesh!' he said. 'Flesh?'

They ignored him. He shrugged and turned back to the

mourners. 'I think, friends, the Hairbeasts are all but extinct. Why these last ones have come here, I don't know. Surely they realize we cannot keep treaty with them now. We'll wait until they sleep and fall upon them then.'

'No,' said Wallbreaker. Stopmouth blinked in surprise.

'No?' Speareye's voice had turned cold. 'Do you challenge my authority?'

'I do not,' said Wallbreaker. He stood to match height with the chief. Gone was the haunted look he'd worn since his wedding, to be replaced by another that Stopmouth knew well: obsession with a mad idea. Even the ancestors, looking down from their grid of campfires above, must have wondered what he'd come out with this time.

'I will bow to whatever decision you make, Chief. I will be the first to leap when you give orders. But, please, as the most loyal member of your people, let me point out some things you might not have thought of in your haste to do the right thing for your Tribe.'

Many in the crowd grinned and Speareye laughed out loud. 'Don't think I can't see you working your spell on me, Wallbreaker! But I will hear you out.'

'We all know the world is not as it should be,' said Wallbreaker. 'Almost every night the Roof lights up with Globes hunting one another. And now this: the terrible destruction of the Hairbeasts.'

'What's so terrible?' shouted Rockface from nearby. 'Peoples disappear all the time, hey? They get wiped out and a new species takes their place. Good eating, I say!'

A murmur of approval greeted his words, but Chief Speareye neither nodded nor spoke.

'This is different,' Wallbreaker continued, 'as you should know, Rockface, with that new tattoo of yours! The Hairbeasts are no weaklings like the Flims. The Hairbeasts have been our neighbours for a long time. They were a good match for the Armourbacks and a welcome buffer against them. Something terrible must have happened for such a strong people to fall so quickly.'

Everywhere hunters nodded.

'The Hairbeasts lost,' he went on, 'because the Armourbacks and the Hoppers attacked them *together*. They *co-operated*. Think about that. The Armourbacks, if they can speak at all, do so without voices – with smells maybe, or signs. The Hoppers, on the other hand, talk in squeaks.' Stopmouth smiled to himself. This was another of his brother's favourite topics.

'But even we and the Hairbeasts, who both have voices, have never been able to understand more than one, maybe two words in each other's language. Even after poor Treatymaker spent half his life with them! Co-operation is impossible between us.'

Speareye laughed. 'You're only proving my point, young

Wallbreaker. What use are these Hairbeasts if they won't work with us?'

Wallbreaker shook his head and lowered his voice to force the spectators to listen. 'If the Armourbacks and the Hoppers have destroyed the Hairbeasts by working together, who do you think is next?'

This thought had been on everybody's mind, but few had spoken it aloud.

'But why would they destroy *us*?' cried Speareye. 'There's only so much flesh any creature can eat!'

'I'm sure these neighbours of ours thought so too,' said the younger man. He pointed off towards Hairbeast-Ways. 'I bet there's a lot of flesh rotting over there right now.' He paused. 'Look, I'm not saying the Armourbacks are planning to attack us, but if they are, these Hairbeasts will surely fight for their lives the same as any living creature. Better. Those clubs break through shell quicker than any weapon we have. We need the Hairbeasts on our side. We're a strong people: we can build up our stocks of food elsewhere. But whatever else we do, we need to keep these Hairbeasts in our streets for the day the Armourbacks come!'

Wallbreaker sat down to a thoughtful silence. At last Chief Speareye nodded his head. 'Your advice is good, young man. We will do as you say for now and take our food elsewhere. As one of our finest hunters, *you* will lead the way. Tomorrow.'

Everybody applauded at this great honour for Wallbreaker. He was young to be leading a hunt. He beamed at them, that famous dimpled smile. Only Stopmouth of all the crowd could see the terror that lay beneath it.

'He'll get us killed,' said Wallbreaker, shaking. 'He's known for it! Those stupid risks of his . . .'

Stopmouth looked down to street level, where Rockface waited with five other men who would accompany them on the hunt.

'He k-kept me alive in H-Hairbeast.'

The other hunters talked among themselves and their voices, though not their words, reached the rooftop. Stopmouth didn't need to hear them to know they were discussing Wallbreaker. The young man had gained a reputation for his spear skills and daring but had never led a hunt before. Nor was it a secret that he hadn't left the human streets in a long time. Too long for someone with ambition.

Wallbreaker held a piece of Globe metal tightly to his chest. His face was pale. 'Tell the men I'm injured,' he said.

Evening was approaching fast; when full dark came, the party would slip into no-man's-land towards Clawfolk territory. The bridge might be watched, so they'd push a tree over the Wetlane and make for the alleys of Flim-Ways well before dawn.

'Y-you're n-not injured.'

Wallbreaker turned an imploring gaze on his brother. 'You injure me then! Here, I'll put my arm between these two blocks. You could step on it hard. Here.' He knelt down on a bed of lichen, scattering the mossbeasts that crawled upon it. 'Do it!'

Stopmouth poked his head over the parapet of the house. 'W-we're c-coming n-now!' he shouted.

He thought back to the last day of his brother's courage. Stopmouth had been sad before the wedding, so Wallbreaker had suggested they go and spy on some beasts. It was a dangerous pass-time, frowned upon as wasteful and, above all, stupid.

'Oh, we're in no danger,' Wallbreaker had said. 'No creature's ever even spotted us before. And the more we know about our neighbours the better we can hunt them, right?'

Stopmouth needed the distraction, but he would have gone anyway. He always did.

They found a nice little tower in Hairbeast-Ways over-looking a square where a party of Hoppers leaped past and even over each other in a complicated dance. Their fur streamed with sweat and their voices squeaked in what Stopmouth imagined to be laughter.

'A game,' whispered Wallbreaker. 'It must be. They're not so unlike us, after all.'

The dance came to a halt and the grey-furred beasts flopped down in whatever position they'd finished in. All of them looked exhausted and yet again Stopmouth realized how clever his brother was, for Hoppers in a state such as this would be easy meat.

Then one of the beasts struggled upright and raised long arms above its head. Strange that it should be first to rise: it looked even more exhausted than the others. The rest of the Hoppers turned all at once to fix it with their gaze. Then they rose, one at a time, and approached while the weak-looking one stayed put, trembling. The first Hopper to reach it locked teeth on what would have been the armpit on a human. It seemed to drink from the wound it had made. After a few heartbeats another took its place, sucking at the same gash. Others followed, most to drink, but some to hug. One even offered its own armpit to the wounded one.

'Amazing,' whispered Wallbreaker. 'I think they use that dance to choose volunteers.'

Wallbreaker had been so excited that day, but he was over-eager to get home in time for the 'Purchase of the Bride' ceremony. So eager, in fact, that he'd led his brother straight into the midst of an Armourback hunting party.

He'd been lost ever since.

Stopmouth turned round to get Wallbreaker moving downstairs. But his brother had forgotten all about the hunt. He'd spotted a pair of battling Globes and was watching them intently as they swerved round each other against the blue glare of the Roof. They weren't near enough for the pieces to rain down on Man-Ways, but Wallbreaker hadn't lost his fascination with the things. Stopmouth followed his gaze in time to see a beam of light lancing from one of the spheres into another. The stricken Globe split neatly in two. As the halves separated, something tiny and dark dropped out and plummeted earthwards. It fell a thousand paces. Then a white membrane blossomed in the air above it.

'It's stopped falling!' whispered Wallbreaker.

'N-no. S-slower.'

'You're right, Stopmouth. It's just falling more slowly. It's heading for Bloodskin.'

Wallbreaker was on his feet in an instant and hurtling down the stairs. 'Let's go!' he shouted to his brother. He grabbed two spears, a water skin and a set of knives, and ran out to where the other hunters were waiting. His wife was there too, but he didn't even take the time to flick her a drop of blood in farewell, and only Stopmouth saw the disappointment and worry on her face.

'A change of plans,' said Wallbreaker to the other hunters. 'We're off to Bloodskin instead. We need to be near that thing when it lands.'

'You're crazy,' said Lowsquat, one of the party's veterans.

He was a man with a family to feed and an ailing wife. 'It's flesh we want, not more of that useless metal.'

'It's n-n-not m-m-met—'

'I'll get you your flesh,' said Wallbreaker. He was breathing heavily. He seemed elated, as if the hunt had already been a big success. 'I'll get you enough to pay Stopmouth's bride price for your daughter!'

Lowsquat was outraged. 'My Brighttooth won't marry a mute!'

'But he's not a mute,' said Rockface. 'Are you, boy?'

'N-n-n—'

'Look,' said Wallbreaker, 'I'm going now. You can all follow, or not.'

He set off at a jog. Relieved, Stopmouth ran after him and presently he heard the footsteps of the others following on behind. The shape had grown in the sky. The black part wriggled like prey in a Flyer's grasp while the white membrane formed a dome in the air above it.

The object wasn't coming straight down as he'd supposed. It had begun its fall over Bloodskin but since then had drifted closer to human territory and now seemed destined to land in or near Centre Square.

Wallbreaker turned back to follow it, but Rockface stopped him dead.

'That thing is safe now, Wallbreaker. It'll come down in our streets. You can look at it when we get back.'

'Yes,' said the other men, clearly angry.

'Enough flesh for my Brighttooth's bride price!' growled Lowsquat. 'That's what you promised. Not that the mute will have her!'

Stopmouth laid a hand on his brother's shoulder and felt the muscles twitching under his palm. Whatever spell had cured him of his fear seemed to have worn off again. His eyes were wild and Stopmouth had a vision of his brother bolting. He couldn't let that happen. He took Wallbreaker aside and whispered in his ear: 'Th-the B-Bloodskin p-plan.'

'What?' said Wallbreaker. 'Oh.' He paused, still breathing too fast. 'The Bloodskin plan. Yes. I remember that one. But, Stopmouth, I couldn't!'

'N-not you. M-me and R-Rockface.'

'Are you sure?'

'T-tell them!'

Wallbreaker and Stopmouth went back to the others, who were muttering angrily. They stopped when the brothers approached, but clearly it would now take something spectacular for Wallbreaker to save his reputation.

'I'll get you more flesh than you and your families can eat,' he said. 'I've promised you that, and I can deliver it. But we all have a lot of work to do before dawn. Stopmouth? Run home – you know what I want you to get. Oh, and bring extra spears if you can find them.'

Stopmouth ran.

When they were children, Wallbreaker had already predicted a glorious future for himself. He'd be a hunter to rival the legendary Traveller: a great man who could sneak alone into enemy streets and return with an entire carcass strapped to his back. Wallbreaker always played the Traveller in their games. He always had a plan. As he got older and began participating in real hunts led by other men, he'd become increasingly frustrated by the lack of forethought that went into them. Sneak around, wait for an opportunity – any opportunity – and pounce! He'd do it differently if he ever took charge, he'd said. He'd bring flesh home in abundance. At last the chance he'd once craved and now dreaded had arrived.

Stopmouth sped home on his brother's orders. He cut through small alleys between the main streets, ducking under skeins of pounded moss hung out by the women to stiffen in the heat. Ahead of him he could hear a commotion in the direction of Centre Square, where the white thing must have come down. He was dying to see what it was, almost as much as Wallbreaker. But it would have to wait. He had other business now. Dangerous business. Already he was sorry for offering to be the runner in the plan, but he was excited too and, like any young man, keen for a chance to impress the older hunters.

* * *

61

The creature swooped down towards Centre Square on its great white wing. Women who'd been smoking flesh ran screaming in all directions while their men tried to get shots in over their heads with slings.

'Don't kill it!' shouted Speareye. 'It's only one creature – we can surround it first!' The beast's shadow soared over ash-covered paving blocks, dyed red from generations of butchery. The men thought it would come down in one corner of the square and ran in that direction, but it banked suddenly and everyone turned, tripping over each other to make for the middle again. The beast hit scant paces from the ancient fountain. In the fading light, it seemed to have shiny black legs, and they ran while it landed, kicking up a storm of sparks. Finally it skipped through a pile of bones and collapsed with the silky wing settling on top.

The men circled around with raised weapons as the creature struggled to get out from beneath its covering.

'Wait now,' called Speareye. 'You'll all be getting your share, but it's my right to kill it.' He stepped ahead of the others, quite close to where the main body of the creature was emerging from its cocoon. The tattoos on his shoulders flexed as he raised his weapon, but he never struck.

'By the Traveller!' he said.

'What is it?' someone asked.

Speareye walked backwards, holding his weapon in front of him. The creature shook the last of the white wing away and all the men gasped together.

'It's a woman!' said Roughnose.

'It can't be,' said Gapsmile. 'It's got no hair! And its skin is too shiny!'

The creature was panting and its bald head glistened with sweat. From the neck down its skin was charcoal black. It was devoid of nipples and genitalia, but it had a woman's figure and a face so disturbingly human, none of the hunters could find it in themselves to strike it down.

The creature moved one hand slowly to its neck and pressed a small wart. Suddenly the shiny part of its skin peeled away – a form of clothing? – and removed any doubt that this was indeed a woman, albeit a strange one. Her body was too young to have ever borne a child, and yet her face made her at least six thousand days old. They all stared, mesmerized by teeth too white to be human and skin a little too dark, too flawless to be real.

She tapped her chest with delicate fingers. 'Indrani,' she said.

'How did you come from the sky?' asked Speareye, regaining some of his composure. 'Are you an ancestor? Have we displeased you?'

The woman shrugged. Her eyes shifted from man to man, passing over the buildings of the square, gaily decorated in the skulls and bones that signified plenty. Beads of sweat began to trickle down from her scalp.

The chief tried several more questions, but got no replies.

'If she can't speak,' said Speareye, 'either she's a beast, and therefore flesh, or she's a half-wit that'll have to be volunteered next time we trade.'

Indrani struggled when they tried to bind her. She had an amazing ability to kick a full-grown man in the jaw from a standing position. It took five hunters to tie her up, and after that they had to gag her, for she shouted at them in mad gibberish and wouldn't be still no matter how many times they told her her life depended on it. None of them used their knives, however: not even the hungriest believed her to be a beast now.

Stopmouth caught up with the party again on the Bloodskin side of the Ways. The women seldom dared gather wood out in this direction, even with the usual hunter patrols to guard them, so the wilderness had taken over in a way it had never managed in the no-man's-land between home and Hairbeast-Ways. Trees grew everywhere, in every shade of purple and red. They had taken over the banks of the Wetlane and their poisonous fruits dragged branches right down to the leaf-littered surface of the water.

The men had made a bridge with a fallen trunk. Now they were up to their knees in dirt, digging and cursing.

'We're nearly ready,' said Wallbreaker. 'Did you bring the skins?'

Stopmouth showed them the Bloodskin-hide mantles he'd pulled from his bed. The smooth red skin glistened under the tracklights as though alive. He'd also brought the preserved Bloodskin head from the main room of the house. Someone had eaten the eyes, but that would go unnoticed in the dark, especially with the rest of the features in such fine condition. So many bright teeth jammed the creature's mouth that many remained visible even after the jaws had closed. Wisps of hair dotted the cheeks, shielding a dozen tiny openings that made up for the lack of a nose.

'Good,' said Wallbreaker. That head had been his first trophy and he'd always been proud of it. 'You'll need to stuff the hides with moss and tie them closed. Rockface has agreed to go with you.' Stopmouth nodded, glad to have such a good fighter to watch his back. Rockface could run too. Not as fast as Stopmouth, but faster than these others.

Wallbreaker showed him where they'd have to jump on the way back. 'You'd better go right over that big rock, or you'll end up impaling yourself on the traps. When you get to the Wetlane, drop everything you're carrying and cross over the log. Don't worry about knocking it away after-wards, you won't have time.'

Stopmouth and Rockface prepared to leave.

'Wallbreaker's explained everything,' said Rockface. He

flexed his massive shoulders and grinned at his young companion. 'You're going to need that famous speed of yours!'

Wallbreaker interrupted them. 'There's one more thing, men.' He put a hand on Rockface's arm. 'I'll have to ask you to leave your spears behind. They'll only slow you down, and we need them here.'

Rockface glared at him. 'How'd you expect us to kill Bloodskins with only our knives, hey?'

'The whole point of the plan,' said Wallbreaker – Stopmouth could almost hear him gritting his teeth, 'is that you *don't* kill them. You run. You lead them here, and *we* kill them for you.'

'I'll run faster if I have a spear.'

'My plan,' said Wallbreaker. 'My plan and you agreed to it.'

Rockface flung the weapon against a nearby tree and turned away. 'Are you coming, Stopmouth, or staying here with *Windbreaker?*'

Stopmouth patted his brother on the back and followed the larger man through the trees. It was completely dark now and they often tripped as they walked along crumbling footpaths covered in vegetation. Fifty types of moss grew here, if not more. They fought for space on the largest trunks and rocks, dying and rotting away with an acrid smell that itched the nostrils.

Stopmouth supposed houses must once have stretched

from the Wetlane right up as far as Blood-Ways, home of their intended prey. He'd no idea how or even why the houses had been levelled. He knew of no power that could accomplish such a thing. Wallbreaker said the trees could do it by themselves, slowly, slowly devouring the buildings, or pushing them under to drown in the earth.

After five hundred paces the cover came to an end. Here it was the trees who'd died, not the buildings. The Bloodskins had cut them down or burned them to form an open space between their homes and the forest.

The two hunters crouched at the edge of the wood and rubbed dirt into their skin. Like everywhere else Stopmouth had seen in the city, streets and lanes criss-crossed Blood-Ways in a grid pattern. Most of these were blocked off, of course. From his hiding place he spied piles of rubble heaped between buildings and jammed into the doors and windows that faced outwards. Only one road on this side had been left free for the benefit of Bloodskin hunting parties. It was heavily guarded, watched from a pair of towers to either side. However, a determined, hungry enemy could find a way into any district with a bit of patience. There were always too many windows and doors. This was why most people in Man-Ways lived as close to Centre Square as possible. It meant enemies had further to go to find prey, and when they found it – in the very heart of hostile territory – one little sound would be enough to kill them.

The men went belly first to the ground and crawled slowly through the darkness towards the nearest buildings. Stopmouth's heart thudded in his chest. He wondered if a Bloodskin guard had already seen them and was pointing them out to others. The creatures had a way of leaping from buildings without suffering harm. He imagined one of them coming down hard on top of him, claws first, its toothy red face stretched into a vicious grin.

They moved closer to the houses with agonizing slowness. Rocks poked through moss into their skin and tree saplings caught at their loincloths. When they reached the first buildings, they kept their backs to walls damp with Roofsweat and sidled along towards the main road out of Blood-Ways. Once everything was ready, they'd make sure the guards spotted them. The enemy would see the Bloodskin hides tied in a bundle to Stopmouth's back and in the dark it would look as if the humans were escaping with stolen infants. The men would feign fatigue or injury. The alarm would sound and the Bloodskin guards would pursue them all the way into Wallbreaker's trap.

But twenty paces from the tower, Rockface leaned closer to Stopmouth and whispered in his ear. 'We're in luck! The barrier has fallen away from this window. See?'

Stopmouth stared at the big man in horror.

'What's the problem?' said Rockface, too loudly for Stopmouth's comfort. 'Your brother's scheme will work just as well if we do this thing for real. And think of the glory! It's been generations since anybody got out of Blood-Ways alive. Here, I'll give you a boost up.'

Stopmouth shook his head violently. Rockface scoffed. 'Oh, you think you can support *my* weight, hey? No, you'll be going first. Come on!'

The man's voice was growing louder all the time. Desperate to shut him up, Stopmouth put his foot into the stirrup of Rockface's hands and climbed into the building. It was madness – Wallbreaker would surely think they'd been killed. And yet, if they emerged from this alive, there would be more tattoos; more admiration and respect.

He clambered into the darkness beyond and reached back for Rockface. Then there was a bit of stumbling around until they found a door looking out onto a deserted lane.

'Me first!' said the big man, and he strolled into Blood-Ways as if he were in Centre Square, looking neither left nor right. Stopmouth did enough of that for both of them. He felt sure that an army would be leaping down from nearby rooftops at any moment. If he simply went back the way he'd come, Rockface wouldn't even notice. But he tried to keep his mind on the tattoos he'd be getting on their return, and the look of jealousy on Lowsquat's face as a *mute* was paraded around Centre Square on people's shoulders.

'You think I want your poxy daughter?' he'd say. And Lowsquat would be the one to stutter in indignation.

Rockface dragged him into a building just as two Bloodskins turned onto their laneway. The creatures were both male, their prominent lower teeth shining in the tracklights.

'If we can find where they came from,' Rockface whispered, 'we'll get their young. We'll be heroes!'

The Bloodskin males passed out of sight. The humans crept round the corner from which the beasts had come. A shock awaited them. Up till now the houses had been in poor repair, but most still had their roofs and the walls stood strong. Here, however, it looked like a giant foot had stepped on them, smashing everything for several blocks. Man-sized chunks of metal jutted from the buildings, while other fragments had torn up the paving on the street. Wreckage of a Globe, thought Stopmouth, and shuddered to think what had happened to any creature unlucky enough to be in the buildings at the time it had struck. If Bloodskins from these houses survived, surely they'd moved out to live elsewhere. But no; Rockface waved his dagger in the direction of the most damaged building of all. Cracks ran up the walls of the house, and the whole top floor seemed to have fallen in. And yet a faint glow shone from the doorway like the embers of a fire.

Rockface pointed at the house again and signalled 'Go!' He crossed towards it on tiptoe and Stopmouth followed, wondering what kind of creature would stay within walls that could collapse at any moment.

The glow led them to a room at the back, strewn with rubble. Half of the ceiling had fallen away, and a huge piece of metal had crashed into the room to hang a few spans above a dying fire. Stopmouth could see thousands of tiny flashing lights inside the ripped metal shell. A single Bloodskin lay sleeping beneath it. Wisps of hair on its face rose and fell above the many little holes through which it breathed. Why was it here? Stopmouth wondered. What manner of creature would endure danger to be close to such a monstrosity?

Then it hit him. This creature . . . this flesh . . . was Wallbreaker to the Bloodskins. He felt dizzy. He had an image of the beast and his brother conversing, having more in common with each other than either had with the rest of their own Tribe. Stopmouth knew they had to leave this house and find a different Bloodskin to hunt. He touched Rockface's arm and tried to signal they should go, but the bigger man simply grinned and moved closer to the sleeper. He raised his bone knife to strike. Stopmouth, without thinking, caught his wrist.

'Are you mad?' said Rockface.

The Bloodskin awoke. Its eyes glinted like the lights in

the metal shell. Rockface knocked his companion away and stabbed down at the beast. Stopmouth never saw if the strike succeeded or not; he was already falling backwards. He crashed into the damaged wall and felt it shake under his weight. He looked up in time to see part of the fragile ceiling give way. A piece of stone twice the size of his head slammed down onto his legs. Pain erupted in him, like knives and teeth together. He saw bone, his own, poking through his skin. He screamed as he'd never screamed in his life. Whether it was the pain or the sight of his ruined legs even he didn't know.

'Shut up!' shouted Rockface. 'For the life of your Tribe, shut up!' Rockface hit him and he did.

Several times his pain woke him, and several times it drove him into unconsciousness again. He caught the rest of the night's events in flashes. Rockface must have lifted him to his shoulders and made a run for it. Stopmouth heard the Bloodskin alarm, a rhythmic clanging sound. But the houses around them had all been destroyed and so the enemy had further to come to catch up with them.

Rockface ran straight down the main street and passed between two guard towers. Every step jolted Stopmouth's ruined legs. Slingstones fell around them. Two struck Stopmouth but hit nothing vital. A third found his legs and sent him back into unconsciousness.

Later he woke again. A pack of six Bloodskins were closing in fast. Their leader had almost caught up with the humans. Its strangely shaped muscles flexed under glistening skin; its eyes and spear pointed straight at Stopmouth. 'Was it your brother we killed?' he mumbled. 'Are you the Bloodskin version of me? Is that why you're so fast?'

They'd reached the trees by now. Stopmouth could hear the slap of branches and felt Rockface's great body heaving for breath.

'You should drop me,' he tried to say.

By now the Bloodskin version of Stopmouth had come close enough to spear its human counterpart and might have done so if it had been more sure of its footing. Stopmouth saw its glittering, intelligent eyes, its lips pulled back in a snarl. At last the spear arm reached back, preparing to strike.

Rockface leaped into the air.

Stopmouth saw the beast falling forward, heard it scream. Then Rockface landed on the far side of the pit with a jolt and Stopmouth was screaming too.

5.

THE NEXT
VOLUNTEER

Wallbreaker's stomach churned at the sight of his brother's smashed legs. The young hunter, converted to flesh and white bone, brought his nightmares into focus and set him to scratching the spear scars the Armourbacks had made in his skin.

He couldn't face it. 'Take him home, Rockface. Take him to my mother's house. Please.' Rockface nodded, though his chest still heaved after his heroic escape.

Wallbreaker and the others got down to the business of butchering the Bloodskins who'd come running into their trap. The humans had done well and their families would gain honour for such a successful hunt.

Lowsquat slapped the hunt leader on the back. 'Six adult Bloodskins in exchange for one human. Amazing! And thanks to Rockface, we even get to keep Stopmouth for trade—'

Wallbreaker almost struck the man with his spear.

'Stopmouth isn't dead.' His head was spinning. Gore covered his hands, and instead of the Bloodskin under his knife, he kept seeing poor Stopmouth.

Lowsquat seemed oblivious to Wallbreaker's anger. 'The funny thing is,' he continued, 'if Stopmouth had lived, there's easily half a bride price in his share – well, it'll be your share now, of course. And if you want another wife, you couldn't do better than my Brighttooth: she—'

Wallbreaker screamed and grabbed Lowsquat by the neck. 'My brother's not dead! You hear me?' He raised his fist, but the others pulled him away and the eldest hunter of the group, Frownbrow, spoke the words all knew to be true.

'Calm yourself, Wallbreaker! Stopmouth was a hero today' – the others grunted assent – 'but we all saw his legs and they'll not heal straight. You must help him do the right thing and bring honour to your family. Don't shame his coming sacrifice.'

Wallbreaker didn't answer, but when they released him, he took up his knife and went back to butchery without looking at his comrades.

Later Frownbrow made a sled of tree branches. The men used it to pull the bounty of flesh back with them across the Wetlane, where shadows rose to the surface to look on enviously.

The return of such a hugely successful hunt ought to have attracted more attention from the Tribe, especially as

Rockface had gone on ahead to announce their triumph. But even the tower guards were facing the wrong way to see them.

'A big white thing came down in the square!' shouted one, a grizzled man almost old enough to volunteer. 'Come back and tell us when you find out what it is!' No one offered so much as a word of condolence over Stopmouth, though Wallbreaker found he could think of little else.

The first streets were deserted, without even children to run alongside begging for scraps or trophies. They heard an uproar from Centre Square and as they got closer, they found their way blocked by growing crowds.

A day earlier, with his brother safe and happy, Wallbreaker would have done anything to examine the mysterious creature first-hand. Instead, his imagination raced down one blind alley after another in search of a way to keep Stopmouth alive, to undo the terrible thing that had happened because he, Wallbreaker, had been too cowardly to take his place at the front. He'd been relieved when Stopmouth had offered to be the runner. And now the poor boy would be volunteering for something else entirely, something final.

The little group's progress came to a halt in the press of the crowd. Wallbreaker felt dizzy with the noise of them, their smells. They were his people, his friends. They were Tribe. But Stopmouth's legs . . . A wave of nausea threatened to push him to his knees in disgrace. He decided to try to make it to his mother's house through one of the side streets, but he was interrupted by the arrival of Bonehammer, Chief Speareye's youngest son.

'Daddy – I mean, the chief – wants you. Quick, he says.'

Wallbreaker was too tired to argue and knew his family would need the chief's favour if Stopmouth was to avoid volunteering. So he allowed the boy to thread him through the crowd to a crumbling storehouse near Centre Square, where confused hunters kept the curious at bay. The Roof was beginning to emit the faint light of dawn and it showed up the new bruises and black eyes sported by many of the guards. The chief had earned some minor injuries of his own. Wallbreaker found him limping up and down angrily in front of the storehouse.

'At last!' said Speareye. He didn't enquire about the hunt. 'I need you to see this . . . this creature. See what you can tell me about it.'

Wallbreaker could think only of his brother, but he stepped into the darkness amidst sides of hanging meat. He could hear the creature breathing as his eyes adjusted. His nightmares were always like this: he imagined the Armourbacks driving him into a dark room, where he'd hear only the scuttling of their young across the floor. He shuddered and struggled not to shame himself.

But already he could distinguish its outline. *Her* outline.

A woman such as no woman he'd ever seen; her skin flawless. She stared up at him and he recognized the terror in her eyes. His first thought was: *We have this fear in common.* And it pleased him. His second thought was to wonder why the chief hadn't claimed her as another of his wives. How could any man resist such perfection? His gaze lingered on her breasts and he saw her dark eyes narrow in response. Then she shouted something at him, something angry and hateful and utterly without meaning.

At last he understood. 'The chief doesn't want you because you're simple,' he said. 'You'll be volunteered at the next trading . . .'

His eyes lingered on the curve of her hips. 'Such a pity,' he whispered.

He reached out a hand to her skin, which got her shouting again. She actually tried to bite him.

'And yet,' said Wallbreaker, 'you came from the sky. I saw it! You came from a Globe. You can't be an idiot, can you?'

Her struggles had brought a sheen to her skin such as he had when he woke from his awful dreams. Wallbreaker felt exhilarated, and for the moment had even forgotten about his brother. He went back outside to the chief.

'Definitely human,' he said.

'But simple,' said the chief. 'We will have to trade her.'

'Yes,' said Wallbreaker. 'Or maybe . . . maybe I could

take her to wife. Since she is without family, I'd have to give the bride price to you, as chief.'

Speareye scoffed. 'No hunter can afford to keep a simpleton! She'll give you children who're twice as bad! Besides, where would you get another bride price so quickly?' But Wallbreaker could see the calculation in his eyes.

The younger man smiled. 'You didn't ask about my hunt, did you, Chief?'

Fever ravaged through Stopmouth's body and had done so for as long as he could remember. Sometimes people came to see him. Rockface brought a gift of flesh. He talked to Stopmouth for half a day, but Stopmouth understood little. On another occasion he heard his mother speaking to Speareye in the next room.

'Come on, Flamehair. You know that leg will never heal right.'

'You don't know that, Speareye. My boy deserves his chance.'

The room swam in front of Stopmouth's eyes. The trophies of his boyhood stared down at him from the walls, the skull of his first kill – an injured Flim Wallbreaker had permitted him to finish off – beside the bones of his father's final victim. For a moment it seemed as though Speareye's voice came from one set of remains and his mother's from the other.

'All I'm saying,' said the chief, 'is that you should prepare yourself. If he doesn't get better, the flesh he consumes now is wasted. Others need it.'

'Wallbreaker brings in enough flesh for all of us.'

'I'll grant you that,' said Speareye. 'His Bloodskin trick has worked with other species too . . . But it'll never work twice with the same beasts. Then he'll have to hunt just like everyone else.'

Stopmouth missed the rest of the conversation, but his mother cried when it ended.

Every day a strange woman came to see him.

'Mossheart?' he asked.

He never saw her arrive or leave, and when she spoke, his fevered mind couldn't hold onto her words. The sickness racked him day and night, but she was always near to press damp hide to his forehead and whisper soothing gibberish.

'I'm not a baby,' he told her. Or thought he did.

Finally he woke up one day with the fog gone from his head. He saw the woman sitting in the corner of his room, and realized she wasn't a creation of his pain, but a real human being.

'W-what's your n-name?' he asked her. She had the shortest hair of any woman he'd ever seen; no longer than a single finger-joint.

He tried again. 'W-why have I n-never seen you before?' The Tribe had a story about a man who'd hidden his mother away for half a generation so she wouldn't have to volunteer. Had this woman spent her entire life indoors? Is that why her skin was so dark?

She wouldn't answer his questions. She simply looked at him. Perhaps, he thought, she was mute. Maybe the gibberish he'd heard her speaking had been part of his fever.

It was only then that he began to notice the abominable itch in his legs. When he pulled away the pounded moss covering, he saw that somebody had tied each broken limb to long straight pieces of metal. Why, he didn't know, but he was relieved he couldn't see bone sticking out anywhere. He reached down for a good scratch, but the woman quickly stood and batted his hands away. Stopmouth couldn't find the strength to fight her.

'Mother,' he called. 'M-Mother!'

No reply. He looked at the stranger again. 'It's j-just us, then.'

The woman tapped her chest. 'Indrani,' she said.

'W-well,' he said, glad she could talk, but suddenly tongue-tied by her strange, dark eyes. And she too seemed reluctant to say anything else after that. He wondered if, like him, she suffered from embarrassment and a twitchy tongue. And so they remained in uncomfortable silence, interacting only when he stole glances at her strange face or when she hissed at his attempts to relieve the itch in his legs.

Stopmouth didn't discover how the woman came to be

in his house until later that evening. Wallbreaker paid him a visit and seemed delighted to find his brother conscious.

'You had me worried,' he confessed.

Stopmouth noticed that Indrani had moved to the corner of the room farthest from his brother. Strange, really, for Wallbreaker had regained the sleek air of confidence he'd lost during his encounter with the Armourbacks.

'How l-long have I been f-f-feverish?' asked Stopmouth.

'You had your little adventure with Rockface twenty-two days ago.'

Stopmouth thought about this. The sight of jagged bones poking through his skin would have left most of the Tribe doubting he would ever walk again, let alone hunt. Twenty-two days was a terribly long time for them to put up with that. To take his mind off it, he asked Wallbreaker to tell him about Indrani.

'Now that's a story!' said his brother. 'Do you remember much of the night you escaped from Blood-Ways on Rockface's back? We all saw this object falling from the sky and I was desperate to get a closer look, but everybody wanted to go on with the hunt.'

'I think I r-remember something like that . . .'

Stopmouth was sitting with his back against the wall. His mind had been clear for no more than a tenth part of a day, but already he was tiring. Indrani came over and helped him to lie down. She kept a wary eye on

Wallbreaker and went straight back to her corner when she'd finished.

'I'll tell you that story,' said Wallbreaker. He grinned. 'I'll tell you how I came to be married for a second time, young as I am!'

Stopmouth looked in astonishment from husband to wife. It was indeed unusual for so young a man to have two women. And yet the Bloodskin hunt would have gained each member of the party a full adult carcass. If Wallbreaker had been able to repeat the success of that even once, it was no wonder he'd been able to afford the extravagance.

'You see, brother, I knew the first moment I heard it that her gibberish was just another form of speech such as the Hairbeasts use among themselves. Now, we've never been able to learn the Hairbeast language. But they're not people, right? We can't think like them without going mad like Treatymaker. However, if another human language existed – and it's not something those farts in the Flesh Council will ever accept! – but if it did exist, I figured I ought to be able to work it out. I've already learned some of her strange words and she's picked up some of ours. Not enough, though. Not nearly enough.' He'd uttered the last sentence so quietly, Stopmouth wasn't even sure he'd heard it.

'Enough f-for w-what?'

Wallbreaker glanced out of the doorway and lowered his voice. 'When I tried to take her to my bed, she struck out at me. She fights as well as most men. Not me, of course, or she'd have broken my jaw! Also, Mossheart is being unreasonable about the whole thing, if you can believe that. She'd be a head wife and her still so young. But no. She wouldn't have another woman in the house. Doesn't even want me to visit Indrani. Madness! So, for now, until I can explain to Indrani that she'll be volunteered if she doesn't find a use for herself, and to Mossheart why she must obey . . . Well, until then, you'll have her here to look after you.'

'The m-metal?'

'Yes, the metal splints were her idea. I was amazed, but I immediately saw how they might keep your legs straight while they healed. She's a match for me, all right! And if we can keep the Flesh Council off your back for another twenty days, she might even have saved your life!'

Wallbreaker smiled at his new wife. She glared back for a moment before turning away. Stopmouth felt himself drifting, but his brother wouldn't let him sleep yet.

'One more thing,' he said. 'This is important: as far as the Tribe is aware, I have full control over her, all right? I will too. I just have to learn to speak to her first.'

But he'd need her co-operation for that, and Indrani didn't look like she'd start co-operating any time soon. Stopmouth wanted to offer to learn her language on behalf of his brother, but already the excitement of the day had been too much for his recovering body and he slipped quickly into darkness.

When Stopmouth woke again, the light coming through the only window had weakened. He felt sure he'd lost at least another full day to sleep. But that was fine. Somebody must have fed him because there was soup caked on his lips and he felt a little stronger than before. Indrani sat in the corner on crumpled hides that looked like they'd been slept on. Stopmouth thought she'd been crying, though the darkness of her skin made it hard for him to tell. He knew she couldn't understand a word he said, but he tried to speak to her with kindness in his voice. 'You are my sister now, Indrani.'

She looked up at her name, but spoke none of her gibberish in return.

Mother and Wallbreaker walked in. They must have heard his voice. Mother seemed more stooped than when he'd last seen her. New lines had spread across her face. Or maybe it was a trick of the light coming through the pounded-moss doorflap behind her that he noticed them now for the first time.

'My Stopmouth, you're awake!' Anxiety filled her voice more than joy. 'Quickly,' she said, reaching for him. 'Quickly! You have to stand! A Clawfolk delegation has arrived to trade. Speareye wants five volunteers. Five!'

'He can barely sit up!' said Wallbreaker. He too looked very worried, and that was when Stopmouth knew to be afraid.

'He has to stand,' Mother continued, 'or Speareye said they could take him!' Stopmouth saw that her hair had gone uncombed and her hands shook.

A voice called into the house from beyond the hide curtain that blocked off the main entrance.

'Hello in there?'

'Just a moment,' said Mother.

'We can't wait more than a few heartbeats,' said the voice. It sounded vaguely familiar. 'We need three more volunteers before nightfall.'

Mother and Wallbreaker didn't hesitate. They pulled Stopmouth up and supported him between them. Indrani shouted something at them and tried to make them put him back. But when three hunters pushed into the room, she seemed to understand and stepped forward to block their way.

'He's standing,' said Mother to the hunters. 'Now go away!'

'That's not good enough,' said one of the men. Stopmouth recognized him as Brighttooth's father, Lowsquat. He was red in the face and sweating. 'The boy has to stand by himself. For ten heartbeats like the chief says. Or else he's not healing.'

Stopmouth's family held him up, but already he needed to sit. The room seemed to spin and what little lay in his stomach wanted to come up again.

'You hear that, son?' whispered Mother. 'You stand for ten heartbeats, that's all.'

She didn't know what she was asking. Far easier to lie down. If he volunteered, they'd let him rest. They'd heap praise and honour on his family, whose futile hope could finally end. He could hear that hope now in his mother's voice. Worse, he felt it in himself: the shameful urge to live, even at a cost to others.

'I'm going to let go now,' said Mother, 'and you're going to stand for ten heartbeats.' Her voice was so determined, he wished he didn't have to let her down. She and Wallbreaker pulled away from him simultaneously.

For perhaps two heartbeats he didn't even realize they'd gone. The strips of metal tied to his legs seemed to support him all by themselves. But then the pain began: like rocks and knives and sharp beaks under his skin. A fire burned in his legs, in his marrow. He screamed and screamed again, but by the fourth heartbeat he was still on his feet. He heard voices counting. Poor Mother! He swayed, and when he righted himself, the pain doubled, first in one leg and then in the other. He had to end it. He had to fall. He felt as if his bones had come apart and were once more poking through his skin.

And then his sweaty face was in Indrani's lap, her eyes the only point of stillness in a spinning room.

'That wasn't ten heartbeats!' said Lowsquat.

'We counted them together,' said Wallbreaker, reaching for a knife. 'That was ten. Now get out!'

Lowsquat was hopping in rage. His fellow hunters placed calming hands on his scarred shoulders. But he wouldn't be still. 'We all know there's a few people in this house who should be volunteering. You hear me, Stopmouth?' There was a catch in his voice. 'If you were a man, you'd know there was only one right thing to do. You'd not let them have my wife instead of you. You hear me, coward?'

'I told you to get out,' said Wallbreaker through gritted teeth.

'I'm going,' said Lowsquat. 'I'm going to get Speareye. Let him judge if Stopmouth can stand for ten heartbeats!'

Lowsquat left, and Mother stood to follow him. 'I'd better be there when he tries to tell the chief his lies. Speareye knows my word is good.' She knelt next to Stopmouth and kissed him on the forehead.

'Live,' she told him. 'Your Tally is far from full.'

'If they c-come b-back,' said Stopmouth, 'I w-will volunteer.' The thought didn't seem half so terrible to him as the idea of standing again. The Clawfolk were said to kill their volunteers quickly and painlessly.

Wallbreaker brought food for them as they waited.

'Look,' he said, pointing at Indrani to distract his brother. 'See how she eats? She closes her eyes and chews only as much as she has to. When I first married her, she wouldn't swallow anything. She sat miserably in that corner and I was sure she'd die and I'd be disgraced for not making her volunteer first.'

Stopmouth saw several new tattoos on Wallbreaker's skin. He wondered if it meant his brother had rediscovered his courage.

'One day this strange new wife of mine lay on the floor, so weakened we thought that was the end of her.' Wallbreaker laughed. 'Mossheart was already celebrating! But Mother held a skull of soup to her lips and – amazingly! – she began to drink. She seemed to wake up then and saw that she was eating. She cried, if you can believe it! But she guzzled down the soup all the same.'

Stopmouth's mind drifted, thinking of this strange girl who hated to eat. He wished he'd had more of a chance to get to know her. But soon Speareye would come and he, Stopmouth, would never last another ten heartbeats on his feet. Better to volunteer at once to honour the family.

When he woke, night had fallen and Mother still hadn't returned. Indrani pulled the hides up to his chin.

'Indrani,' he said. She smiled with teeth so straight he thought they'd been carved. He pulled one hand out from

89

under the coverlet and weakly tapped himself on the chest. 'Stopmouth,' he said.

'Shtop-Mou.'

She spoke like a baby with its first words. Perhaps in her strange way she was a child still and, like a child, would someday learn proper speech.

A day passed and Speareye still hadn't come for him. Mother hadn't returned either. To keep from thinking about that, Stopmouth tried to teach Indrani some proper talk. She seemed glad of the distraction, although she kept her distance. In spite of her best efforts – and she was trying hard – he spent the best part of a day teaching her no more than a dozen words: hides, house, hands, legs, metal, urine . . .

Rockface came to visit with one of his children, a boy three thousand days old or less.

'This is Littleknife,' said Rockface, his manner subdued. The boy began to poke about, staring openly at Indrani. He had a small spear that he dragged around the room after him. Presumably his father had also crafted him a dagger which the Tribe had used to name him. He even wore a loincloth, unlike other children the same age. A proper little hunter.

'I'm glad you lived, Stopmouth. I thought we'd be losing you for sure. But then I heard – I heard . . .'

'R-R-Rockface, I—'

But Rockface had come to speak his piece and it all came out in a rush: 'Everyone's proud of your mother, Stopmouth, very proud. The chief asked for volunteers to help us get Home and . . . Well, many a woman her age would have had to be dragged. Flamehair still had a thousand days in her or I'm no judge.'

It was formula. Just formula. The one you used with the relatives of anybody whose volunteering hadn't been forced. But Stopmouth could see that Rockface meant every bit of it. The big man turned as he was leaving. 'We will hunt again, Stopmouth. I thank your mother for giving you back to us.'

He left before his words had fully sunk in.

6.

CANDIDATES

'**O**ut!' said Indrani.

A few days earlier she'd removed the tips of two spears and had wrapped hide around the top of the shafts. She'd taught him how to stumble about the house using them for support so that Rockface and even Wallbreaker laughed at the sight of him and his 'wooden legs'. Stopmouth couldn't say why, but his brother had grown increasingly bitter of late and it came as a great relief to see him smile.

But now Indrani was keen to get Stopmouth using the crutches beyond the confines of the house.

She nudged him towards the street. Her hair had grown since they'd first met, taking away some of her strangeness. And she'd picked up one of Mother's old loincloths to wear. But she still couldn't hide the darkness of her skin or the unnatural brightness of her teeth.

'Out, you!' she cried when he pretended reluctance. By

the time they'd crossed the threshold they were both giggling like children. Stopmouth hadn't seen the Roof properly since his injury and the blue glare left him turning away and blinking spots from his eyes. When they finally cleared, the first thing he noticed was a Globe, drifting all by itself against the vastness of the Roof. No more battles in the sky, he thought. And grinned. No more Indranis either!

She was having a hard time with life on the surface. She tended to drift into periods of blackness, moaning things like 'Nothing in my head! All gone!'

'What are you talking about?' he'd asked her once, but she didn't have enough Human words to answer so maybe that was what she meant.

'You'll learn,' he'd said. 'You'll speak as well as m-me in no t-time at all!'

Often he heard her up on the roof of the house, shouting streams of gibberish in the direction of passing Globes. He'd hear threats in her voice and anger turning to a desperate pleading that tore at his heart.

And yet these episodes never took her for long. Indrani had a sense of mischief and fun that Mother would have loved to see. She delighted in hiding Stopmouth's crutches and provoking him to laughter by almost any means possible. She was a better friend than any he'd had before, for unlike Wallbreaker she spent all her time with him. Even better, he rarely stuttered in her presence: she was the only person he'd ever met who spoke worse than he did.

It was a wonderful feeling and he hoped that when she finally accepted her fate and moved into Wallbreaker's house, he could visit her every day. But not yet. He didn't want to lose her yet.

She followed him into the light and threw pebbles at him as he tried to stay upright and hobble a house-length in each direction. He wished the chief were here to see him, but the only onlookers were curious Flyers on nearby buildings and a couple of older women who walked past quickly, frowning in disapproval.

'More walk!' she cried. 'More!'

He gasped, 'Enough!'

Indrani took pity on him and helped him back to his bed of hides and pounded moss.

'Now,' he said, 'm-my turn to torture you.' He picked up a needle. 'What's the w-word for this?'

He laughed when she rolled her eyes Roofwards and groaned.

Fifteen days later Stopmouth finally got a chance to earn his keep again. Like most of the recovering injured, he worked for the Tribe by taking turns in the watch towers, receiving food as payment. He preferred to take the night watches, for the streets seethed with tension and fear these days, while the hunting seemed poorer than ever.

The older man he shared his watch with – Bridgecrosser – flexed his hand right under Stopmouth's nose. 'See this?' His voice was gruff, as if he constantly needed to hawk and spit. 'I told you it was getting better. Another week babysitting you and I'll be back hunting.'

Stopmouth smiled in the fading light of the Roof. Bridgecrosser's hunting exploits had never gained him more than sneers in the past. But Stopmouth enjoyed the older man's company well enough. Night was falling and only the grid of tracklights – barely enough to see by – remained to help them in their watch. Below stretched the no-man's-land that had once led to Hairbeast territory. It lay clear of saplings to the front as far as the Wetlane, but in some areas further down, stands of trees had been allowed to cross the water as they did on the Bloodskin side.

'Why do you think the Hairbeasts were never replaced?' asked Bridgecrosser. 'My dad used to talk about the time they ate the last of the Semplit. Took no more than a couple of days for the Flim to turn up. There was a big, bright flash – he said you could see it from these here towers – and then ... Ha! Thousands of Flim with no idea where they were! We ate well in those days, Stopmouth. Took those stupid beasts five tens to learn they had to eat us to live.'

Something on the ground below flickered at the corner of Stopmouth's vision. Had some creature moved in the trees? He interrupted Bridgecrosser with a touch on the elbow. 'W-what,' he said, 'w-w-was . . . ?' He reached reflexively for the Clawfolk-shell horn, but didn't blow the alarm. Humans rarely hunted at night, and never in Hairbeast-Ways – not since the alliance of Armourbacks and Hoppers had driven them out. At the same time, enemy raids into human territory had grown more frequent. Chief Speareye had ordered the roofs of more buildings to be manned overnight, but extra guards meant fewer hunters and less flesh to go round. So the chief had requested more volunteers. One day he'd visited Stopmouth to 'see how he was recovering'. Luckily that was Stopmouth's first day of walking without the crutches and Speareye hadn't been able to force the issue.

'It's Flyers,' said Bridgecrosser excitedly. He wasn't even looking in the right place. 'Wow, you see them? There must be tens of them! What are they doing here?'

Flyers made excellent scavengers. Their colourful formations had hovered over Hairbeast for days after the destruction of its people, and Stopmouth dreaded to think what their arrival in Man-Ways might herald now. Something terrible was coming. He felt sure of it. His palms were suddenly clammy around the shell and he almost blew the alarm, but all he'd seen was the tiniest of movements amongst the trees and he needed to be certain.

Bridgecrosser shared none of his concerns. He was still rambling on about the Flyers. His young companion wanted to shout at him to ignore them and look down instead, but nerves had turned his traitorous tongue to gristle in his mouth.

Then he heard it: the tramp of feet. It wasn't coming from outside the walls. It was coming from the very heart of the Ways.

'Wow,' said Bridgecrosser right at his ear. 'I think a Flyer's going to land on our tower!'

Stopmouth heard shouts of alarm from guards on the far side of the road. Then a draught of cold air passed over his back and Bridgecrosser cried out. Stopmouth looked round to see the old hunter's legs disappearing into the air, a Flyer's claws piercing the man's chest.

The beast looked to be struggling under the weight. Stopmouth lunged for Bridgecrosser's ankles and missed. The man was screaming, and other screams echoed from the tower opposite and from nearby streets. Bridgecrosser's feet bumped once against the parapet and then the Flyer released him over the road, where he landed with a sickening impact.

Stopmouth heard the beating of more wings overhead. He rolled away in time to see another Flyer swoop over the spot where he'd been lying, striking sparks from the roof with its claws. He pressed the shell trumpet to his lips and blew for all he was worth. Two other trumpet blasts echoed through the streets. The second was cut short mid-blow.

Now he rose to his knees, and suddenly the trumpet shattered in his hands, struck by a flung spear. He looked up to see a Flyer perched on the wall, its flaky wings spread as if to offer an embrace, its huge black eyes staring into his. He felt as if he were disappearing into them, like a child burying itself in its mother's lap.

Distant shouting brought him back to himself. He plucked the Flyer's spear from where it had fallen and his enemy fled at once. By now the muscles of his healing legs were trembling and sweat beaded every part of his skin. He looked over the parapet for the source of the screams and nearly fell back in horror at what he saw: a large party of Armourbacks was retreating past the base of the tower under a desultory hail of slingshot and spears. They were driving at least five entire human families before them – people he had known his whole life. He saw Brighttooth among them, and her two younger sisters.

So far, less than ten hunters had arrived to confront the enemy. They hung back in confusion, knowing they were outnumbered.

Stopmouth hefted a rock up onto the edge of the tower's wall. Once he would have had little problem lifting it, but in his weakened state it nearly drove him to the ground. He balanced it on the edge and pushed. He didn't pause to watch where it landed. It might be for the best, he thought, if he hit one of the prisoners by mistake. He moved for another rock, every muscle crying out for rest. A Flyer, perhaps the same one he'd chased away earlier, swooped down and landed on the wall before him. Stopmouth grabbed the spear and was surprised the enemy didn't retreat. Almost too late, he dropped to the roof. A line of fire seemed to open along his back as another of the beasts swooped in from behind.

He clambered to his feet, but the Flyers had gone again. When he looked back over the parapet, he saw one Armourback lying crushed under his rock. The others had moved out of range.

The number of hunters below had risen to twenty now, and Speareye had arrived to marshal them. 'There are more men on the way, boys! We just need to catch them before they cross the Wetlane!'

Stopmouth felt dizzy. Something was nagging at the back of his mind. Surely, he thought, the Armourbacks must have known they'd be seen and pursued. They must have known that the humans would be able to gather lots of hunters in a short space of time.

'S-S-Speareye!' he shouted. 'Ammmmmb-bu-bush!'

Speareye looked up, his face a mask of fury. 'You think I'm stupid, boy? We won't follow them anywhere we can't see where we're going.' He led the hunters out. There were thirty of them now, double the number of Armourback attackers, who were already crossing the bridge. Stopmouth had never seen so many hunters charging together at one time. They screamed their fury, loosing slings and waving spears. The sight was glorious. It stirred his blood, even though he knew it must be a mistake.

He saw the Armourbacks trying to get their prisoners to move faster. Two children fell into the Wetlane in the rush to get them across.

But help was coming. The hunters closed half the distance between them and the enemy in a dozen heartbeats. Then Stopmouth saw shadows moving out of the trees on the human side of the Wetlane. Hoppers! Perhaps as many as two dozen of them. He shouted a warning at the top of his lungs.

Too late. The hunters didn't even look behind them. They threw themselves at the Armourbacks, crashing into the enemy line. These days many of them had spears like Stopmouth's, and a number of beasts went down under the assault. But twenty heartbeats later, at twice the speed any human could run, the grey-furred Hoppers tore into Speareye's followers from behind. Stopmouth shouted again and again, a wordless, useless alarm. Many other hunters had gathered below him, milling about. Some were crying. Others wanted to save their friends, but Wallbreaker walked among them, his strong voice calling them back from certain death.

The slaughter had almost ended. And then a number of Hoppers suddenly fell back.

Stopmouth screamed, 'W-W-W-Wallbreaker!'

His brother heard and saw what he was pointing at. As always, he understood immediately what had to be done. He called the other hunters from their grief and had them form a line with slings and throwing spears at the ready.

Stopmouth had seen a small knot of humans under the leadership of the brute, Crunchfist, break through the Hoppers. The faster enemy gave chase, but the humans kept together and sold themselves dearly.

'We must run to them!' shouted Rockface. 'We can't leave them!'

'No!' said Wallbreaker. 'You'll get us all killed! No!'

Stopmouth knew that Rockface intended to disobey, but Crunchfist's group was almost in range now. Stopmouth saw Crunchfist lift a Hopper from its feet and break its back over his knee. Looking at him, Stopmouth knew a Hero possessed him.

'Loose!' shouted Wallbreaker. Everybody did. Three Hoppers and a human went down under the attack. The enemy paused. 'Again!' More stones and spears rained down. The Hoppers grabbed up their dead and ran, leaving Crunchfist and two other members of the hunting party still breathing, though one of them looked certain to volunteer before dawn.

Nobody interfered as the enemy butchered the bodies of Speareye and his hunters in full view. They portioned out the flesh among those of their prisoners still living and forced them to carry it back towards Hairbeast, while relatives wailed and men shook their fists.

Stopmouth's weakened legs gave way. If the Flyers had come back for him then, he couldn't have resisted them.

Panic reigned throughout the Ways for many days after the disaster. Never before had they faced such a devastating, organized attack from an enemy. People didn't go outside any more without first scanning the air for Flyers.

Corpses from that night were still turning up. The Armourbacks had killed many in their beds, and others had died when they struggled with their captors. The human population had lost perhaps as many as forty hunters in total.

One in a hundred, thought Stopmouth as he hurried across Centre Square. Like everybody else, he wondered if humanity would soon join the Hairbeasts on the edge of extinction. He hesitated before the House of Honour, the only building on the square unadorned by charcoal or trophies, its grey walls kept clean of moss and climbing plants. He'd been meaning to come here since the first time Indrani had taken him out on his crutches. And yet . . .

'What are you waiting for?' The elder of Rockface's two wives, Watersip, stood in the doorway. She pursed her thin lips and wagged a finger at him. She was almost as tall as her husband. 'I know you want to come in. We don't bite, you know.'

Her hands, like all women's hands, were heavily callused from pounding moss for cloth; she reached out with them and pulled him into the House of Honour before he could protest.

'Look what I found outside!'

Three other women smiled up at him, all in various stages of pregnancy. They sat where they could amidst piles and piles of Tallies, each stick representing a life spent in honour, a soul that might someday return. The house had four other rooms just like this. It also had a place for broken Tallies, but nobody liked to think about that.

In one corner, Mossheart wept, ignored by all the others. Lots of people were weeping these days, Stopmouth supposed. She didn't look up at him and he didn't know what to say to her even if he could have won control of his tongue.

'He was waiting outside,' said Watersip. 'Thought I was going to take a bite out of him.'

'You should,' said Frownbrow's wife, Treesinger. 'With those blue eyes he looks almost as tasty as his brother.'

Stopmouth blushed amidst the women's laughter, his tongue a stone. He wished he'd never come, or at least that he hadn't hesitated at the door. But the truth was, hunters feared the House of Honour. Bad luck followed any man foolish enough to touch a Tally stick, and tales were told of Dryspear, who'd ruined his life by coming here and falling in amongst the stacks of sacred wood.

'Forgive us, Stopmouth,' said Treesinger. She was old to be having a child, her face lined by thousands of days of mischief and good cheer. She was carving new Tallies from a pile of branches that the other women were stripping for her. 'We shouldn't make fun of you—'

'You mean, *you* shouldn't!' said Watersip. 'A woman in your condition . . .'

Treesinger smiled, deepening the crinkles at her eyes. 'Yes, I'm a bad girl, it's true.' She put down the Tally she'd been carving and reached up to take Stopmouth's hand. 'You did the right thing coming here. I thought, after the bad times we've had, there'd be a lot more visitors.' She shrugged. 'Wait here. I know exactly where she is.'

Treesinger stood carefully, one hand on her swollen belly. The top of her head reached no higher than his chest. She ran her hands over one pile of Tallies near the door.

Stopmouth shivered. Somewhere in that stack, preserved from rot by berry juice, might lie the Tallies of the Traveller, or Treatymaker or other great Heroes of the Tribe. No man could tell one stick from another. But a woman might. It was said they could even use them to tell which marriages would produce bad children.

'There,' said Treesinger, plucking one from the pile.

She held it up before his eyes, careful not to touch him with it. His mother's Tally, a stick no longer than his forearm, marked all the way up with tiny slashes in complicated designs.

'Do you see this little cross, Stopmouth? No, that one's Wallbreaker; the second one, see it? That's you.'

'My b-birth?' He felt tears coming to his eyes. How he'd missed her.

'Of course not! Birth days are never marked. This was when you were accepted into the Tribe. Your naming day. I remember it well, because there were many who didn't want you named.' He'd have been volunteered quickly if that had been the case, but Mother had protected him, it seemed, and not for the last time.

'She was so happy you'd been saved,' said Treesinger. 'She smiled for tens of days afterwards.'

'Well,' said Watersip. 'Good thing they kept him. My Rockface says the lad's a fine hunter even if he is a bit simple.'

'He's not simple,' Mossheart said suddenly, her beautiful eyes rubbed raw with crying. 'It's just his tongue.'

Watersip opened her mouth, but Treesinger silenced her with a look that said: *Don't upset the girl – you know how she gets.*

But Mossheart was already upset. She got up quickly and pushed her way out of the house, almost knocking Stopmouth into the Tallies behind.

Treesinger shook her head. 'That brother of yours . . . Why can't he be as charming at night as he is during the day?'

The other women laughed again, but this time Treesinger looked serious, holding the young hunter's gaze and resting her free hand against his shoulder. Stopmouth had never felt more uncomfortable in his life.

'Stopmouth, am I the only one who thinks she should have picked you instead?'

He pulled away from her, stumbling outside into the glare.

By now Wallbreaker had organized many successful ambushes and was respected enough that when he asked people to travel from building to building shoring up the barricades broken by the invaders, they readily agreed and even seemed grateful for his orders. He often met with sympathetic hunters. Some of them had served on the Flesh Council and took him seriously despite his age. He was busy, always busy, but he still had time for Stopmouth and Indrani, although she never seemed to welcome his visits.

'We'll have to kill the Armourbacks,' he said to Stopmouth one day.

'Of c-course!'

'You don't understand, brother,' said Wallbreaker. He'd been supervising the building of new defences. Dust picked out the muscles of his body, hiding the tattoo of Bloodskins falling into a pit of spikes. His voice cracked for want of water, but he was too intent on what he was saying to drink from the skull at his hand or to even pour it over the blond hair plastered to his scalp. 'We'll have to kill them, even if we don't get to eat them.'

The concept was a strange one, but once Stopmouth had swallowed it, it seemed to make perfect sense. The Armourbacks had learned to co-operate with other species. Even now that the humans had a few Hairbeasts living among them, co-operation between the two was non-existent.

Stopmouth had tried, of course. He was teaching Indrani adult talk and she now understood much of what he said. But when he tried to teach the Hairbeast refugees, they ignored him. He never stuttered in front of them, but it didn't matter; it was as if they couldn't hear half the words he spoke. Once, when he grew too persistent, a large male butted him with its chest, knocking him flat. Only the mythical Treatymaker had ever managed any kind of communication with the Hairbeasts. It was said that even he'd understood them very poorly indeed, unable to copy some of the sounds they were making. They'd captured him as a child and, for motives known only to themselves, had failed to eat him. In the end they'd sent him home, half mad, dressed in sweltering furs and almost incapable of speech with his own kind. Almost.

'The Hoppers will also have to die,' said Wallbreaker. 'And the Flyers too.'

The brothers sat in the doorway of their mother's house. Inside, Indrani was performing kicks and punches at a hide bag she'd strung up to the roof. Strange behaviour.

Stopmouth didn't want to tell Wallbreaker that Indrani made him do the kicks too. 'For to get unsick,' she said, 'and to be . . . to be . . .' She flexed her arms.

'Strong?'

'Yes. Strong.'

So Stopmouth kicked and punched, just not where anybody could see him. Especially not his brother.

'Y-y-you were s-s-saying?'

'What?'

Wallbreaker had lost track again. He kept looking over Stopmouth's shoulder at his new wife, seemingly fascinated by her strange exercises. Stopmouth wanted more than anything to leave the two alone together, except he knew Indrani would make him pay for it later if he did. And he didn't see what good it would do anyway. She spoke enough Human to understand Wallbreaker's demands and still she refused to share his blankets or even talk to him about her origins. Sometimes Stopmouth wanted to shake his brother. 'You have Mossheart waiting for you every night! How could you possibly want another woman?'

But he knew that Wallbreaker had great ambitions, and

keeping two wives at such a young age could bring him the respect he needed to realize them. Having one of those women refuse him, however, would have the opposite effect entirely.

Stopmouth tried to bring Wallbreaker back to the conversation they'd been having. 'Too many Ar-Armourbacks,' he said, 'with Flyers and H-Hoppers. How c-can we b-beat them?'

Wallbreaker turned his eyes back to his brother and sighed. 'We have to learn from them,' he said. 'That's the most important thing. See how well they worked together? Armourbacks, Hoppers and Flyers combining their different strengths? It's as if they were one body. When humans go on a hunt, we don't work together half so well, and we are only one species. I tell you, brother, if we don't learn from the Armourbacks, we deserve to feed their young.' He shuddered. 'I need to become chief. I don't think anybody else can learn from our enemies the way I can.'

Stopmouth agreed, except he wondered how a man too terrified to approach an Armourback could possibly defeat them.

'Tomorrow at the meeting I will put myself forward as a candidate.'

'But, Wallbreaker . . . If s-somebody else w-wins, he could make you v-v-volunteer next trade!'

'I will win,' Wallbreaker told him. 'And when I do, I won't waste any hunter strong enough to challenge me!'

And if you don't win, Stopmouth thought, you'll be too clever to keep around.

Fifteen days after the death of Speareye, the weakest men, and even a few women, were sent to guard the watch towers. Every male old enough to hunt crowded into Centre Square and trampled the smoke fires to make more room for themselves. The only woman present was Speareye's wife Housear, who, being pregnant and unaffiliated with any of the potential candidates, had convened the meeting. Other women crammed onto nearby roofs and into surrounding windows to try and watch the Choosing.

Two hunters hoisted Housear onto their shoulders and her little boy, Bonehammer, blew on a Clawfolk trumpet to silence the crowd. The strain of recent events showed on her face, especially around the eyes. It would be hard for her to feed her children now, and the younger ones might even be refused names and volunteered if things became desperate. Nevertheless, she kept her voice steady and brave.

'Speareye,' said Housear, 'is waiting for us with all our ancestors and he hunts the ancestors of our enemies.'

The crowd murmured its agreement. Not even death would keep great Speareye from the hunt.

'We must now find a man to lead us out of trouble and bring us Home; a man the Heroes will possess in times of need, as they often possessed my husband. Let those who would take the place of the chief step forward.'

Wallbreaker pushed through the crowd to the front. One of Speareye's deputies followed him, a man named Lingerhouse who'd lost most of his family in the Armourback raid.

Then the crowd parted of its own accord and Crunchfist passed through. Everyone applauded him, even Wallbreaker. Crunchfist seemed to have no skin; only tattoos. Muscles that would have put Rockface to shame bulged and rippled all over his body. Whispering began. Here and there, men told tales of Crunchfist's exploits. How he had made his first kill while still a child; how he had broken a Hopper's back across his knee; how he had been separated from his hunting pack once only to return after eight days dragging a Bloodskin with one hand and a Flim with the other. People said he was the only hunter who still dared enter Hairbeast territory. Stopmouth remembered him on the night of the disaster, breaking through the enemy almost single-handed, his body possessed by a mighty Hero, maybe even the Traveller himself! Stopmouth was filled with excitement at the thought of Crunchfist as chief. He had a brutal nature, but that's what the Tribe needed now, and with Wallbreaker whispering in his ear, surely the glory days of humanity could not be long in returning.

After a suitable pause, during which no other candidates presented themselves, Housear asked each of the three men if he truly wished to lead the Tribe.

'I wish to withdraw from the contest,' said Lingerhouse. 'I am sure that Crunchfist will feed the Tribe better than I could. I support his candidacy and will be a part of his pack if he will have me.'

The crowd applauded. Wallbreaker joined in, much to Stopmouth's relief. Surely he would be next to withdraw.

Crunchfist curled his lip. 'No, old man, I will not have you in my pack. Go back to your place quickly or I will remember you next time we need volunteers.'

Lingerhouse opened his mouth, but thought better of it and pushed himself angrily back into the bewildered crowd.

'And what of you, Wallbreaker?' said Housear. 'Do you also wish to withdraw?'

'Withdraw!' shouted someone from the back.

'Why should I?' asked Wallbreaker, his voice shaking. 'I am going to win.'

Crunchfist laughed, but some hunters applauded his bravado in the face of death. From a nearby window Mossheart began weeping, but only Stopmouth noticed and his heart went out to her.

'Change your mind, Wallbreaker,' Housear

commanded. Her face was stern in the flickering light of nearby torches. 'We need every hunter we can get. The ancestors will not approve of you throwing your life away.'

Wallbreaker didn't reply.

'Very well,' she said. Then she turned her face Roofwards. 'I speak to Speareye now! I call to you, husband! Two men would take your place, and you must show us which of them can better feed us. Choose us a man strong enough to lead us Home!'

She turned back to the candidates. 'You can take five men each. You have a day and a night to bring flesh back to Centre Square. Whoever brings the most flesh will show himself worthy of leadership. Now, pick your men.'

Crunchfist shouted first, asking for men to join him. He rejected most of those who showed up. Finally, however, he had five heavily muscled hunters, one of whom was Rockface.

Crunchfist grinned at his new pack. They were clearly the strongest hunters in the Tribe. Then he turned and pointed at Wallbreaker. 'His ambush trick won't work on any of our neighbours now!' he shouted. 'And when the Tribe needs volunteers, I will remember anybody who joins him! I will remember your wives! I will remember your children!'

Rockface looked at him in disgust. 'I have changed my mind,' he said. He left the group and moved to stand with Wallbreaker while Crunchfist could only blink in surprise.

'Will you have me, Wallbreaker?' asked Rockface. 'I would have joined you first, only . . . Well, with all your plans, it's too easy, hey? We spend more time digging ditches than hunting!'

Lingerhouse joined Wallbreaker too, as did Stopmouth when he saw nobody else had come forward. He felt sick in his stomach, though, for he knew Crunchfist kept his promises.

'Only three?' said Wallbreaker, raising his voice. 'Nobody else wishes to join me? Good, very good! Three is already too many to share the glory with. Three makes it easy! But you shouldn't be afraid to join us now. Crunchfist already has four of us to take vengeance on. Too many names for even his great brain to remember.'

The bigger candidate lunged for Wallbreaker, but Housear's guards put themselves between the two.

'After,' she said to Crunchfist. 'After you win, you can do what you want.' Then she turned to Wallbreaker. 'You were the first to put yourself forward. Choose your direction.'

'Flim,' said Lingerhouse. 'Has to be Flim!'

But Wallbreaker pointed to his rival. 'I think the loser should choose.'

Crunchfist's face had turned purple, but he wasn't as

stupid as Wallbreaker had implied. The big man forced a smile through the tattoos on his face. 'That was your last mistake, fool. I choose Flim.'

'Very well,' said Housear. 'Go and prepare yourselves.'

Each of the hunters nicked themselves and flicked a drop of blood in her direction.

'Your blood has come back to me,' she intoned, 'and so will you. May Heroes possess you all. May the flesh of your bodies return to the Tribe.

'The hunt begins at first dark.'

7.

THE WETLANE

'You're mad,' said Lingerhouse to Wallbreaker. He looked like a volunteer who'd only now discovered that his leg wasn't broken after all.

'Oh, we're mad, all right,' Rockface told him. 'The strangeness never ends with these two brothers, hey, Stopmouth? But don't you worry, Lingerhouse, Wallbreaker will get us flesh. It'll be boring, though, as boring as moss.'

'I hope it is,' said Wallbreaker. 'And Rockface? Please don't do anything to make it interesting this time. I'm asking you this as a special favour.'

They went to Wallbreaker's house, where Mossheart joined them. She didn't look directly at her husband as she served them dried Armourback flesh. Rockface complained at its bitter taste, but Lingerhouse tore into it with satisfaction, thinking no doubt of his lost family.

'This won't be a standard hunt,' said Wallbreaker. From

under the hides where he and Mossheart slept he pulled a large rope net that Mossheart must have worked on for tens of days. Humans rarely used such tools for hunting. Most forays took place in nearby streets controlled by Treaty species such as the Hairbeasts or Clawfolk, where nets were more likely to trap an ally than a meal. Besides, women had better things than weaving to do with their time, such as smoking flesh or pounding skins for clothing.

Wallbreaker spread out the net and demonstrated how each of its corners was fastened to a rope. The four ropes came together to form a single, thicker rope. He showed them another cord too, slender this time, tied to a wicked hook of jagged Armourback shell.

'You look worried, brother.'

'I rem-m-member you t-t-talking—'

'It's a good plan, Stopmouth!' Wallbreaker said firmly. 'It is. All we need is plenty of rope. And here we have it, all right?'

Stopmouth's heart sank. He'd heard all Wallbreaker's hunting schemes during his life. Some were dangerous, some suicidal. This plan, however, was just plain silly, and its failure would see all of them condemned by the new chief at the next flesh meeting. But he was committed to it now unless he ran away. He fantasized such an escape for himself until the stupidity of it made him laugh out loud, and the others regarded him with worried expressions on their faces. He wondered what they'd say if he told them what he'd been thinking.

Only the legendary Traveller had ever left home. He'd returned after a journey of fifty days, during which he'd seen many wonders and lost the nine best hunters in the Tribe. After telling his story, he was promptly volunteered – nobody wanted to perpetuate such madness. But the tale lived on, and later generations of young men prayed for his spirit above all others to possess them in times of need.

No, there'd be no more running away for anybody. All they could do was stick with Wallbreaker's plan and hope for the aid of a Hero.

When night fell, Wallbreaker gathered up his small party and headed out of the gate towards Bloodskin until they reached the bridge. Under his instructions, they chopped up a fresh Flim corpse and forced a bloody gobbet of it onto the shell hook.

'What now?' asked Rockface, licking his fingers.

'Now comes the easy part,' said Wallbreaker with a wink. 'You see how I've weighted the ends of the net with stones? Well, we'll throw it into the Wetlane so that it spreads out as it falls.'

'Won't that alert the Wetlane beasts?' said Lingerhouse nervously.

'We *want* to alert them,' Wallbreaker told them. 'When a hunter falls into the Wetlane, he makes a splash, doesn't he? And he makes more splashes as he struggles to get out.'

'Ha!' said Rockface. 'And then they come for him. But this time it is we who'll be waiting for them!' He slapped Wallbreaker on the back. 'Another slimy trick, but this one I like! I've always hated those Wetlane beasts and never seen one caught.'

And so the hunters stepped to the edge of the murky water. They saw nothing there except reflections of the pale tracklights and the tiny impacts made by falling Roofsweat. The splash of the net seemed enormous in the night, although Stopmouth felt sure a man falling in would have made more noise. He shrugged; it was up to Wallbreaker now.

He joined his brother and Rockface. The three of them moved away from the Wetlane, paying out the rope attached to the net behind them while Lingerhouse stayed on his belly near the bank. The older man controlled the more slender rope with the hook on it. He twined a good length around his wrist for fear of losing it and lowered the rest into the water above the spot where they all hoped the net would be lying on the Wetlane bed.

'Now we wait,' Wallbreaker said. 'It could be a while – I don't even know if any of the Wetlane beasts are night hunters.'

The men settled down. Nothing moved but for clouds of little mossbeasts – harmless as long as you didn't swallow them – and the only noise was the regular buzz of Rockface's snoring. The men hadn't slept since the previous evening and Stopmouth found the tracklights blurring in his vision, as they had on the night of his brother's wedding to Mossheart. So much had happened since then, and yet whenever he walked the streets, his eyes still sought her out. It was hard to believe that Wallbreaker now cared only for the strange Indrani.

'I got one!' shouted Lingerhouse.

The other three sat up, Rockface rubbing furiously at his eyes.

The rope in Lingerhouse's hands sprang taut. 'Pull!' shouted Wallbreaker to the others. 'Pull in the net!'

Suddenly Lingerhouse was jerked off his feet and disappeared into the Wetlane. His three companions stared as the water churned. Then Rockface grabbed up a spear and started running towards the bank.

'No, Rockface!' shouted Wallbreaker. 'It's too late! The rope! Pull the rope!'

He and Stopmouth started pulling together while Rockface hopped about helplessly on the Wetlane bank, staring into the water. Finally the net caught on something. The brothers began dragging it in, but it fought back. Their feet slipped on the ground, bare soles dragged painfully against roots.

'Rockface!'

The big hunter snapped the shaft of his spear over his knee in impotent rage and came back to them. He gripped the rope in front of Stopmouth, anchored his feet against a half-buried rock and heaved like ten men, his eyes bulging, his face a vision of fury. *A Hero has possessed him*, thought Stopmouth in awe.

Sure enough, the edge of the net appeared above the bank of the Wetlane. Something black and glistening struggled within, but Rockface wouldn't be denied and dragged it over the edge almost by himself.

The three approached it with spears at the ready. They didn't need to use them. The creature in the net thrashed a few more times before joining its ancestors. It was half as big again as a man and had black, oily skin. Its mouth was full of teeth clamped around a chewed-up arm. When they turned the monster over, they found the rest of Lingerhouse underneath, his face the very image of terror.

'Great plan!' said Rockface angrily. 'Brilliant!'

Wallbreaker had turned white; he was shaking. Nevertheless, he ordered the other two to grab hold of the rope with him to draw the shell hook back out of the water.

Then they hauled the unfortunate Lingerhouse and the Wetlane beast back to Centre Square, where Housear and other pregnant women (though not Mossheart) waited to judge the contest. Housear tried not to look impressed, but the others oohed and aahed, touching the monster and

121

wondering what its flavour might be and how it should be cooked.

Meanwhile a runner was sent to try and find out who had the rights to Lingerhouse's flesh.

'Let's do the bridge near Flim now,' said Wallbreaker.

'How?' said Rockface, still angry. 'When there were four of us, we could barely keep the thing from dragging us all into the water. What can we do with three? Shall we ask that only small beasts take the bait?'

'I have an idea for that,' said Wallbreaker. 'I should have thought of it before, but all new plans need a bit of testing before they work out.'

'Oh yes, testing! I'm sure Lingerhouse was grateful to be your test!'

They walked out through the gate towards Flim. The other team was probably out there somewhere searching for unwary creatures. Stopmouth thought it unlikely they'd return with one body at a time as Wallbreaker's pack had done. They'd stockpile the flesh somewhere and bring it all home together.

At the next Wetlane, before throwing in the net, Wallbreaker made sure they used spare ropes to anchor themselves to roots. Their fear kept them alert, and as soon as they saw some creature had taken the bait, the three of them pulled in time to Wallbreaker's shouted count, almost like a crowd of women pounding skins.

They worked hard through the night, moving from Wetlane to Wetlane. In this way they caught four of the original oily creatures and a shelled monster twice the size of a man that looked like a cousin of the Clawfolk.

'This,' said Rockface in disgust, 'has got to be the most successful hunt ever since the time of the Traveller. Four of us in one night and only once in danger. It can't be right.'

A fifth of the night remained for hunting, but nothing else was biting. 'This will never work again,' said Wallbreaker. 'They know about us now.'

Finally, with the Roof brightening, they pulled back the rope. It was incredibly light this time, for something had sheared off the net and looped the ends of the rope through the eye-sockets of a human skull.

'That's definitely it,' said Wallbreaker. Stopmouth nodded. He wondered if what they'd achieved would be enough to save their lives.

Over the course of the morning they dragged the rest of the kills back to Centre Square, where the pregnant women were waiting. The ladies had butchered the Wetlane carcasses into neat bundles that could be fairly measured against Crunchfist's booty. A clean spot had been marked out for this purpose, but as yet the great hero had failed to show up.

'He'll be here,' said Rockface. He sounded almost glad.

The square filled with curious, excited people as the

morning wore on and still Crunchfist's pack failed to arrive. It was dark again before the assembled humans could bring themselves to admit that their best hope for leader wouldn't be coming back. On top of the disaster of twenty nights before, it was almost too much to bear.

Housear was lifted onto the shoulders of her guards. She didn't have to hush the crowd, for they were already silent, many blinking like frightened Hairbeast pups before the slaughter.

She tried to keep her voice steady, but every now and again her eyes would flick towards the edges of the crowd as if expecting somebody.

'Speareye has chosen his successor,' she said. 'He has brought meat to Wallbreaker's spear.'

A very muted cheer arose. Wallbreaker got to his feet. 'I have brought you flesh!' he said. 'Flesh no one ever hunted before. That only I know how to hunt.' There was no reaction. Stopmouth could see the sweat on his brother's lip, see the way he clenched his fists. Wallbreaker's voice turned hard. 'But if you don't want me for a leader, I will accept your decision above that of our ancestors who have chosen me.

'I admit that I feed you tonight more through trickery than through strength. So shout now, any who believes he knows any better than the spirits, and I will step down. Shout, curse you! Shout!'

Nobody spoke. Feet shuffled; eyes looked away.

Wallbreaker nodded. 'I am the first to admit that Crunchfist is our strongest hunter. I had planned to let him live, because I needed him at my right hand, the way even Speareye did. Therefore, if you still want me as your chief' – murmurs of assent – 'my first act will be to organize a search party for Crunchfist and his group.'

The hunters applauded this with more enthusiasm.

Wallbreaker turned to Stopmouth and Rockface. 'Get some sleep, you two. We need to find out what happened to him. I'm sending you out tomorrow.'

'Great,' said Rockface, delighted. 'A proper hunt!'

Stopmouth could only shake his head in disbelief.

8.

INDRANI

Stopmouth came home to find Indrani sleeping in the hall. Perhaps she'd become cold waiting for him, because she'd taken his blanket to throw over herself. More strangeness, he thought. He was too tired to fight her for it and he needed to sit down. So he left her there and passed into the bedroom. His injured legs had healed quickly, yet when he touched them in the darkness, they felt puny under his hands and the muscles trembled with exhaustion.

He found he couldn't sleep. He kept seeing Lingerhouse lying dead in the net; he saw the man's half-chewed arm in the Wetlane beast's maw.

Just as these images began to fade and his eyelids started drooping, he was jerked into wakefulness by Indrani calling his name.

'What?' he asked, alarmed by the fear in her voice. 'What is it?'

She launched into a stream of gibberish and he realized she still slept. He lay down, fully awake again, his heart hammering. He cursed her. He'd need all his energy to search for Crunchfist tomorrow.

At last he slipped into a dream to find his mother waiting for him.

'Oh, cheer up!' said Rockface, slapping the wind out of him with a thump on the back.

'W-w-w-why p-p-p—'

'You're doing that thing with your voice again, boy! You know I can't understand a word you say when you do that.'

'P-p-p-pick m-m-me? Why m-m-me?'

'Oh, there's no reason why Wallbreaker shouldn't pick you to find Crunchfist. You're recovered well enough for a little hunt, hey? Wallbreaker knows that. Besides' – Rockface grinned – 'he probably thinks you need to get out a bit after spending so much time on your back in the company of a beautiful woman.'

'W-what w-woman?'

'What woman? You're joking, boy! Everybody looks at her! Indrani, I mean. You must know. Everybody! There's not a girl in the Tribe has skin like hers, hey? And I don't just mean as dark as hers either. There's not a flaw on it. And her teeth are so bright! And that body! By the ancestors, it must be the way she runs all the time, the way she's always kicking at things—'

'M-m-married!' said Stopmouth, who was growing increasingly uncomfortable with this conversation.

'*She* doesn't think she's married! It's one of the reasons no one wanted Wallbreaker to win the chieftainship. Oh, he's always been popular, but you can't respect a chief who doesn't even rule his own wives . . . Now, Watersip – you've met my first wife, haven't you? Well, she says Indrani likes you. She says it happens a lot when a woman cares for a wounded hunter. Besides, Watersip says you're a handsome lad – good skin, straight teeth and blue eyes. You could've had any girl in the Tribe if they didn't know there was something wrong with you. Could be that's why Wallbreaker's sending you out today when you're still not ready.'

But Stopmouth knew his brother better than Rockface or any of his wives. 'He t-t-trusts m-m-me. That's w-w-why I'm p-p-p-picked.'

Rockface laughed. 'That must be it,' he said. 'Who listens to women's silly talk anyway, hey?'

They set off in search of Crunchfist's trail. The tower guards told them where the missing party had entered the woods near the Wetlane. The two hunters found a path and followed it to where a tree trunk had been pushed over the water. The tracks were fainter on the other side.

'This is where they started to get cautious,' said Rockface.

Stopmouth thought they should get cautious too – Crunchfist was no fool, whatever else. But Rockface just plunged on and Stopmouth had to struggle to keep up. He managed it better than he'd feared. His strength was definitely coming back.

The trail led into Clawfolk territory, which bordered Flim. Chaos awaited them there. Clawfolk skittered in every direction on spindly legs, even bumping into the humans in their haste. Stopmouth tried to ignore the great panic and study the creatures. It was something Wallbreaker had always urged him to do and he'd want a full report when they got back. Each of the beasts had five legs, one of which was hooked at the end and used for hanging from the sides of buildings or for dragging prey back to Claw-Ways. Right across their long flat bodies, patches of yellow shell alternated with a dozen wet openings that sometimes seemed to be mouths, sometimes eyes.

Now, a great many of the creatures had embedded stone spikes into their hook claws, and once or twice the hunters had to jump aside in order to avoid being sliced open. When they came to the far edges of Claw-Ways, the reason Crunchfist hadn't returned became obvious. Flyers circled high above the streets of Flim-Ways. Armourbacks stood in the towers.

'The Flim are no more,' said Rockface. He shrugged. 'They were no challenge to hunt, anyway.' Even so, Stopmouth thought the big man looked shaken. They plunged back into Claw-Ways, hardly looking where they were going, so that they almost ran into a group of Bloodskins. Stopmouth didn't think he could have outrun them in his present condition, but luckily for the careless humans, the beasts failed to spot them and the men ran on.

They reached home, sweating heavily, heads reeling. When people pestered them for news, they ignored them and made straight for the chief's house.

Wallbreaker had already moved in all his possessions. He was waiting for them amidst a pile of junk metal. He kept sorting through it, ignoring their presence for many heartbeats. He had even failed to hug them on their safe return. He was chief now, Stopmouth thought; he couldn't be seen to favour his brother over any other hunter. And perhaps he was unwell, for his skin shone with perspiration as if he too had just returned from a patrol. Eventually he climbed up onto a fur-covered block that Speareye used on special occasions, and had Mossheart bring them bowls of water. Stopmouth saw that her belly had begun to show. He grinned at her but got no response, and she left quickly.

Then the two hunters gave Wallbreaker a full report of what they'd seen. He surprised them by smiling at last.

'This is good news, my friends, not bad as you seem to

think.' He got down from Speareye's seat and began drawing in the dirt of the floor. 'We are here . . .' He made an X. 'The Armourbacks and their Hopper friends started here . . .' Another X. 'Now they've moved into Hairbeast and Flim, separated from home by Clawfolk and Human. Stupid! So stupid! They must think themselves as powerful as spirits.'

'But there are s-s-so m-many of them,' said Stopmouth. 'Three s-s-species of them. And they have already k-k-k-killed so many of our h-hunters.'

'Sure,' said Wallbreaker, 'but every time they fight somebody, they lose a few of their own. Even the Flim must have killed some when they were taken. And the Hairbeasts would certainly have killed a lot. Our enemies have spent too many lives too foolishly, and we will be the ones to finish them off!'

'I like this talk of their foolishness,' said Rockface, 'even if I hate Armourback flesh.'

'You'll have to get used to the taste!' said Wallbreaker. 'We all will.'

His confidence was inspiring. Rockface left, grinning, and was sure to spread the good news far and wide. Stopmouth hung around for a few minutes afterwards. He wanted to talk to Wallbreaker about the rumours surrounding Indrani, to assure his brother there was no truth in them. He didn't get a chance.

'Not now, brother,' said the chief. The confidence he'd displayed in front of Rockface had disappeared. 'I need to consult with my best warriors about the fight that is coming.' He waved the back of his hand towards Stopmouth. 'We'll talk another day.'

Stopmouth had no choice but to go. He felt a tightening in his gut as he walked home.

Indrani was waiting for him with the roasted flesh of a Wetlane beast. He looked at her, really looked at her, and she looked back; straight into his eyes. She was not Mossheart. Mossheart didn't have such fine cheekbones, nor black hair which, while still short, was lustrous. Mossheart had crooked teeth like any normal woman. She'd never seen him as anything other than a path to Wallbreaker.

He took his food outside to break the spell. When he sat in the doorway, Indrani came and squeezed in beside him. He should have pushed her away. But how could he explain that to her? He'd never minded before, never been as aware of her as he was now. As they ate together, people watched and whispered.

Desperate to distract himself from her proximity, Stopmouth told her what he'd seen in Claw-Ways. Her Human was improving and he thought this time she might understand most if not all of what he was saying. Not that she'd care much: every time in the past when he had begun to tell her about hunting, she'd told him in broken Human that she didn't want to hear about it. 'Not want you talk about bad men do,' she always said.

Today, though, she ate her flesh and listened, sensing his fears. After a few minutes her expression changed from one of reassurance to shock. She jumped to her feet like a panicked Flim.

'Armourback!' she spluttered. 'Armourback work to Hoppers? Work to Flyers?'

'Work *with* Flyers.'

'You never tell me!' She ran into the house, then out again, eyes wild. 'They have the – the . . . No word for it! My head is empty. They have a metal . . . a metal thing they use to talk to Hoppers. You understand, Shtop-Mou? They cannot have this thing!'

'I'm sorry, Indrani, I don't understand. We have metal too. There are bits of Globes all over the place now.'

'Not metal, Shtop-Mou!' She clenched and unclenched her fists. 'A thing of metal, a very different thing.'

Stopmouth could only shrug, while she became more and more frustrated with his lack of understanding and her own lack of speech. She looked like a woman whose child was to be volunteered. She stopped for a moment and screwed her eyes shut, muttering in her baby talk. He saw her look up to the Roof with her deep, black eyes. Then she pointed at it. 'See the . . . the Globes? They are of metal, yes?'

'Yes.' Even the shape of her arm caught his attention now.

'I come out of Globe, yes? You see I come, yes?'

'Yes.' The hair on her head had grown back, but none showed on her skin. He didn't want her to catch him staring, but she had shut her eyes again, struggling for words. 'The Globe is a thing of metal that goes into air. The thing the Armourback has is a different thing of metal that talk Flyer talk to Flyer, Hopper talk to Hopper, yes?'

He had no idea what she meant. And yet . . . A metal object such as a Globe allowed the human Indrani to fly. Could not a magic object exist that would allow beasts to understand each other? If the Armourbacks had got their claws on such a treasure, it would explain why they had suddenly been able to make common cause with two other species. Stopmouth jumped to his feet, excited at last for reasons that did not shame him.

'By the ancestors!' he exclaimed. 'This thing . . . this *different* thing. If we c-can take it away from the Armourbacks, they won't be able to talk to the H-Hoppers any more?'

Indrani nodded.

'You must tell W-W-Wallbreaker.'

'No!' she shot back. '*You* tell to him!' The mention of Wallbreaker's name had worked its usual sour magic on her features. Lovely features, he thought, and turned away from her to calm the beating of his heart. This woman was not just married to his brother, she was married to the chief. For her to be living with another man was an unprecedented scandal among the Tribe, and Indrani had only been allowed to get away with it so far because she had fallen out of the sky. As her speech improved and the novelty wore off, Wallbreaker would be left with no choice but to volunteer her. That decision might have already been taken – the Tribe had lost its greatest hunters. It needed flesh more than ever if it was to survive. Stopmouth had to stop thinking about Indrani, stop looking at her. He had to get her living with Wallbreaker at all costs or see her sacrificed.

'Indrani, *you* must tell W-Wallbreaker. The Tribe won't take the threat seriously if it comes from me.'

She pursed her dark lips and hissed some gibberish at him. But finally she turned and walked towards Centre Square, making Stopmouth scamper to keep up.

'It can't be true,' said the chief when Indrani told him. They'd found Wallbreaker and Mossheart alone in their house. In spite of the presence of his first wife, the chief's eyes had lit up when Indrani arrived. Then he saw Stopmouth too, and smiled more than seemed natural. Mossheart turned her back and took the stairs for the roof. She didn't return.

After a clumsy silence, Wallbreaker questioned Indrani as closely as her broken speech would allow. His lingering stares made her uncomfortable at first, but gradually his fascination with the subject had him hopping in his seat with excitement and Stopmouth grinned to see his brother returned once more to himself.

'If they only have this one metal thing, this . . . let's call it a Talker . . . Yes, Talker sounds right. But if they only have one, then how can the Armourbacks and their friends be in three separate areas at once and still work together? When the Armourback chief takes the Talker out of an area, co-operation there must stop.'

'Only n-need it when p-p-planning,' said Stopmouth.

'True.' Wallbreaker formed his lips into a genuine smile. 'And if we can attack them in a place where they don't have the Talker, they won't be able to adapt their plans quickly. We could really hurt them.' Then he frowned. 'Tell me, my wife, if they can talk to Flyers and Hoppers, could they talk to others as well? Bloodskins, Clawfolk?'

'Can talk with all,' said Indrani, and added, 'Not wife of you!'

'Why n-n-not us?' said Stopmouth quickly. 'Why n-n-not the H-Hairbeasts?'

'Dear brother,' said Wallbreaker, his tone almost sneering, 'if you invite everybody to the feast, there's no one left to eat.' He stroked his chin. 'Perhaps there's no point in attacking them, after all. What's to stop them replacing their losses through alliance with yet another species? No, the only way to survive this is to find the Talker and seize it for ourselves.' Wallbreaker turned his gaze back to Indrani. 'Go home, wife,' he said.

'I not your wife. I never say it!'

'I want to speak to my brother alone. Goodbye, Indrani. Go home.' She scowled, but left them.

Wallbreaker fixed his gaze on the younger man, until Stopmouth felt himself squirm. *I've done nothing wrong!* But the gaze didn't shift for what seemed like tens of thousands of heartbeats.

'How are you healing, Stopmouth?'

'W-w-well.' Stopmouth felt himself relax. 'I r-r-run every d-d-day.'

'Good,' said Wallbreaker. 'You would have been volunteered long ago had I not been able to keep you fed. And Indrani too. A lot of people want her to volunteer, you know. Especially the women. But I married her out of kindness. To keep her safe. And you safe too, because she has no small talent for healing. Some people would find it very funny if, after all that, the chief's brother were to betray him with his own wife.' Wallbreaker laughed. 'Some fools are saying that you are already betraying me. Can you believe that, Stopmouth? They say you're laughing behind my back!'

'N-n-n-never!'

'Why not? Don't you find her beautiful?' Stopmouth

could only look away. Wallbreaker got to his feet and shoved Stopmouth violently with both hands, knocking him back hard so that he hit the wall and slid to the floor, winded.

'Why, Stopmouth?'

'I d-didn't—'

'I didn't say that you did.' His voice turned to a whisper. 'But you want to. Don't you? What is it about my wives, Stopmouth? I would have paid bride price for you to the father of any girl you wanted. But no. Always *my* women. First Mossheart and now poor, unnatural Indrani. I'm a laughing stock. I'm the only chief who can get the Tribe through the horror that's coming. But I can't be chief if I allow this situation with Indrani to go on. You understand that, Stopmouth?'

'W-will you v-v-v-volunteer m-m-m-me?'

'Who do you think you're talking to?' shouted Wallbreaker suddenly. 'Crunchfist?'

Then he calmed again. 'Not a bad idea, Stopmouth. But I will waste none of our people for selfish reasons. No brother of mine will volunteer until he's too old to lift a spear. In fact, if we could gain control of the Talker, no human would ever have to volunteer again. We could co-operate with other strong peoples. Even' – he grimaced – 'with the Armourbacks . . . No, I won't waste you, Stopmouth. Let's make a deal. I don't want Indrani. I'd willingly set the ugly beast aside and allow you to marry her.'

Stopmouth tried to prevent a smile from spreading across his face and failed. He couldn't remember a moment in his life when he'd been more happy. He reached out to hug his brother, but Wallbreaker threw him back again, even harder than before.

'No, Stopmouth.' He was speaking through clenched teeth. Why was he still angry? He'd just said he didn't even want her. 'Not so easy! If I set her aside for you, my chieftainship would be ruined for ever. This will only work if I can provide us with a victory so stunning that no hunter would dare to question my manhood. You understand? If you want Indrani, then I want the Talker.' His eyes bored into Stopmouth. 'Someone's going to have to get it for me.'

'W-who?'

Wallbreaker just kept staring.

9.
THE ALLIANCE ATTACKS

Stopmouth carried the last of Mother's hides to the new house near Centre Square. He wasn't sure he liked it: the buildings were smaller here and other houses crowded in on either side. To tell the truth, nobody wanted to move, but Wallbreaker had ordered the Tribe to pull in as close together as possible. 'For protection,' he said. 'A smaller perimeter will be easier to defend.'

A number of families had disobeyed. The chief just ignored them. 'They'll come round,' he muttered, 'when they've wasted a few more lives.'

Stopmouth still felt bad about what had happened between them and desperately wanted to patch things up. However, the chief was always busy and only spoke to his brother to give him instructions. He seemed to have orders for everybody these days, even the children.

One day he told the Tribe's women to stop pounding skins for a few days to build barriers instead. 'I want them blocking every street within a short walk from my house,' said Wallbreaker. He showed them where, always making sure that this new border had plenty of space in front of it so that intruders wouldn't be able to leap across from nearby buildings. Men were drafted in as well. Traps were dug in the streets, both inside and outside the barriers; boulders were hoisted onto roofs. As work progressed, accidents reduced the number of mouths to feed and created volunteers to keep the others strong.

Stopmouth's own strength came back to him as he worked, and new muscle developed where little had been before. He showed other men how to make spear-points from Armourback shell and soon every fragment of it in the Ways had been used for weapons.

Now and again word came through from the families who'd stayed beyond the protection of the new walls. One day a hunter visiting his uncle discovered only blood. Other homes were found abandoned too. In the end the last survivors moved into the centre.

Now all hunting parties left with Wallbreaker's permission and hunted only where he ordered them to go.

'I can't stand this,' said Rockface one day. His had been the last family to retreat from near the old border. 'I found my infant playing with a pair of Hoppers. They were leading her away. Couldn't even be bothered to carry her!' He grinned. 'I made her a cot out of one of them.'

He watched Stopmouth filing at a piece of Armourback shell for a time. Then he stood up again and wandered restlessly from one side of the small room to the other. 'I can't bear it!' he said finally. 'Crunchfist wouldn't have retreated like this, hey?' Then his eyes lit up. 'Say, Stopmouth, since you and Windbreaker don't seem to be talking much these days, how about the two of us sneaking into Clawfolk to see if we can't sling a Flyer, hey? It'll be like old times.'

Stopmouth could never think of Rockface's 'old times' without a shiver of fear running up his spine. But he needed the big man: no one else was willing to go along with Wallbreaker's mad scheme to steal the Talker. Rockface, on the other hand, had *begged* to go.

I must be crazy, thought Stopmouth. And yet the young hunter prayed every night that an opportunity to capture the magical device would arise soon. If he survived, he, Stopmouth, would have a chance to seek happiness. In the meantime Indrani, who'd learned enough Human by now to understand the peril in which she'd placed both herself and Stopmouth, had finally agreed to avoid further scandal by moving into Wallbreaker's house. She'd been promised her own room and would pretend to obey the chief. Stopmouth was to keep his distance. When the Talker was found, Indrani would be free to live where she pleased, while Stopmouth would be free to woo her.

He hadn't shared the last part with her. His stutter didn't

like the idea of wooing and silenced any attempts to broach the subject. But things would be different after the Talker. He felt sure of it.

He sighed, smiling.

'Thinking of our coming adventure, hey?' asked Rockface, souring the mood again.

Right on cue, Rockface's boy, Littleknife, ran up to them, covered in sweat and dust. 'The chief wants to see the two of you at once. You're to bring your weapons.'

'Thank you,' said Stopmouth, his stomach churning.

Rockface whooped. 'See you there!' he shouted. He flung the child over his shoulder and ran off. Stopmouth collected his latest spear and a favourite sling. He didn't bother with stones or water skins – he'd find plenty of both waiting for him. Then he moved out into the crowded streets of the reduced perimeter. News travelled even faster than in the old days. People buzzed with excitement and fear. Stopmouth didn't pause to ask what was happening. He could guess well enough.

Wallbreaker was waiting for him with Mossheart. The chief had no smile for his brother. A cold nod was all. In the background Indrani busied herself pounding hides where anybody could see her. She never looked up at the sound of Stopmouth's voice, but he thought she stuck to her task with more single-mindedness than was natural. Her hair looked tangled and filthy. Not like her. But who had time for combs these days? Suddenly he realized he was staring. Mossheart smirked, but her husband was positively shaking, as if poised for violence.

Stopmouth lowered his eyes and was relieved when Rockface arrived, too excited to feel any of the mounting tension.

Eventually Wallbreaker spoke, more calmly than his brother could have imagined possible. 'Our scouts have spotted large numbers of Armourbacks and Hoppers moving together outside the walls of Hairbeast-Ways. You realize what this means?'

'They'll try to take us,' said Rockface, 'before they take the Clawfolk!'

'Oh, certainly that,' said Wallbreaker. Since becoming chief he'd worried less and less about showing contempt for those who didn't see things as quickly as he did. 'More importantly, the object we seek, the Talker, is in Hairbeast-Ways. It has to be to co-ordinate all that moving about. And yes, Rockface, they're coming for us. Maybe even tonight.'

'You w-w-want us to l-l-leave n-n-now?'

'Yes, dear brother. N-n-now.'

Stopmouth staggered as though the world had suddenly lurched under his feet. He felt the eyes of Mossheart, Indrani and Rockface on him. But not Wallbreaker's. The chief looked only at the hides on the floor. 'Of course,' he muttered, 'if you don't think the reward is worth the risk, you can always stay here instead.'

'Is not worth risk!' shouted Indrani suddenly. She threw down the hides she'd been working on and stormed out of the room.

'That one's mad,' said Rockface, in forced good spirits. 'People will sing of our deed long after the Traveller's been forgotten.'

Stopmouth gathered himself. He took a deep breath and swallowed the words that first jumped to his lips. Instead, he said, 'Wallbreaker, w-w-when . . . if I c-c-c-c—' He took another breath. Never in his life had it been so difficult to speak to Wallbreaker. 'If I come b-b-back, p-p-promise we will be b-b-brothers again?'

Wallbreaker nodded curtly, and then, as if not trusting himself to speak, he waved them out of his presence.

Stopmouth and Rockface jogged to a house on the perimeter nearest Flim, where friends helped them over the wall.

'You're brave lads,' said one of the hunters, but he was shaking his head and Stopmouth knew the man thought they were crazy.

On the far side of the barrier, Stopmouth and Rockface circled back towards Hairbeast, keeping to the shadows. It was the middle of the day and even in the shade sweat sheened the hunters and soaked into their loincloths and tool-belts. They kept moving, regardless. A few Clawfolk skittered past, stalking one of the surviving Hairbeasts. Finally, after a quick check of the Roof for Flyers, they ducked into a crumbling house that looked as if it would collapse on any creature daring to shelter in it. Parts of it were rigged to do just that. The top floor, however, was trap-free and a lot less dangerous than most of the other buildings in the area.

The men filled their water skins in a nearby channel and dragged them up to a small shelter on the roof that was built to look like rubble from the air. Stopmouth hoped it worked. He'd been having bad dreams about Flyers since the night of the disaster.

'We'll have a fine view of it when it starts!' said Rockface happily. His companion nodded. A wide street led away from the house straight to the new human border. Another house had been prepared for them on the Clawfolk side of the perimeter in case the enemy had decided to come from that direction instead. But the roads were narrow there and the lines of sight more restricted.

Stopmouth dug out a store of smoked flesh. 'Ugh,' he said. 'A-A-Armourback!'

'There'll be a lot more where that came from soon enough,' said Rockface. He too grimaced when he chewed on the flesh.

'We should save some for later, hey? It'll be so boring waiting here. For all we know, the Armourbacks mightn't even bother turning up!'

Within minutes of finishing the snack, the big man was on his back, eyes closed and snoring.

Stopmouth watched the empty streets and distracted himself with daydreams of Indrani. They didn't seem so impossible now. Wallbreaker had promised, hadn't he? Stopmouth imagined the fine skin on her arms, hairless and gently curved. He imagined her lips and the strangely perfect teeth hidden behind them.

Something caught his eye: a pair of hunters were racing back from the direction of the old perimeter. The man in front had already thrown away his spear, so intent was he on escape.

Another movement. Stopmouth almost shouted to warn the men but, remembering why he was there, bit his tongue. Three Flyers were swooping down towards the running humans. Coloured wings folded inwards and the creatures dived. Just when it seemed as if they'd crash into a building, they pulled sharply upwards and released the rocks they'd been holding in their claws. The first man's head burst open. His companion raced away, running for his life. To Stopmouth's relief, the second hunter made it to the walls, where a hail of slingstones drove the Flyers away.

There could be no doubt now. The Armourbacks were coming.

A tenth of a day later, or maybe a fifth, the air filled with a dozen more Flyers. They glided high above Man-Ways. Now and again they'd swoop out of sight behind the walls. Stopmouth saw one of the creatures rise up with a child in its claws until something knocked both it and its prey out of the air. He expected to hear the sound of human cheering. None came. Perhaps the child had died in the fall.

Now the streets began to fill with Hoppers and Armourbacks. Other Flyers arrived to perch on nearby buildings.

'What's going on?' said Rockface, waking.

'Hush!'

Stopmouth tried to count the enemy below him. Impossible, of course, but there didn't seem to be as many as he'd expected. Had they really suffered such tremendous losses in their attack on Flim? If so, surely they couldn't afford more of the same now! But then he remembered the amazing organization this strange alliance had shown on the night Speareye had been killed.

The rest of their force must be circling round to the other side, he thought. After several tries, he managed to communicate this information to Rockface.

'So how will we know which of the two groups has the Talker?' asked the older hunter.

Stopmouth shrugged. Perhaps the ones with the Talker could be spotted by their superior organization. Then again, such a group might just be following previous orders. Or maybe the Armourback chief was even smarter than that: maybe it had used the Talker to teach prearranged signals to all the species under its control. However it was done, the discipline was perfect. Tens of Armourbacks passed in a line through the streets below with tree trunks on their backs. Hoppers hopped alongside with sacks of what might have been water skins or smoked flesh. After the enemy fighters, the two humans saw another strange sight: hordes of Armourback and Hopper females escorting rivers of young.

'Can't leave them behind,' said Rockface, 'or the hunters'd come home to nothing!'

There were definitely more beasts than Stopmouth had at first guessed. The small vanguard had grown tenfold, and more creatures were still arriving.

'W-what w-w-w-ill they all eat?' whispered Stopmouth.

Rockface didn't answer. He didn't have to.

The enemy moved to occupy houses. Downstairs, something hopped into the hallway. A rumbling sound shook the building, followed by gratifying Hopper screams. Up and down the street, dust emerged from other houses too, along with further cries of pain.

Stopmouth fell asleep sometime after dark. He didn't wake until the Roof had filled with light again, although a small square patch of it remained black where a Globe had once struck it. Armourbacks and Hoppers combed the streets below him, looking for rocks or bricks, which they carried to the tops of the sturdiest buildings. This activity went on for a whole quarter day until Stopmouth imagined some of the roofs must have been groaning under the extra weight.

'What next?' asked Rockface.

Next wasn't long in coming. For a while the air had been mostly empty. Now, hundreds of Flyers converged from every direction towards the piles of stones. Each one descended and took a rock in its claws before rising again. They were so numerous it seemed they would blot out the light of the Roof. They wheeled in the sky without any Flyer ever bumping into its companions. Then they sped in the direction of Man-Ways.

The men watched in horror as humans fell off the walls under a rain of stone, knocked senseless or killed outright. Screams reached their ears a heartbeat later. Flyers who'd dropped their burdens returned to the stockpiles in search of more. One human had fallen from the wall into enemy territory. He lay there, moving his head from side to side, his legs obviously broken. Stopmouth winced in sympathy. A group of five Armourbacks made a run for the body, probably hoping to get there before slingers came back to the rampart above. All five disappeared into a pit-trap before they'd got halfway.

'Spikes!' said Rockface with a smile. 'Your brother sure knows where to put them!'

The bombardment continued for many heartbeats. In the midst of it, a Flyer landed on the roof of their building clutching a stone. Rockface grabbed a spear, but Stopmouth held the man's arm. Rockface turned to him in anger, but relaxed almost immediately when he saw Stopmouth's pleading face. He raised a hand in apology.

The Flyer took off again, leaving a few shreds of dried skin behind it. Something glinted in its claws, and suddenly Stopmouth realized it hadn't been a stone after all, but a small sphere of metal.

His jaw dropped. The Flyer swooped low over a crowd of Armourbacks and Hoppers. 'Attack!' it screeched. Was it talking Human? 'Attack! Or I take your children instead! Attack! Use the trees! Remember, human flesh belongs to Flyers alone!'

The Armourbacks and Hopper fighters surged towards the human positions. Hoppers leaped over pits with ease; Armourbacks bridged them with tree trunks. When they reached the base of the walls, humans emerged to push rocks on top of them or fire slingshots. Flyers dived at the humans, but they too were shot at and several fell from the sky into Man-Ways.

The enemy fell back in disarray until only a few angry Flyers remained hovering over the defenders. When the

Armourbacks and Hoppers had reached a safe distance, the Flyer with the metal sphere in its claws swooped over them, screeching for more stones to be brought to the rooftops.

'Try and watch where that one lands,' Rockface whispered. But the Flyer didn't seem to have any one perch. Once again Armourbacks and Hoppers gathered stones and stockpiled them on the roofs of houses. By the time they'd finished, Rooflight had faded. The Flyers gathered in flocks on the same buildings that held their missiles, but this time they stayed to rest and groom each other. It appeared that the attack was over for the moment.

The two hunters witnessed an exchange of wounded between Armourbacks and Hoppers. The Hoppers killed the Armourback wounded one at a time, dismembering each corpse before pulling forward the next victim.

The shelled beasts, on the other hand, preferred live food, and the high screams of Hoppers kept Stopmouth awake for some time after. He wondered what kind of effect it must be having on the relatives of those same Hoppers. Surely they must have wished for better allies.

Stopmouth woke later with Rockface's hand over his mouth. The big man smiled and whispered directly into his ear: 'Let's find that Flyer with the Talker, hey? The only guards they've posted are at their perimeters. They'll never be expecting us!'

Stopmouth's eyes widened. This was exactly what he'd

been afraid of when Rockface had asked to be part of the mission. They couldn't risk it yet. They had to wait until the enemy was weaker. He shook his head violently. They didn't even know which roof that Flyer was hiding on!

'We could be stuck up here for days while the fighting goes on,' said Rockface. 'Besides, this should be easy, and if we don't see the Flyer, we can always find an Armourback to knock on the back of the head, hey? What will my boy think when I tell him I hid while others were keeping him safe?'

Rockface didn't wait for a reply. Stopmouth sent a quick prayer to the ancestors, then followed despairingly through the maze of traps he himself had helped to set.

This is madness! he thought. He should have stayed on the roof and left Rockface to risk his own neck, although if Rockface were seen coming out of this building, Stopmouth would be doomed in any case.

On the ground floor they found two Hopper legs and one arm jutting out from under a pile of rocks. The beast had set off the trap on the stairs. Rockface pried a spear from its grasp. Its point had been made of human bone, and grips had been fashioned in the haft to fit a Hopper's long fingers. Rockface grinned, happy as a child, making Stopmouth even more nervous.

Immediately outside their doorway, two more of the furred beasts slept, entwined. They made Stopmouth think of Indrani for some reason. He winced when his companion stabbed each of them quickly in the eye and moved on. Death, but not for food, not for survival. It seemed strange and wasteful.

A fire burned at the next intersection. More Hoppers slept here, a large crowd, and Stopmouth grabbed the big hunter's shoulder before he could advance on them. Rockface looked hurt, as if the very idea he would do something to endanger the mission were absurd. Instead, he pointed at a nearby building and signalled 'Go!' Stopmouth didn't understand. Rockface signalled again, then made for the doorway and straight up the stairs, leaving his young companion with no alternative but to follow.

Stopmouth understood when they reached the roof. Three Flyers slept with heads curled under flaky wings. They were surrounded by the small stones they used as missiles and the shredded remains of a meal that might once have been one of Stopmouth's neighbours. None of them had the Talker. Rockface pointed to one of the Flyers, which was sleeping off to one side, and then pointed to Stopmouth. The younger man, knowing he had no choice in what came next, nodded.

He climbed carefully over the piles of rocks, heart pounding, worried they might skitter beneath his feet. He could see the creature's blunt snout poking from under its wings. A faint, rhythmic buzz issued from it, which didn't stop until he wrapped one hand over its face and another around its skinny neck. A quick twist, a snap, and the creature was no more. Rockface had also killed one of the beasts on his side, but he seemed strangely reluctant to finish the other. It had wakened before he could attack it, and now he stared into its big, dark eyes, frozen to the spot. Slowly the creature spread its wings.

Stopmouth slipped his bone dagger from its sheath. He would get one throw. If the creature even screamed, they were both dead. He flung the dagger and watched it spin in the air. It seemed to take days to reach the target. When it did, the hilt and not the point struck home. The creature fell from the roof, stunned. Rockface shook himself, but otherwise wasted no time in grabbing up his weapons and running down the stairs to finish the Flyer off. It had fallen on the opposite side of the building from the door. So when they reached the ground floor, they sneaked round the corner of the house. And froze. An Armourback had found the Flyer and was shaking it as if to wake it. Rockface was about to charge, but Stopmouth pulled him back. He pointed to his sling repeatedly, until Rockface sighed and nodded.

The shot was perfect. The Armourback dropped even as the Flyer's wings began twitching. There was no stopping Rockface this time. The big hunter rushed forward and ended yet another life. But not for food.

A thought came to Stopmouth, the type of thought that must have come to Wallbreaker every day. He took the fallen Armourback's spear. On the way back to the hide, he jammed the weapon deep into the corpse of one of the two Hoppers that Rockface had killed outside their building. He left it there, jutting from the body where it couldn't be missed.

Another attack was well under way. Flyers bombarded defenders from a safe height, while below, lines of Armourbacks battered the shaky wall with tree trunks. Humans had never built anything before, certainly not in Stopmouth's lifetime. So rocks quickly came loose and tumbled into the street. Some crashed into the attackers, but not enough to drive them back. Rockface cried out when he saw what was happening, his voice lost in the collapse of an entire section of the wall.

Ancestors save us! thought Stopmouth.

Tens of Hoppers leaped through the gap into a great cloud of dust. Armourbacks followed them, although many of these disappeared down another pit just inside the wall. They were quickly replaced.

Stopmouth thought of Indrani and Wallbreaker and of what the enemy would do to them when they were caught. He saw Rockface biting his lips and clenching his hands and knew the big man was thinking about his own family: two wives and their children who lived by the strength of his arm. So when Rockface tried to run down into the street, the younger man was ready for it and tackled him around the knees so that both fell into a heap.

'N-n-n-ot over yet! C-C-Centre Sssssquare!'

Rockface threw him off, but didn't run. Everyone in the Ways had been drilled to retreat to a new line of defences at Centre Square when the wall fell. They'd be safe still. For a time.

The chief's original idea had been to make the enemy pay such a heavy price for the attack that they'd give up and choose some less fortified victims. But Stopmouth realized this was never going to happen: the Flyers seemed to be completely in control of the attacking forces, and their own losses were very light. What was to stop them simply choosing other allies after the Armourbacks and Hoppers had spent themselves? But, as usual, Wallbreaker had another plan, a darker one. For it to work, the humans would have to hold out at least a full day longer.

The air carried the sounds of desperate struggles all the way to the hideout: the clashing of weapons; human and Hopper screams. Sometimes the men even heard the booming cries of Hairbeasts, and many of their Armourback victims stumbled back to camp with smashed and splintered shells. Once again Wallbreaker had been proven right. But the men saw more and more enemies filing into Man-Ways, until soon only their wounded remained outside. The stronger of these began dragging the weaker back towards their own lines.

A few times Stopmouth saw Armourback young running on four stubby limbs to swarm over dying Hoppers. Other Hoppers chased them off, perhaps because they felt the victim might yet recover, or perhaps they were just angry with the Armourbacks and the torment they caused those they fed upon. Stopmouth couldn't tell.

'The waiting is killing me!' said Rockface. 'They could all be dead in there.'

'No,' said Stopmouth.

Half a day passed and still the two men had no indication of how the battle might be going inside the perimeter. Every now and again, wounded enemies would stumble back through the wall carrying others of their kind. Often, too, it was a human corpse they brought. At one point a Hopper hopped by below with Speareye's youngest child, Bonehammer, over its shoulder. The boy was pale but for a bright slash across his throat.

A Flyer swooped over the Hopper and screeched at it until it dropped the boy and hopped back towards the battle. The Flyer flew off with the child in its claws.

'It's begun,' said Rockface, horror and awe in his voice. 'Wallbreaker's really going ahead with it.'

Finally, to the hunters' great relief, night fell, and the

enemy began streaming back out of the Ways towards their own lines.

Armourbacks and Hoppers dumped corpses of all kinds, including a few Hairbeasts, practically beneath the building in which the two men were hiding.

The Flyer with the Talker in its claws flew low again over the gathered ranks of its allies.

'Human flesh belongs to Flyers,' it screeched in perfect Human, and the only way Stopmouth could tell a beast had spoken was because he'd seen the creature. Someone clever like Wallbreaker would be able to use that to his advantage when planning more of his strange hunts.

The other corpses and injured were to be divided equally among the Flyers' allies. At one point a fight erupted when an Armourback tried to drag off a Hopper still strong enough to resist. Beasts on both sides were wounded until the Flyer leader put an end to it.

Stopmouth saw the corpse of Mossheart's friend, Redcheek, hauled into the air. He'd had last seen her dancing around the fire at his brother's wedding, laughing and making eyes at Waterjumper. Her only smile now was a gash across the throat.

'What a beauty,' said Rockface sadly.

'B-b-brave,' replied Stopmouth. Even if his brother's plan worked, Stopmouth worried that the Tribe could never recover from the loss of so many of its young.

The sounds of squabbling and gorging came from every direction. Neither of the hunters ate. Both watched the Flyer chief feeding itself to a standstill on a nearby building. They were half afraid it would move away afterwards. Instead, it tottered into a corner of the roof and lay down.

When the humans hazarded a look over the parapet of their house, all they saw in every direction was sleeping enemies. Stopmouth didn't try to stop Rockface leaving this time, but padded after him through shadows towards the building where the Flyer leader had made its perch.

Outside, he stood on something soft that shifted under his feet. He stabbed blindly down with his weapon until the movement ceased. It was the place where he'd left an Armourback spear in the corpse of a Hopper the night before. He hoped the furred beasts would blame their allies for this killing too, rather than seeking out any humans in their midst. In either case, it was another creature he wouldn't eat. He consoled himself with the thought that he had yet to commit a waste as great as the one Wallbreaker had planned. In spite of his disgust, right now, in the midst of his enemies, he hoped his brother had done more than just plan it.

They climbed the stairs to the roof, where four Flyers waited. The creatures hadn't placed head under wing as they normally did when they slept. Instead, they lay about the roof, wings twitching uncontrollably, big eyes staring up at the sky. They seemed to have succumbed to some strange kind of fit. The two humans stepped over the remains of Redcheek's corpse and made the easiest kills of their lives. Blood ran hot onto their hands, sticky and delicious. But they didn't dare lick it off. Wallbreaker had said that if the battle went badly enough, he'd call for volunteers and have them eat handfuls of mossbeasts until foam came to their lips. Then they were to be killed and left where the enemy might find them. One human corpse might account for ten beasts or more. Quite likely there were dying Flyers on half the rooftops of the area.

Stopmouth didn't have time to mourn the waste. He prised the Talker from the leader's grasp. It fitted easily into his hand, warm and alive, like the tiny head of a newborn.

He signalled to Rockface, swearing to himself that if the older hunter went on another killing spree, he could do so without Stopmouth's help. They needed to get back to the hide and stay there until they could sneak home. But no sooner had they hit the street than they heard it: 'Humans!' An Armourback had *shouted*, if shout was the right word for creatures that spoke without sound. Whatever the explanation, the men understood it well enough to start running for their lives.

Stopmouth took the lead. His instincts pushed him away from Centre Square, where traps would be waiting in the dark. He'd grown up in these streets and knew alleys and turns that the enemy had never seen. Nevertheless, if a few Hoppers took up the chase, the men would be caught in moments. The young hunter's original home lay no more than two hundred paces away. He ran in that direction, sometimes leaping over huddles of the sleeping enemy.

The pursuing Armourbacks got caught in a crowd of Hoppers just waking with the commotion, adding to it. Some of the females nestled young against their armpits, feeding them with their own blood perhaps.

The milling about and the high-voiced demands of the furred beasts gave the humans time to duck into a doorway. But Stopmouth knew they weren't in the clear yet. He remembered what it was like to be hunted by Armourbacks, how the creatures could run for ever, how relentless they were. And soon the whole area would be swarming with them.

What would Wallbreaker do? he wondered. He remembered his brother pleading pitifully for his life the day he'd been caught. But Wallbreaker didn't have the Talker then. He'd have found a way to use it.

The Armourbacks were having more trouble getting through the Hoppers than expected. The furry beasts seemed angry with their allies over something, and that's when the young hunter knew what he had to do.

'H-h-help!' he shouted. 'The A-A-Armourbacks are attacking us!'

The Hoppers heard this in their own language and reacted angrily. They threw themselves at their allies and a fierce battle ensued. Stopmouth led Rockface through a house and out of a window at the back. No enemies roamed here and they could proceed more slowly, shell spears at the ready. Every time they came to a junction they looked carefully up and down the street. Surely they weren't far now from the edge of enemy occupation. They could find an empty house to hole up in until the fighting had ended.

With immediate danger behind them, Stopmouth began to relax. Every muscle ached, especially those of his left hand, which clutched the precious Talker. This was his marriage, his future. His Tribe's future. This would light the fires in any woman's heart, no matter how strange or beautiful.

And then a sudden, shocking pain lanced into his shoulders. It grew worse as claws jerked him into the air. The Talker shot out of his grasp and rolled down the slight incline of the street. A moment later he hit the ground with the body of a dead Flyer on top of him. Rockface pulled it off and jerked his spear free.

'We should have been looking up too,' said the big man cheerfully, but Stopmouth was searching around desperately for the metal sphere.

'It rolled that way,' said Rockface, pointing.

Stopmouth picked up his weapon and ran down the hill

after it, new wounds burning across his back. He saw the Talker hit a kerb and roll off to the left. He sprinted round the corner in pursuit and stopped dead. Six Armourbacks, probably among those who'd been set to guard the enemy's perimeter, stood around the precious sphere, no doubt wondering if it really was what they thought it was. Six. One on one, with its powerful shell, an Armourback almost always beat a human hunter and would stand a good chance against two.

Stopmouth trembled. The creatures still hadn't seen him, but it didn't matter. He felt crushed, empty. He stood in the middle of the street waiting for the enemy to notice him and claim his useless life. Then Rockface was charging past him, screaming at the top of his voice. Stopmouth hesitated only a heartbeat before joining the other hunter.

Humans had always possessed a longer reach than the Armourbacks, and now they had a new advantage. *Crunch!* Two shell-tipped spears ripped through armour and pierced vital organs. Stopmouth tore the haft of his weapon free, leaving the point in the body of his victim. Never mind. He swung the staff around and struck an Armourback that had turned to face Rockface in the back of the neck. The creature collapsed without a sound, although Stopmouth heard its scream in his head. Two others came for him, little eyes burning red. His spear-shaft couldn't pierce their shell but he managed to strike the legs out from under one of them and avoided the thrust of the other. Rockface, with two victims behind him, finished the standing beast with a knife through a slit in the armour.

The last of the creatures didn't even try to regain its feet. The hunters killed it between them.

Six! They had bested six Armourbacks! Stopmouth took in great gulps of air; sweat streamed down his body and stung his eyes. He'd never felt so exhilarated in his life. Almost as an afterthought, he retrieved the Talker and the two men jogged out of enemy territory. Already Stopmouth was imagining how he'd recount the story to Indrani and how he would surely win her when Wallbreaker finally put her aside.

10.
A BITTER
HOMECOMING

As it happened, the men had to wait the best part of seven days before they could return to their homes. They watched Hoppers and Armourbacks slaughter each other with no thought of food or survival. Eventually Clawfolk coming from one direction, and humans from another, mopped up what remained of the alliance. Stopmouth was sure they'd all be eating bitter Armourback flesh for some time to come. No matter. He'd be getting to see Indrani again soon: her dark lips, her eyes as compelling as a Flyer's. He could marry her in a way that Wallbreaker hadn't. He could win her consent.

Stopmouth had expected cheers at his return. Instead, he and Rockface were greeted with stares in the bone-filled streets from men with new scars and tattooed boys barely large enough to lift a spear. Rubble cluttered the alleys, and everywhere women smoked huge quantities of flesh over fires.

Rockface asked after his family, but nobody seemed willing to answer until he shook the truth out of an exhausted hunter.

'Watersip,' said the hunter, 'she volunteered to poison the Flyers. This was after the Armourbacks had . . . when the rest of her family . . . I'm sorry, Rockface. She was brave. She still had a thousand days left in her, she—'

Rockface refused to believe it. He dropped the hunter in the dust and ran off home, shouting the names of his wives and children.

Stopmouth looked after the other man, his heart filled with pity. Whose ancestor could Rockface be now? It was a horrible thought, but not the only one. Who else had died? he wondered. Who had he, Stopmouth, lost? He tried not to dwell on this question as he picked his way towards the chief's house. The streets had been so altered by traps and fallen buildings that when he reached Centre Square, he barely recognized it. Blood spattered many of the walls, and the half-butchered corpses of enemies littered the ground, sure to go to waste. Worse, old Tally sticks had spilled out of the doorway of the House of Honour, some trodden on, some even broken! The souls to whom those sticks belonged would never make it Home. Nobody had taken the time to clean up this outrage or even to hide it. Nobody.

Then he saw Wallbreaker and Mossheart stepping out

of their house together. Wallbreaker looked like he hadn't slept in tens of days. He was thinner than Stopmouth had ever seen him and he had dark patches under his eyes. When the chief noticed his brother looking at him from across the square, he cried out as if he'd seen a spirit. He hobbled over the intervening space to hug Stopmouth in evident relief. Had all been forgiven? Were they brothers again as the chief had promised they would be? His joy seemed real; Stopmouth could feel it in the strength of his embrace. Many heartbeats passed before Wallbreaker even asked about the success of the mission.

But when he did, activity in the square came to a halt. It was as if people were only now remembering why they hadn't seen Stopmouth during the battle. Men and women edged closer, almost timidly. Not like humans at all. Stopmouth looked to the edges of the gathering crowd, hoping to spot Indrani there, smiling at him. Why couldn't he see her? He felt a sudden reluctance to pass the Talker over to his brother, mingled with fear for her safety. What if she'd been made to volunteer during the battle?

But he knew these thoughts were unworthy of him. If he couldn't trust his brother, the world had lost all meaning. So he reached into the pouch and pulled out the fist-sized sphere of metal.

He said: 'I h-h-h-ave it h-h-h—'

And the Talker said: 'I have it here!'

Some of the people applauded; many wept until Wallbreaker waved for silence. They obeyed instantly.

'We are few now,' the chief said. 'No more than a thousand' – Stopmouth's jaw dropped even as his brother's voice grew stronger and louder – 'but we are the bravest thousand humans that have ever lived!'

He raised the Talker. 'With this ball of magic whose capture I planned, I can promise our survival! More! I can promise that none of our children's children will ever have to volunteer! Ever!'

A great cheer followed.

Stopmouth's head was still reeling with the thought that so few of his people had survived. Too few in such a dangerous world. And he still couldn't see Indrani.

He tried to ask Wallbreaker about her, but couldn't make himself heard above the crowd.

'We have all been brave,' shouted the chief, 'but none more so than my brother, Stopmouth!' The people agreed with enthusiasm. 'He and Rockface will have new tattoos for this! Although I don't know where poor Rockface will find the space!'

'I bet his wives know!' shouted someone in the crowd. There was some laughter, but this was quickly hushed by those who knew the fate of Rockface's family.

'I will also reward my brother by keeping a promise I made to him the last time I thought I'd lost him. I will find him a bride!' Stopmouth's heart soared. 'The Tribe needs children now, new hunters, and more women to build our walls and smoke our flesh. I will personally pay the bride price for Stopmouth to take his pick of any of the unmarried women of the Tribe!' More cheering followed, real cheering, as if the people only now realized they'd won and were finally safe. In the midst of fierce backslapping, Stopmouth was wondering what Wallbreaker had meant by 'unmarried women'. Had he already set Indrani aside? Had she died in the fighting? But he didn't dare ask such questions in public. So, when Stopmouth got the chance, he pushed his way through those who tried to hug him towards the chief's house, where Wallbreaker had already retreated. Stopmouth didn't enter. If Indrani waited within, he couldn't be seen with her. Not yet. But he had to know that she still lived. He couldn't bear the thought that she lay in some larder, perhaps the larder of this very house. He rested one hand against the lintel for support. Unless he could talk to his brother, alone, he had no way of finding out what had happened to her. He called a few times with no response from within. The celebration started by Wallbreaker's speech had grown rowdy enough to drown out his voice. Perhaps that was why no one came to the entrance to greet him. He could come back in a tenth, or sooner if the singing stopped.

Behind him, people were taking flesh from the smoking fires and dancing around them. A few even jumped the flames as though this was a wedding. Most were discussing the power of the Talker in excited voices. They smiled when Stopmouth passed, but knew they'd never get a story out of him with his twitchy tongue and left him alone.

He wandered through a few laneways until he came to his new house. Blood had dried into the dirt of the floor and a small clump of what might have been Hopper fur lay in one corner.

The hides were mostly undisturbed. He sat on them, watching the light outside, hoping the celebrations would die down soon.

After an eternity had passed, he made his way back to his brother's house. Centre Square hadn't emptied, but most people were here now to eat. Before the siege everyone had preferred to take their meals in family groups, but the fighting had brought the survivors together.

He called out for Wallbreaker, who appeared from behind a hide curtain of the thickest sort. The chief nodded at his brother, but didn't smile as he had in public or invite him inside. Wallbreaker was wearing a pouch on his belt with the Talker in it. Good, thought Stopmouth. His speech would be clear. He'd need that.

The Talker spoke in Stopmouth's voice: 'When are you going to be setting her aside?'

'I'd be a cruel man indeed to set aside any woman in the present circumstances,' the chief replied. 'I couldn't do that to either of my wives.'

Stopmouth stood and stared, unable to believe what he was hearing. Wallbreaker made as if to step back inside, but Stopmouth found his voice again and called him back.

'You made me a promise!'

'Stopmouth, you know I only made that promise because Indrani didn't want to be here at the time. I had no intention of forcing her to stay. But during the fighting . . . well, I saved her life and she was sufficiently grateful to—'

'That's a lie!'

'Keep your voice down!' hissed Wallbreaker. 'You made a promise of your own, remember? Do you want the whole Tribe to hear?'

'They'll surely wonder why you're not inviting your own brother into your house, but instead keep him at the door!'

'I don't invite anybody in here any more. They all know that. It's the best way to protect my family.'

'This is madness! Let me see Indrani. If you won't allow me in, then send her out here to tell me of her decision herself. I'll accept what she says and I'll leave you alone.'

'I am your chief,' said Wallbreaker, face burning, 'and you will do what I say in any case! But I don't want to fight with you, my brother. I never wanted to fight with you. Not over a woman. They've always found me more attractive than you, you know that. I thought you'd come to accept it by now.' He reached out a hand to Stopmouth's shoulder, but Stopmouth shook it off angrily. He wanted to hit

Wallbreaker. Not like when they fought as children, but to really hit him. He knew he could strike hard: he'd gained muscle of late, while Wallbreaker, if anything, seemed to be losing it.

'Look,' said Wallbreaker, 'Indrani can fight. Most people even call her Mankicker now. Do you honestly believe that I could have obliged her to show her gratitude if she hadn't been willing? Do you think I could keep her here against her will?'

The barb struck home. No one could make Indrani do anything she didn't want. They'd have to kill her.

Stopmouth dropped his head as Wallbreaker continued. 'So many women in the Tribe need husbands now, Stopmouth. They'll admire you when they see the tattoos I'll give you. And what of the widows who need protectors to avoid volunteering? Why, at your age you could have two wives if you wanted!'

Stopmouth stumbled away without answering. What he wanted right then was to die.

Over the next few days, humans began to pick up the pieces of their lives. Most families had been required to provide volunteers during the fighting and others had disappeared entirely. So there were many weddings and a great deal of building to enforce the new perimeter that Wallbreaker had established. Hunters spent their time competing with

Clawfolk for the corpses of Hoppers and Armourbacks that kept turning up, dreading the day when this easy flesh ran out. There were so many orphans around now that the chief had ordered older hunters to hold classes in Centre Square in place of missing fathers.

Stopmouth hardly noticed the changes. He ate little and walked lots while his imagination invented heart-wrenching conversations with Indrani: 'Why did you choose him? How could you choose him? You wanted me!' Although Indrani had never actually said so herself. He needed answers to these questions. He wanted her to see him again, to remind her of what she'd rejected. Perhaps then she wouldn't be able to speak the words that would surely kill him. Oh, he knew many who'd lost far more than he had, and from time to time he sent prayers to the ancestors to watch over Rockface and other mourners. But he couldn't prevent his thoughts from returning to Indrani.

In his mind's eye he saw the way Wallbreaker had always watched her with such hunger. It hurt, and he couldn't stop feeding the hurt until it filled every waking moment.

By day he walked through Centre Square as often as possible. He took to burning Armourback shell into spearheads at a place where he had an unrestricted view of the door to the chief's house. After several tens he realized that Indrani never went outside, not even onto the roof. A person couldn't live like that. It wasn't natural.

She was probably inside now, he thought, giving Wallbreaker answers to all the questions he'd ever posed, laughing in between; coy, kissing. The thought burned and came back again and again to burn him further.

One day he followed Mossheart as she set out from the house alone. Her child wouldn't be long in coming now, he thought. She waddled in the direction of her older sister's home. He caught up with her before she reached it at a place where the Hairbeast refugees had painted some of their strange blood designs on the gable end of a house.

'C-c-can we sssspeak?'

She grimaced when she saw who it was, no echo of friendship left in her eyes.

'The chief has told you to stay away, Stopmouth. So stay away. Find a woman before people begin to talk about you. Some of them already do.' She began to move off again.

'W-w-why won't she l-l-leave the house?'

'She obeys her husband,' said Mossheart bitterly. 'As I do. Neither of us has any choice.' When she walked off, he called after her, but she didn't stop.

Of course Indrani had had a choice! She'd been a strange but powerful fighter who could kick the height of a man's head. Lots of men had been afraid of her, and even Wallbreaker couldn't stand over her ten tenths of the day.

Once again he wondered if she were dead, or horribly injured and next on the list of volunteers. He wondered too why Wallbreaker never permitted anyone into the chief's house any more. Surely, if he'd won Indrani's loyalty for himself, the smart way to quell all those earlier rumours would have been to show her off as she prepared his food.

Stopmouth realized there was only one thing to do: he'd have to go and see for himself.

When night fell, he moved into the streets behind Centre Square. Here the back of the chief's house faced onto a laneway with a ground-floor window for the ventilation of smoke.

Stopmouth lifted himself onto the sill. The embers of a dung fire inside gave just enough light for him to see that the room was empty. He sighed with relief. This part at least would be easy.

He was about to crawl forward when he noticed something: an old spear-shaft had been left on the inner part of the windowsill – right where he would have had to put his hands as he climbed inside. He reached to push it out of his way, but the fire burst into life again and frightened him into stillness. In that moment he saw that the piece of wood under his hand was no ordinary old spear-shaft. One end of it connected to a hide rope, hidden until now by a rim that framed the window and disappeared into the shadows of the ceiling.

A trap! Wallbreaker's speciality. Perhaps it was just a

leftover from the battle; many houses had been protected in this way, although it was surely strange that something so dangerous should still be here when the threat had passed.

Stopmouth climbed carefully into the room without disturbing the spear-shaft. He saw nothing more suspicious amongst the shadows than racks of smoked flesh and a few tree branches ready for cutting into tools.

In the next room at the back of the house, Mossheart slept, breathing noisily. A few flames danced in a fire pit, throwing light onto the delicate curve of one cheek. She looked as beautiful as on her wedding night. An arm stretched out from under the hides, resting on what might, in her dreams, have been a shoulder. His heart melted and for a moment he was once more the boy who had loved her in desperation. He shook his head, ready to move on. But then he saw the first signs of Indrani's presence. In the corner, something black and shiny rested against the wall. He stepped over to it carefully and picked it up. A smile came to his face. It was part of the strange costume Indrani had arrived in. It must be. A bent container, just the right size for one of her feet. He had just turned it over to examine the sole when he heard a movement and froze. Mossheart had stirred in her sleep. His mouth turned dry and his heart thudded *bang, bang, bang* in his chest. But she seemed to settle again at once. He put down the foot-covering and moved on.

The next door brought him to what had been the meeting room before Wallbreaker had stopped inviting guests into his home. No fire here, no sounds of breathing. Nothing.

One last place to check, he thought. It lay in front of him, hidden by a hide drape across the entrance. He steeled himself for what he might find now: his brother and his love entwined on the floor. He'd leave as soon as he saw it, but he didn't want to add to his humiliation in Indrani's eyes by being caught. No matter what was in that room, he vowed, he'd keep silent. He could cry all he wanted when he got home.

Careful, he thought. Careful . . .

Remembering the spear-shaft on the windowsill, Stopmouth checked for traps again, and amazingly found a piece of ligament twine tied at ankle height across the doorway. Nothing fatal. But in your own house! Another piece of ligament stretched across at neck height and Stopmouth had to duck between the two as he pushed the curtain aside.

He heard more breathing in here, one person only. It was a hoarse rattle, a constant struggle. With no fire to guide him and the window blocked up, he had to get down on his knees and crawl towards the sound. His hand found the damp palm of another person in the dark. The fingers didn't move under his.

'Indrani?' he whispered. 'Indrani?' The person didn't

wake up when he shook her by the shoulders. Her skin burned under his touch and every few seconds a twitch passed from her body into his hand. It reminded him of something. But what? Then it came to him. In his mind's eye he saw the rooftop where he and Rockface had recovered the Talker. He saw the dying Flyers with their staring eyes and trembling wings.

This then was how Wallbreaker kept her at home. Stopmouth wanted to cry out, to scrape at the walls until his palms ran bloody. It's a mistake, he thought. Wallbreaker didn't do this. Nobody could do this. Indrani was always so ignorant of even the most basic things, like a child. And like a child she might have forgotten to brush mossbeasts off her food if any had crawled onto it.

And yet a person would need to eat whole handfuls of them for this to happen.

He lifted the woman onto his shoulders with far too much ease. Perhaps this wasn't Indrani after all. Indrani had muscle on her frame. He moved to the doorway and tore the curtain out of his way. He nearly dropped his burden right there. Mossheart stood in the hallway looking straight at him. Shadows covered most of her face, giving her the look of a skull.

'Good, Stopmouth,' she said. 'I thought you'd never come! And on a night when Wallbreaker is off working on plans for an alliance with the Clawfolk. Good!'

She pointed a shaking hand at the body on Stopmouth's shoulders. 'She is destroying my husband.' Her voice was almost a screech; tears tracked down her face. 'He was never so frightened before *she* came to this house.' Stopmouth didn't try to correct her. He edged past her towards the main entrance.

Mossheart's skull turned to follow him. 'I almost don't recognize you any more, Stopmouth. You're filling out, more of a man than a boy.' She shrugged, as if to say, *The past is no more.* 'Once Wallbreaker finds out she's bewitched you, he'll have to volunteer you both.' Was she smiling? 'I think after that . . . he'll be able to sleep again.'

Stopmouth left through the main entrance, not caring if anybody were awake to see him. He was sure Indrani was dying, so it seemed less important to him in that moment that he too was as good as dead; little more than walking meat to be traded to the Clawfolk.

II.

THE LONGTONGUE

In Centre Square the smoke fires had burned down to the embers. He removed Indrani from his back to get a good look at her. She blinked slowly through drooping lids and didn't respond to her name when he softly called her. White flecks of foam speckled her chin and glittered in the low light of the ancestral fires in the Roof.

He didn't know what to do. He'd only gone to Wallbreaker's house to see her, to talk to her and suffer her scorn. Looking at her now, he realized that if she wasn't already dying, his stupid rescue had surely condemned her. And himself too.

Unless . . . He couldn't believe the idea that settled in his mind just then. As if the ancestor of an enemy had wormed its way into his head and whispered: *Sneak back into the house. Murder Mossheart. Murder Wallbreaker on his return.* He shook off the alien thought, knowing no human was capable of such a thing. No, he'd find another way. He wasn't as clever as Wallbreaker, but he'd think of something.

He took Indrani into his house and built a fire. He found a cloth to wipe her face, then ruined his good work spooning broth into her mouth. For a while he just watched over her, expecting Wallbreaker at any minute. But her rasping breath drew first his pity and then his eyes. He found he couldn't look away. Sometimes when she spoke, full of excitement, she clenched her teeth behind open lips, fiercely, but fierce in the way a child is fierce; all innocence and enthusiasm. That look never failed to make him smile. She wore it now in her illness and he imagined her standing proud before the enemy ancestors that assailed her, wishing he could be with her.

He touched a hand to her damp forehead. Without meaning to, his palm slipped down to cup her face and passed from there to play idly with her perfectly black hair.

'Indrani. P-poor Indrani . . .'

He wondered again how long it would take for Wallbreaker to come back. The first place he was likely to search would be here.

When the broth was gone, Stopmouth packed up his weapons and two empty water skins. He wouldn't be able to carry much more if he had to take Indrani as well. He hefted her onto his shoulders and went out into the night-time streets. His shuffling steps echoed off the walls as he stumbled towards an empty building near the new perimeter. The windows here had been blocked, of course, but one particular barrier had been made weaker than the others so that it could be easily removed from the inside.

He heaved Indrani up onto the windowsill, climbed past her and pulled her down after him. He made no effort to close off the barrier again: he doubted whether it was even possible. Besides, he wanted any pursuers to think he'd gone towards the now empty streets of the Hairbeasts.

Half the night had passed and Indrani got heavier with every step he took. Her breathing rasped in his ear and her drool soaked into his shoulder. He still had a long way to go before he could rest. He circled the old perimeter until he came to a house that had been prepared for himself and Rockface on the Flim side. If the Armourbacks and their allies had chosen to attack from newly conquered Flim-Ways instead of Hairbeast-Ways, the two men would have hidden here rather than the place they'd used for stealing the Talker.

He stepped round the traps on the stairs, which hadn't been disturbed, and found with relief that no one had touched the food caches either. There was so much flesh from the great battle that nobody had yet needed to come for it.

He laid Indrani down on the old skins that had been left here. Then he curled up in a corner and was asleep in an instant.

Stopmouth woke with a knife against his throat. The glare from the Roof was so strong that for a moment he couldn't see who held it.

'He promises he'll give an extra wife to whoever brings Indrani back,' said Rockface. 'What do you think of that? And me a widower, hey?'

Rockface gave off a foul odour – his teeth were going bad, and for the first time Stopmouth realized that the bigger man might soon lose his great strength. Nor did he look like a person used to a good night's sleep: his eyes were bloodshot and baggy. Soup caked the sides of his mouth.

'I was s-s-sorry about W-W-Watersip and Q-Quicksmile,' said Stopmouth. 'They s-still had a th-thousand days left in them.'

'Yes,' said Rockface sadly. 'Yes, they had.' He put away the knife. 'The men are already checking in our old hide, the one we used for stealing the Talker. It was sneaky of you to leave by the Hairbeast route, but they'll come here next. This is not a good place for you.' He studied Indrani, his bloodshot eyes blinking slowly. 'You should move to another building, hey? I'll help you carry her, although she looks ready to volunteer no matter what you do for her now.'

They took Indrani and the blankets to another house nearby. Then they carried over the food and Stopmouth's few weapons. As they left, Stopmouth triggered a trap on the stairs by lobbing a rock onto the appropriate step. Half the roof collapsed. He didn't want any of his old friends setting it off by mistake. Besides, they'd use up more time wriggling through the rubble to get to the rooftop.

'Stopmouth?' said Rockface. The younger man nodded and waited. Rockface was always so easy to read. Right now his face had screwed up as if he'd found a particularly tough knot of gristle in his broth. 'Wallbreaker thinks you and I are in league. He tried to have me followed this morning. And . . . and there's something else . . . Wallbreaker said . . . Well, it's a message, I suppose. He said that if you come back to the Ways without her . . . If it's just you by yourself, he'll forgive you. He'll deny the rumours that you took her and say she ran off alone. He even told the others they were only looking for her. He's letting on she's feverish and doesn't want to volunteer.'

The two men turned to look at Indrani. She'd gone way beyond feverish. She burned under the attack of an army of enemy ancestors. And yet Stopmouth remembered how well she'd taken care of him when people had wanted him volunteered. He could do no less in return.

For some reason this thought cheered Rockface. Maybe he needed the distraction. 'Oh, you're always getting me in trouble, Stopmouth! But it's the type of trouble that's good for a man, hey?'

Rockface didn't leave immediately. 'I almost forgot! They found Crunchfist.'

'The b-b-body?'

'No! That's the amazing thing. He's alive. All his pack were killed by Armourbacks in Flim-Ways and they damaged his leg so he couldn't run. But he managed to hole up there, and even with all his wounds, he caught a few to keep him company while he healed.'

'W-W-Wallbreaker?'

'Oh, he locked him up in the old wedding tower. He's within his rights, hey? Crunchfist is a failed candidate. But people aren't happy about it and Wallbreaker won't be able to trade him until food gets really short.'

Or maybe, thought Stopmouth, Crunchfist would eat a few mossbeasts. The unloved chief couldn't afford to keep a living hero around for long. Especially one as dangerous as Crunchfist.

Rockface clapped the younger hunter on the back and left the way he'd come.

Afterwards, loneliness swept over Stopmouth. He grew angry at his brother and then cried because he'd lost him.

He spent the rest of the day building a shelter on the roof. Sometimes he saw hunters pass by, human or Clawfolk. Once he even saw a pack of Bloodskins. He wanted to shout the alarm, but couldn't. Nor did he dare light a fire to warm Indrani when they ran out of soup.

He looked up to where a pair of Globes floated almost directly above him. It was strange how there always seemed to be at least one of them near Indrani. The Roof darkened, its panels turning from searing blue to grey and then black, the grid of tracklights slowly brightening. The Globes never moved the whole time. Finally he turned away to examine the supplies.

They had eight strips of dried flesh between them. Each strip could sustain a hunter for a day. He tore off a chunk of it and chewed and chewed until his aching jaws had turned it to pulp. He mixed this with water in the base of a Flyer skull and poured it into Indrani's mouth.

'We're done for,' he said as he massaged her throat. 'We can't go back, and yet where else can we go?'

Then again, if Wallbreaker were to die somehow . . .

That horrific thought again. How could a human kill another when everyone needed everybody else? When the Tribe had been so far reduced as to hang on the verge of extinction? Humans didn't kill their own kind unless to put them out of their misery. From time to time the chief could simply order a hunter to volunteer for the good of the Tribe. In this way even adulterers and other criminals contributed to everyone's survival.

Stopmouth knew he couldn't murder Wallbreaker, not even this new Wallbreaker who could look at a brother and not see him. Nobody else was sharp enough to save the Tribe; nobody else could come close.

A terrible smell distracted Stopmouth from his musings. Indrani had soiled herself. He cursed and realized he should have thought of that earlier. At least it was a sign of life.

Over the next few days his meat supply dwindled. Hunting parties still passed in the streets below, but they were looking for flesh and not criminals. By now Indrani had ceased foaming at the mouth and her body rarely spasmed as it had at first. They both needed flesh. Stopmouth could think of little else, even though he knew he had no right to live.

When night fell, he took his spear and sling, a supply of stones and a water skin. He spent a few minutes studying the streets from roof level before setting out. He'd never hunted alone before. In the Tribe, only Crunchfist had survived such stupidity more than once.

He headed for the Wetlane, always keeping to shadows, ducking into doorways if he thought he heard any movements. Then he did hear something: human voices. He stayed stock-still and waited, hoping a gurgle from his stomach wouldn't give him away. A trading party was coming back from Claw-Ways. Three of the creatures accompanied the humans, but the beasts couldn't have been volunteers for they weren't bound and they even carried weapons embedded in their hook claws. So Wallbreaker had used the Talker to make an alliance! Stopmouth changed direction to avoid getting too close to the group.

He decided to head for Flim in the hope that a few Armourbacks or Hoppers might be left there. If nothing caught him, he could at least scout out the area and return the following day.

He reached the Wetlane at the Clawfolk end of the old perimeter, but stayed on the human side until he came to a place in the forest where an old tree had fallen over it. Both humans and Flims had used the trunk in the past as a route into each other's territory. Now Stopmouth crossed it and sneaked through the woods until Flim stretched before him like a curtain of black moss. No fires brightened the night and the towers appeared unguarded. Nevertheless, because both his life and Indrani's depended on it, he ran hunched over towards the first buildings, as if thousands of eyes were searching the night just for him.

He'd covered no more than fifty strides when a light brighter than the Roof exploded into the air around him with almost physical force.

He dropped his weapons and fell to his knees, pawing at his eyes. 'I'm blind!' he screeched, heedless of who or what might find him. He lay down and wept for hundreds of heartbeats, palms pressed against his face. When finally he pulled them away, garish spots danced in front of his eyes. But at the edges of the spots his vision was clearing. A short time later he could see well enough to run over to the first wall, panting with terror. Only then did he begin to question what had happened.

The old people had spoken of something like this. What was it? What? Then he grinned. He couldn't believe his luck.

'Of course!' he whispered.

In the past, whenever a species had been hunted to extinction, new victims appeared to replace the old. Enough new creatures would arrive to fill every room of every building in the area. Those numbers would decrease very quickly until the new arrivals learned to defend themselves. But as long as their ignorance lasted, every nearby species would be sending hunters to profit from the bonanza.

Stopmouth decided not to bother sneaking in through a window, and ran instead for the main gate. He wouldn't have to fear other hunters with so much easy flesh to be had.

The streets of Flim-Ways lay silent and empty before him. Good, he thought. Good! New beasts were always said to arrive in their sleep.

He entered a street containing only ruins. But near an intersection, three houses stood together wholly intact.

'Mustn't get greedy,' he told himself. Depending on their size, the weight of an adult might prove too much for him and he didn't want to risk hanging around to butcher a corpse. No, what he needed to find was a family. He could spear the young and bring back enough flesh to keep himself and Indrani alive for weeks.

The first house of the group of three had no hide curtain across the door. Stopmouth approached cautiously and peered into the hallway. He couldn't see a thing. He poked the spear inside.

'Stop wasting time!' he scolded himself. Just this once he was on a hunt with nothing to be afraid of. His mouth was watering at the thought of new flavours. It was almost too much to bear. He stepped into the darkness of the hall. Away from the tracklights he could see very little apart from two shadowy openings. He was about to enter the first of these when his spear-tip encountered something soft and yielding that seemed to be stretched across it.

He was reaching out a hand towards the strange substance when a noise from the street stopped him cold. He turned towards the doorway, trying to bring his spear to bear. It took several heartbeats to work loose. By that time he could already see the Hopper charging in through the main door at him, a knife in its hands. The spear came free, but he dropped it when the Hopper cannoned into him. Its knife cut a red line up his left arm. Its body knocked him flying back into a wall, winded, helpless.

Stopmouth couldn't see the creature's face clearly in the dark. He wondered if its eyes were filled with triumph and hatred for the humans that had brought doom to its race. It raised its knife for the killing blow.

And paused.

The creature seemed to be straining against something, its breath coming in quick little wheezes. It lifted its second hand to the first, which held the knife over its head as if waiting for one of its fellows to take blood from its armpit. Now its whole body shook. When it raised powerful legs from the ground so that its full weight hung in the air, Stopmouth thought he was dreaming. The Hopper jerked and spasmed before the young hunter realized that the creature was caught in something so thin it couldn't be seen in this poor light.

Stopmouth decided to make a run for it. Whatever beasts lived here, he no longer felt the urge to hunt them. He tried to sit up, but he sprang back against the wall, held by some kind of stretchy moss that stuck to his skin.

Meanwhile, in spite of its struggles, both the Hopper's legs were now entangled too. It stopped all movement for several heartbeats until its breathing had slowed slightly. Then it renewed the assault, more determined than ever. In the end, even its head became entangled.

Stopmouth decided not to struggle as the Hopper had done, yet he had no idea how to free himself. So far, the sticky substance had only caught the skin of his back, and perhaps part of his loincloth. He stretched a little, testing the bounds of his trap. The floor didn't stick to the soles of his feet. That was a start. He stretched a little more. His left foot brushed against something on the floor, something that rolled away from him. His spear! To reach it he had to lean back further into the sticky moss that held him. It welcomed a whole shoulder into its embrace and didn't let go again. His ear became stuck, as did strands of his hair. Panic rose within him. He wanted so badly to pull away. His breath came quicker and quicker until he and the piteous Hopper kept perfect time.

Stopmouth tried to will himself to calm down. His left foot touched the spear-shaft again. He dragged it towards his free hand, leaning more and more into the moss. It covered his eyes now, gluing them shut. It was all he could do to keep his mouth free of the stuff.

In another part of the house, something began to stir, something that scratched and skittered. The Hopper heard it too and renewed its useless thrashing.

Stopmouth shifted the spear round until he had the Armourback-shell point in his hand. He was frightened to cut into the moss in case the blade got stuck too. Instead, ever so slowly, sticky strands parted under the edge until he'd freed the lower half of his face and most of his right arm.

The skittery-scratchy noise came closer. Whatever kind of creature it was, it had left the front room of the house and seemed to be climbing the walls.

The Hopper screamed once. Then again. Warm liquid splashed across Stopmouth's back. Every instinct told him to tear himself free. Instead, he kept on sawing. His hand shook under the spear-shaft while something squelched and slurped behind him. More skittering, closer now. Stopmouth cut the last of the strands from his eyes and face. He jerked himself violently away, ripping hair from his head, leaving the loincloth behind him with its weapons belt.

A shadow clung to the roof where the Hopper had been. Dark skin glistened in the poor light of the hallway, but the beast's shape remained vague. Stopmouth held the spear up in front of his face. A powerful blow hit the centre of the shaft, almost knocking him back into the moss. Another strike and the wood snapped in his hands.

The young hunter was breathing heavily, trying to choke back his fear. He was about to die and the only question was how brave a fight he could make of it. He threw the bottom half of his broken weapon to one side in case he slipped on it. The moment the shaft struck the floor, a long part of the creature lunged after it, striking repeatedly. Stopmouth prayed he wasn't misreading the situation and took a gamble. He flung the rest of his spear up at the roof behind his head. It stuck to the moss, bouncing up and down. The beast scrambled towards it and Stopmouth ran for his life.

The creature came charging after him. It must have struck at him because he felt a light, burning touch on his shoulder. Then he dived through the door and rolled onto his feet. He turned to look behind him, but the monster had drawn back into the shadows of the doorway.

Heaving and sweating, Stopmouth wanted only to run home and throw himself on his hides to sleep. A squeal stopped him. Looking down the street, he saw a Bloodskin leaning halfway out of the window of a nearby house. It had got itself caught in something and Stopmouth had a good idea what that might be. His skin crawled and he felt sorry for the beast. Creatures must be coming from all over now in search of easy prey, but they were becoming prey themselves.

Flesh, thought Stopmouth. Indrani would need flesh and he'd be in no condition to get it for her over the next few days.

So he turned back to the Bloodskin trapped in the window. It was probably pleading for help, its snarl of teeth clacking together rapidly. But Stopmouth heard other Bloodskin cries from within the building and guessed that no aid would be coming any time soon. He snapped the creature's neck quickly. From the room beyond, he heard thrashing and guessed there was at least one more beast in there that would have been glad to have its neck broken round about now. But Stopmouth didn't have time to worry about that. He stole a bone knife from his victim's belt and began carving strips of red flesh from its arm. Then, he heard the skittering-scratch of the new beasts as one of them entered the room beyond. The last Bloodskin renewed its struggles until an impact like the smack of a drum brought them to an end.

Stopmouth's time was running out. He was halfway through an elbow joint when the knife, and the rest of his kill, were jerked into the darkness of the house. A spray of warm liquid drove him back from the window. Then a black, shiny-skinned head pushed outside. It had eyes, but they stayed closed and Stopmouth wondered if they could open at all. A round, toothless hole made up the rest of the head while the body remained invisible. Stopmouth kept himself out of what he thought of as arm's reach. The head swayed from side to side on the end of a rigid-looking tubular neck. Oh, how he wished for a sling!

'There's no m-more flesh for you here tonight,' he said.

The mouth opened even wider. Instinct drove Stopmouth to the ground. The air whistled above him as a black line, like a spear, shot out of the creature's face and impaled the air above his head. The tongue shot back as fast as it had emerged. Stopmouth lay transfixed for many hundreds of heartbeats before the new beast pulled back into the building.

He grabbed the two poor handfuls of Bloodskin flesh

he'd been able to cut and staggered back to the gate of Flim-Ways just as the Roof was beginning to brighten with morning.

He walked across the moss to the trees and from there went to the fallen trunk across the Wetlane. He heard human voices coming the other way and hid himself. He was surprised it had taken his people so long to send a hunting party to the new beasts, and wondered if this was perhaps the second or third. He hoped not: the Tribe couldn't afford many losses.

They passed him in single file, six hunters, from veterans down to boys. All wore tattoos from the recent fighting. Stopmouth felt wretched. His muscles tensed – not for running away, but for leaping out to join those who should have been his comrades. Only with great effort did he hold himself in check.

Most of the men wore a tool-belt and a loincloth of supple grey Flim hide, marvellous material, cool against the skin and gone from the world now for ever. The hunters chatted almost gaily, excited and unafraid of the still innocent flesh that awaited them in old Flim-Ways.

When they'd wandered a good thirty strides up the track, Stopmouth shouted after them.

'Wait!'

They turned towards him and almost jumped out of their skins when they saw who it was.

'N-n-no c-c-closer!' said Stopmouth. He hoped they'd remember his fame for speed and wouldn't see any point in pursuit.

An older man named Trapsetter, who was surely the hunt leader, dropped his spear and stepped forward a pace.

Stopmouth was relieved to see how little interest they had in him. If anything, they shuffled their feet and kept glancing towards Flim. Trapsetter calmed them until they'd heard Stopmouth out. The fugitive's nerves and stumbling tongue tried their patience and even his own. Every moment he spent with them increased his chances of being captured. Yet he couldn't bear to see these men he'd known all his life stolen from the Tribe that needed them.

At last his message seemed to get through. Trapsetter sighed and scratched his balding head.

'I cannot believe these . . . these *Longtongues* are as dangerous as you would have us believe, young man. They are blind, you say?'

Stopmouth agreed.

Trapsetter scratched some more and finally nodded. 'We will be careful, Stopmouth. More careful than you have been at any rate.'

Some of the group sniggered until Trapsetter glared at them. 'If I thought we could catch you, we would. We'd take you straight back to your brother. The Tribe is in sore need of volunteers. But we will hunt for you another day, I think. For now, I'm grateful for your advice and if it proves useful, I will speak out for you when you are captured. But you are wrong to make us waste good hunters chasing you. Nobody can survive on his own, Stopmouth.'

The hunters turned for Flim without quite so much bounce in their step as before. Even as they passed out of sight, Stopmouth heard Trapsetter ordering silence.

The man had told him the truth. No one could survive without the Tribe. His experiences that night had proved it. With a heavy heart he sneaked back into the hideout he shared with Indrani.

12.
IN THE RUINS

Stopmouth was climbing the stairs with two skins of water when Indrani screamed. He dropped his burden and burst up through the hatch. He looked around for beasts, but saw none. He scanned the sky for Flyers. Nothing. Indrani was wide awake. He'd dreamed of this moment, waited days for it. She looked over at him and screamed again.

'What's wrong! Are you h-hurt?'

She backed away, obviously still weak, and huddled in the farthest part of the shelter. Her hand found the hilt of a bone knife and she held it up between them, the point shaking as though the knife weighed more than she did.

'What's wrong, Indrani?'

She shouted at him in her baby words. Then she dropped the knife and fell over sideways with foam at the edges of her mouth. Stopmouth placed her back on the hides and sat over her for some time afterwards. A generation previously a man of the Tribe had been volunteered by his family because he couldn't recognize them any more. Is this what it had come to? Had he stolen her for nothing? Trapsetter had said Stopmouth would never survive by himself, and he never felt more alone than he did at that moment.

As he was making Indrani comfortable again, he couldn't help thinking about all the flesh the pair of them represented. It was selfish to keep it from those in need; those with a chance at life.

He cast about for something to distract himself from these thoughts. All he found was a couple of Globes up high near the Roof – there always seemed to be one above him these days, so he ignored them. Instead, he relaxed into a daydream where the Tribe was in such need of hunters that, far from wanting to trade him, they welcomed him back with open arms. Everybody was cheering, as they'd done when he'd returned from Hairbeast-Ways in time for the wedding. Mossheart and Rockface laughed and Wallbreaker embraced him. A smile crept across Stopmouth's face, but he lost it when he realized there was no room for Indrani in this picture. Nor was he sure he'd be able to stop himself assaulting his brother if Wallbreaker tried to embrace him.

Indrani's eyes fluttered under their lids. Delicate eye-lashes, longer than those of normal women. His smile returned. Who needed normal women?

'I will keep you safe,' he told her.

Around midday Indrani woke again and winced when she saw him.

'Where we are?' she asked in Human language.

'You were s-sick,' said Stopmouth. 'P-poisoned.' He was always amazed at how little he stuttered in her presence.

'Ah. Can I have drink?'

He handed her a skin. She had difficulty with the weight, but when he leaned over to support it for her, she dropped it and jerked away from him.

He stepped back, as frightened himself as Indrani looked. Was she about to start babbling again? She picked up the skin as though nothing had happened. She had less difficulty with it now, having spilled half its contents.

'You didn't say where are we.'

'We are in the old p-p-part of the Ways. I . . . I am sorry, Indrani. I have done something v-v-very stupid. I stole you out of Wallbreaker's house and now we will b-both d-d-d-die.'

Indrani shocked him by throwing back her head and laughing until she was too weak to laugh any more. Later, when Stopmouth cut up some of the remaining Bloodskin flesh, she looked at it in disgust.

'If you knew what I w-w-went through to bring you that f-f-food, you wouldn't t-t-turn your nose up so easily!'

'Keep it, then!' she said. 'It is good I die.'

'I don't understand.'

'No,' she said. She closed her eyes and spoke wearily. 'I sorry you die, Stopmouth. I sorry you and me cannot go home to our Tribes.'

'Tell me about your Tribe,' he asked, more to make peace than anything else.

'Your brother always ask. Always, always. But even if I tell, there are not the words in his head to see.' She pointed at the Roof and the Globes which hung directly overhead. 'My Tribe is there. My Tribe watches me and it laughs. Many there are glad I hurt. Many are not, but quiet now. Very quiet. Afraid to ask for me.'

She seemed terribly sad.

'Your T-Tribe live in the Globes?'

'No,' she said. 'Globes are . . . No, we live in Roof. I tell only you this who save me. Not Wallbreaker.'

Stopmouth hid his delight at these words by studying the Roof. Sometimes from the tallest towers he'd seen how it curved down towards the horizon. Tribal legend spoke of how the Traveller and his band of hunters had almost reached it before disaster had struck. He told Indrani the story, but she just smiled and shook her head.

'The Roof never, never comes to here!' she said.

Her smugness angered him and he was on the point of storming off to hunt when she opened her eyes wide and sat up.

'Wait, Stopmouth. I'm sorry. You are right. The Roof not come to here, but there is one place where here reaches to Roof. You must walk many, many territories to find this one place.'

So it was true after all! The Traveller had found the end of the Roof! Stopmouth imagined going there himself, climbing inside and looking down on Wallbreaker from above. What strange creatures must live there, and what hunts could be had! No wonder Indrani turned up her nose at the flesh here below. A pity, he thought, that no human could ever survive such a journey. Even the Traveller had only seen the place from a distance. And he alone of a band of ten fierce hunters had returned to tell the tale.

'Stopmouth,' said Indrani, answering his grin, 'I see you think as I do. You must to take me there!' She put one hand halfway to his, and then, with a shiver, withdrew it. 'You cannot go to your Tribe, but my Tribe, if I go there, must to take me. And you too if you are with me.'

'Sure,' he said, delighted to see her smile. He knew she'd change her mind when she recovered her strength. For now, it was enough to share impossible dreams as he and Wallbreaker had done so often. But Indrani hadn't finished yet.

'The Roof is many distant from here,' she said, 'with many eaters of flesh.' She made a disgusted face. 'We cannot to go without the Talker. We must to get the Talker back from . . . from him.'

Stopmouth gaped at her. Did she really think he'd sacrifice the Tribe's one chance at survival to save himself? Obviously it was the fever talking and not her. And yet Stopmouth was young. He was stronger than he'd ever been in his life and in love with an extraordinary woman. He watched her as she collapsed back into exhaustion and at that moment knew he would do anything to keep her safe, even if it meant crossing half the world.

'I know where I m-might find another T-T-Talker,' he said. 'T-tell me if I'm r-r-right.'

Stopmouth couldn't look at the walls around Bloodskin without a tremor of horror. The last time he'd stood here, Rockface had led him through this very window. A tenth of a night later he was lying with blocks of stone embedded in his legs. He swallowed back his terror and poked his spear through the gap. It was still unblocked, so he heaved himself up and crawled inside. There, he waited for his eyes to adjust before moving forward. The house hadn't changed since his last visit. No creature made its home there, except perhaps the tiny ones who lived in the moss and who, according to Wallbreaker, ate only plants and not each other.

He came to the door onto the street and listened hard for sounds of Bloodskins.

When Indrani heard that he meant to come here, she

had shouted at him and called him a fool. Then she'd wanted to come with him.

'It is my fault,' she'd said. 'And I fight good!'

'You're still too w-w-weak, Indrani,' he'd replied, not wanting to hurt her feelings. Really, he thought, she'd slow him down. He couldn't hunt with somebody too afraid to come within touching distance of him.

As he looked out onto the terrible streets of Blood-Ways, he wished he'd given in and let her come. What harm, he thought, if they both died here instead of at some other point on the mad journey she'd proposed? And if he didn't make it back, what chance of survival would she have anyway, surrounded by enemies and unable to hunt?

He heard nothing – the Bloodskins in this area must have all been asleep. He retraced his footsteps from the night of his injury: up one long street of mostly empty houses; round the corner to where the wreckage of a Globe had reduced the buildings to dangerous rubble.

When he stood in front of the house where his legs had been smashed, his memories so terrified him that he lingered in the dangerous open for many heartbeats before slipping inside. A great quantity of rubble cluttered the doorway, more than he remembered. Holes gaped in walls and sometimes he could see twisted bars of metal underneath. They flaked under his hands. Stopmouth found his way back into the room where he'd had his accident. No fire lay in wait for him this time; only darkness. He tried to slow his breathing and listened intently to the sounds of the house. All was still.

He unpacked the equipment he'd brought. First he removed the hides, which he stretched across the ruined doorway to the room. Rubble had already blocked most of it and for that he thanked the spirits. Next he used a bit of tinder and some scraps of wood he found in the hallway to light a small fire of his own.

Shadows danced about the walls, but now Stopmouth could see the wreckage above him. A curtain of metal hairs still hung from the hole in the ceiling, while the rest of the Globe had slipped deeper into the room. He could reach it just by raising his hands and standing on his toes. The metal was sharp in places, sharp enough to cut his thumb when he touched it. The whole thing looked unstable, as if it still had farther to fall. This worried him, especially when he thought about what had happened the last time he was here. But if he and Indrani were to have any chance of survival, there could be no turning back. So he licked the blood from his thumb and set about the task of building a pile of rubble tall enough to stand on. It looked very shaky when he'd finished. Tiny fragments, like the ones he used to chip off walls as a boy, lay everywhere. At that moment he had a memory of Wallbreaker scolding him for damaging masonry before either of them had ever dipped a spear: 'You shouldn't, Stopmouth,' Wallbreaker had said. 'I know you can't see it, but someday there'll be no more buildings. Nobody knows how to make them – certainly no human. Well, maybe I will.' He'd grinned then, his dimples already prominent. 'See all those straight lines on the forest floor, brother? Houses once upon a time. Definitely houses.'

Stopmouth's pile of rubble now reached almost to the black maw of the torn Globe. He lit a torch from the fire and climbed to the top, wary of standing straight until he'd passed under the jags of metal.

Here, bright colours danced in the light of the flames. He saw designs that would have bamboozled the Hairbeasts: curls and glinting lines. Strange, strange shapes packed the insides of the Globe. When he reached up, his hand found most of the surface to be soft, like skin over layers of fat. Tiny black designs ran across some areas and seemed to move from the corners of his eyes. He pulled at several items. Nothing came loose, although once the entire Globe creaked as if it were about to fall down on top of him.

Stopmouth wanted to spend more time investigating these wonders. Here, at last, he'd seen something that Wallbreaker never would. But he'd come for a reason, so he stopped fumbling about and whispered the phrase Indrani had taught him.

'Acteevate!' he said.

Nothing happened. He cursed himself as Indrani had

cursed him with words he'd never taught her. 'Easy!' she had said. 'So easy it is! Activate! Activate! Activate! Just say it!'

Three little sounds and it had taken him the best part of a day before he could approximate Indrani's pronunciation.

'Perhaps I n-n-need one of your ancestors to p-p-possess me,' he'd said. She cursed him even more, and although she was still weak, she looked as if she wanted to hit him.

He tried again, making a special effort with the 'i' in the middle of the word.

This time a pale yellow glow appeared at the far end of the Globe. Indrani had taught him what to expect, but he still dropped the torch in surprise. Luckily the light from above remained steady. But how to reach it? If he had a spear in his hand, and if he stretched and held the spear at the base of its shaft, still he'd fall short of the target. Also, from what Indrani had told him, the object couldn't be detached from its hiding place unless he touched it with the warmth of his hands.

He would have to climb.

He knew from his earlier investigations that plenty of handholds awaited him should he really need them: shafts of metal, ridges of various other materials. They all seemed strong enough to support his weight, but every time he tested one, the entire Globe complained with a screech.

He decided he'd have to risk it. He and Indrani would

die without a Talker and he certainly couldn't take the one owned by the Tribe.

Stopmouth found two sturdy handholds and pulled himself up. The body of the Globe creaked and he heard a rain of dust and other fragments falling just out of view. It all reminded him too much of his accident. He forced himself into perfect stillness until his breathing calmed. 'It's not going to happen again,' he told himself. Then he pushed up further towards the glow, never putting too much weight on one side or the other. Halfway up he stretched out a hand for the sphere and couldn't quite touch it. One foot was balanced on a padded, slick surface, the other on a series of tiny protrusions that dug painfully into his sole. Then the Talker stopped glowing.

Stopmouth cursed. 'Actovite!' Nothing happened. 'Acteevate! Acteebate!' He cursed again and decided to climb up further to retrieve the thing by feel. He raised his left leg in search of another foothold, forcing the protrusions under his right to dig even deeper into his skin. He shifted slightly to ease the pressure and something went *click!*

The whole Globe came alive and started shaking. The grip under his left hand became hot. Then he heard metal shrieking and stone collapsing. The wreckage, with Stopmouth inside, fell the last body-length to the ground. The young hunter survived the initial impact, but above him a metal object came free and smacked him into unconsciousness.

He woke in stifling darkness. His head pounded, and when he touched it, his hand came away sticky. He heard something beating against the metal shell that encased him. For a moment he thought it was Rockface come to carry him home. Same room, different accident. Part of him wanted to laugh. The banging came again from the outside of the craft. And he heard voices now, Bloodskin voices.

'It is a human. I found hide across the door. And look, embers from its fire.'

'It did not hunt well. It did not come for hunting. It was sent by others of its kind. To be absolved of a crime perhaps.'

'Perhaps. But how can I eat it if it has buried itself under here? The flesh will rot and the spirit will never leave this place.'

'Who can explain beasts?'

Stopmouth understood every word that was spoken. When he heard the Bloodskins leaving, he reached around in the darkness until he found the little sphere that had knocked him unconscious. The Talker, of course. He marvelled once again that a metal object could feel so alive. 'Activate!' he said, finding the word came easily to him now. In the emerging glow he looked around again at the inside of the Globe. He wished the sphere could give off a stronger light and, to his surprise, it did just that.

As children, he and his brother had often trapped moss-beasts under skull bowls. Wallbreaker always wanted to leave them there with no moss to see if they'd eat each other. He was surprised that they never gave in to appetite. Instead, after a few days, the creatures simply stopped moving. Like Stopmouth would now. How terrible to die here, he thought, his flesh uneaten!

Stopmouth found he could just about stand in the confines of his prison. He pushed and prodded several surfaces in the hope that something would give way. Nothing did. He sat again and his eyes wandered. Eventually they came to rest on the tiny black designs that covered many of the surfaces. Had Indrani painted them herself? What did they mean?

He jerked his head back in shock, bumping it painfully. The designs suddenly made sense to him, speaking through his eyes. The Talker, of course. It was as if somebody had found a way to draw a voice!

'Rear Armament' said one design. 'Forward Armament' said another. Although his eyes could 'hear' the words, they still seemed like gibberish to him. He couldn't understand why a person would need separate weapons for front and back. Still, the drawn voice fascinated him and he followed the little symbols around the craft: 'Ext. View, Rear. Ext. View, Int.' 'Home.' 'Emergency Rations. Press Once.'

Stopmouth pressed the little symbols several times, but nothing happened, not even when he pounded them with his fist. Then he remembered the protrusions that had dug into his foot earlier and how they'd caused the whole craft to shake when he'd stood on them. He found the button he'd accidentally pushed beside little symbols that said: 'Thrust'. He wouldn't be touching that one again! But there were other buttons where it said 'Rations' and, sure enough, when he pressed them, a panel magically slid open. He whooped. This death was turning out to be more enjoyable than he'd expected. Unfortunately he found no rations inside the magic panel, only packets of a stone-like substance that crumbled in his hands and smelled dangerously sweet: like rotting Hopper flesh. He didn't dare consume any of it.

He looked around for more symbols, sometimes pressing buttons to no effect, until he found some words that stopped him dead: 'Emergency Escape Hatch: Press Once'.

Was it possible? Not daring to breathe, Stopmouth pressed the nearest protrusion. *Bang!* The Globe shook and wisps of smoke puffed into the air around him. A small gap, which might have been larger had the shape of the Globe not been so badly altered, lay open at the top of the craft. He struggled through it, sweating heavily, holding the glowing Talker out in front of him. When he'd freed head, shoulders and both arms, he paused for a rest. It was then, half trapped in the opening, that he noticed the two Bloodskins standing in the doorway of the room.

'Will I kill it now?' asked the shorter of the two, its wispy-haired face twitching.

'No. Can't you see the glow? It is already a spirit.'

'Yes,' said Stopmouth, terrified. 'A spirit. You should go.'

The creatures stayed in the doorway, breathing slowly through rows of tiny holes above their mouths. Their muscular legs shifted beneath them and Stopmouth was sure they were about to spring at him across the room. Finally, however, the Bloodskins looked at each other and the shorter one said: 'We are sorry for you. I will mark this building so none will come here again.' They turned away and loped out of the building.

When Stopmouth was sure they'd gone, he wriggled the rest of the way out of the Globe. Now, if only he could get the Talker back to Indrani without getting killed!

He had no idea how much of the night he'd spent unconscious, but when he looked out of the window, he detected the first hints of dawn in the panels of the Roof. He sprinted back the way he'd come. Four Bloodskins lounged with spears against one wall of a street. He shouldered his way through the centre of the group before they could react, running towards the house through which he'd entered the area. Already behind him he could hear the

Bloodskins giving chase. Obviously these ones hadn't heard that he was a spirit to be left alone.

He ran in through the doorway and down the hall to the back room of the house, the Talker lighting his way. Almost there, he thought, when he saw the window waiting for him. Then he put his weight on the wrong stone. It gave way under him and he fell flat on the floor. He skinned both knees, barely keeping hold of the Talker. By the time he regained his feet, the Bloodskins were already piling into the room and he knew he'd never make it through the window without a spear in the back.

Four beasts spread out. He'd left his own spear on the floor of the building where the Globe had crashed and had no idea what had happened to his knife. No doubt the Bloodskins thought this would be the easiest hunt of their lives. Stopmouth raised the glowing Talker, hoping to frighten them, but he'd spoiled the spirit trick earlier when he'd pushed through their group on the street. Now, though they hesitated, they handled their weapons as if they meant to use them. He thought of flinging the Talker at them in defiance. Then inspiration struck him: 'Brighter!' he commanded. 'Brighter than the Roof!' The sphere obeyed immediately and the Bloodskins screamed and pawed at their eyes. Unfortunately Stopmouth hadn't known what would happen either, and he had forgotten to look away. Spots danced in his own vision, but he felt a draught from the window at his back and stumbled towards it. He fell outside, got up and set off in a limping run to where he thought the trees must be. His vision had started to clear by the time he'd reached safety.

He ordered the glow to stop and looked back towards Bloodskin. A hunting party had set out to chase him down. He laughed, for he had a good lead, and no Bloodskin could run as he did, even with skinned knees and bruised feet.

When he got back to the hide, he met Indrani on the stairs. She'd gathered his last Armourback-shell spear and a knife he'd been making from the same material. 'Thank all the Gods, you've returned safely!' she said in her child talk. He was surprised it made sense to him – not because he'd forgotten the Talker magically translated everything, but because, for the first time, it confirmed that her baby words had been a proper language all along, something he'd never found easy to believe. Humans spoke Human just like Bloodskins spoke Bloodskin. Now a new world was opening up to him where there could be many human languages, many for the Bloodskins and every other beast in the city.

'What are you doing with my spear?' he asked her, shaking his head. 'Don't tell me you were coming after me – you don't even know where Bloodskin is!'

'I know more about the geography of your world than you ever will, you ignorant savage.' She grabbed the Talker out of his hand and stormed back up the stairs, stumbling slightly in her weakness.

In the days that followed they made preparations for their journey to the place where the Roof touched the land. Stopmouth was fortunate to catch an unwary Huncher by speaking to it through the Talker and luring it down an alleyway. The little sphere also helped him trade the corpse of that rare beast with the Clawfolk for a wide variety of flesh types that he and Indrani would need to keep healthy in the first twenty days of their journey.

Meanwhile Indrani rigged up a sled that would allow them to pull their supplies along with them.

'How long will it take us to reach the Roof?' Stopmouth asked her. He was still amazed at how the Talker filtered out his stutter completely. It filled him with such confidence that sometimes his tongue didn't stumble in the first place.

'I'm not sure,' said Indrani. 'Fifty days? First we must find the river and follow it to the sea.' She'd already explained that a river was a quick-moving Wetlane, while the sea was a body of water too large to cross.

'You know, Indrani,' he said, 'we don't have enough food to make such a long journey. I'll need to hunt and . . . I don't like to ask this of a woman, but I'll need you to help me.' Indrani gazed at him with the utmost horror on her face. Stopmouth had been afraid of that: by tradition, a woman could butcher flesh, but never hunt it. He pressed on. 'So far we've been lucky to eat at all, not to mention have enough to trade. Without the Talker we'd be weak from hunger already.' He waved an arm vaguely in the direction of Flim-Ways, where they planned to start their journey. 'Out there, we won't know the streets or the forests or the beasts. We'll die very quickly unless we learn to hunt as a team.' He didn't add that they were likely to die anyway, well before they ran out of food.

'I can't help you with the . . . the flesh,' she said, a look of disgust on her face.

'I appreciate that it isn't a woman's work,' he said patiently, 'but Indrani, you need to understand that—'

'It is *you* who need to understand!' she said, smacking her fist on the floor where she'd been sitting. 'They see everything I do! Everything! I cannot kill just for food! They mustn't see me kill!'

'It's not like I'm asking you to kill humans, Indrani!'

'I'm not one of you, Stopmouth,' she said with finality. 'I am not a savage.' That word again.

'What about the Globe that hunted your Globe across the sky the day you came to us?' he asked. 'It was trying to kill you, wasn't it? Was there a savage in that Globe?'

'No, Stopmouth. The person who hunted me was *evil*, but I assure you he was no savage.' She turned away from him and started fussing with a piece of rope for the sled. He stared, as he always did, at the beautiful dark skin of her shoulders, the lustre of her hair.

'So,' she said, unaware of his gaze, her little hands working the rope, 'we are decided. You will do the killing and I will be the guide. We leave tomorrow.'

13.
THE QUIET WALLS

Stopmouth heard a noise on the ground floor. He crouched next to the trapdoor, spear ready, while Indrani snored softly in the background. He smelled Rockface before he saw him; a blast of rotted teeth wafting up the stairs. The young hunter sighed in relief.

His visitor waved him silent before he could utter a greeting.

'It's only a tenth of a night before dawn,' the man whispered, fetid breath right up close to Stopmouth's ear. Indrani slept on, oblivious. 'They know where you are now. They know you have another Talker – the Clawfolk you traded with let it slip to Wallbreaker.' Rockface tried a grin. It didn't work too well on his sad, filthy face. 'I can tell you, your brother was *very* surprised to hear you still lived! Trapsetter said you looked half mauled to death by those Longtongues when he saw you. He was grateful for your advice – says it saved them a few hunters, but he said you were done for.'

'Rockface, what did . . . ?' He could feel himself stuttering, but the Talker smothered every mistake with its magic. 'What did Wallbreaker say when the Clawfolk told him I lived?'

'The chief? Ah, he just shrugged! Nothing else! But Frownbrow's wife—' Rockface stopped and blinked. 'His wife said she never saw anybody look so sad and so relieved at the same time. However, now that he knows you have such a precious item . . .'

Stopmouth cursed. Much remained to be done before they could leave this place. Dried and salted sides of meat hung in the back rooms of the house. These would all have to be packed onto the sled. At least his equipment wouldn't take long to store. There'd been too little time to prepare. Apart from the Armourback-shell knife and spear, Stopmouth's only other possessions consisted of a bone dagger, some water skins and a crude new tool-belt he'd been working on to replace the one lost in Tongue-Ways.

However, it was too late to worry about these things. He shook Indrani awake and in moments they were packing as much as they could onto the sled while Rockface hopped around in excitement.

By the time they'd slung ropes over their shoulders and begun to drag their burden from the hide, the Roof was already brightening with the early light of dawn. The sled made a lot of noise in the quiet streets, scraping over bare rock, splashing through ancient drains. Rockface ran ahead every few beats to scout out a path. Once he chose to run back the way they'd come instead, and when he rejoined them, he said, 'They've found your house!'

With a bit of luck the hunters wouldn't discover the fugitives as quickly – the hard surface of the streets made it difficult to track creatures except when they passed over swathes of moss. Even then, Stopmouth hoped that the strange tracks of the sled would confuse their pursuers. Perhaps it would, but it also slowed the runaways, particularly Indrani, still weak from her bout of poisoning. She sweated heavily and Stopmouth feared she might collapse at any moment. But after the twentieth part of a day they reached the old perimeter with its empty towers. The woods waited to shelter them no more than a short walk away.

'The trees seem closer to the walls now,' said Rockface, eyeing the mass of red and purple branches.

'They grow so quickly here!' said Indrani between deep breaths. She too benefited from the power of the Talker, her strange accent replaced by a voice that never made mistakes.

Stopmouth turned to Rockface. 'Thanks for the warning. I'm sorry I'll never see you again.' He meant it too, for although Rockface's thirst for danger scared him, he owed the man his life many times over. Also, unlike Wallbreaker, the big hunter's thoughts were never bitter or hidden. Stopmouth embraced him, but Rockface refused to hug him back.

'You're not dead yet, Stopmouth! You've survived worse than a night in the forest! I'll come back for you tomorrow and help you find another house.'

'Rockface . . . We won't be turning back when we reach the trees. We want to follow in the footsteps of the Traveller: we want to see where the Roof touches the ground.'

Rockface stared at them, mouth agape. 'But . . . how long will it take?'

'Fifty days,' said Indrani.

Rockface looked down at the sled, mouthing numbers under his breath. He shook his head, his face all concern. 'We'll need more supplies. You haven't had time to gather up enough for the three of us, hey? And I'll need my own tools – yours are too skinny for my fingers.'

Stopmouth tried to hide his shudder at the thought of Rockface's company on such a journey. He still had nightmares about what the big man considered to be 'excitement'.

'The Tribe is short of good hunters now, Rockface. It needs every man it can get. It—'

'Stopmouth,' he said, in a blast of desperate bad breath, 'you mustn't be ashamed to ask. Of course I'm coming.' He lowered his voice. 'Besides . . . I need you as much as you need me. The thought of you two stuck out here has been the only thing keeping me going. That house of mine . . .' He shook his head as if to dislodge an insect. 'Don't wait for me. I'll collect what we need and catch up in a day or so. Now that I know where you entered the trees, it'll be easy to track you.' And with that he was gone.

'I think that man is crying,' Indrani said. Her skin shone with sweat and her eyes seemed too bright.

'Don't be ridiculous,' said Stopmouth's translated voice. 'That's Rockface you're talking about!' But his own eyes were stinging as they took up their hide ropes again. When they'd reached the trees, he turned once to look back at the walls and towers of Man-Ways. It seemed to him he knew every crack, every crumbling brick or clinging lump of moss.

One day, he thought, I'll see all this again. I'll see it from above.

Indrani's jaw had dropped when Stopmouth first told her that the Flims had been replaced by the Longtongues.

They'd been sitting in the shade of some old Flim hide and Stopmouth had made a casual remark about the species that had provided it. He made a lot of casual remarks these days, something he hadn't done before he found the Talker. Speech was turning from a source of terror into the sweetest of pleasures. He tried to stay near the Talker whenever possible, filling silences with useless chatter as if the magic sphere might be snatched away again at any moment. And so one day he'd wondered aloud whether the Longtongues might provide skins anywhere near as useful as those of the extinct Flims.

Indrani was still too weak to jump to her feet, but she made a brave effort. 'The Flims have been replaced?'

Her voice rose to a screech that had Stopmouth praying no creature had heard her.

'Why haven't my people come for me then?' she asked.

He didn't know what she meant. Extinct beasts were *supposed* to be replaced. Only the Hairbeast streets hadn't been filled after the demise of its owners. That extinction had happened around the time of Indrani's arrival. Stopmouth looked at her now and wondered for the first time what connections might exist between this most beautiful of women and all the strange things that had occurred over the last two hundred days. He asked her if the arrival of the Longtongues meant things were finally returning to normal, but she wouldn't answer.

She spent most of that day with her arms clasped about her knees, staring accusingly at the nearest Globe. When he suggested she do some work, she uttered an obscenity which the Talker translated for him in full sexual detail.

Many days had passed since then. Now the spirits had decided that Indrani should see the Longtongues for herself.

When they came to the end of the trees, Flim-Ways seemed totally empty. No guards waited in the towers. It looked as if the two humans could just stroll down the main street, and perhaps, by day, they could.

'Do we cross, or do we go round?' asked Indrani.

Stopmouth wanted to go round. He felt fear knotting his muscles at the thought of the beasts that waited behind those quiet walls. But already they could hear the shouts of a large party of human hunters in the distance. The sled hadn't covered their tracks as effectively as he'd hoped.

'They'll catch us in no time if we take the long way. Unless we abandon the supplies.'

'If we do that, we're dead anyway,' said Indrani.

He nodded and took a deep breath. 'Then we go through. I think I understand the dangers of the Longtongues better than the hunters do.' At least he hoped so.

They set off across the cleared area between the trees and the wall. The footing here was treacherous – small pointed rocks hid under beds of moss, while old branches awoke from their graves to pull at the sled. Indrani tried to help free it whenever it got caught, but her hands seemed barely strong enough to lift themselves, and it was left to Stopmouth to finish the job.

Just as they were staggering through the gates, Stopmouth heard somebody cry his name. He turned back to the forest and saw a group of hunters emerging from it. Wallbreaker walked at the front and Stopmouth swallowed back his anger. At least, he thought, if anybody feared to follow them into Longtongue, it would be his brother.

'Let me speak to you, Stopmouth!' the chief shouted. 'I'll come forward alone.'

'No weapons!' Stopmouth called back. He dropped the rope connecting him to the supplies and quickly reached to check on the Talker. 'No tricks either!'

He was aware that Indrani had also dropped her rope. 'I'll kill him,' she snarled.

'Wouldn't your people be angry?' asked Stopmouth, alarmed. He didn't blame her, but they both needed to be calm. His brother was already on the way over. Behind Wallbreaker, the other hunters stayed under the trees and leaned on the butts of their spears. Stopmouth could almost sense their reluctance to get any closer to Tongue-Ways.

Wallbreaker stopped about fifteen paces from them. He pointed at Indrani, who was now holding Stopmouth's bone dagger.

'Keep that creature-bitch away from me, Stopmouth!'

Lines creased his brow like a cracked old building and his hair looked tangled and filthy.

'You look tired, Chief,' said Stopmouth. He felt some of his anger ebbing away.

'Am I still your chief?'

Stopmouth considered and finally shook his head. 'I don't think I even want you for my brother any more.'

Wallbreaker nodded and looked no happier about it than Stopmouth. He pointed at the new Tongue-Ways. 'Are you really going to let those creatures have your flesh instead of your own people? Could a son of my mother do such a thing? I'm sure you don't plan on getting killed, but you, me and the spirits know you can't avoid it. And what will happen when the Longtongues get hold of a Talker? Children lured into the night? It's a nightmare, brother, a nightmare, and I know about nightmares.' He shivered visibly, then pulled himself together and fixed Stopmouth with a steady gaze. 'Not a heartbeat goes by when I don't miss you, brother. Not one! But it would've been better for all of us if you'd volunteered instead of Mother when your legs broke.'

Once Stopmouth would have given way. But not now. Not with a Talker of his own; not with Indrani watching. He looked his brother fiercely in the eye.

'You'll lose hunters if you chase us in here.'

'Maybe,' said Wallbreaker. 'And if it was just your flesh you were wasting, I wouldn't send anybody after you. Especially if you brought that faithless woman with you!'

'I'll kill him!' Indrani screamed. Stopmouth put out a foot and tripped her as she ran past. He knelt quickly and grabbed the knife she'd been carrying. Then he helped her to her feet while Wallbreaker looked on, drinking her up with his eyes. For once she didn't resist Stopmouth's touch. Under his hands every one of her muscles trembled. She was still weak from her illness and had exhausted herself dragging the sled.

'Whether we die today or not, Wallbreaker, we're never coming back, be sure of that.'

'Good,' said the chief. 'But, as I said, it's not your puny flesh I want. You must hand over the new Talker. Give it to your Tribe, Stopmouth. Otherwise we *have* to come after you.'

Stopmouth reached down to the Talker again. Then he turned his back on his brother. He and Indrani picked up their ropes and passed under the towers into Tongue-Ways while Wallbreaker shouted after them, 'You leave me no choice, Stopmouth! The women will break your Tally and make a ghost of you! Do you want that? Do you?'

Stopmouth didn't want that at all. Ghosts were not allowed back into the Tribe and might even be buried uneaten. But he suppressed his shudder and pulled on the ropes.

'They'll catch us before we get more than a thousand paces,' said Indrani, puffing.

'Five hundred if they don't hesitate,' said Stopmouth. 'But they will hesitate.'

Not a creature moved in the streets. Stopmouth looked

around as his body began to remember its fear. Small, flat-roofed houses surrounded him, no different from those at home . . . Except that here every door seemed a drooling maw, and the windows stared down greedily at the little humans passing beneath. Stopmouth felt his breath catch. They couldn't turn back now, he knew that. So he steered the sled and Indrani towards the same house where he and the Hopper had fought until the sticky moss had imprisoned them both.

'We're going inside,' he said. Indrani threw him a frightened look – he'd explained the horrors of the Longtongues to her in great detail. 'It's either that or abandon all our supplies. I'm hoping the hunters will look on it as suicide and won't follow us in.'

'It *is* suicide!' she said. But she kept hold of her rope and listened carefully to his instructions.

'Touch nothing,' he told her. 'If you're tired, don't lean back against the walls. And they've got good hearing, so don't scream.'

She already sounded like she wanted to. 'Won't the creatures be waiting for us just inside the door?'

'Not at this hour,' said Stopmouth. 'Their skin is perfectly black and their eyes don't open. I think they must be night hunters.'

'You *think*!'

'Sssh! Remember what I said about their hearing!'

They were standing right at the front door. Behind them, they could see men nearing the base of the towers. The pursuers halted their advance, each looking at his companions, hopping from foot to foot.

'I'll go in first,' Stopmouth said. 'Stay at your side of the corridor.'

They lashed the guide ropes over the centre part of the sled, using them to secure anything that might fall off. Then, with Stopmouth at the front, they tilted it sideways and carried it into the hall, careful not to touch anything. The interior was utterly silent, the only movement flecks of dust dancing in the Rooflight of the doorway. Blinded by the daytime glare, Stopmouth imagined all sorts of shapes hiding in the blackness; in particular, the smooth, weaving head of a Longtongue, opening its mouth in readiness to strike.

Once inside, they lowered their burden to the floor and Stopmouth indicated that Indrani should climb over the sled to join him. She'd had a long day for somebody so recently ill. As she clambered across, her foot caught on a joint of cured flesh and she fell forward, her hands grabbing at his shoulders. He caught her, and the two of them went down together, winded, but with neither of them uttering a sound. Stopmouth's head finished no more than a handspan from the wall, with its curtain of translucent moss. It vibrated ever so slightly under his breath. Indrani saw it too.

She slid off him, eyes wide, and he had to clamp a hand around her wrist to stop her retreating too far in the other direction.

It was then that he noticed the two hunters in the doorway.

'Runaway lovers!' said the first, a man of Rockface's generation known as Redtooth. He boasted precious few teeth now, but his frame was still lean and muscular and his hair, spiked with grease, gave him a fierce, alien appearance.

'Shut up!' said the other man, skinny and jerky in his movements. 'These things have pretty good hearing.'

Redtooth ignored him and strode into the hallway. Stopmouth was amazed the man hadn't been killed long ago, but he bore no obvious scars and several elaborate tattoos curled around the bulging muscles of his arms.

He advanced into the room and casually raised a spear.

'Redtooth!' cried the jerky little man. 'I can't move my arm! Redtooth! Call the others!'

'We don't need the others, Flimfodder. The chief has offered us wives if he doesn't have to come in and do the job himself.'

'Redtooth! Please!' The little man known as Flimfodder had made the mistake of struggling, and now both arms and the leg he'd tried to push away with were fatally entangled. As Redtooth looked back, distracted, Stopmouth hopped to his feet and took out his sling. When the big hunter turned round again, he let fly with a stone. It hit Redtooth's hand with an audible snap. The man howled and dropped his weapon.

'You should leave, now, Redtooth,' said Stopmouth. He had already fitted another stone into the sling and he spun it lazily. 'I'll hit a leg next time. Then I'll pin you to a wall and leave you stuck there like your friend.'

'You're mad,' said Redtooth, but he picked up the spear with his uninjured hand and retreated, careful not to touch his pleading companion on the way out.

'You're trapped too, Stopmouth!' he called over his shoulder. 'We can wait outside for you. You won't beat five men!'

'Please, Redtooth,' said Flimfodder. 'Please!'

Redtooth left.

'Why did only two come?' whispered Indrani.

'I'd say Redtooth offered,' replied Stopmouth. 'And Wallbreaker was only too glad to accept. He's frightened at the best of times. Besides, he's already lost one hunter chasing us and he'll find it hard to justify that.'

'I can hear you!' Flimfodder shrieked, filling the house with the noise of his struggle. 'I'm not dead! Help me!' He continued to pull and fight until the moss covered most of his body. Then he just hung there, weeping, ready to be eaten. Stopmouth tried not to listen to him, but it became increasingly difficult as night approached and still no Longtongue came.

'We must help him,' he whispered to Indrani.

'No! We'll be killed! You said we could just wait until the hunters had gone.'

'We can't leave another human like that! Think of the Tribe!' She looked at him blankly. 'You're the one who always says she doesn't like to kill!'

'This isn't killing,' she said, as if offended by his implication. 'We will be watching a man pay for past crimes. It is not for us to interfere.'

Stopmouth decided she was joking. She had to be.

Finally night fell, and something stirred in the front room of the house. Flimfodder, who'd been silent for several tenths, began to weep again and beg for help. Stopmouth wanted to tell him to shut up and above all not to make the moss vibrate with his struggles. But he kept quiet for fear of alerting their 'host'.

The trapped man could see through the doorway into the front room. His eyes widened and he thrashed.

'Be still, my dinner!' said a voice.

'Please!' cried the man. 'Please!'

'You are not a Longtongue, much as I wish you were. I have been too long without challenge. And yet you speak! I am happy to hear speech as I feed!'

The skittering grew closer. Stopmouth couldn't see the

234

moss without daylight from the doorway to help him, but he thought he could sense it shaking with the creature's approach.

'What species are you?' asked the Longtongue from the next room. Stopmouth gripped his spear with his left hand. The right held a loaded sling. He could feel Indrani's frightened breathing fast against his shoulder.

'Please!' said the man again.

Before Stopmouth could react, a dark line shot from the door of the front room and smacked Flimfodder in the stomach. It sent him bouncing madly in the moss and elicited still more screams.

'What species, dinner?' said the Longtongue again.

'Human,' cried the man.

'How do you speak our language, human?'

'A thing of metal . . . I don't understand how it works.' Stopmouth expected Flimfodder to give away his and Indrani's position at any moment, and yet the man, for all his terror, still thought of them as Tribe and would bear pain to keep them safe.

'Thing of metal . . .?' mused the Longtongue. 'Ah! You mean technology! How I miss it in this place! Once my body pulsed with such devices as you describe. We only had to call for food and beasts like you would come walking into our moss. And then the delicious struggle! Technology! We will die without it in this place. You are only my second meal, though I have called and called in my dreams.'

The creature skittered closer. Stopmouth thought he could detect the shadow of its head in the doorway. He didn't dare send a slingstone after it until he was sure of his target.

'Tell me, where is the translator of which you speak? Tell me before I enjoy your pain.'

The skinny hunter's voice turned to a whisper. 'Will . . . will you let me go if I tell you where it is?'

The creature didn't answer for some seconds, as if the man had uttered something particularly cryptic. Finally it said: 'You do not understand, human. I will hurt you very much before I eat you. First I want you to tell me where the translator is.'

The man laughed hysterically. He tried to bang his head against the wall in what might have been an effort to kill himself, but the moss held him firm.

The creature poked its head out of the doorway and Stopmouth spun the sling and released. He heard a soft *thwack!* But instead of falling, the head pulled back.

It's dazed, thought Stopmouth. He ran to the door of the front room, Armourback-shell spear in hand, and dashed through, careful not to touch the sides.

To his horror, he discovered that the moss didn't have to stay near walls, but could also be stretched across the middle of a doorway like one of Wallbreaker's traps. He was stomach-deep into the stuff before he'd stopped running.

'Another human dinner!' said the voice. 'It fights as the food beasts fought our ancestors. It has learned to hurt.'

The Talker translated the creature's words, but they weren't words of sound, so Stopmouth had no idea where in the darkness his enemy lay. He did know, however, that it could strike with its tongue at any time. Would Indrani help if he called out? The creature would understand his words and he didn't want to give her position away. From the corner of his eye he saw her stepping closer, a knife in her hands.

Stopmouth strained to hear his enemy over Flimfodder's whimpers. A little light was seeping through the room's one window, but revealed nothing except that the creature wasn't near it. The moss began to vibrate around him.

It's walking towards me at stomach level.

'You will feel great pain now, human dinner,' the beast said.

Stopmouth steadied his spear and held it directly in front of his chest with the long spearhead vertical to his body. A sudden impact drove the shaft into his stomach and knocked him sprawling in the moss.

Screams filled his head. The spear was ripped out of his hands and the screams redoubled. Stopmouth felt sure that the creature's neighbours or relatives would come running at any moment. But this wasn't Man-Ways and nothing came. Finally there were no more screams for the Talker to translate and he hung in his moss cradle, bouncing gently.

'Indrani,' he called. 'I think it's dead. Bring the Armourback-shell knife, but don't come too close.'

It took the best part of a tenth to cut himself out and another tenth to free Flimfodder. The man stank of dung and collapsed as soon as he'd been released. Stopmouth wondered if Flimfodder's experience this night would make him turn out like Wallbreaker or if only a man with his brother's imagination could be destroyed by such a thing.

Outside in the darkness, Longtongues scurried up and down the street, their black skins glistening with droplets of Roofsweat. Each kept its distance from the others, and if they exchanged greetings, the Talker didn't see fit to translate them. At one point they saw one Longtongue chasing another, two patches of black running across the night. 'Be my mate!' cried the chaser. 'I will bring you pain! Be my mate!'

The two shadows skittered out of view.

None of the humans dared sleep. As the night wore on, they watched the comings and goings of the area with growing fascination. Sometimes there were fights, carried out to the death and in utter silence, started for no reason that any of the humans could perceive. More often the creatures simply streamed past each other. Many left through the perimeter gates. These returned towards morning, with moss-wrapped burdens on their backs that writhed and twitched. Stopmouth wondered if Rockface had followed along as he'd threatened to do. Perhaps he lay now in one of those cocoons.

By dawn the streets were empty again and enough light shone through the windows for them to get their first clear picture of one of the beasts. The body lay in a pool of blood in the front room. Its long, shaft-like tongue had split in two around the tip of the spear. Tiny limbs gripped the tongue, as if the creature had been trying to stem the bleeding. The sight upset Stopmouth, though he couldn't say why. Then he noticed something strange.

'There's no moss on the blood!' he cried. Nor had the blood dried as human blood would surely have done by now. Stopmouth asked the others to move out of his way. He took two steps back and dived across the room towards the corpse.

'Are you mad?' shouted Indrani.

The moss caught him no more than half a man's height from his target and held his lower body immobile. He stretched out with one hand and just managed to dip a finger into the pool of blood. It tingled but didn't hurt. When he touched his finger to the moss, the threads parted as though made of water. He freed himself in seconds and proceeded to melt the rest of the moss between himself and his companions.

'Help me butcher the Longtongue,' he said.

Flimfodder cleared his throat. 'I should go.'

'No!' said Stopmouth. 'Not without your share of flesh. We can't carry any more than we've got now. You could take some of the organs perhaps . . .'

The two men worked on the corpse, while Indrani stood back uncertainly. When they'd finished, the hunters shared what might have been a liver between them. Stopmouth knew Indrani was squeamish about blood and besides, internal organs had always been the preserve of hunting men and pregnant women.

Flimfodder slung a full third of the flesh over his shoulders. But Stopmouth wouldn't let him go until he'd cut the man a square of hide and soaked it in the beast's blood.

'Keep this with you for the way back. I'm sure they've put moss around every tree between here and home.'

Stopmouth felt a little catch in his throat as he said the last word. He pushed it aside as Flimfodder thanked him profusely and promised to speak well of him to the Tribe.

With three full tenths of the day gone, they set off through the eerie streets of Tongue-Ways. The houses became steadily larger, moving from four rooms to five, and soon to eight or ten. Some houses had balconies, others roofs that sloped or resembled upside-down bowls. The designs varied widely from one area to the next, and once the two of them walked down a street where every house differed from its neighbours and where all of them had extra walls that enclosed, in addition to the building, a large empty space.

'People used to grow things in those spaces,' said Indrani when he asked her. 'Things like moss and trees.'

'People?' asked Stopmouth. 'You mean beasts, surely.'

Her voice rasped in her throat. 'I mean people. The Deserters lived here, before any beasts came.'

'Deserters,' he repeated. She'd made the word sound like the worst curse she knew – almost the way a man of the Tribe would say 'waster' or 'hoarder'.

'Who were they?' he asked, wondering how he couldn't have heard of other humans living so close to home.

'I need water,' said Indrani. She refused to look at him as she drank, wiping her lips slowly afterwards.

'Won't you answer my question, Indrani?'

'We can't stay here,' she said.

'Indrani!'

'Oh, Stopmouth, what do you care now? It was long ago, long before your time, all right? The Deserters were . . . just greedy people who got what they deserved. Now, please can we move? I hate this place.'

'Sure,' he said. 'Sure.'

Even so, they made slow progress. Every few minutes they had to stop to let Indrani rest. She was breathing too quickly and her face shone with sweat.

'I don't think we'll get out of the area before nightfall,' he said. 'We should pick another house. As long as we stay quiet, we won't have any problems with our hosts.'

'No!' said Indrani. 'I can see the last towers now. I won't stay in a building with one of those!'

Stopmouth didn't blame her. They'd been lucky last time, and the idea of going through it all again made him sick in his belly. He just didn't want to be in the street when night fell and every Longtongue in the vicinity came looking for its breakfast.

But by the time they were struggling up to the base of the last set of towers, a full tenth of daylight remained.

Here they found huge skeins of moss blocking their exit.

'Strange,' said Stopmouth. 'I thought that Longtongues, by their nature, would *want* other creatures to come into their Ways.'

Indrani nodded, too exhausted to speak. She watched as Stopmouth cleared a way through the moss with a piece of blood-soaked hide.

Beyond, a dusty path led to a Wetlane bridge made of stone. The path became a road on the other side, which was bare of houses and ran all the way to an enormous building on the horizon. It looked as if the whole of Man-Ways could have fitted into its spiky vastness. Thousands of small flattened mounds lay between it and the two travellers, as if a giant had stepped on all the other buildings of the area and draped them with thousands of days' worth of vegetation and rotted tree trunks.

Indrani took one glance at this and looked like she wanted to bolt back into Longtongue and beg one of the beasts to invite her in for the night.

'We're staying on this side of the Wetlane,' she said shakily. 'We'll travel parallel to Longtongue until we find the river.'

Stopmouth saw no reason to disobey her as there was no cover on the far side anyway. So they moved into a stand of trees near the Wetlane, where Roofsweat hung on the edges of every leaf. Indrani flopped onto a green bed of moss and fell asleep.

The young hunter took a few moments to stare at her beauty. She was so sweet, he thought, her body curled up, her hands in little fists next to her face. She'd fallen from the Roof: a land of spirits and miracles; of adventures to make even those of the Traveller seem poor. How pale this world must look to her. No wonder she sometimes gave in to bitterness. No wonder at all.

He turned his attention back to Longtongue. He expected the beasts to come out hunting here the way they'd gone towards human territory the night before. However, only a few arrived and these started running to and fro between the towers. Stopmouth didn't know how they did it, but he felt sure they were making new moss and blocking up the road again. The road home.

He felt a sudden upsurge of loneliness. To distract himself, he watched the Longtongues and wondered what could make such solitary creatures co-operate. Why were they so eager to block off this entrance into their territory? But he hadn't slept properly in days, and before he could answer his own question, he too fell into a deep sleep.

14.
DIGGERS

Stopmouth woke to find Rockface poking through the contents of the sled. He had blood all over his face and half of the Longtongue flesh looked like it had already been eaten.

The big man grinned to see Stopmouth awake.

'Those Longtongues are delicious, hey? You made quite a discovery. We should hunt a few more of them before moving off.' He licked his lips and threw over a lump of fresh meat to his young companion.

'Oh, it's so good to be out again!' he said. 'I was sick of all that sneaking around your brother makes us do. Really sick of it. And I miss . . . There's nobody there I miss now.'

'Rockface . . . how did you . . . ?'

'Oh, I came around the edge of the territory un-fortunately. I knew that when Windbreaker had the entrance blocked off, you'd be coming straight out the other side.'

Stopmouth didn't know what to say. Indrani's eyes were open too, he saw. She shrugged, still looking a bit weak, and suddenly he was glad to have the bigger hunter along to help with the sled.

The three exiles spent the day walking under trees along the banks of the Wetlane. Sometimes the woods opened up on the far side to reveal an endless line of mounds, without any other obstacle to soften the yawning horizon. Looking at it felt like leaning over the edge of the Wedding Tower with the parapet crumbling under your hands: dizzying, frightening, thrilling. The sounds were different from home too. Here, the mossbeasts seemed larger, some growing to a finger-length, their colours brilliant against the trunks of trees, their chittering audible in all directions. It hit Stopmouth, for the first time, that he might be following the footsteps of the Traveller into a legend of his very own.

The sled caught on every possible obstacle, even seeming to invent some of its own. Indrani cursed and kicked the back of it. But Stopmouth was glad to see her like this again, convinced that her full recovery lay only a few days away.

He was uneasy too, however. He kept expecting to see curtains of Longtongue moss between the trees, and when they found none, he remembered how the creatures had desperately blocked up their streets the night before. He asked Indrani what could make them act that way, but she only said: 'A mistake, Stopmouth. It's all a mistake.' He didn't feel reassured.

The woods thinned as they walked. Trees became scrawny and sparse, with swathes of rotted leaves, slimy underfoot. Whenever they paused to rest, it was the woman who rose to her feet first and urged the hunters to hurry. She looked sick. Her face shone with sweat and sometimes even the noise of a falling leaf was enough to make her spin round. Whatever had scared the Longtongues had got to her too.

'Do you think we're being stalked?' Indrani asked at one point. Rockface jogged back to check, but found nothing. They moved on.

The final few trees of the wood leaned drunkenly in all directions, their branches dripping with rot. Opposite the Wetlane, nearby houses in Tongue-Ways seemed to be sinking into the earth.

And then they saw the Flims.

Stopmouth had thought the creatures extinct. But here, just outside the woods, they found two of them, trapped and as easy to hunt as flesh on a spit.

The green, scaly beings lay in soil up to their waists. Their clawed hands rested flat against the earth and their heads drooped to one side like the trees and the buildings had done.

'Let's get our spears,' said Stopmouth.

'No!' shouted Indrani. She grabbed his wrist. Her palms felt damp against his skin. 'No,' she said again, voice lower this time. 'Not these. I can't explain this, Stopmouth. It's not that I don't want to, it's that I can't. Please. These are not to be touched.'

Rockface snorted. 'Flims are no challenge even when their legs *are* working, hey, Stopmouth?'

The younger man ignored him. 'So what then, Indrani? Are we to just leave them for somebody else?'

'Somebody . . . something else already has them. Don't you see?'

She began dragging one end of the sled and Stopmouth had to be quick about picking up his rope before she spilled the contents onto the mossy earth. As they passed close to the Flims, one of the beasts lunged for the sled. Indrani yelped, but the creature missed and whatever the danger might have been passed. When Stopmouth looked back, he saw the two beasts had resumed their previous deadened pose.

'Not much of a threat,' said Rockface. 'But if we hadn't got a sled crammed with flesh, we'd have had to take them anyway.'

As they walked, the mounds on the far side of the Wetlane became less overgrown. Sometimes the roof of a house stuck out of the ground at no more than hip height. 'I think we're leaving the rotten area behind us,' said Stopmouth. But then the Wetlane they'd been following took a sharp turn to the right. A wide area of land free of houses opened up in front of them. As far as the eyes could see, figures of various creatures lay planted in the earth. Sometimes only a head poked up from the ground. Sometimes it was an arm, and in one case Stopmouth saw the kicking legs of a buried Pio. None of the creatures showed any interest in its neighbours, and the only sound was a barely audible moan that seemed to travel up through the soles of Stopmouth's feet to lodge in his bones. A foul smell hung over the area, even at a distance.

The humans covered their noses and stared at this strange spectacle running off to the horizon. 'I don't see how we can get past this place,' said Stopmouth. 'Not if they intend to grab us as those Flims did back there.'

Indrani had no answer. She gazed at the planted field with a strange mix of terror and shame. Even Rockface was looking unsettled.

'We could go back,' Stopmouth suggested, 'into Longtongue, travel that way . . .'

'No.'

'What then? It's not like we can just climb into the Wetlane!'

Indrani said nothing for a few breaths. But then she smiled. It was the first smile Stopmouth had seen her give since he and Rockface had found the Talker. Her entire face lit up and he drank in the sight of her gratefully.

'We must go back to the trees,' she said. 'We will build a *raft*.'

'A what?'

'It's a way to move on water used by savages long ago. Like a sled.' She laughed. 'You're the only savages I've got. You'll have to build it for me.'

Stopmouth was woken by a rumbling sound. The humans had wasted the rest of their day moving back out of the rotten area and finding a wood to hide in. They were meant to begin searching for logs then, but exhaustion and darkness had caught them first.

The young hunter grabbed his spear and sat up. Dawn hadn't yet arrived and the others slept on, snoring gently. Had he imagined the sound? He stared into the underbrush of the woods, but nothing stirred. Then he heard it again. He felt it through the soles of his feet. It was the earth itself that growled, a great rumbling that grew more and more pronounced until the ground seemed to ripple under him. It woke Indrani, filled her face with fright. Rockface rolled over beside Stopmouth, a knife in each hand.

A moment later several trees fell down and the soil beyond them exploded upwards. Tens upon tens of creatures surged out of the hole that had now appeared. They ran low to the ground on four legs, their features hard to distinguish in the dark. There were so many of them they spread out on the land beyond the trees like a carpet of moss. There was something strange and unsettling about their skin – under the tracklights it seemed to ripple, as though alive in its own right. Then the beasts began to dig, each in a separate place. Soil fountained above their heads, and in a dozen heartbeats all had disappeared from view with only a shower of dirt to show that they were still there, still digging.

The noise stopped. The creatures reappeared, all at once, and rushed for the hole from which they'd originally emerged. When they returned, they brought prisoners – beasts of every imaginable shape and colour. The Talker translated their voices: cries for mercy, yells of defiance. However, once each had been planted in the soil, the screaming ended and was replaced by groans.

'They won't scream any more,' Indrani whispered. 'They're in too much pain now. The Diggers' young are eating them from below, but slowly, slowly. Their food stays alive right up until they reach the brain – a thousand days of agony. Not even the Roof knows how the Diggers keep them alive that long.'

The humans watched the horrific spectacle until dawn. Indrani kept saying 'Sorry,' under her breath, though Stopmouth didn't know who she was apologizing to. Just as the Roof began brightening, the last of the Diggers ran back into the hole from which they'd emerged. The earth rumbled and then stilled. For a time the groans of the planted creatures continued, but soon they too were at peace.

'How do we make this *raft*?' Stopmouth asked.

Indrani explained in a distracted kind of way, and together the men dragged a few of the smaller fallen trees – those no thicker than Stopmouth's two arms – closer to the bank of the Wetlane. They snapped off the branches and tied the logs together with hide ropes from the sled while the glittering mossbeasts of the area flew around them like puffs of shiny smoke.

'By the ancestors,' said Rockface, 'it's worse than working on one of Windbreaker's ditches!'

Indrani glared at him, but soon the companions had created a little platform as long as a hunter with his arms stretched out and no wider than a child doing the same thing.

When they pushed it onto the water, Stopmouth clapped his hands in delight.

'Look at that, Rockface! Look at it float!'

It was like a moving bridge: a way to pass over the domain of the Wetlane beasts without having to enter it and submit to their mercy. It frightened him too, though, for it would be so easy to fall off.

He kept the raft close to shore with the butt of his spear

until they'd loaded their supplies onto it. It sank lower into the water with every joint of meat they added.

Rockface shook his head and grinned. 'We must be mad! Anyway, I'm not getting on that until I've been into the bushes one last time. Might as well lighten the load, hey?' Nobody answered. 'I'm going into the bushes,' he repeated, winking heavily. 'To lighten ... the ... load!' When they didn't laugh, he shook his head as if in disappointment over the slowness of their wit, and moved off into the trees.

Indrani wrapped the Talker in a square of hide and tied it around her neck. Stopmouth had intended to carry the little sphere himself. He wasn't sure he could live any more without the gift of proper speech it brought. But Indrani shook her head.

'You're supposed to be the hunter. Do you want this thing getting in the way?'

Yes, he wanted it, but Indrani gave him no time to ready an argument. 'Hold my hand,' she said, 'while I step onto the raft.' Even so, she hesitated to touch him, looking at his hand as though it would bite her.

'Why do you hate me?' asked Stopmouth. 'Before I went to find the Talker, you used to lean against me. We laughed all the time. You stroked my face when I was sick, I remember. Now it disgusts you to even look at me!'

She made no answer. Eventually, with a heavy heart,

Stopmouth held out his hand again and helped her onto the raft. He followed her, and when Rockface came back and climbed aboard – gingerly for all his earlier joking – the little platform rode so low in the water that only half a thumb's width separated them from the creatures that even now shadowed the depths beneath. Stopmouth hadn't expected them to come so quickly and sent a quick prayer to the ancestors that the beasts would be too confused by the strange object to attempt an assault. Besides, apart from turning back, the humans had no other way of avoiding the land of the Diggers.

Stopmouth pushed a long pole he'd cut earlier towards the bed of the Wetlane and used it to nudge them awkwardly away from the bank. The water was still, but even so he struggled to get them moving in the right direction. As the raft spun in a slow circle, Stopmouth saw a huge panting creature standing at the same spot on the bank from which they'd launched themselves. For a moment he tried to guess what manner of beast it was.

I know it, he thought. I know what that is. But trees shadowed it, and his poor control set the raft to turning again. By the time he could safely look back, the figure had gone.

'I think we're being followed,' he said to his companions.

'Diggers?' asked Rockface.

'No,' he whispered. 'I think . . . I think I saw Crunchfist on the bank.'

'You look scared,' said Indrani.

'Do you even know who Crunchfist is?' asked Stopmouth. 'Wallbreaker must have sent him to bring us home.'

She shrugged. 'He's missed his chance now. He'll never get past the planted bodies.'

The two hunters, however, shared a worried glance.

After the initial awkwardness they began moving at an easy walking pace. The Wetlane beasts shadowed them for a while and then left them alone, perhaps thinking the platform another one of Wallbreaker's tricks.

Stopmouth gained in confidence with every shove of the pole. He found standing up made the job easier, allowing them to pick up speed. Mossbeasts flew around him in a little cloud and the rotting trees of the forest seemed ten days' travel away. For a moment he forgot who he'd seen on the bank. He even forgot Indrani's scorn for him. The raft glided over the water as smoothly as a Globe and the hunter found himself grinning widely. Why had nobody thought of this before? Why hadn't Wallbreaker thought of it? The ride was so smooth that Rockface had fallen asleep and Indrani lay exhausted, shading her eyes from the hot blue light of the Roof. Stopmouth, however, felt wonderful. Muscles he rarely used ached, but it didn't feel like hard work. His young body sang with happy effort.

We are strangers here, he thought. Just out of sight a whole world must be hiding, with streets he'd never know and unimaginable beasts feasting on exotic flesh. How many Ways could there be between here and the Roof? How many species? The idea should have frightened him, but instead it filled him with a great excitement that only grew with every push.

The trees on the bank turned rotten again and his cheeriness died with them. Soon fields of planted bodies replaced more natural growth and stretched for a long walk on both sides of the Wetlane. He saw no humans imprisoned here, but there were plenty of Longtongues and even the heads of a few Armourbacks sunk deep into the soil. The Talker filled his ears with a chorus of squeals and groans.

'Can't we turn that thing off?' he asked Indrani.

She shook her head, looking sick. The air stank of waste and rot, worse than the latrine trenches in Man-Ways, worse than anything Stopmouth had ever smelled in his life. Rockface awoke, gasping for air.

'By the ancestors, what's making that stench?'

It was strong enough to make everybody's eyes water. Stopmouth wiped his with the back of his arm and tried to study the scene as dispassionately as Wallbreaker would have done.

Most of the bodies hung listlessly, but some waved arms or tentacles or even flippers at the air as they cried out in endless pain. They all seemed to be evenly spaced, one separated from the next by the length of an arm. Nothing grew in the gaps between, not the tiniest sapling or wisp of moss.

'Would you look at them all?' breathed Rockface. 'You know, we should kill a few, hey? Even the Armourbacks aren't that cruel.'

'I never thought it would have spread so quickly,' said Indrani. 'We didn't mean it. A bit of excitement, we thought. That was all. We knew we could control them if we had to.'

Stopmouth had given up asking her specific questions some time before and was surprised by this opening up.

'I've always wondered why my people haven't come to save me,' she continued. 'But if this is the reason, I can't say I didn't earn it.'

'What did you do?' he asked.

'You don't have the words to understand it.'

'I do, the Talker—'

'Ah yes! The Talker. The greatest miracle of our Tribe! Do you know, Stopmouth, that we have things of metal so small that if they were to grow a hundred times, you still wouldn't see them? Things that swim in our bodies to keep us whole. There are things of metal – *machines*, I should say – that built the Roof itself, and all we had to do was give them the orders to begin.

'Some of them can make life. They can redesign us to live where we choose, how we choose; to die when we want in a way that pleases us. Stopmouth, my Tribe has machines for everything. Everything! And of all of them, only the Talker needs to be this big.'

The raft sailed past a field of creatures that resembled hairy humans with twisted horns on their heads and eyes that glittered green in the fading light. It had been some time since they'd seen anything moving in the water. Stopmouth was becoming more and more anxious to find a place to stop for the night, but knew Indrani would never agree to it so near to the Diggers' victims.

To distract himself – to distract all of them – he asked, 'Why then does the Talker have to be so big? Is changing words so much more difficult than making a world?'

'Oh no,' she said. 'Changing words isn't so hard. Recognizing a particular sound, swapping it for another – that was easy even for your ancestors. Reading what happens in your head and the heads of all the beings around you, now *that* is difficult. Finding equivalents in one culture for the basic concepts of another – that is *really* difficult. I say the word *vegetable* and the translator tells you something like 'edible moss'. So, yes, it's a miracle, but it's a dangerous miracle. It makes you think you understand beasts and you never do. When it comes down to it, you can't even understand your own species.'

Stopmouth shook his head. 'I understand everything you say, Indrani. Maybe not always before, when you were trying to speak Human. But with the Talker it's easy.'

'Oh, really?'

Stopmouth nodded and was amazed to see her mouth turn up into a snarl. He feared she would use the bone knife on him and maybe Rockface thought the same thing, for the bigger man lifted one arm as if to restrain Indrani. But it wasn't necessary.

She said, 'If a woman says the word "rape" to a man, the little Talker in the man's head comes up with several matches, none of them correct. You're just a savage, Stopmouth. Rape means nothing to you but a good time. But not even the most civilized of men will ever know what rape is to a woman.'

'Indrani, what did Wallbreaker . . . ?'

She didn't answer. Stopmouth's head was reeling. It made a lot of sense now. Wallbreaker had been wary of Indrani's fists and her strange, high kicks, but he could fool anybody into doing anything.

'Did he weaken you with poison?' asked Stopmouth. 'Did he trick you into eating mossbeasts?'

'No,' said Indrani, not looking at him. 'That was my idea. After.'

Stopmouth felt ashamed. He wanted to tell her that not all savages were rapists; that he, Stopmouth, wasn't one.

Surely she knew that already! She'd been ill and at his mercy for days and he'd done nothing but care for her. He didn't want to believe Wallbreaker was capable of such things either, in spite of all he'd seen, but one glance at Indrani's face told him otherwise.

Rooflight was already beginning to fade and still the fields of planted beings continued along the banks of the Wetlane. In the distance Stopmouth saw a dark line that might have been trees. He prayed fervently that this was so.

'Look!' said Rockface. 'A Digger!'

Sure enough, a triangular head regarded them from the edge of the water no more than two hundred heartbeats distant. Its great, flat claws gripped the lip of the Wetlane and its long, perfectly round snout dripped clear liquid that hissed on impact with the water. It stared at them, if 'stare' was the right word for a creature with large but empty eye-sockets. Stopmouth remembered how the Diggers' skin had seemed to writhe on their bodies the night before. As he got closer, he saw the reason why. A hundred thumb-sized grubs scurried over the creature, into and out of its ragged ears and the empty sockets of its eyes.

'They're its young,' whispered Indrani. 'They'll keep feeding on it until it can find them another host. Then it will mate again.'

The creature had powerful-looking hind legs and it flexed them now as if it might try to leap aboard.

Stopmouth poled them further from the bank, unable to understand how the beasts survived like that.

As the humans passed directly in front of it, the Digger said: 'Attack.'

All beasts planted nearby obeyed at once. A multitude of appendages reached for muck or stones and flung them at the raft. Most of the missiles landed way off. Many didn't even reach the Wetlane, while others threw up plumes of water to either side.

A clod of earth broke over Stopmouth's head, but he kept pushing them along. Stones struck him in the shoulder and Indrani yelped a few times. Rockface growled back at the enemy. He returned any missile that came near him with as much force and accuracy as he could muster from a kneeling position. He got close to the Digger a few times, but it seemed unperturbed.

Finally, when they'd passed a dozen paces beyond it, the creature said, 'Stop.' Its empty eyes followed them until they were out of sight.

'A display of power,' said Indrani with a shiver. 'It was struck as often as we were, I think.'

They came up to the trees in full darkness, but still Indrani wouldn't let him stop. When he claimed to be too tired to continue, Rockface took over the job of poling them along. The big man was even more clumsy than Stopmouth had been, and surprisingly nervous, perched on the edge of the raft.

'Those trees are still pretty sickly,' said Indrani. Stopmouth didn't think she was much better herself. She had gained some strength, but looked like she could have done with a few more days' rest before setting off. If we get past the Diggers, he thought, we can hole up for a while. Then his only problem would be keeping Rockface from turning back in search of special Digger trophies. He sighed. At least he'd finally found one thing the big man feared. Rockface was sweating much more than would have been expected and he kept his gaze away from the water as much as possible.

'Let me take over for a while,' said Stopmouth. 'Go on, we'll need your strength for later. And I enjoy it.'

'If you're sure,' said Rockface, handing over the pole immediately.

Stopmouth *wasn't* sure. Exhaustion and pain were quick to replace the pleasure of his earlier exertion. Roofsweat started falling shortly after that. It brought some relief. It also saved his life.

Just as the trees were looking healthier, something grabbed the pole and yanked hard. Stopmouth's slick palms lost their grip and he fell forwards onto Rockface, one hand clutching at the straps that held the logs together, the other landing in the water. Indrani shouted a warning and he pulled his arm free just as a pale head, all eyes and teeth, surfaced, lunged and sank.

For a beat all was calm. Stopmouth had knocked the

wind out of Rockface. 'Sorry,' he whispered as the big man struggled for breath. The pole was floating away from them. Stopmouth got to his knees and used his Armourback-shell spear, point first, to pull it in closer.

Then something battered into the bottom of their raft, making them sway wildly. Stopmouth had to give up on the pole to lie flat on top of the supplies. The battering was repeated again and again. The creature or creatures struck mostly in the same place, as if hoping to create a weak spot. Perhaps they could see one already, a crack in a log or a frayed lashing. More of them seemed to be joining in on the assault. A flurry of thumps came that rattled every log and loosened the hide ropes holding them together.

'Get away!' shrieked Indrani. Stopmouth couldn't see what had frightened her, but she rolled over towards him. As the raft tipped up, a log at the high end came loose entirely and floated free.

'Untie another!' cried a 'voice' from beneath them. Stopmouth saw a delicate white arm with writhing fingertips pulling at the rope directly under him. He shoved his dagger into the gap between logs, felt it bite, 'heard' a yelp of pain. But the raft continued to spin and twitch and shudder under a dozen different attacks.

'We'll have to give them the food!' said Indrani.

'We're dead without it!' he said. But it didn't matter

and they all knew it. Another log was starting to come loose.

'Hold me steady,' he said to Rockface.

A few quick cuts removed the hide that kept the food safe. Then the three humans could only watch as their chances of surviving the journey spilled into the water, one precious joint of flesh at a time.

A frenzy ensued. It seemed as if the creatures were fighting amongst themselves.

By now the humans were clinging together on the three shaky logs that hadn't been torn free. Rockface, still underneath, had a dagger in one hand and his eyes fixed on the water, waiting for an opportunity to strike. Stopmouth could feel Indrani's rapid breath, wet against his ear.

'Behind you,' she whispered. He wanted to spin round, but knew it would have killed them all. However, it wasn't an attack she'd spotted – some kindly ancestor had sent the steering pole floating back towards them.

'I can't reach it,' he said, 'even with the spear.'

'I'll do it,' said Rockface. 'Let me up!' His efforts to rise shoved Stopmouth onto Indrani and nearly over the edge. The raft swayed and dipped.

'Enough! Rockface, please!' said Stopmouth. 'You can't reach it either! Somebody will have to lean out over the water. Somebody the others can hold onto . . .'

He could tell by the increased rapidity of Indrani's breathing that she knew who that person had to be.

The battle for their supplies seemed to be calming down now. Perhaps the creatures would be sated with what they'd already won, perhaps not.

Rockface held Indrani by the waist as she leaned out towards the pole, her shadow stretching over the reflections of the tracklights on the surface of the water. Stopmouth kept them balanced by sitting as far back as he dared.

'A bit more,' Indrani said, straining, brushing the pole with the butt of the spear. All other activity in the Wetlane had come to a halt and Stopmouth wanted to scream at her to hurry up. Rivulets of sweat ran down her face, dripping into the water like invitations. She passed back the spear and lifted up the pole.

'Watch out!' yelled Rockface.

A white head appeared and two arms, tipped with a nest of tentacles, reached up as if to embrace her. Indrani yelled and swung the wood at them. As the beast ducked away, she shoved the pole into the water and pushed the raft a man-length closer to the bank. Rockface drew his knife and slashed at the water where the creature had been, yelling the worst insults he knew: 'Waster! Hoarder! I'll eat those eyes for you! Flesh rotter!'

Whatever differences the creatures may have had earlier

were forgotten, and everywhere their white forms were streaming towards what remained of the raft.

Stopmouth threw his weapons and tool-belt over to the shore. It wasn't so far now, but something was fighting with Indrani for control of the pole. She smacked the creature over the head with it even as more tentacle-like fingers were reaching up out of the water. She had to let it go.

'Jump!' Stopmouth said to the others. 'Jump!' Indrani did, while he struggled to keep them steady. Even so, she almost capsized them. Hands were already reaching up from below, plucking at his ankles, loosening the remaining knots. Rockface had a snarl fixed to his face. White arms clustered around him. 'Jump!' screamed Stopmouth again. Rockface ignored him, slashing and stabbing. 'Please, Rockface! Do you want to end up like Lingerhouse?' *Half eaten, trapped in horror at the bottom of Wallbreaker's net.* Some of the fury left the big man's face. 'Please, Rockface, we need you! Jump!'

Rockface roared. His great fist pummelled once against a pale row of eyeballs. Then he tore himself free and leaped ashore, even as one of the last three logs came away from the raft.

Stopmouth's heart was beating now, faster than the drums at his brother's wedding. He couldn't get up without falling in; he couldn't control the raft. Terror ran free in his blood. Why hadn't he jumped himself? Why should he be the last one left here, where the others couldn't even help him?

'It's better to drown them first,' said a 'voice' beneath him. 'Pull it down and fill its lungs!'

'One more knot,' said another.

'Stopmouth!'

The beasts sounded happy. 'It's coming loose. I have it now!'

Something poked Stopmouth in the face. He saw it was the end of his spear, and he grabbed onto it for dear life. Indrani and Rockface pulled the raft in with desperate strength. The creatures, surprised perhaps at the sudden movement, reacted slowly. Stopmouth shook off their clutches and brought his legs and body onto the shore, one arm trailing behind him on the raft. To right and left, other figures were struggling out of the water too.

'Leave them to me!' shouted Rockface, running to head them off. 'They're mine!'

But the beasts hadn't finished with Stopmouth yet. One creature, pale and slender of body, surged out of the Wetlane and fixed the needle teeth of its jaws about the young man's biceps. The pain and the beast's weight dragged him back to the water, where shapes were rising and jaws opening.

Indrani screamed with rage. She still had the Armourback-shell spear. She plunged it deep into the chest of the creature on Stopmouth's arm, and although it didn't let go, the two humans together managed to wrestle it ashore.

The hunter felt its grip release and he rolled away, clutching at his arm, almost delirious with pain and terror.

'I can't breathe,' said a 'voice'. 'I'm dying. I can't breathe.'

Stopmouth's arm was bleeding profusely. 'Shut it up,' he said. 'Kill it!'

But he heard a splash, and when he sat up, the creature was nowhere to be seen.

'What . . . ?' For the first time since the arrival of the Talker, he was speechless.

'It was frightened,' said Indrani.

'Frightened?' He couldn't believe it. He looked around. Rockface stood panting fifty paces further up the bank. He was covered in scratches and bites, but none of the enemy had managed to scramble ashore. Stopmouth turned back to Indrani. 'But what are we going to eat? It might have kept us alive.'

Indrani shook her head and pointed upwards. 'They're watching me, don't you see? Every awful thing I do down here will make them less likely to take me back. And . . . and that beast's no different from you, Stopmouth. It's an intelligent, suffering being. I couldn't kill it, I—'

'You did kill it!' he shouted.

'Go easy,' said Rockface, walking back towards them.

Stopmouth ignored him. 'You stabbed it through the chest with my spear. It's being eaten, right now, by its own kind!'

She started crying then. Great sobs that pulled at his

heart. She didn't move away when he wrapped his bleeding arms around her, but nor did she hug him back. Instead, she soaked his shoulder with tears.

'It's not so bad,' said Rockface, patting her back from the other side. Stopmouth didn't contradict him, although he knew they'd all be dead in a few short days.

'Not all the flesh was lost,' Rockface continued. His voice was surprisingly gentle and Stopmouth remembered how caring and careful he'd always been around his son, Littleknife. 'I still have a roll of Clawfolk meat in the pouch on my tool-belt. And we'd have wanted to do a bit of hunting on this trip anyway, hey? What was the point of bringing more than we could carry? Now we get to chase something fresh, something no human has tasted since the Traveller!'

Indrani pulled away from both of them. 'I don't want to kill things. I don't want to eat them.' Her weeping got worse. 'It's wrong. I can't do it any more.'

Stopmouth didn't know what to say. He remembered his own mother's words whenever he refused the flesh of some evil-tasting creature as a child. He repeated the admonition to Indrani: 'If you don't eat flesh, you're killing yourself,' he said. 'You're weakening the Tribe.'

'I have no Tribe,' she said. 'They'll never take me back now.'

'We are your Tribe, Rockface and me!'

'You're only savages.' The Talker had never found a good word in Human for that particular concept, but it hurt him as nothing else could.

'You've taken flesh like the rest of us savages,' he said. 'And we had to kill extra so you wouldn't go hungry. Those beasts died at your hand even if you were too much of a coward to lift the spear yourself!'

She wiped her eyes with the palm of one hand. 'You're right. It's too late for me now.' She took a deep shivering breath. 'I will hunt with you tomorrow.'

Later Stopmouth took the risk of lighting a fire. He felt Indrani needed it and he certainly did. He baked all Rockface's Clawfolk flesh, seeing no point in trying to save any for the morning.

That night, for the first time, Indrani ripped into her food as if she were really enjoying it. She ate with relish and asked for more when she'd already put enough away to keep Rockface quiet. But there was no more. She shrugged and lay back, firelight dancing over the perfect lines of her face even as Rockface's first snores tore through the night. Stopmouth watched her, thinking, surely she was too beautiful to be real.

'Are you truly human?' Stopmouth asked. He hoped she'd open her eyes and look at him. Another part of him wanted her to keep them closed so he could watch her without making her angry.

They stayed closed.

'I'm human,' she muttered. 'As human as you are, anyway.'

'What do you mean?' he asked, puzzled.

She lifted her head. 'None of your men have hair on their faces. You live on a diet of pure meat, most of it non-human. Your women never die in childbirth. You rarely get sick, any of you. And all of a sudden *I'm* the one who's not human?'

'Well,' he said, confused by her strange words, 'I only asked because . . . well, you mentioned something about my ancestors yesterday. As if they were different from yours.'

'You don't really want to know.'

'I do, of course I do.' Wallbreaker would want to know, but never would. It was a thrilling thought.

She nodded slowly. 'I'm not sure, Stopmouth. You're so different from your ancestors.'

It was a cruel thing to say. 'I am?'

'Yes. Very different. You see, they were cowards. They were *deserters* and thieves.' That word again, deserters. Uttered as if there were nothing worse in all the world. 'They stole everything from my people and left us to die. They deserved this gods-forsaken world and everything that happened to them since. But you don't, Stopmouth. You're—'

Stopmouth felt his face grow hot. He was dizzy. She

271

mustn't have meant it, she couldn't have. To speak ill of the ancestors was like . . . like wasting food, like murder. And the hypocrisy of it! He and Indrani were the ones deserting their Tribe. They were the thieves, stealing their own flesh from the needy. Stopmouth turned away lest his forefathers see her through his eyes and force him to avenge them. Perhaps she apologized afterwards, but he didn't listen. He waited until she slept. Then he was up on his knees, begging forgiveness on her behalf until sleep took him.

15.

AN ANCESTOR'S WRATH

That night the ancestors sent Stopmouth many bad dreams. He was a criminal, they informed him, who'd stolen his flesh from the Tribe to run off with a woman who despised him.

'You're just a savage; a potential rapist.'

He tried to block out their voices, but Mother was among them, and his half-remembered father.

'If Indrani hates us who are the marrow of your bones, your flesh, your heart, then what must she think of you?'

He opened his eyes, praying desperately that the night had finally ended. But darkness still reigned under the trees with the patter of Roofsweat playing softly on the branches. He wasn't the only one visited by nightmares: big Rockface was sobbing in his sleep. How terrible to lose your whole family all in one go. During the day Rockface smiled and joked and blustered. Yet sometimes it didn't seem real to Stopmouth and he worried about the man. Many in similar

273

situations had simply volunteered. But not Rockface. His whole chest shivered with grief, his deep voice now so childlike.

And Stopmouth heard something else: a sound of jerky movement. He looked over to Indrani and saw that she'd gone. She liked privacy for when she made water, but she wasn't so stupid as to go unarmed. She'd taken his tool-belt with its weapons and left the Talker behind.

More movement. A struggle, he thought.

Stopmouth grabbed his spear and surged to his feet.

'Rockface!' He kicked his companion awake. 'Up! Up! I think something has taken Indrani!'

The ground he stood on trembled slightly, but he had no time to worry about that. He placed the Talker about his neck and helped Rockface to his feet. Both men padded towards the movements as quickly and quietly as they could.

'That way!' said Rockface suddenly, and started running through the whipping fronds of darkened trees. Stopmouth chased after him. He too could hear sounds ahead now.

Something whipped past his ear and shattered against a nearby tree. Then Rockface cried out and fell over. The young hunter sidestepped and half fell behind a solid trunk. He could hear more impacts through the wood. Slingstones? His heart was hammering. He wondered for a moment if Indrani had lost her mind and started attacking him with his own weapons.

'Rockface? Rockface?' There was no answer and he couldn't see his companion from where he hid.

The vibrations in the ground were getting stronger.

'Come out, Stopmouth,' said a man's voice.

The young hunter felt his gorge rise. Crunchfist. He should have been expecting it. The ancestors seemed to inhabit the man constantly and kept him alive through everything. What better vehicle could they have for the punishment of law-breakers?

'Your woman gave me more trouble than the Longtongues I killed on my way here. She nearly broke my nose. I will enjoy her while you cower behind that tree.'

'What do you want from us, Crunchfist?' Underneath the protection of the Talker, he stuttered worse than he ever had before.

The earth rumbled. Back towards the edge of the wood, a number of trees started listing to one side, sinking into the ground.

'The Diggers are coming,' said Crunchfist, his voice harsh against the *drip-drip* of Roofsweat through the branches. 'They've been tracking me since I took a bit of flesh from their fields.' He didn't sound in the least bit concerned. Trees began falling, some of them breaking in half with a great cracking noise. Stopmouth pictured the

Diggers underground, struggling through the roots with empty eye-sockets and chewed-up skin, while their own young ate them alive. He wondered why they hadn't simply surfaced outside the forest and run the last few hundred paces. And yet, in spite of the route they'd chosen, the beasts were getting nearer. When they reached the clearing where the large hunter waited with his prisoner, there'd be nothing to stop them.

'It's very simple,' said Crunchfist. 'Your coward brother wants another metal toy. He'll have to forgive me publicly if I get it for him. Then he'll have an accident and I'll be chief. But first I'll give him a full account of how I enjoyed his woman.'

'I'll swap you the Talker for her,' said Stopmouth as Crunchfist must have known he would.

But both of them had waited too long. Somewhere below ground the Diggers had found a corridor free of roots all the way to the clearing where the big hunter waited with his prisoner. Stopmouth's tree leaned back so suddenly it knocked him over onto his side. He saw soil fountain into the air between himself and the other humans. He heard Crunchfist curse above the din and saw Indrani collapse to the ground as he released her. Diggers with writhing skin and powerful claws surged out of the hole towards Crunchfist before he could run from them. He bellowed as the ancestors filled him with anger and inhuman strength.

Stopmouth could only watch helplessly. He wondered how he could use the distraction of the attack to sneak in and rescue Indrani. Seeing her endangered swallowed all the anger he'd felt for her only a few hours before. He realized that no person in this world was more precious to him. She'd suffered terrible crimes at the hand of his family and it was his sacred duty to see her safe now. But the Diggers were on all sides, scrambling towards the man who'd stolen from them, and there was no way through.

Crunchfist was fast as well as strong. He worked his spear like a club, sweeping beasts into heaps with the butt until he saw a opening. Then the pointed end found throats or empty eye-sockets. He fought with fury, snarling and snapping like a Bloodskin. Spitting curses. The Diggers were no weaklings as the Flims had been, and Stopmouth counted at least ten in their hunting party. But incredibly the big man drove them back towards their hole, receiving only small wounds and scratches for every one of them he put out of the fight. But he was weakening. Stopmouth saw one Digger tear a gash in his calf and Crunchfist almost went down, staggering and swaying, biting his own lip bloody with pain. He flung his spear straight into the head of an enemy before wringing the neck of the one that had injured him. He used this corpse as a bludgeon. Another creature ducked under it to score him across the ribs.

Stopmouth hated the man and feared him above all

others. But when he saw Crunchfist in trouble, a human fighting heroically against beasts, he knew he had to intervene. Only two of the original attackers remained, but the earth was rumbling again and Stopmouth felt certain more of them were about to climb out of the pit that separated him from the other humans. It was no wider than a man lying down, and if Stopmouth positioned himself at the lip on his side, he might just be able to spear the Diggers from behind as they emerged.

Crunchfist dispatched the last of his enemies and staggered back towards Indrani. The shaking of the ground was intensifying and Stopmouth was about to shout across the pit to offer the man the Talker again when something incredible happened: eight of the creatures Crunchfist had 'killed', including the one with the spear jammed in its body, seemed to have revived themselves enough to begin crawling or rolling back towards the pit.

'How?' asked Crunchfist when he too saw it.

A great *crack!* filled the air and three trees on the far side of the clearing toppled over. The upper branches of one of them scratched Stopmouth all along one side of his body, cutting him off from Indrani even more. To get to her now, he'd have to climb through branches and over the trunk. And he'd need to hurry: even as he watched, a new pit opened up behind the other humans, and Diggers clustered at its edge.

Crunchfist roared his frustration. He picked up his prisoner and flung her body at the beasts to scatter them. Stopmouth screamed. He fought through clinging, sopping branches, knowing he'd never make it in time. One of the creatures, perhaps to disable her, had already shoved claws deep into one of her calves.

'Give me the Talker!' shouted Crunchfist. 'Give it to me and I swear by all the ancestors I'll save her. I swear it. Let me never go Home if I lie.'

Stopmouth didn't hesitate. He threw the pouch over the tree and the first pit. Crunchfist nodded once, his great frame leaking blood from a dozen wounds. Then he charged straight in among the beasts. There were fewer of them and they must have sensed the battered remains of the first party. But they showed no fear.

Stopmouth didn't wait to see what happened. He was desperately trying to climb onto the fallen trunk and it blocked his view of the fight. He heard Crunchfist's shouts and sometimes the grunts that indicated fresh injuries. The younger man's spear kept getting in the way, yet he didn't dare let go of it. In a dozen heartbeats he'd made it onto the trunk and all of the carnage became visible.

Dead beasts lay everywhere, but they'd left red slashes of revenge all over their enemy. Now the big man was wrestling with one of two surviving Diggers. Such was his weakness, the contest was an equal one. But not for long: the other surviving creature, its hind legs broken, crawled towards the struggle, intending perhaps to hamstring its opponent.

Stopmouth had too many branches to get through to join the fight. So he steadied himself on the trunk and pinned the crawling Digger to the ground with a mighty throw of his spear. Crunchfist needed no help with the last beast. He snapped its back over his knee.

'Good,' said the big man, looking up. Already some of his 'dead' opponents had begun dragging themselves back to the pit from which they'd emerged, yellow grubs wriggling frantically over their skin. 'You gave me the Talker and I have saved your woman as I promised.' With visible effort, he picked up Indrani. Her leg wound was bleeding freely and would need to be bound as soon as possible.

'Leave her there,' said Stopmouth. 'I will tend to her when you're gone.'

Crunchfist laughed. 'And what am I supposed to eat for my journey home? Do you think I'll risk one of those' – he kicked at a crawling Digger – 'coming alive in my belly?'

'You promised,' said Stopmouth. He was already looking for a way down through the rest of the branches to challenge the weakened hunter.

Indrani groaned and blinked her eyes. Crunchfist transferred her to his left arm. With his right, grunting in pain, he wrenched the Armourback-shell spear from the body of a twitching Digger.

'You'll be needing this,' he said. He flung it, point first, straight at the younger man. Stopmouth jerked to one side, but the tree swayed beneath him and he fell backwards in amongst the clinging branches. He too was not as strong as he should have been, and he struggled far too long to free himself and recover his weapon. Dawn was brightening the Roof by the time he'd made it into the clearing. Some of the 'dead' Diggers had disappeared underground. The others, perhaps five, lay unmoving, and the grubs that had once crawled all over them had fallen off the bodies and were nowhere to be seen.

His stomach rumbled. He remembered Crunchfist's comment about the Diggers coming alive in his tummy, but for all his fears he knew he'd need his strength to track the man and find Indrani. The shell tip of his spear sliced easily through Digger flesh. It was riddled with little grub-sized holes, but he put that out of his mind and forced himself to chew the tough flesh and swallow. A horrible thought came to him: Crunchfist would be hungry too.

He jumped to his feet. And stopped. What about Rockface? Crunchfist must have hit him with a slingshot. After all he'd done for Stopmouth, surely the least he was entitled to was that a friend should consume his flesh.

Stopmouth shook himself out of his reverie. Indrani couldn't afford to wait. He followed bloodstains into the forest. The trees seemed to close around him, almost bringing night again. Pungent moss, unlike any at home, hung from every branch and quickly bathed him in a cold slime. Tracking became extremely difficult. Crunchfist, in spite of his injuries, had gone to some effort to cover his trail, and several times the younger man would have lost it entirely had it not been for a curious thing: he kept finding items from his own tool-belt. His sling lay caught in the branches of a bush; his needle glittered in a stray shaft of Rooflight. Part of him wondered if the other hunter were leading him slowly into a trap, but that was more Wallbreaker's style than Crunchfist's. No, it had to be Indrani, calling for help.

He stumbled on, ignoring a thousand scratches and a throbbing pain in his left biceps. The ground squelched beneath him here and the cloying smell of rot hung in the air. By nightfall he still hadn't caught them. He was getting desperate.

The trail finally ended when Stopmouth found Crunchfist's bloody knife. Hidden in the undergrowth around it lay the entrances to three tunnels. The beasts must have picked their way carefully through the roots to get here, for above ground there were no signs of sagging trees. It was a perfect ambush. Stopmouth's legs wobbled beneath him. He allowed himself to fall and lay still on his back, watching the tracklights of the Roof. He didn't need to go looking for Indrani any more. He knew where she must be.

The young hunter forced himself to wait for daylight, trying for sleep and failing. When dawn brightened the Roof,
he shoved Crunchfist's knife into his belt and made his way
to the forest's edge. He could see the border of the Diggers'
territory from here.

Stopmouth walked into the open, passing over the roofs
of sunken houses to the place where the bodies began. They
were thick in this area, with no room to walk between them
and only the odd lump of rock sticking up here and there.
The stench was incredible, even worse than he remembered
it: like a mixture of vomit and human waste. It was so strong
that the young hunter had to stop to force clumps of
pounded moss into his nostrils and take deep breaths until
the nausea had passed.

Sometimes little bits of equipment lay scattered around
the listless victims. The Diggers obviously had no use for
anything other than their claws and hadn't bothered collecting them.

The young hunter found Crunchfist first. On a human
face the agony suffered by all the surrounding creatures was
obvious. The man said nothing, looked at nothing in
particular. Yet his eyes bulged out of their sockets, and while
his body hung motionless except for the odd twitch, his
nostrils flared and his lips were drawn back as far as they
could go. The soil only rose to his thighs, and around him

were scattered his broken spear-shaft, the Talker and bits and pieces from his tool-belt.

'Crunchfist?' No answer came, nor even the faintest hint of recognition. Stopmouth was anxious to find Indrani. Like Crunchfist, she was a new arrival. The young hunter hoped that meant she'd be somewhere on the edge of the crowd too. But he needed the Talker and he didn't want to leave any human in this kind of agony, even Crunchfist. So he gripped his spear firmly and shoved it straight into the big man's heart.

'Mother!' said Crunchfist. 'Oh, Mother!'

'Hush,' said Stopmouth. 'You'll bring them on me.'

Crunchfist grabbed the spear-shaft and pulled it deeper into himself before a surprised Stopmouth could let it go. He fell off-balance into the big man's embrace. Arms twice the size of his own squeezed tight.

'Mother,' wheezed Crunchfist. Nearby, other creatures began to take up the call. Stopmouth could barely breathe, and the clumps of moss in his nose only made matters worse. He struggled, pushing and prying at the immovable arm holding him. The vision at the corners of his eyes began to darken. He forced himself not to think about air, not to waste his energies on useless struggles. Instead, he tried to turn his kneeling legs into a position where he might push away with them. The soil was too slippy for a proper grip. He needed . . .

'Mother!'

Mother indeed. He could see her smiling. She hadn't died at all, then. Her embrace was firm and loving. Far away he could feel his feet scrabbling, slipping. It was tiring work and neither he nor his mother could see the point of it. Better to rest, to sleep. Then one of her arms fell away and the grip of the other weakened. Stopmouth took in a gulp of air, the glaring Roof swimming above him. He felt himself sliding backwards.

A familiar voice said, 'I can't believe it. Look, Stopmouth! I cut his throat and the poor man's still alive, hey? Stopmouth?'

'Rockface?' He sat up. The first thing he saw was the blood bubbling far too slowly from a gash in Crunchfist's neck. One of the hunter's arms lay on the ground where Rockface had hacked through it. He was still trying to speak – the same word, 'Mother', mouthed again and again – as the other prisoners around him lapsed into silence.

Rockface hunkered down beside Stopmouth, the smell from his teeth covered completely by the stench around them. A thatch of dried blood clumped the hair down one side of his head, but he smiled, as though delighted to be in this fine place.

'Let's find Indrani, hey?'

She'd been buried sideways on. She also tried to squeeze the life out of Stopmouth and called for her mother. But

Rockface pinned her arms while Stopmouth dug up the soil with Crunchfist's blunt knife. The earth writhed with yellow grubs, most no larger than his thumb. A few had grown to the size of his hand, and these tried to dig themselves out of his way with tiny limbs. But not for long. They curled and died without any intervention on his part while the imprisoned beasts around him continued calling for their mothers.

Blisters and wounds of many sizes covered Indrani's skin beneath the level of the soil. None appeared very deep. Even the wound in her calf caused by the adult Digger seemed shallower than it should have been.

'Are you all right?' he asked.

'Mother,' she replied. She struck at him clumsily until they'd pulled her ten strides from the rest of the prisoners. Then her eyes closed and the agony left her face.

Rockface offered to carry her.

'No,' said Stopmouth, although Crunchfist had squeezed the strength out of him. He heaved her onto his shoulders and staggered back to the rotting forest edge, while the big man trotted ahead. Behind them, a wild variety of beasts continued to suffer in their shared torment. A disturbing desire tore at Stopmouth to turn round and dig them all up, no matter that they weren't human. He knew it was stupidly dangerous and wrong besides, for surely none of those he rescued would have hesitated to hunt him. No, each species must look after its own.

Indrani's condition didn't change until they reached the cover of the trees. Then she made a terrible choking noise. Alarmed, he dropped her to the ground. Her whole body spasmed and she came up on her hands and knees, choking and coughing. About fifty little grubs sprayed from her throat onto the mossy soil. Many of them wriggled for a moment, trying to bury themselves perhaps. But one by one they fell still.

Indrani's eyes were open, looking straight at him. 'I knew you'd come,' she said. Then she lay down on top of the mess she'd made.

Stopmouth took one of the grubs and held it up to the light. The colour already seemed darker. It felt slimy and a little warm.

The hunter shrugged and popped it into his mouth.

'Good eating!' said Rockface. He shoved a whole hand-ful between his own jaws and sucked noisily on the juice. Then he placed one grub in his ear and one against the orbit of an eye. 'Look at me, Stopmouth! What am I, hey? Take a guess!'

'Careful, Rockface, we need to save some of those for Indrani. She'll be needing her strength.'

'Oh, you're worse than your father, boy. Too full of strange thoughts to have a laugh. I remember one time, old Toecracker hid your father's portion of the kill and he was too embarrassed to admit he couldn't find it. We watched him go round and round the fire, pretending he was just restless, and I laughed so much I wet myself. That was my first hunt as a man. It was the best time I ever had.'

Stopmouth felt his face go red. 'So he was just the butt of your jokes, was he?'

'Oh no! Well, yes, but we loved him, you know? And I mean *all* of us. Look! Look here.' He lifted up his arm. Down one side of the big man's stomach, between the tattoos of a spitted Hopper and a dying Flim, lay a thin white line Stopmouth had never noticed before. 'I shouldn't be with you now, hey?' He pointed up at the Roof. 'I should be up there, me and many others, if it wasn't for your dad.'

The big man surprised Stopmouth by wiping his eyes with the back of a huge hand. 'And you look just like him, you know? More with every passing day.'

Stopmouth didn't know what to say. 'Um, Rockface? I do have a sense of humour. With Indrani, we—'

'Oh, I know, boy! And that's as it should be. And now that you've rescued her, she'll be wanting to jump the fire with you in no time, hey?'

Stopmouth went red again. He turned away in embarrassment and delight.

The humans kept to the forest after that, for the difficulty it would cause the Diggers if they chose to follow them. At first the party meant to travel only by day, where speckled light guided them between the boles of twisted trees. The forest seemed beautiful then. Mossbeasts chirruped in a chorus that Stopmouth had never heard at home and saplings burst out of luminescent clumps of blue moss. Wallbreaker would have been fascinated by the whole thing, and even Rockface exclaimed in wonder at all the new colours. But in the three nights that followed, the beasts always knew where to find their quarry and sleep became impossible. As soon as the Roof darkened, faraway trees would come crashing down and Stopmouth would lift Indrani onto his shoulders and stagger on.

'Let me walk!' she whispered sometimes. She did her best, but she didn't get far with her wounds. It was quicker just to carry her, leaving the scouting up to Rockface.

'We're lucky they don't like to travel by day,' she said at one point. She wouldn't talk about her sufferings when the Diggers had buried her, but the shame that used to fill her voice when she'd spoken of them had been replaced now with hatred.

'It's the light,' he replied. 'I think it kills the grubs. If I thought it would hurt the adults too, I'd risk using the Talker on them.'

'No, you're right. It is just the grubs that fear the light. I knew that before, but I must have forgotten it.'

Stopmouth looked at her, wondering how a person could lose such a vital piece of knowledge. She returned his gaze, her face a mask of exhaustion, as his must be. They were resting at midday, believing themselves safe from attack. Rockface had gone ahead a little in search of the signs of pursuit. He seemed to have recovered from the knock on the head, but even he would need more food soon. They'd eaten the last of the grubs that morning. From now until their enemies finally caught up with them, the party could only get weaker.

'Is there nothing else you remember about the Diggers?' Indrani shook her head.

'Are you sure, Indrani? Like, how do they know we stole you back from them? How do they always find us when night falls? And what trick did Crunchfist use to get through their fields of bodies?'

She sighed and shook her head. 'Stopmouth, can you remember the first words you spoke to your mother?'

He shrugged. 'I doubt I was good at speaking even then. I don't know. Why is it important?'

'I don't remember my first words either. Not here on the surface of the world. But my people rely on the Roof to remember for them. It knows everything. You need only ask it.' As she spoke, her fingers wandered over the wounds of her legs, scratching and picking at scabs. 'The Roof is more than a place, Stopmouth. It's knowledge too. All the knowledge humans have ever learned. It keeps our memories safe for us so we never need to forget anything. But then it gets hard to tell sometimes which bits are in our heads, and which are in storage.' Her legs were bleeding now under her busy fingers. He pulled them away, taking her hands in his. She jerked out of his grasp, almost cowering away from him.

'I'm sorry,' she said, seeing the hurt on his face.

'No. I'm sorry. I'm sorry for what my people did to you. My brother . . . I would never—'

'Oh, Stopmouth, I know! You saved me from him. I know you wouldn't hurt me.'

'I won't let the Diggers have you either,' he said. 'Let the ancestors witness. I *will* find us a place where we can live and be safe.'

She smiled at him, the weariness disappearing from her face. He dared to touch her cheek, his heart thudding as much as it did in a fight. Indrani didn't pull away this time, but she said, 'Rockface is signalling us, Stopmouth. I'll try walking again.'

He nodded and dropped his hand. It felt warmer than the rest of him, as if it were tingling.

In spite of his promises, the young hunter didn't really expect them to survive much longer, and he contemplated finding a way to ambush their pursuers while he and Rockface still had some strength. But although he didn't know it, the ancestors had taken pity on the small band of humans. The ground began to slope upwards away from the Wetlane and the trees grew scrawnier, like grasping hands bent against the slope. Soon the forest had fallen behind them altogether. The ground became lumpy, and brown moss replaced the more colourful varieties of before. Stopmouth groaned at the sight of the hill stretching ahead of them, knowing they couldn't possibly keep going. But Indrani surprised him by smiling.

'There must be rock underneath,' she said. 'They'll never follow us here! Oh, thank the gods! We've escaped! We've beaten them!' She was shaking with exhaustion now, every step marked with agony across her face. The others fared little better. Even Rockface had stopped talking and looked thin and stooped. But Indrani was right. By the time night had fallen they were walking along something she called a *ridgeline* – a chain of *hills*, like muscles of earth flexing skywards – with no sign of pursuit.

Below them, in the direction from which they'd come, lay a ribbon of reflected light that could only be the Wetlane, made tiny by distance. From the other side of the ridge they saw a dark line of buildings, with here and there the orange glow of cooking fires.

Indrani threw herself on the ground to sleep and so missed out on the other gift the ancestors had chosen to bestow on them that evening: right in their direction of travel, no more than two days distant, a section of houses suddenly flashed, brighter than the Roof. The two hunters fell to their knees, eyes momentarily blinded. 'Oh, thank you!' Stopmouth said. 'Thank you!'

It seemed almost too good to be true.

16.

THE NEWCOMERS

Days and nights of frantic, painful travel brought them to a point on the ridgeline directly above the area where the new beasts must have arrived.

The city here differed greatly from Stopmouth's home. Rather than being divided into clearly defined Ways, the streets clustered in an unbroken line along the length of a strange, noisy Wetlane known as a *river*. From this distance the buildings looked battered and worn, hunched together like unwilling volunteers on a final journey.

Smoke rose into the air and Stopmouth feared it meant the new arrivals had already adapted to the shock of their situation and were organizing themselves. He hoped they still had a lot to learn. The humans were far too weak to pose a threat to any creature versed in the arts of survival. Hunger and various injuries had worn all three down to the point where a single Hopper would have picked them off gratefully.

Indrani, in particular, had reached the end of her strength. She had walked most of the way there despite the agony brought on by her wounds with every step. She never once complained. A few days of hunger and travel had turned her from a woman back into a child, her fat all gone, her muscles fading.

Stopmouth shook Rockface by the elbow, surprised at how long it took to get a reaction out of him. The hunter had been delighted by the flash two days before. Since then his nights had been bad and he tired quickly during the day. It was almost as if he didn't want to find vulnerable new beasts waiting to save his life.

'We need to hunt,' Stopmouth told him.

'For who?'

'For us . . . For Indrani.'

She had already flopped to the ground, and even before the men had finished speaking, she curled up behind a small ridge. Stopmouth watched her settle. He longed to hold her, to look her in the eyes for what might be the last time.

'I will not fail you,' he whispered, wondering if something as bad as the Longtongues waited for them below. But a pain in his gut told him it was time to leave. She was lying on top of the Talker and the thought never crossed his mind to take it from her.

The hunters set off on trembling legs in search of flesh. A few painful falls on the scree taught them to walk where the moss grew until the vegetation thickened again and brightened in colour. In the distance smoke was still rising from somewhere among the houses by the river. They moved low along the ridgeline until the smoke was directly opposite. Then they crawled or skidded from bush to rock until they neared a stand of trees. They never reached it. At the last moment the sound of a snapping twig sent Stopmouth diving for cover. Rockface was still standing in the open and his young companion had to pull him down behind a boulder.

'I thought you wanted to hunt,' muttered Rockface. But he said no more.

Stopmouth was breathing hard by now, every part of his body caked with sweat and dust. He counted off a few dozen heartbeats, praying Rockface hadn't been seen.

He hadn't. When Stopmouth poked his head round the edges of the boulder, he saw four beasts with their backs to him. They were spindly, with such smooth white skin he immediately baptized them 'Skeletons'. They had four arms, which tapered off into supple triangles of flesh rather than hands.

The beasts carried well-crafted spears and were crouching low amongst fallen branches for what could only be an ambush. What perfect targets they made! But they were too many for a pair of exhausted hunters. The men had no choice but to wait them out in the hope they might leave some scraps of their kill behind them. Stopmouth passed the time wondering whether their head, as in humans, was a weak spot. He imagined himself scooping out the brains. His mouth watered.

At last something seemed to be moving in the wood, something clumsy and large.

A creature emerged blinking into the light. Stopmouth almost choked. This was no beast. It was human, a real human, with skin as dark as Indrani's and strange, grey-coloured hair. He carried a belly such as Stopmouth had never seen in his life, being almost as large as a child all by itself. Sweat poured down the man's face and he stumbled right into the waiting beasts.

They didn't attack. Instead, they rose up smoothly to either side of their victim, as if they were playing with him.

Suddenly Rockface bellowed, 'Leave him alone!' Stopmouth nearly jumped out of his skin. But when Rockface stumbled to his feet and shambled off towards the beasts, Stopmouth gladly followed. They wouldn't leave one of their own to die so cheaply. The beasts turned as one to face the new threat, ignoring their previous quarry. Before Rockface reached them, his foot caught on something hidden in the undergrowth and he went down just in front of Stopmouth. The young hunter leaped over his companion to stand in front of him.

His short charge had left him exhilarated, full of the

rush of battle. If the beasts had come for him straight away, he might have been all right.

Instead, they looked him up and down, each with a quartet of glistening, pupil-less eyes over a tiny drooling mouth. Two stood close enough to him that he could have reached out and tapped them on the white domes of their heads. The other pair waited further off, still flanking the startled fat man. The beasts looked calm, as if nothing in all the world could scare them. Stopmouth realized how little he knew about these creatures, how heavy the spear felt in his hands, how tired he was. His heart hammered; his limbs trembled as fear began its whispers. He could still turn and run back to Indrani. They might live a few days more . . .

'The sharp end,' said Rockface, stirring at last. 'See how they like it.'

Stopmouth stepped forward quickly and punched the shell spear straight through the chest of one of the two beasts nearest him. They were slow to react and he had all the time in the world to withdraw the point and swing round the blunt end at another creature's head.

'G-get up, R-Rockface!'

'I am, I am.'

The last two Skeletons exploded into action. One bore down on Stopmouth at great speed. Its legs bent backwards rather than forwards; its tiny mouth worked furiously, spilling drool.

The beast threw its own spear even as it ran. The hunter felt it whistle past his ear and then the creature was pushing aside Stopmouth's weapon with one pair of arms, while the other swung at him with knives. He stumbled backwards, released the shaft of his spear and allowed the unbalanced beast to fall past him.

It used three arms to push itself up, fending him off with the fourth. Stopmouth grabbed it where the wrist should be. He held the arm in place and kicked at the join. It snapped very easily, but the beast made no sound. Instead, it used the hunter's spear against him like a club. One strike across the chest knocked the wind out of the human and drove him backwards. The creature moved awkwardly now, distracted by pain perhaps. Even so, it managed a blinding cut to Stopmouth's scalp and the exhausted hunter might have died then had the fat man not come into the fight, shouting and throwing pebbles. When the Skeleton looked behind it, Stopmouth snapped the remaining knife arm and wrenched back his spear. The beast died without a sound.

Stopmouth looked around for Rockface and found him resting against the boulder they'd been hiding behind.

'I needed that,' said the big man, managing his first smile in days.

'W-w-why didn't y-y-ou—'

'What are you saying? Maybe you should wait until we get the Talker back.'

'W-w-why d-d-didn't you h-help m-me?'

'Oh! You know you wouldn't have wanted me to. Pity that fellow spoiled it for you, hey?'

Stopmouth looked at the fat man, the man who *couldn't* be here. He was still yelling in gibberish and throwing stones at the last dead Skeleton.

'Are you from the Roof?' asked Stopmouth when he'd caught his breath. Blood ran down over the young hunter's face from the wound in his scalp. 'Have you come looking for Indrani?' He could scarcely credit his eyes. Another human! He wanted to embrace the man. But the newcomer abruptly turned away from him. He sat down on a boulder near the one Rockface leaned on. Then he began to cry.

'You're alive!' said Stopmouth. 'We won!'

He was about to offer the man his choice of the four kills when another crashing sound approached from the forest. A look of abject terror spread over the man's face. Stopmouth was worried too: he didn't think he had another fight in him.

'We should flee,' he said.

But the shapes struggling through the trees were human too. Five men, soft-looking, though not fat. They wore hides . all over the lower halves of their bodies and the heat must have been intense. Each carried a long branch freshly broken from a tree.

'We're safe now,' Stopmouth said.

The man's fearful expression never changed. He stumbled to his feet and broke into a shambling run, weighed down by his wobbling belly. He fell over after no more than a dozen paces.

'A law-breaker,' said Rockface. 'Like us.'

'Y-yes.' For some reason it made Stopmouth sad.

He didn't intervene when two of the men picked the fat one up by the arms. Another member of the group, no more than a boy with new scars across his right cheek, approached the hunters, excitement on his narrow face. He gabbled frantically for a few seconds and then, quite distinctly, said: 'Wok-faze! Shtop-Mou! Shtop-Mou!'

Stopmouth, though light-headed from lack of food and blood, laughed. 'Yes! Rockface and Stopmouth! How c-could you know that? Who are you?' His early experience with Indrani had taught him to point, but even so, the boy looked at him blankly. Then he too was grinning and tapping his own chest: 'Yama!'

The others, however, weren't amused. A heated discussion ensued with some of them gesticulating angrily towards Stopmouth. He hoped they'd sort out their differences quickly and give him something to bind his wound. Rockface wouldn't be much help: he'd closed his eyes and seemed to be ignoring the newcomers.

While Stopmouth waited, he cut a slice of the bone-white flesh from one of the kills. He was surprised to find the body didn't bleed red like all other creatures he'd known. Instead, a milky liquid seeped slowly over his fingers, still warm. It tasted sweet, the flesh firm and delicious.

He was about to cut more when a blow to the face knocked him over. A balding man he took to be the leader waved his stick at Stopmouth. He made chopping gestures and pointed back in the direction from which Stopmouth had come.

'We're not leaving without our share,' said Stopmouth, angry now himself. He climbed unsteadily to his feet and levelled his spear. Of course he wouldn't use it! He was so glad to see other humans, he would never dream of attacking them.

The bald man felt differently. He threw a clumsy swing in Stopmouth's direction. The hunter dodged. He reversed his spear and sent the man tumbling into the arms of his friends.

'We're not leaving!' he said again. He could see the bald man wanted to have another go at him. He was spitting and shouting while his companions held him back. Finally he quietened down and the others let him go. They grabbed the unresisting criminal and all six moved away without taking any of the kills for themselves. The boy, Yama, nodded and smiled as he left. Stopmouth nodded back, very confused.

He slid to the ground beside one of the Skeletons and cut away as much flesh as he thought they could carry.

'R-R-Rockf-face?'

The big man's eyes were still closed and sweat covered his limbs. Stopmouth pulled him away from the boulder to find a large gash in the man's back, still bleeding freely. His opponent must have reached round behind him and caught him with a blade. Why hadn't he said anything?

He used the big man's own needle to stitch him up.

'Your uncle taught you well,' said Rockface, breathing hard against the pain.

'Y-y-yes.'

He pounded some moss to remove the juices that would sting Rockface's wound. Then he used it as a bandage, tying it on with a strip of hide.

'Tell me something, boy. Why is your tongue always broken when you talk to me, but to those strange people it's as smooth as your brother's? They can't even understand you.'

Stopmouth had wondered the same thing back when he'd tried to teach Indrani to talk. He shrugged and cut some slices of Skeleton meat for himself and his companion.

'Don't waste any on me, boy. I'm about ready to volunteer, hey?'

'N-n-not d-dead yet.'

'Yes, I am. Back home they'll already have broken our Tallies and declared us ghosts. And I can't . . . I can't even be an ancestor now.'

Such talk frightened Stopmouth. It wasn't like Rockface, not like him at all. He made the big man eat a little, then he packed as much meat as he felt they could bear and heaved Rockface to his feet.

They staggered up the hill together. Stopmouth hadn't been able to stitch up his own wound and was weaker than he'd thought. After no more than a few paces he dropped one of the four limbs he'd been carrying. By the time they found Indrani, still asleep where they'd left her, his head was spinning and the pair bore no more than a single leg between them.

He woke with a pounding headache. Rockface had collapsed into sleep as soon as they'd returned and he still snored. His wound had been rebandaged with fresh moss and it looked as if the big man had a few thousand days more in him.

Stopmouth felt Indrani next to him, her cool hand against his forehead. She tutted. 'That wound you came back with may have induced a fever in you.'

'I'm not feverish.'

'Not now. But you were last night. I was worried about you. You were mumbling all sorts of mad things.'

'What are you talking about, Indrani?'

He'd been exhausted on their return, he remembered that much. He'd woken Indrani and the two of them had gorged themselves on sweet flesh as Rockface slumbered beside them. He'd tried to tell her what had happened while she stitched his wound, but his head had been reeling and she'd made him lie down.

'Oh, you said you'd seen humans,' she told him. 'Which is impossible. And I should know. Unless we're moving in circles, of course!'

He still felt a bit groggy and wondered if he really had dreamed the whole episode or if the ancestors had sent him a vision. Indrani bit into one of the last scraps of Skeleton flesh and smiled beautifully. 'Well, this is real enough!'

His face reddened. 'It is good, isn't it?'

Apart from a portion they were saving for Rockface, no more than a few bites of food remained and Stopmouth regretted all the good flesh they'd abandoned on the way back. 'If you don't believe me about the humans,' he said, 'we'll have to go and visit them. I know it wasn't a dream. I've been feverish before, remember?'

'I do remember,' she said wistfully. 'You looked so much like a child then! An innocent among savages. The first flesh I willingly allowed past my lips was the food I chewed for you.'

Stopmouth laughed. 'Oh, come now. What did you eat before you came to us? Air? Rooflight?'

'Only savages,' she said, 'eat flesh. *Civilized* beings eat other things made from plants.'

'You can't live on moss and trees! They'd make you sick!'

'I never said we did!' She seemed exasperated. 'There are other plants besides those. *Rice*, fruit, *vegetables*. To kill a being and eat its flesh is the most evil and terrible thing a creature can do! It's obscene!'

Stopmouth offered her the last morsel of Skeleton flesh. She swiped it from his hand.

'I know,' she said, stuffing her mouth. 'I know!'

They lay down in silence while they digested their meal. From here the humans could look back over some of the great distance they'd travelled. The air rippled in the morning heat and a light mist, soon to burn off, hung over the Wetlane. Tiny grey shapes, probably buildings, dotted the horizon. Stopmouth imagined them sinking into the Digger-riddled earth and shuddered.

He didn't feel well. His head was spinning and he began to question again whether he'd really seen the humans or if his wounds had induced a fever in him. Yet there was something in the way Indrani sat, the way her eyes darted about, that suggested she wasn't entirely sure of her own point of view either. She looked like a woman who insisted her child still lived in spite of the puddle of blood on her floor.

'You came from the Roof,' he said at last. 'Why couldn't other people have done the same? They certainly looked more like you than me.'

'People don't come here from the Roof,' she said. 'Oh

yes, every thousand days or so we get an idiot who feels more holy for having beasts eat him . . . But groups? Never.'

'And yet—'

'Even if a group did come, a big group . . . The world is vast, Stopmouth. Huge. What are the chances that we'd run into them? It's impossible.'

'It's not impossible,' he said. 'They could have placed themselves in our path on purpose. Like . . . like an ambush or something.'

The idea seemed to throw her off completely. She stared at him for a dozen heartbeats before a look of pure horror came over her face. 'Or someone else . . .' she whispered. 'Someone else could have sent them here, right where we are. Oh, by all the gods!' She scrambled to her knees. 'We've got to go! Quickly!'

'We can't,' said Stopmouth. 'Well, Rockface can't and I won't leave him here. We all need rest. Another day, Indrani, please. They'll still be there tomorrow. We'll be stronger then, I promise.'

She looked at the wound she'd bound herself only the previous evening. Blood still oozed into the moss bandage and sweat beaded Stopmouth's brow.

Indrani nodded and sat down, but he could see the tension in every muscle of her body. Surely, he thought, the idea of finding humans right where they needed them was the best possible news? And yet she looked so frightened.

There was so much about her he didn't know, whereas she seemed to know everything about him and his people.

'Indrani, why did you call my ancestors "Deserters" the other night?'

'I . . . I shouldn't have said that.'

'Because it's not true?'

'Stopmouth . . .' She was still staring at the horizon, dragging her hands through the stony soil of the ridge.

'Please find some question other than that,' she said finally. 'Please. It's not that I don't want to tell you things. I do. More than you can imagine. Sometimes I look at you, at your cleverness, all that strength and energy, and I think . . . I almost think you could be one of us. And then I see you killing. You enjoy it. Don't deny it! I see you kill, and in your own way you're magnificent, but you could never, never be civilized.'

'Because I hunt for food?'

'Partly, yes.'

'You have hunted for food.'

'I know,' she whispered.

'And ten heartbeats past, you grabbed a piece of flesh out of my hands. Didn't you like the taste? Because if you can be a savage, maybe I could be civilized. It's possible, isn't it?'

They looked each other in the eye and he saw tears in hers. But she didn't flinch away from his gaze. She nodded and wiped the back of one hand across her face.

'And anyway, what has my being civilized got to do with the "Deserters"?'

'I . . .' She cleared her throat. 'I insulted your ancestors the other night. I'm sorry. Your people have your stories, like we have ours, all right? It's just that my stories would stop you wanting to come to the Roof with me. They could even make us enemies—'

'Never!'

'You say that, but if it happened, I'm not sure I could—'

'It can't happen,' he said. 'I just want to know.'

She leaned forward towards him, almost as if she wanted to kiss him, and his heart beat faster, waiting for that moment of joy. Her face paused a handspan from his own.

'All humans, Stopmouth, came from the same world. And bad things happened there. But it was a long time ago and you are so far above all that, so . . .' Her eyes were fixed on his for the longest of moments. Then she jerked her head back as if she'd just caught herself before stepping over the edge of a tower. She sighed, rubbed her face, then looked up once more.

'You've done everything for me, Stopmouth. It has cost you your home and probably your life.' Her eyes began to tear up again and he fought hard to keep his own from responding. 'Even so, I will beg this one last thing from you, dearest Stopmouth. Please . . . Please don't ask me to tell you this story. And if we live to meet other humans, if they're real . . . I'm begging you, don't ask them either. I can't offer you anything in return, but—'

'I don't want anything, Indrani. I lo—'

She touched his lips with a finger. 'Thank you.'

And then she was in his arms, bawling like a whipped child, until she closed her eyes and he laid her down beside Rockface.

He couldn't sleep himself afterwards for all the thoughts she'd stirred up in him. The story Indrani was keeping from him fascinated him and he wondered how she thought that simply telling it would make him hate her. But more amazing still was the sight of Indrani lying so near and the recent feel of her in his arms. He'd sacrifice everything for that. He already had and he knew that nothing could ever make him break his promise to her.

17.
ALLEY FIGHT

The Bloodskin tattooed on Rockface's back was as realistic a depiction as Stopmouth had ever seen. It was charging in for the kill, baring a mass of tangled teeth. As the big man limped down the slope in front of him, Stopmouth felt a flash of fear. He remembered clinging to that broad back, a Bloodskin just like that one reaching for him. Rockface had saved his life then, and not for the last time. But today the beast would have caught him easily: the big man was limping, his normally cheerful mouth twisted in pain that remained private except for the odd escaping grunt.

All around the little party, morning mist was fading with growing heat from the Roof. Clumps of coloured moss fought eternal battles over brittle crumbles of stone. A moss-beast whizzed by on tiny wings. It hovered for a moment at Stopmouth's ear. Then it swung away off down the ridge and out of sight. Looking for food, he thought, his own stomach rumbling. His wound stung a bit beneath its bandage, but it was healing quickly under Indrani's care.

Her touch was always so gentle with him, even when she spoke bad things against his Tribe. He couldn't blame her for that, after what she'd been through. But he hoped her sufferings would soon fade from her memory and she would come to his arms again for more than crying.

She stopped for a moment to drink from their only remaining water skin and caught him looking.

'You're not angry with me, Stopmouth?'

'No!'

'It's just when you scowl at me like that . . .'

'I wasn't— I mean, I didn't know—'

She smiled and handed over the water skin. 'We're still friends, right?'

If only she knew! It was all he could do to nod without reaching for her and scaring her off again.

They set off along the ridge until they came in sight of the fire that seemed to burn constantly down by the river. They followed its smoke, as Stopmouth had before, moving downhill from cover to cover.

More beasts roamed the area today. Not skeletons this time. These ones ran on four legs, although they looked as if they could rise to a head-height above a man if they wanted to travel on two. They had tiny eyes perched atop pointy skulls and rust-coloured, scaly skin. Human body parts dangled from hide ropes tied to their backs. They must have had good hearing, for when Indrani gasped in horror, they stopped. She managed to keep quiet long enough for the beasts to decide they'd heard nothing and move off again downriver. Nor were these the last danger between the three humans and their goal. All the land around seemed to swarm with enemies. Only a dozen heartbeats after the first sighting, Stopmouth spotted a hunting party of Skeletons in the distance. They too appeared to have been successful, dragging dead women behind them by the ankles.

'I told you there were humans here,' said Stopmouth. Indrani didn't reply. Her face had turned white. 'They're not much good at defending themselves,' he added. He told her about the pathetic weapons the two hunters had faced two days previously, and the equally pathetic fighter.

They tiptoed through the forest until they reached the first, unguarded walls. The road here had been barricaded a long time before, but hadn't seen repairs in generations. They climbed over it easily and stepped into the empty street beyond.

Everything about the houses here screamed 'old'. Older by far than those Stopmouth had grown up in. Many were dressed in a loincloth of their own rubble, and moss blanketed every wall as far as the second or third storey. It grew thickly here, bunching around cracks and forming little mounds over fallen-in roofs. Where two varieties met, red with purple or deep green, little eddies of colour would form, each apparently trying to grow over the top of the other. Throughout the area, narrow streets crossed with even tighter alleys. Most of the latter were impassable, blocked by generations of dying buildings. In one case, two houses leaned across the gap towards each other, making a bridge of their outer walls.

The party moved from door to door, careful of ambush. They saw no one. Finally they heard crying. A child no higher than Stopmouth's waist sobbed and wailed. She stopped for a minute when she saw them. Then she started up again.

'Hush,' said Indrani. 'Hush! Where's your mother?'

Dried blood smeared the child's forehead although she didn't look injured. In fact, red splashes decorated most of the street. When the girl made no answer, Indrani took her by the hand and pulled her along as they walked towards the river. Soon they heard more crying; the keening of grown women. Almost every corner boasted human bones or pools of blood. Even Rockface woke from the stupor he'd been in to ask, 'How could this happen? How?'

The way opened up into a wide square where hundreds, maybe thousands of humans lay jammed together around a bonfire, crowding even nearby roofs. Stopmouth gaped in wonder at the bizarre and beautiful colours worn by these people. Not even the mossbeasts of the Diggers' forest had been so brilliant. In particular, the women seemed to shimmer in skins that covered them from neck to foot. But the heat must have been terrible, for only their arms and faces felt the air. Stopmouth couldn't tell one person from another at first. Maybe he didn't want to, for when his eyes finally began catching on details, the pity was nearly enough to make him turn and run. A woman, her limbs like sticks, crawled on all fours as if searching for her missing eyes. A haggard boy prayed loudly to spirits Stopmouth had never heard of. He had the look of madness on his face. Nearby an infant clutched vainly at the legs of a man who, it seemed, could not look down; could only stare ahead, unblinking. Volunteers ready for the pot.

There were many others like this, weeping or fighting over trifles, wailing or begging. All looked terrified, and no amount of coloured cloth could hide it.

The hubbub died down at the approach of the new-comers. A woman next to Stopmouth whispered in his hearing: 'It's the witch! This is her fault!'

'You!' The bald man who'd attacked Stopmouth two days before pushed through the crowd, stepping on people who couldn't move away fast enough. He sweated heavily and stumbled as he emerged. Hair grew on his face and it almost looked to Stopmouth as if his head were on upside down. Like many of the other men (but none of the women), he had stripped himself to the waist. He had so little muscle that his skin seemed to hang about him in flaps without so much as a single tattoo to relieve the ugliness.

'He mustn't have eaten lately,' whispered Stopmouth. 'Maybe none of them have.'

'But,' asked Indrani, 'why are they even here?' She too was sweating.

The bald man pointed dramatically at Stopmouth and spoke loudly enough for the whole square to hear him. 'I told you lot not to come back with your savage ways! We will not descend to your level! We will not waver!' He turned to Indrani. 'As for you,' he sneered. 'Witch! You have my pity. You will never leave this place! Not if you die a thousand times!'

Rockface roared and stepped forward. Indrani grabbed his shoulder, making him wince. 'We're going now,' she said. 'We've seen enough.' She pushed Rockface back in the direction from which they'd come. Then she took Stopmouth by the hand and began dragging him and the child with her.

'Wait!' Stopmouth freed himself from her grip and turned to the crowd. 'What's going on here?'

'The savage has a Talker!' somebody exclaimed.

He ignored them. 'We found this little girl with no mother. You left her in the streets to die! What must your ancestors think of you?'

Many of the watchers looked ashamed, but the balding man scowled. 'We will not be staying here, savage! Death will save us, and the girl too if you would just let her be!'

'Yes!' said somebody at the back to approving murmurs. 'Let her be!'

'No!' said somebody else.

The balding man looked around for the rebellious voice. A young woman on a rooftop, every bit as beautiful as Indrani and large with child, stood up.

'I shouldn't be here in the first place!' she cried. 'I never believed any of your drivel.' And then she stumbled backwards. 'Ow! Let me go, Grandmother!'

Stopmouth didn't know whether to be more shocked by the fact that an adult had a living grandmother or by the sight of the old woman herself: bone-white hair over skin as wrinkled as a brain.

'You're ready for cremation already!' the young woman said. 'Why did I have to die for your beliefs?'

A riot ensued up on the roof as other family members pulled her down and tried to shut her up. She continued to shriek insults until the others beat her into silence.

'We're going now!' said Indrani. Stopmouth allowed her to drag him as far as the next street, still with the little girl in tow and Rockface limping along behind.

'Who are these people?' he asked her. 'This is madness!'

'They're a group that prays a lot to spirits. I'll tell you more when we stop.'

They picked out a building and sat in the shade of its lintel. A curtain of moss helped keep the glare away and was still damp and cool with the remnants of last night's Roofsweat. All around them, the buzz and whirr of insects soothed away the human sounds of the square. Stopmouth gave the little girl a drink of water and she curled up and went to sleep immediately. Rockface moved to sit beside her, resting one hand gently on her back. He was breathing heavily, exhausted by his wounds and the short trip they'd made to get here.

'Who were those people?' asked Stopmouth again.

Indrani didn't answer at first. She looked sick and afraid, as if her worst nightmares had all come true at once. 'There are plenty who think like them where I come from, Stopmouth. They are people who claim to love spirits more than they love themselves. Some of the fools even mean it, I suppose . . . We have a special word for them: *religious*.' She pronounced it the way she pronounced the word 'savage', as if it hurt to speak it. 'Some of them were the ones who rebelled up on the Roof – that's when you saw the Globes start fighting. But these ones are the kind that don't like to fight, or say they don't. Their legends tell them that if they eat the flesh of another living creature, they must be eaten themselves one day. That's why they don't defend themselves.'

Stopmouth was still mystified. 'They're going to be eaten anyway. Every creature is eaten in the end, so they might as well start defending themselves and live a bit longer, am I right?'

'Of course he's right,' said Rockface. He patted the other hunter weakly on the back as if to say: *See how well I trained him?*

Indrani sighed. 'Stopmouth, I don't know how to explain this to you, really I don't. But it's not this life those people are worried about. If they eat flesh, then when they're reborn they—'

'What do you mean, "reborn"?' Stopmouth wondered if the Talker, unable to give the appropriate meaning, had thrown in the first word it could find.

She sighed again. 'Just trust me on this, all right? It doesn't matter if you don't understand what I'm talking about, or don't believe it. Just accept that *religious* people imagine they will have other lives after they die—'

'As ancestors?'

'No, Stopmouth. As people, or beasts or trees. Don't look at me like that! That's what their idiot leader meant when he said I'd never leave here. I have eaten flesh, so he thinks I'll be reborn here and devoured here again and again until I learn not to consume others. He's sure that if he dies without flesh passing his lips, he'll pay off whatever crime against the spirits condemned him to be here in the first place. The next time he's born, it will be to a kinder fate.'

This was just about the most amazing thing Stopmouth had ever heard. He had questions, lots of questions. He didn't get to ask them.

A band of men and women more than a dozen strong found them. The boy, Yama, who'd recognized Stopmouth and Rockface when they'd fought the Skeletons two days before, smiled and stepped forward out of the group. He still carried his stick, but he looked more haggard and the scars on his cheeks were crusted with blood. The others hovered at his back, men twice his size, as if they thought Yama would protect them.

'Great hunters' – he dropped the tree branch and bowed with his palms flat against each other and raised in front of his face – 'I've watched your people my whole life, although the elders told me not to. Ha ha, I bet they all wish they'd watched you now! None of the stinking cowards have eaten for days.'

'And what have you eaten, Yama?' asked Stopmouth.

The boy ignored the question. 'You're quite good,' he said. 'At hunting, I mean. I know I'd be good too if I had a proper spear like you do. Then I could feed myself and any wives I had.'

'Good boy!' said Rockface. 'You hear him, hey? Stopmouth?'

Another man stepped forward. He was one of the grey ones with scraggly hair sprouting strangely from the front of his face and a voice like two stones scraping together.

'Oh, enough of this!' said the grey man. 'I am Kubar, one of the elders this little fool has been mocking. We need your help, savages. You murder for food and we have women here, starving people who need you two to feed them.'

Stopmouth felt his face grow hot. He was sick of being called a 'savage'. Also he noticed that some of the group before him cast hateful glances towards Indrani. He'd heard people call her a witch earlier and didn't like that either.

'We need to get going,' he said.

'Ridiculous!' said Kubar. 'Have you no feeling for your fellow humans? No feeling at all? The beasts are here every day, picking us off. But at night' – he shuddered – 'at night they come in big groups. The white ones with four arms. The ones with tongues that will wrap around a child and snatch her away. The red ones that can run on four legs or two. They herd away hundreds of us at a time and butcher them in a street nearby where we can hear everything! Sometimes they just run at us with their knives and kill and kill until they grow tired. And you . . . you refuse to help us? There were ten thousand of us only a few days ago, and now we are a fifth of that. In a few more days we will all be dead.'

'Isn't that what you want?' asked Stopmouth. 'To be reborn?'

Kubar looked away. He was filthy, his hair matted with moss and dirt, his hands shaking with hunger or fear. '*I* do not want to die,' the elder whispered. 'Not like that. Last night some of us formed a circle and fought back. I don't think we even scratched any of the beasts, but they let us be in favour of others who were weaker. We will be reborn as mossbeasts or worse for what we did.'

Stopmouth had a momentary vision of himself and Rockface leading these few back to join with Wallbreaker. However, remembering the hazards of that journey – Diggers, Longtongues and Wetlane beasts – he knew that none would make it. He wasn't sure what his party could do to save them, especially with Rockface wounded. He looked at Indrani.

She sighed. 'We could do far more for these people if we got to the Roof. They can't survive here. Even if they did, sooner or later the Diggers will come and that will be that . . .' She shrugged. 'Oh well, they need your help now and I suppose you'd better give it.'

'Of course we'll help them!' said Rockface.

'Rockface, you're injured,' said Stopmouth, 'and I'm not sure I'd be much good to them.'

Indrani snorted in disbelief, sending a warm glow through his body. The others looked at him imploringly. One twitchy young man even went down on his knees and held shaking arms outstretched in Stopmouth's direction.

'All right,' he said at last. 'We'll do our best. Rockface?'

'Ha! I knew it! Just like your father!'

The newcomers looked relieved, breaking out into a babble of prayers and weeping. Stopmouth had to speak up to be heard above them. 'But are there no others who want to live?'

'Oh yes,' said the elder. 'Many others.'

'Good.' He looked round and spotted the boy Yama. 'You – could you . . . please go back to your people and tell all those who wish to fight . . . all those willing to *eat*, to come here. Bring any sticks you have. And make sure you get back to me before dark – that's when most of the attacks will take place.' The boy whooped and ran off.

Stopmouth left the weaker ones under Rockface's protection. He took the rest of the new humans scouting. It would have been better if he could have sent them collecting sticks or bones for weapons, but he didn't trust them on their own with so many enemies around. They didn't trust themselves either. They milled about, their terror and exhaustion evident in every movement, each afraid to be the last in line.

'Keep your eyes peeled! We need a few buildings we can isolate from the rest and defend.'

He found what they were looking for next to the wildly rushing river. A complex of buildings, three storeys high, formed a U shape around a blind alley. Very little moss clung to the smooth material of the walls, as if it couldn't get a grip, or didn't like the taste. Stopmouth looked up three storeys and couldn't see a single crack in the facade. That would have been unusual at home, but in this area it seemed a miracle. Best of all, the flat roofs overlooked the only unblocked entrance to the complex on three sides.

'Perfect,' he said. 'And look at all that rubble!' At some time in the past a house across the street had collapsed and many of the stones had obligingly rolled over towards the small opening of the U.

He piled up some heavy rocks and began carrying them one by one up to the roof. The others, apart from the injured Rockface, followed his example, groaning under unaccustomed weight. When he saw they were getting the idea, he limited himself to supervision, hoarding his energy for the night to come. Nobody complained. These people who'd begged the savages' protection seemed to fear him. But Indrani . . . they *hated* her. Still, when she grew exasperated at them and shouted, they leaped to obey.

'These fools seem to think they can just lie down and leave all the work to others!' she said to him.

'It's not that,' he replied. 'They don't have the strength for this. They need flesh.'

'And courage.'

And rest too, they needed rest. After half a day they'd managed a few dozen rocks and he doubted he'd get any more work out of them short of killing them.

Kubar had scraped his hands raw with the stones he carried. Splinters and fragments of stone jiggled in the strands of his beard. 'Where's that young idiot, Yama?' he asked, his voice even lower with all the dust in his throat. Nobody knew. Some of them had families the boy had been supposed to collect and bring here. No more than a tenth of daylight remained. Many of them wanted to go back to the square.

'None of you are leaving!' said Stopmouth. 'I'll find Yama for you.'

'But who will protect us here?' asked Kubar. 'No offence to your big companion . . . but he's gone to sleep. Look at him! He couldn't fight off a child in that condition.'

'Indrani will be in charge,' Stopmouth said.

'What?' She hadn't expected that.

'You can fight, Indrani. You terrified our hunters back home with your kicks, remember?'

'I can *defend* myself, Stopmouth. Against humans.'

'It's the same thing,' he said, although it wasn't. But he knew she could do the job. He pressed the Armourback-shell spear into her hands. He didn't plan on being gone long enough to need it. More importantly he wanted her to be safe. In spite of the things she'd told him the day before, the thought of harm coming to her was too much to bear. 'Bring the people to the top of this building,' he told her. 'Keep quiet and drop rocks on any beasts that come into the alleyway. They'll find easier prey and leave you alone. All right?'

He left her stuttering in protest and ran towards the square. It felt wonderful to stretch his legs, to see the buildings glide past almost in a blur. Beneath his feet the thick moss of the area hid wobbly stones and other hazards. Nothing slowed him down; it felt like nothing could.

He ran on until he heard the shouting and weeping of the crowd.

Night is approaching, he thought. They know what's coming. He passed several half-butchered corpses on the way. Mostly old people with that strange grey hair. None of them was the boy and he didn't stop.

The square itself heaved with panic. People on the outer edges tried to push closer to the centre. The weak finished on the outside or screamed as those with more strength walked on top of them. If Yama and the families he was supposed to bring with him were hiding in this mass, Stopmouth would never find them.

'Yama!' he shouted at the top of his lungs, but doubted he could be heard more than a few body-lengths away.

Stopmouth ran into a nearby building and climbed the steps three at a time. From the roof he could see right into the centre of the crowd. He didn't find Yama but he did see the bald-headed chief of these people. The man rested against a huge, squat building which bordered the square on the river side. Young men kept the crowd at bay. Others crossed sticks in front of the entrance to the building. It looked like they had imprisoned somebody inside and Stopmouth had a good idea who it was.

He left the roof and moved into side streets and alleys, trying to find a route that would bring him to the river. He heard it, roaring constantly in the background, but this wasn't much like the Ways he'd grown up in – the lanes here kept twisting away in strange directions, confusing him even as the Rooflight grew fainter. Finally he cut through the hallway of a house and emerged from the back window to see the river no more than twenty body-lengths distant.

Here lay the back end of the huge building that the chief's men had been guarding. It had a few windows, but they were small and high. No way through there, he thought. He kept walking around the building until he saw a place where a house had collapsed against it, one precariously leaning wall forming a natural ladder.

Lumps of concrete cracked under his feet as he climbed. Some fell away in a spray of powder and stones. Once he reached too far for a handhold and slid a full body-length, braking painfully with his bare skin while the whole structure shuddered. It was Bloodskin all over again, except this time he made it onto the roof before the wall came tumbling down.

He could hear the people in the square beyond the

building. The sounds of panic were already reaching fever pitch. He knew he didn't have much time. Tonight neighbouring beasts would aim to cripple the new arrivals, maybe even exterminate them.

He searched about frantically for a skylight. When he found one, it was so dark inside that he couldn't see any stairs. Maybe there weren't any.

'Yama?' he called. His voice echoed into the darkness, but the building was so large that even if the boy was inside, he mightn't hear him. Stopmouth dropped a stone through the skylight. It struck something almost at once, so he lowered himself over the edge and let go.

Stairs! Thank the ancestors!

He descended them carefully while his eyes adapted to the darkness. This too reminded him of the night he broke his legs. 'Yama? Yama?' he called.

At the bottom he started moving in what he hoped was the direction of the guarded doorway. He reached a large open space where the last of the Rooflight trickled in from the high, small windows he'd seen earlier.

'Yama?'

A voice called back something in gibberish. Stopmouth ran towards the source of it until he could see the guarded doorway and hear the noise of panic from the square beyond. 'Shtop-Mou?'

Yama's silhouette bowed, outlined in a sheen of

perspiration. Around him other silhouettes waited, perhaps a hundred of them, or two hundred. Men and women both. Why had the chief placed the rebels here? Surely this was the safest place in the whole area, with the crowded square buffering it from attack?

Outside the screaming began, first at one end of the square and then the other. Yama's people began murmuring among themselves, their fear almost palpable. Then came a scream from *within* the building. Gurgling and short. Another shriek nearby, and a wave of panicked bodies ran for the guarded doorway. White shapes danced through the back of the room, their skin glowing gently.

Stopmouth grabbed Yama. 'Why are we running from so few? We have to fight them!'

The urgency if not the meaning communicated itself. Yama did some shouting of his own and grabbed a few of the fleeing men. The Skeletons were getting closer. Stopmouth picked up a piece of masonry and charged in the direction of the enemy. His stomach churned with the old fear and he prayed the others would follow, knowing he was dead if they didn't.

His rock crashed down on the glowing head of a Skeleton. He grabbed its spear as other white figures converged on him. But then the rest of the humans arrived in a ragged charge, throwing rubble. Stopmouth saw two Skeletons stagger while another went down altogether. The rest retreated, one group fending off his men while another dragged away human corpses. They all disappeared into the floor.

Back home, Stopmouth and his comrades might have pursued the enemy in an effort to save the bodies. Not here. He didn't know how many more entrances to this place lay hidden in the darkness. They had to get out. He thought of bringing the people up onto the roof, but the stairs he'd dropped onto didn't quite reach the skylight. He imagined the chaos of exhausted people trying to lift each other up while those at the bottom of the stairs were savaged by beasts. The panic alone would cost many lives. No, he'd bring them out through the square, where the enemy would find easier targets and where he could at least see his way.

He grabbed Yama and showed him the spear he'd captured. The boy nodded, his grin flashing in the light from the door. He called out gibberish until the others began collecting abandoned enemy weapons.

The next step would be harder. Stopmouth pressed a strip of white flesh into Yama's hand. The boy squawked and flung the morsel away. Stopmouth grabbed him and forced his fingers to close around another piece, still warm from the corpse. Stopmouth could hear him almost whimper at the thought of what he was about to do, but slowly, without any further help from the hunter, he raised the meat to his mouth. Stopmouth heard him swallow, almost gagging. But his voice was firm when he shouted at the others – most of whom were older than him – until they lined up nervously before Stopmouth. Some got sick as soon as the flesh passed their lips. It didn't matter, thought Stopmouth: now they would have to fight.

He led them to the door. Guards still blocked the way with sticks. They were big men by human standards, but Stopmouth could see they were soft. Sweat beaded their skin while their heads swivelled now one way, now the other, following whatever was causing the screaming in various parts of the square. The balding chief knelt just in front of them, his hands over his eyes.

Stopmouth stepped between the guards. They jumped, but stood back from the tip of his new spear. More of the newly armed prisoners pushed in behind him.

The chief and Yama began shouting at each other, but Stopmouth ignored them, appalled by what he could see: a great boiling mass of humans, under attack from all sides by a bewildering variety of beast species, but weaponless and helpless as babies.

Several alleyways lay free of attack and sometimes people ran into them to escape. Stopmouth felt sure that more creatures lay in wait there, grateful for easy prey.

He shook Yama out of his argument with the chief and

indicated a side street leading around the prison towards the river.

'We're going that way.' Any other path would take them across the swirling crowds of the square.

Stopmouth moved off with his allies behind him. Three of the guards came too, and women and children ran to join them. A riot began in the middle of the square as tens rushed to follow.

Stopmouth halted the group at the mouth of the alley. It looked clear, but that meant nothing. He pulled three spearmen to the front along with the guards and their pathetic sticks. He made others pick up rocks.

'Slowly does it,' he said, moving forward.

The hissing of the river grew louder. Halfway down, one of his men dropped his spear and clutched at his neck. He fell and slid backwards into a doorway. People shouted in fear. Then Stopmouth felt a tightness around his own left ankle. His leg was pulled from under him and he crashed onto the stone-covered street. He too began scraping towards a doorway, where a pair of red eyes flashed in the darkness close to the ground. He called out for help, having dropped his spear, but all he heard were screams. People were falling everywhere; some were being trampled.

He jerked his knife free of his belt and cut the cord around his leg. He was surprised as hot blood spilled from it. The glowing eyes leaped towards him. He flung up his weapon and had it knocked from his hands by a slime-covered limb. Then talons were pushing him down, digging into his shoulder. Jaws opened hugely against the tracklights.

Stopmouth heard a crunching sound. The creature slid off him. A young man helped him up and returned the dropped knife. He tapped his chest, as if he knew Stopmouth couldn't understand him, and said, 'Varaha.' He was as good-looking for a man as Indrani was for a woman, with a strong jaw, deep black eyes and a winning smile. Varaha showed not the slightest hint of fear and didn't even appear to be sweating. All over the alley, humans who didn't know how to fight were flinging stones and jabbing awkwardly with spears. The slimy-skinned beasts who lay in wait couldn't have been expecting such numbers or resistance. They died quickly, having killed no more than twice or three times their number.

'You!' shouted Stopmouth at the former prison guards. He showed them Varaha's kill. 'We need to take that corpse.' He mimed it for them, but they just looked at him stupidly until Varaha growled them into obedience. Men further back picked up another corpse of their own accord. Then the whole band moved on, squeezed at the back by ever growing numbers of refugees.

Stopmouth reached the river without further incident. Behind him, humans were still pouring from the mouth of the alleyway. Far more of them had followed than he'd been expecting. They'd chosen life above all the teachings of their wrinkly old men. Even the chief had come, tears in his eyes, his face so anguished Stopmouth could only pity him.

But it wasn't over yet: predators had followed prey and screams echoed from the back of the alley. Stopmouth tried to organize his hunters to form a defensive line. Too many people were pushing past, driven by the slaughter at their backs. He might as well have tried stopping the rushing waters of the river. Over their heads he spied the rust-coloured beasts standing on their hind legs, sweeping great claws through human flesh. A mist of gore blurred the air around them.

Blood flowed out of the alley in gutters. He wondered briefly if that was what gutters were for. How many humans had died to produce so much blood? How many beasts would feed on them and for how long would they be satisfied?

People were still pouring out of the alleyway. By now the beasts must have been walking on a carpet of bodies. They were only twenty paces away and the young hunter knew they wouldn't stop until they'd weakened the humans beyond the point of recovery.

He shouted for Yama, but couldn't see him in the chaos. So he gathered a group of the terrified new hunters, most armed with no more than rocks. Varaha came too and helped him shove the men into position as close to the mouth of the alley as possible.

Suddenly the last survivors had passed, and Fourleggers, plastered in gore, exposed their bellies to human vengeance. After such easy slaughter, the organized ambush took them by surprise. The young hunter gutted one of them before they even knew they were under attack. Rocks and stones flew into the mouth of the alley, knocking the enemy off balance even as Stopmouth charged them. Other humans ran with him, yelling their hatred, and amazingly the beasts turned tail and ran for their lives. There had only been a dozen of them in the assault to begin with. Almost all of them escaped.

The young hunter sagged against a wall.

He heard Varaha calling out something to the humans behind him in a strong, rich voice. When he turned, the man was grinning and everybody was staring at Stopmouth as if he was some kind of hero. Varaha spoke again and the young hunter heard an approximation of his own name in amongst the gibberish. The crowd cheered, many with damp eyes. Then they rushed forward to hug him, and tears were streaming down his face too. It felt so right. Like home, except better, for here he wasn't Stopmouth the stutterer, Wallbreaker's harmless brother – here he was the man who'd saved their lives.

He knew that if only he could protect these people,

make them protect themselves, his little group would have a home again. He and Indrani could be together and no man could say otherwise.

And there was another thought lurking at the back of his mind: 'I won't have to go to the Roof. I won't have to live among those who hate my ancestors and hate me!'

18.
THR⊕UGH THE
FIRE

Stopmouth found Indrani's band safe and sound the next day. He'd been hoping for a hug when he saw her. Instead, she yelled at him and punched him hard enough to set his head ringing. Then, with no words of explanation, she bathed his cuts and bruises, tenderly and with great care not to hurt him further. Better than a hug, he thought to himself, although it wasn't really. At least she'd lost her fear of being close to him.

All around them joyful reunions were taking place. Anxious faces sought relatives and friends. Many tears were shed and throats, raw from days of fear, found the strength to cry some more. There were a few orphans too, like the little girl Stopmouth and Indrani had saved. The Tribe will be their family now, thought Stopmouth. And mine too.

'We were attacked last night,' Indrani told him. 'They were the four-legged ones with the red scales. We beat them off.'

'Did you kill any?'

'Oh yes!' But the beasts had been too canny to leave corpses behind them.

'They waited until we ran out of stones,' said Indrani. 'Then they stole back their dead.' She hung her head. 'It was my fault. They knew we were low on rocks because I shouted at the people who were supposed to push them over the edge. The Talker translated what I said.'

'You stayed alive,' he told her. 'That's what counts. And we have flesh aplenty now!' He looked around. 'Where's Rockface?'

She looked worried. 'His back hurts, he says. He threw more rocks than anybody last night, but it made him scream. Towards the end he tried to pick up one that was too big for him. He wouldn't give up and we had to drag him off. He's sleeping again.'

'Mother always said sleep could heal a man,' Stopmouth replied. Still, the injury worried him more than almost anything else. What if it was permanent?

The young hunter started organizing relays of women to carry the flesh back from the scene of last night's battle and picked out strong men to guard them. Others were set to replenishing the supply of rocks on the roofs of the U-shaped complex of buildings that people were already calling *Headquarters*. Against the moss-covered stone of the surrounding houses, its walls gleamed, almost like the coloured clothing the women wore. Only the windows of the lower two floors, plugged with bungs of crumbling rubble, marred the perfection. Still, the unblocked openings of the upper storey gave glorious views of rooftops and river and would allow enough light for women to do their work throughout the day.

Indrani had hinted that Stopmouth's ancestors, the so-called Deserters, had created this magnificent place and every other building under the Roof. He couldn't imagine how. They must have been like these people's gods to do so. He wondered how long a man might spend smoothing even a tiny section of this wall. How could they spare the people for it? How many hunters had it taken to feed them all? He shook his head.

He turned to look around at his new comrades. Not all members of this strange Tribe were making themselves use-ful: many were too weak to carry more than themselves. Even now some of these refused all beast flesh. Strangely they had fewer qualms about eating human meat.

'And why should they?' said Kubar, his grey beard even wilder than it had been. People looked up at the sound of his gravelly voice. Many seemed relieved to find him alive. 'These were our friends,' he continued. His skinny arms had muscles of a sort, unlike most of the other humans. 'We didn't hurt them and they would have wanted us to have their bodies now that they are gone.'

For the time being Stopmouth was happy as long as the other hunters ate. They needed weapons too. A dozen more knives had turned up in the alley and he suggested tying them to the ends of sticks to form makeshift spears.

As bands of flesh gatherers returned from the alley, Stopmouth pulled the hunters aside and divided them into groups, making sure always to combine spear carriers with stone throwers. It was only the combination of the two that had saved them all the night before. He sent some of the men back to the alley for any corpses that hadn't already been taken. Others were to patrol the perimeter of Headquarters.

'You're not to attack the enemy,' he told each group. 'They've been hunting all their lives and will kill you if you go too near.'

'Why not?' said Yama. He sported scars on his arms to match those on his cheek. He showed them to any woman who glanced in his direction. 'We beat them last night. We can do it again!' Earlier Stopmouth had seen the boy stuffing his face with flesh and laughing as older men retched.

'It doesn't matter if you can do it again,' said Stopmouth. 'If you lose one fighter and they lose ten, it's still a loss we can't afford.' The boy just shrugged, then shouted at 'his' hunting party to follow him.

Stopmouth didn't think the beasts would risk an assault on armed humans that day. They'd be too busy butchering their enormous kill and transporting it home. No, he thought. For another day or two at least, the tiny human community would be fine as long as nobody got caught outside alone.

He went to check on Indrani, who'd been trying to organize the collecting of wood for fires. She had gathered up orphan children for the task and was trying to marshal them and keep them from wailing.

'It's not so easy when you keep the Talker to yourself all day,' she complained.

'But surely these are your people!'

She curled her lip. 'Some of the younger ones speak a little of my tongue. But I can no more understand their speech than you could a Flyer's. These . . . these spirit-lovers' – it seemed the worst insult she could imagine and Stopmouth wondered if, for once, the magic of the Talker had failed to come up with a good human word for it – 'they are not my Tribe. They've had all the benefits of *civilization*, all the knowledge, and still they've turned their backs on it.'

'Ah,' said Stopmouth, 'that might explain why some of them look at you with such hatred. One of them called you a witch, I remember.' This had been worrying him.

Indrani laughed so much that nearby conversations stopped. Perhaps it had been a long time since they'd heard a loud human voice that wasn't screaming.

'That's not why they hate me, Stopmouth, not at all.

That's not why three of their weakling old men have already tried to kill me.'

Stopmouth's jaw dropped. 'I didn't know . . .'

'I don't need you to protect me from the likes of them!'

'Of course not!' He clenched his fists, wondering who'd attacked her. He couldn't bear the thought of losing her now that they'd found a home. 'But what have you ever done to them?'

Her eyes took on a distant look. 'I did my best for them in the Roof, Stopmouth. I always remember thinking how awful it must be for them, trapped by the words of grumpy old fanatics when all the wonders of *civilization* were there for the taking. So I made sure their children went to proper schools where the madness of their beliefs could be challenged. I forced medical checks on them and fought to free their women.' She shook her head. 'They always paid me back in hatred, Stopmouth, and now, although they know it's impossible, they hold me responsible for their presence here below the Roof. Me! And I was always the one who spoke out against it whenever it was suggested. But maybe I should have kept my mouth shut.' Her voice turned to a whisper. 'Maybe I wouldn't be here if I had.'

Stopmouth's mind was swirling with strange ideas, some of them frightening, some merely hurtful.

'Why . . . why *are* you here, Indrani?'

She shook her head. 'I always ask myself that. Always.

Every day I have a different answer. Every—' She pressed her hands over her eyes and stumbled away from him. She didn't want to cry in front of the people, he suspected, but many had seen her anyway and some had openly sneered.

'What are you looking at?' he shouted at them.

For now he had plenty of other problems to deal with. No one seemed to know about even the simplest of tasks and they looked to him for orders as if he were a chief like Wallbreaker or Speareye.

It's because Rockface is injured, he thought. Otherwise he's the one they'd be looking to for help.

A few of those charged with bringing flesh from the alley got lost on the way and were never seen again. Screaming matches broke out in the confined spaces between and within families. The balding chief, too weak to stand, continued haranguing his subjects from a pile of cracked stone blocks. And nobody wanted to butcher the corpses they'd fought so hard to win. Most were too squeamish even to touch them. Stopmouth gathered up his hunters for the job as they returned from the alley.

'Oh, let me do it!' said Yama. He had a funny smile that only ever lifted the left side of his mouth, maybe because the scars on the other side had stiffened his face. 'But I want to start with the corpse of my stepmother.' A lot of the men broke into smiles until the boy stared them down. They thought he'd meant it as a joke. He took a knife and went off whistling to find the woman's corpse.

Another willing helper was the handsome Varaha, who'd saved Stopmouth's life in the alley. He looked totally relaxed, not in the least bit tired or even hungry. He wore a crafty wooden necklace, but had abandoned most of the other clothing these people wore except for a loincloth he'd improvised for himself. 'Now that we're in this game of murder,' he said, 'we might as well play it to the end.' Every woman's eye was on him and Stopmouth wondered what Indrani thought of him.

'It's not murder, Varaha. We have killed only beasts!'

The man shrugged, smiling brilliantly. 'Sure. But, well . . . All my life I have believed it to be murder to kill another living creature for food. Oh, I used to watch your adventures, Stopmouth! Avidly sometimes. But I was a teacher before I came here, and one thing I learned is that even *your* carnivorous ancestors would have considered it murder to kill a being that could think as well as they!'

Stopmouth handed the man a sharp stone. He had a sudden urge to ask Varaha for the story of his ancestors, in spite of the promise he'd made to Indrani. What harm could it do? But he kept his mouth shut until the teacher bent over a corpse and began hacking at it.

Meanwhile Indrani's crews had finally learned to identify the stones for making sparks. She showed them how to pound the juice out of moss to make kindling and growled when they demonstrated a clumsiness that had once been hers. All of them were weary, their bright clothing filthy from the knees down. Surprisingly, even the most squeamish showed no qualms about putting bodies into the flames.

'We need to be careful,' Indrani warned Stopmouth. 'Some of those idiots are trying to cremate the bodies rather than cook them.' This idea seemed like madness to him, but several times before the night was out, corpses were burned beyond use. Some people even tried to sneak to the river with the ashes, but their pitiful screams a tenth later deterred the others.

Finally the awful process produced enough to feed them all for a couple of tens. The last struggle was to try and convince everybody to eat. It wasn't as difficult as Stopmouth had feared. The survivors were all people who'd chosen life over their beliefs. And so, when the delicious (to Stopmouth) odours of roasting meat filled the air, most partook, even if only to swallow a few scraps.

Sounds of retching continued long into the night.

Strangely, he couldn't sleep. He should be exhausted – and he was! His body ached from numerous wounds and every muscle quivered with fatigue. But he was too happy to sleep. He'd found a home. The bodies lying nearby, the clumsy lookouts he'd picked, all were Tribe to him now. Hopeless, they were all hopeless and probably doomed, but they had more chance of survival than his little party had of reaching the Roof. At first he'd been worried about the hatred many of them felt towards Indrani. And yet, even as they'd conquered their fear of flesh, they would soon learn to value Indrani's courage and strength. They'd need her almost as much as he did. Only one thing remained to make his happiness complete.

'Are you awake?' whispered Indrani from her bed of moss next to his.

He smiled. Would it happen now? He pictured her beautiful lips touching his. If it could happen anywhere, surely it was here in the bosom of their new Tribe. He'd often thought she'd never want anything more to do with men. But the further they'd walked from Wallbreaker, the less fear she had of him and the closer they became.

'I'm awake,' he said. He reached a hand out towards her, not daring to open his eyes. His stomach fluttered as warm fingers intertwined with his.

'I'm glad,' she said. He thought he knew what she meant. For a while they lay like that. He'd waited so long for this moment, so long for a chance to tell her his feelings. He felt himself drifting off and forced himself alert again. It had to be now!

'Indrani?'

'Mmmm . . .'

'Don't go to sleep, Indrani.'

'Mmmm . . .'

'I – I want you.' She was awake now: he felt her hand snake away from his, even as his face burned. 'I mean, I want you to jump the fire with me, that's all.'

There was a pause. Nearby, Indrani's collection of orphans stirred and muttered in their sleep.

'Oh, Stopmouth.' Her voice sounded terribly sad, but he didn't dare look over at her. His heart was hammering and there was a churning sickness in his stomach. He had his answer and he wanted her to stop speaking.

She didn't. 'Ever since I came here, I've had one horrific experience after another.'

'Am I horrific? Because—'

'Of course not!'

'Because I thought you liked me. Back before Wallbreaker—'

'I *do* like you, you idiot! How could a woman not? In every way, you're beautiful. Every way. But jumping the fire with you would be like . . . like surrendering to this place. Like becoming part of it. Do you see? You told me before that I was acting more and more like a savage and you were right. But oh, the gods know how I hate it! The only thing that allows me to live with myself now is the thought that one day I might get home and put an end to this whole disgusting system. I can't believe I used to be part of it.'

'The Diggers?'

'Yes,' she whispered, 'and other things. Things we've promised not to talk about.'

The Deserters.

Neither spoke for a while, each immersed in their own suffering. Then Stopmouth said, 'Was there never a moment when you might have . . . when you wanted to . . .'

'To kiss you? Many times. All the time.' She took his hand. 'Sitting beside you in the doorway, or watching you learn to walk again . . . And the way you'd throw your eyes Roofwards when I messed up the words you were teaching me. Yes, I wanted to kiss you. I even used to wonder about it when we talked, watching your mouth and thinking how soft your lips must be.' She paused. 'But I can't see you anywhere except the surface, Stopmouth – it's this awful place that makes you beautiful. And it is awful. Beings arrive civilized, and either they become savages or they die, because there is no in-between.' She clutched his hand more tightly, squeezing with both of hers. 'Oh, Stopmouth . . . I swear to you, I swear it, if you could show me some way, any way, we could build something better here than what we have now, nothing could stop me jumping the fire with you. By the gods, I'd walk *through* the fire to be your woman.'

The thought only deepened his despair. 'I could be more civilized, Indrani. You could teach me.'

She sighed. 'You couldn't be any more civilized than you are and still survive. No, this place is irredeemable, I think. I must get to the Roof.'

'How?' He raged in himself that such an impossible dream should keep them apart. 'We tried walking there and look what happened to us. If we hadn't been lucky enough to find other humans, we'd already be dead.'

'It wasn't luck,' she said. 'I'm sure of that. In my first days on the surface, while you slept through the fever of your broken legs, I expected rescue at any moment. My side in the war, the *seculars*, had most of the Globes, and we had thousands of fighters stronger than Crunchfist. It would have been easy for them to get me out. I thought they'd come through the ceiling of the house, or scoop me right up from the street. As your poor legs recovered, and nobody came, I feared the *religious* must have beaten us. There was no other explanation for why they left me there. Day after day amongst dangerous savages . . . And then one time, you told me the Flims had been replaced. We must have been the victors after all, because the rebels would never have done that. Yet still my people ignored my pleas. I couldn't figure it out; my heart was broken and I lost all hope of returning until you promised to take me home.'

'I was only trying to cheer you up,' he said. 'I knew we'd never make it. The Traveller had the greatest hunters in the Tribe with him and even he came back alone.'

Again, pressure on his hand. 'I know,' she said. 'But now somebody has gone to a lot of trouble to keep us alive.'

'How can you be sure, Indrani?'

'I'm being watched, Stopmouth, and I don't mean the Globes. They want more than an entertaining death from me; I just don't know what it is yet. I'll tell you the rest when I'm sure. For now' – she released the grip on his hand after a final, brief squeeze – 'we should sleep.'

'How?' he wanted to ask. His heart hadn't felt this empty since he'd thought her Wallbreaker's lover. How could he sleep? But he did try. Right up until the first panels of the Roof began to brighten.

19.
A PLAN

Rockface had cleaned himself up for the first time since before he and Stopmouth had won the Talker from the Flyers. His arms had thinned somewhat, but there was still enough muscle there to cause tattoos to writhe like the creatures they represented: Flims and Bloodskins, Hoppers and Armourbacks; all had met his spear. Even his eyes had lost the dullness of previous days.

Stopmouth was so delighted to see him back to his old self that he ran from the training session he'd been giving with Varaha. For the first time ever he hugged Rockface like a family member.

The man nodded solemnly. He waved at the exhausted newcomers. 'These people are useless,' he said. Nearby men and women hung their heads at his translated words or pretended to fuss with the tatters of their ruined clothing. 'But they still need food in their bellies, hey?'

Stopmouth nodded. The flesh from the alley fight would run out soon and things would become desperate.

'Good.' Rockface pointed at the Talker. 'You'll find it easy to make treaties with that thing at your belt, hey? When you do, I want to be your first volunteer.'

Stopmouth stared. All talk in the vicinity died.

'It's my back.' The big man bent forward as far as he could, showing how little give remained. 'I'm nearly as useless as the rest of them. And without descendants I have no place in the world and—'

'No, Rockface.' Stopmouth was appalled. 'I need you! And these people need you too. They need you to train them!'

Rockface shook his head angrily. 'They can't even speak properly without the Talker, hey? They're slow and stupid. Weaker than children. A man's father and uncles should teach him to hunt. I'm neither to these people. All I can give them is my flesh, while it's still good.'

'Rockface, I—'

The bigger man gripped him by the shoulders. 'It's for you and Indrani I'd be doing it, Stopmouth. You know that, hey?'

'But—'

'You want to wait till it's needed. OK, I understand that. But when the time comes, I want the honour of being the first. I should have done it long ago, Stopmouth, but your father took my place. He had a thousand days left. At least a thousand! What would he think of me now if I did less? A man should charge all his days, hey? Not be hanging back.'

He limped off before the younger man could say another word.

'More rocks!' shouted Varaha at a group of exhausted men. Sweat plastered their dark skin. Their hair, deepest black or sometimes grey, stood up in wet clumps where they'd pushed it away from their faces. The handsome young teacher had matched them rock for rock, but was breathing only a little harder than normal.

Stopmouth's group looked no better than Varaha's. Their arms sagged under the weight of the long sticks they used for spear practice. Moss juice stained everybody's feet, for in the whole area there didn't seem to be a single piece of road free of growth. This was only the second day of proper training and already he was beginning to agree with Rockface: the task was hopeless.

'They're so weak!' he said to Varaha during a break. 'The ones with the grey hair are the worst!'

'They're just old,' said the teacher. 'That man there, the one you sent for a run when he dropped his spear – he's nearly twenty-eight thousand days old.'

Stopmouth almost choked on the bone he had been gnawing. 'Impossible!'

Varaha arched his perfect eyebrows. 'You really didn't know, did you? We thought you were just being cruel, as only a Deserter can be – no offence! You have saved all our lives and we have chosen this cruelty for ourselves.'

Stopmouth had seen somebody called 'Grandmother' on his first day here, but hadn't been able to take the idea seriously. Back home, any hunter too weak to contribute to the Tribe would have had the self-respect to volunteer long before. Like Rockface would do if Stopmouth couldn't find a way to change his mind. But these people had only ever lived on the Roof. What need could there be to volunteer when anybody could just go out and grab a handful of moss or whatever it was they ate?

He shook his head. 'But even the younger ones are weaklings,' he said.

'Unlike you,' Varaha said, 'they haven't been hunting all their lives.' He smiled that knowing smile of his. 'It's a miracle you came to us, Stopmouth. Of all your Tribe, you are the one I would most have wished to help us.'

Embarrassment washed over the young hunter. And something more. His crippled tongue had always left him an outsider at home. But not here, not with the Talker nearby; even when he didn't have it, his tongue could run every bit as fast as his legs sometimes. Nobody understood him then, of course. But he'd picked up a few words of his new Tribe's language – 'hurry!' and 'spear' – and these he uttered clumsily, but without stutters. He sighed. 'It will be a miracle if we survive more than a few days anyway.'

'Ah,' said Varaha. 'So there's no point in me taking a wife just yet?'

'I didn't know you were thinking of jumping the fire!' He'd have his choice of women, that was for sure. Stopmouth had overheard how they talked about him, forgetting their terror at the sight of his sculpted jaw.

'Let's just say I've had my eye on somebody.'

'But who?' asked Stopmouth.

Varaha laughed, startling a few of his resting crew. It shouldn't have done so – the man wore a look of perpetual amusement, as if everything he saw around him was part of a huge joke. He was one of the few adults with the strength and the inclination to play with Indrani's orphans and always seemed to be giving them his food. Even now he tucked away the meat his friend was sharing with him, refusing even a bite of it for himself.

He patted Stopmouth on the shoulder. 'This woman is a delicate matter, my friend, and it's not worth broaching if we're all going to die.'

Stopmouth thought of his own 'delicate matter' and how she'd refused to jump the fire with him. Oh, Indrani hadn't rejected him outright! She'd more or less told him he wasn't civilized enough for her, but also that she didn't want him any different. A number of times he thought she'd been on the verge of changing her mind. Then she'd shake her head and bite her lip in that way that she had and go and find something else to do. The last few nights she'd slept beside her orphans. Away from him. Of course it hurt. It hurt too that the young men who were supposed to hate her couldn't help looking in her direction. How long, he wondered, before she started looking back? They were civilized people, after all, unlike him. He sighed and put the memory away, realizing Varaha was still talking to him.

'Now, tell me really, Stopmouth . . . You don't think our hunters will be good enough by the time we run out of food?'

The hunters in question glanced up nervously from where they lay flopped on a carpet of moss. They didn't look ready for another bout of torture with their instructors, let alone a real hunt.

Stopmouth shook his head. 'Every time a species is exterminated, a new one appears in its place, right?'

'Right,' said Varaha.

'The new species is very plentiful at first. They fill every house in their Ways. They walk or crawl the streets and don't know how to defend themselves. They don't even know they're supposed to defend themselves.'

Apart from the Longtongues, he thought.

'So creatures come from all over for the easiest hunting of their lives. They get as much flesh as they can, although it never keeps for long. Sooner or later the new species will either learn to fight back while there are still enough of them to survive, or—'

'Or,' said Varaha, 'they get wiped out and another new species replaces them. More easy hunting.'

'Exactly,' said Stopmouth. 'There aren't many of us left now and we're not too good at fighting. Even if our neighbours suffer losses, it might be worth their while to finish us quickly.'

Varaha sat back and digested that. 'So,' he said, 'we have to make it not worth their while. Is that it? We make it costly to hunt us.'

'Exactly,' said Stopmouth. He sighed. 'They'll probably realize they can destroy us through simple attrition over a thousand days anyway. I just hope they're not that patient.' He stood. 'You and you' – he picked out two grey-haired men – 'go and . . . go and do something else.' They hobbled off before he could change his mind.

He cast a cold eye over the other six. They'd already spent half a day carrying rocks to the tops of buildings. When they had finished their training with him, they'd work until dusk making pathetic weapons along the lines of the ones captured from their enemies. Other parties of men were out gathering wood. Meanwhile the women spent their days endlessly, and with great distaste, sharpening bone or running here and there on Indrani's 'rock' drills.

Stopmouth couldn't see any of this group surviving even

a skirmish. Unless . . . unless he concentrated on those who already showed some talent and left the weaker ones to support them.

'I've just had an idea!' he said to Varaha.

He left his new friend working with the hunters and went in search of the fierce boy, Yama.

He found him butchering the old chief's corpse for a group of grateful women. Most of them couldn't watch and held hands over their mouths and noses, with their faces turned to the wall. The chief himself looked shrivelled and wasted.

Yama greeted Stopmouth with a grin. 'My stepfather,' he explained. 'He wouldn't touch a mouthful of what I got for him. Now he's mine!'

Yama forced open the jaws of the corpse, reached in his hand and pulled out the tongue. He waved it at the old ladies, spattering blood on them. 'Who wants this then?'

One of the women burst into tears. Her hair was as grey as that of the corpse and her eyes were red from days of weeping and horror. A vicious sadness tore through Stopmouth as he thought of his own mother and how her sacrifice had saved him. He wanted to strike the boy for his disrespect. But it wasn't his place to do so. Instead, he said, 'I need to talk to you, Yama. Come away. Leave the chief.'

'You're the chief now.'

'Me?'

'Sure, everybody says so. With Rockface injured, you're the best killer, right? Oh yeah, you're not Crunchfist – he'd have been something! But I saw how you and Rockface took down six Armourbacks between you and I was *so* jealous. I thought I'd never get my chance.'

'You . . . you sound happy to be here.' It was all he could say. His mind was still reeling with the idea that these people thought of him as their chief. His own people would have laughed at that.

'Happy?' continued Yama. 'It's a dream come true. Stopmouth, I can't wait until you really stamp your authority and get things working right. Flesh meetings, tattoos, wives . . . I'm going to have lots.'

'But I thought the Roof was paradise.'

'Oh yeah, sure. If you like sitting in your room all day, not even allowed to watch hunts. If you like crowds and food shortages.'

'Food . . . shortages? Isn't there plenty of moss?'

Yama laughed. 'Oh, who wants moss when you can eat flesh, right?' His eyes were bright; his scars too. 'I always knew I'd love it when I got used to it. Anyway, it's all falling apart up there. You heard about the rebellion, right? Ha! You probably got to see more of it than I did! Our stupid sect don't believe in fighting and wouldn't take part. Look at the good it did them. They didn't even join in with the Long War against the beasts.'

'Ah, so there *is* hunting above!'

'Sure, but don't worry, Stopmouth, you're not missing anything. It's mostly just human machines against the machines of beasts, until one of ours gets through and a world dies. Not that we ever get to watch.'

Stopmouth was shocked. 'A world cannot die! Surely not!'

Yama laughed and called out to all those standing nearby. 'Hey, there's a Deserter here says a world can't die!' He shrugged when nobody laughed. 'Fools. But you must know about your people killing the human homeworld, right? How they took so many resources from it, it couldn't support life any more? Indrani must have told you.'

'My Tribe could never have done such a thing,' said Stopmouth. And yet his people had produced Wallbreaker and allowed him to lead them. How many like him had appeared before? To what depths had they sunk?

'It's why we all hate you,' Yama continued. 'You doomed the planet and then took what little remained to escape. You left our poor ancestors to die.'

'Yama, I did no such thing.' His ears were ringing. He felt dizzy. He'd promised Indrani not to ask about these things. He had to shut Yama up.

'Of course not, Chief. You know what I mean. But what really gets me is how you can even bear to be around that witch, Indrani. After what she's done to—'

'Enough!' Stopmouth roared. 'I won't hear another word against her!'

'But you must know what she did before she—'

'I said "enough"!'

He would keep his promise to Indrani at all costs. And the cost was great. Instinct told him there were things here he needed to know. He wanted to grab Yama by the shoulders and beg him to finish the story. Slowly he got control of himself and managed to calm his breathing and the tone of his voice.

'Yama, I didn't come here to talk about these things. I've heard about your gang.' He tried not to let his lip curl as he spoke – the elder, Kubar, had told him how the boys used to terrorize the old and the weak up on the Roof.

'If any of them still live, bring them to me. And bring the ones you used to fight against too. Meet me on the roof of this building at nightfall.'

Stopmouth left the boy to his butchery, trying to drag his mind away from the supposed crimes of his ancestors. He'd deal with that some other time. He had a hunt to plan and he'd need more than a few vicious children if there was to be any chance of success.

Three buildings made up the U of Headquarters. The entrance, at the base, could only be reached by passing between the 'arms'. There were many other doorways, of course, but great metal barriers blocked them and Varaha assured Stopmouth that no living creature had 'the right to open them'. Whatever that meant. Even with the help of the Talker, he couldn't get sensible answers to a great many of his questions. But it was well that no beast would ever force open the doors, for behind them, human families lived higgledy-piggledy, one on of top of the other, jammed together like the fangs in a Bloodskin's mouth. Easy meat.

As night fell, Stopmouth met with about forty other hunters on top of the building at the base of the U. Here the roof was lower by half a man's height than the roofs of the 'arms' to either side, and as his people arrived, he heard them jumping down: the slap of many feet on a mossless surface; the murmur of curious voices.

He was bitterly disappointed to see that Rockface hadn't come, in spite of a big effort to get him involved. Of those who had turned up, perhaps a dozen had accompanied Yama and were so young they'd never have been allowed to hunt at home. Indrani was there too, and often as Stopmouth talked, the men's eyes would slide in her direction, making him grit his teeth. Adding to this was the sight of Varaha sitting near her. He looked at her most often of all. She only glowered in return. It was as if something had happened between the two of them to which Stopmouth wasn't privy. An argument perhaps. The thought should have cheered him, but did not. Varaha and Indrani were each perfect examples of their sex. A couple, Stopmouth thought, that just hadn't realized it yet.

Indrani introduced a pair of younger women she'd brought along with her.

'These two tell me they know how to use a sling,' she said. 'Their father gave exhibitions in the ancient martial arts of his ancestors.'

'Have they ever killed with their slings?'

Indrani snorted. 'We should take what we can get, Stopmouth, and be grateful for it.'

The two women – Sodasi and Kamala – bowed before him. They were pretty and their deference flustered him. He'd forgotten that many of these people considered him a chief. He pulled Indrani to one side and asked her if she'd heard the same thing. She seemed very agitated, perhaps as a result of her possible falling out with Varaha.

'Well, of course you're the chief, Stopmouth.'

'But I'm not like Speareye—'

'No, because he's not here. You are. Now stop waiting for people to be quiet. Tell them to shut up.'

'Are . . . are you all right, Indrani?'

'Of course I am. Now, if you want these fools to live, you'd better give them orders, because you're the only one who knows what needs to be done.'

She was right. The chief was supposed to be the guide,

the great provider. He looked up. 'Please,' he began. And then, 'Quiet!'

As Indrani had promised, they settled down. It was like magic. He looked around from face to face. Their skin shone silver under the tracklights, glistening here and there where cool drops of Roofsweat had hit them.

'Sooner or later,' he began, 'a large number of beasts will come here to finish what they started.' The men looked up at him with dark, foreign eyes. Many, such as Kubar, the ex-holy man, creased their brows. But not Yama. The boy was grinning his lopsided grin and nudging his followers.

'Thanks to Indrani' – scowls on faces everywhere – 'we've made this place so dangerous for them that if they attack us in force, they'll suffer heavy losses. The night we fled from the square—'

'We won that night!' said Yama. Others nodded and cheered and Stopmouth hadn't the heart to contradict them.

'That same night,' he said, 'a small group of beasts attacked this place and got rocks thrown down on their heads.' Another cheer. 'And we could do it again. We could hold off ten times those numbers . . . But it wouldn't do us any good.'

He paused to see if they'd understood.

'Surely,' said Varaha, 'if we teach them to leave us alone . . .'

'Oh yes, we'll teach them that,' Stopmouth continued. 'But not yet.'

Forty men and three women stared at him in puzzlement.

'When Indrani drove the enemy away from here, she and the other defenders stayed up on the roof. They pushed rocks over the parapets and twice they had to roll them down the stairs. They made maybe five kills. If they'd come out from hiding instead, if they'd engaged in hand to hand, the beasts would have butchered them all, even Rockface. Anybody can push a rock, but not all are skilled with the spear.'

'We only had one spear!' said Indrani, glaring at him.

'It's not an insult, Indrani! You did what you had to do! As I said, you'd have been killed.'

Yama interrupted him. 'They didn't kill us when we charged into the alley!'

Stopmouth nodded. 'We did well that night. But I tell you, if we'd followed them all the way back to the square, they'd be eating us even now; Skeletons and Fourleggers fighting over our guts.'

A shiver ran through the audience and Stopmouth was glad of it. 'My point is this: after Indrani's victory here, the enemy didn't leave any bodies behind them. Not one! Back home, when a hunter claimed to have killed a beast, people asked to see the flesh. If he couldn't produce it, if he'd come without it, we cursed him for a wastrel and a coward. Back home . . . in my old home, "a waster" is the worst thing you can call somebody, even worse than calling him a "hoarder". Do you see? Killing is pointless if it doesn't feed us. We need to eat. Flesh is life, and a victory that leaves us hungry is just another defeat. That's why I say now, when the beasts come for us over the next few days – and they will come; they *will*! – we'll leave the others to mind children and drop rocks. You and I have other business.' He paused for breath, surprised by the rivers of sweat on his skin, amazed they were still listening. 'We will make sure that every beast who dies here stays here. None can escape, none! Your Tribe . . . *our* Tribe will survive!'

They cheered him, rushing over with back slaps and hugs and hopeful eyes. Their words were becoming un-intelligible, however. Indrani had the Talker with her and she was walking back to her orphans. Varaha too had disappeared.

20.
WELCOME TO
THE TRIBE

'Good throw,' said Stopmouth. Most spears had landed close to the target, although only Varaha's had pierced the rust-coloured skin. As always, he grinned, flexing his muscles to make his comrades laugh. Stopmouth's mind kept going over and over a conversation he'd had with the man before. Varaha had said he wanted to take a wife, but had refused to name her. 'This woman is a delicate matter,' he'd said. Stopmouth couldn't get those words out of his head.

'Gather up your spears,' he said.

That's when the children started screaming. Stopmouth's blood turned cold. Had the great attack come already and caught them unprepared? He gripped his own spear and started running for the alley that opened into Headquarters. He'd forgotten to order the men to follow, but he heard them coming on behind him. He dodged round half-built walls at the mouth of the alley and passed out of the glare into darkness, trying desperately to see what was going on.

The screams tailed off as he entered the main hall, to be replaced now by shouting. He slowed, the hunters crowding in behind him. As his eyes adjusted, he made out the figure of Yama, waving his spear dangerously in the faces of those around him while children snivelled.

'What's going on here?' asked Stopmouth.

Amazingly they all stopped talking at once. He covered up his surprise by looking around. The elder Kubar was here, scowling through his beard. Other adults stood with him, including Indrani, her orphans spread out behind her. And there was something else, but the light . . .

His stomach flip-flopped. 'What's that?'

Nobody spoke. The creature was smaller than most of the surviving children. It had rust-coloured skin, Digger-like claws and a triangular head with tiny eyes on moveable stalks at the top. A Fourlegger, an infant. It couldn't be anything else.

'Kill that at once,' he said, appalled.

'What do you think I've been trying to do?' cried Yama.

The children all wailed and many of the adults shook their heads. 'Are we to murder children now too?' said Kubar. 'We found it clinging to its mother, who, I might add, you probably slaughtered. What harm can the creature

368

do? The children love it. They need something like this after what they've been through.'

Stopmouth shook his head, wondering if he'd ever teach these people survival. For all he knew they'd been hiding the thing since the battle of the alley.

'Do you want me as chief or not?' he asked.

None of them said anything, but most nodded and the hunters behind him murmured their assent.

'Then stand back,' he said. 'All of you. Go ahead, Yama.' Stopmouth would content himself with watching because he knew how keen the boy was to get a kill of his own.

Yama grinned. 'I'm going to cut you, little Fourlegger,' he said. 'I'll cut you slowly.'

The small creature dodged in amongst the weeping children. 'I'll rip those eye-stalks right off your head . . .'

Stopmouth remembered his own terror lying on the raft. He remembered the white Wetlane beasts calmly discussing how they meant to kill him while the Talker translated every word. It had been an appalling experience.

'Just . . . just do it, Yama, don't talk about it.'

Yama caught up with the little Fourlegger and might have speared it. Instead, he seemed content to whack it with the shaft so that he might chase it further. He struck it again, sending it tumbling in amongst a group of orphans, his face alive with excitement. But when he'd pushed the children aside, he found it had gone.

'Why didn't you just kill it?' asked Stopmouth, trying to control his fury.

'I . . .'

Stopmouth felt something scratch the back of his leg. He turned to find that the Fourlegger was using his body as a shield. He picked it up, not quite sure what he meant to do with it. It wasn't even as long as his arm. Its body felt warm on his skin and it shook as a child might when afraid.

'You do it quickly,' he said to Yama, 'or I'm giving the job to somebody else. You don't play with death because it always wins.'

'I will,' said Yama. 'Quickly. It won't get away again.'

At that moment, Stopmouth felt something warm and wet on his hands. At first he thought it was blood. Some of the adults smiled in spite of themselves. A child giggled.

'Filthy thing,' said Yama. 'Give it here.'

Stopmouth hesitated. How often had he seen this? Human infants wetting themselves, soaking the adult holding them while everybody laughed? This creature . . . this baby should have been killed the moment they'd found it. But instead it had been playing with human children for days, sharing flesh, sharing warmth.

'Enough,' he said.

Yama seemed not to listen. His eyes were wide with excitement. He grabbed the Fourlegger by its slender neck and thrust with his spear.

Stopmouth pulled the beast out of the way. Then, with his free hand, he tore the boy's weapon from him and pushed him to the ground.

'Enough, I said!'

Yama scrambled to his knees. His eyes took in all the staring faces around him. 'What kind of a chief are you?' he cried. 'You're a joke. A joke! You can't even make these old ones volunteer.' He climbed to his feet and pushed his way through to the stairs, pausing once at the doorway. There were tears on his cheeks and his voice cracked as he spoke. 'Where are the tattoos? Where are the wives?' Then he was gone.

The room fell quiet. Stopmouth put the Fourlegger down carefully. 'Welcome to the Tribe, little one,' he said. Everybody applauded, but all he wanted was to clean his hands. *Yama's right*, he kept thinking. *I'm a fool.*

Beast flesh turned on makeshift spits until the air filled with delicious scents. The Tribe was using the last of the food from the alley before it rotted and the whole thing had turned into a feast, with singing and jokes. Everyone was eating their fill. Laughter drifted from group to group as people worked hard to forget their awful new life and the imminent attack that would probably end it.

'Go on!' somebody shouted, soon joined by others. They urged a lovely girl out onto the lowest roof. She seemed shy at first. However, when she started singing, her voice was as rich as the flesh of a Hairbeast pup and her haunting words had everybody crying for their lost home.

'This is your home now,' Stopmouth told himself, angrily wiping his eyes. Tomorrow he would carry out his plan. The trained hunters – the best of a bad lot – would go to their hiding places and might well be stuck there for days. Most likely they'd be slaughtered. But they *had* to try.

The girl bowed to cheers and Kubar took her place. His gravelly voice told the story of some kind of spirit that could take human form. People stared in rapt attention, but even with the Talker, the new chief couldn't really see the point of it. He was relieved when Indrani came over to sit beside him.

'Don't worry,' she said. 'You'll like the next bit.' And he did. This Tribe had no drums to play, but people made music with their mouths and women – only women – danced. Their hands moved in intricate patterns, flexing constantly at the wrist. They twirled in place, smiles lighting them up and hiding their worries.

'Why don't you dance?' Stopmouth asked Indrani.

'I don't know how.'

'Just wave your hands about. It can't be hard.'

Indrani laughed. A real laugh such as he hadn't heard from her in the longest time. He didn't want her to dance anyway. They sat together as they had in the days after they'd first met, their bodies so close he could feel the warmth of her skin. Oh, to put his arm around her! But he didn't want to spoil the dream, especially now that he feared she loved somebody else.

'Every one of those movements has a precise meaning,' she said. 'Believe me, neither you nor I will be dancing with this lot any time soon.'

They ate and listened to the strange music. Afterwards Indrani put her hand on his chin and turned his face towards hers.

'Stopmouth, I came here tonight to apologize.'

'About wh—'

She shushed him. 'Let me say my piece before I lose my nerve, all right? What you did with the Fourlegger . . .' All of a sudden she hugged him. She whispered, 'I am an idiot, Stopmouth. Blind. Anybody can be civilized in a civilized place. But you . . . to overcome all that and . . .' She couldn't finish the thought. Carefully he surrounded her with his own arms, hardly daring to believe that she wouldn't pull away.

When the fires burned low, grey-haired men and women walked from hearth to hearth visiting. They only spoke to others of the same age.

'I think we'll have some weddings soon,' murmured Indrani against his shoulder. 'Spirit-lovers are so backward they have to get their parents to set it up for them!'

Stopmouth tensed. 'And what do your people do?'

The sound of her voice carried a smile. 'I don't know about the men, but we women wait for a hunter with a bulging loincloth to come and sweep us off our feet.'

Stopmouth swallowed. 'Um, any hunter?'

He felt her shaking against him in the dark and for a moment he thought she was crying for some lost hunter of her own Tribe. But then the laughter escaped and his face burned. He was totally at a loss about what to do until he remembered the line the older hunters at home had told him to say in this situation: 'I'll be gentle.'

She fell over, laughing all the harder. Eventually it stopped, and when she turned to face him again, her good humour seemed to have become mixed up with other, less cheerful emotions.

'You should pray to your ancestors, Stopmouth, that *I* will be gentle with you.'

She bent close to him and pressed her mouth to his, warmth against warmth, her lips so soft. Stopmouth heard gasps from somewhere behind him. Indrani sighed and pulled away. 'I'm a little too ... too modern for these people. Or too primitive.'

She took him by the hand away from the fire until they found an undisturbed corner at the base of the U where somebody had dumped swathes of pounded moss.

He tried to pull her to him again but Indrani resisted, confusing him.

'I'm not my brother,' he said.

Bizarrely it turned out to be the right thing to say. She relaxed, and together they lay down and kissed, hands roaming, bodies pressed together.

Later, much later it seemed, he rested on his back while his body cooled and drops of Roofsweat mingled with his own.

He watched the tracklights until they blurred under his drooping eyelids. Home at last, he thought. People around him again and a woman to hold. An amazing woman such as his ancestors might have loved. But something still bothered him.

'Why me?' he asked. 'Why not . . . Why not Varaha?'

She opened her eyes. She seemed fully awake all of a sudden. 'What has *he* got to do with anything?'

The venom in her voice was such that he knew the man was no rival to him and he dropped the subject. Soon the beautiful woman, *his* woman, relaxed into sleep.

21.
A PLAN GONE WRONG

S topmouth kept utterly quiet. The Slimer sniffed loudly, its fat head bobbing from side to side. It was an ungainly creature to his eyes – its short fat legs were good for one quick leap from ambush, but they also gave it a lurching gait that made the creatures almost helpless in the open. A thin black tongue flickered in and out of perpetually open jaws, licking walls, the ground or its own slimy hide.

The creature sniffed again. Perhaps it hadn't yet learned to identify human smells, or perhaps its sniffing was just some beast ritual. In any case, it never once looked in Stopmouth's direction as it climbed onto the roof.

Stopmouth saw the Slimer poke its head over the parapet as he himself had done no more than a thousand heartbeats before. It stared across the road towards Headquarters. Maybe it was eyeing up the defences. The young human hoped so. He'd designed them to look weak, especially the wall thrown across the mouth of the alley. Stones were clumsily piled, one on top of the next, as though built by children with no idea of the terrors waiting in the world beyond.

Stopmouth could have killed the beast. Instead, he watched it turn back downstairs and prayed it would soon return with a few dozen relatives. It was either that or lose Rockface. Human food stores were running out and the Tribe badly needed the mass attack Stopmouth had predicted.

'They'll think we're not ready for them,' he'd said. The beasts would be surprised by the ferocity of the defence and shocked to find their retreat cut off. It was a great plan. But only if the neighbours took the bait. Otherwise it was the humans who'd be desperate for food, making foray after foray into enemy territory until attrition wiped them out.

Stopmouth's tummy rumbled. Thoughts of fatty flesh filled his mouth with saliva.

'If you see an opportunity to kill,' he'd warned his men, 'don't take it! Let them think we're too disorganized to post guards beyond Headquarters.'

Stopmouth had sent his less able men along as protection for the women gathering water. As a special favour he'd asked Rockface to mind the children.

'Why don't you just let me volunteer, hey? I warn you,

Stopmouth, don't insult me by keeping me alive beyond usefulness. My wives would weep with shame to see it.'

'I won't,' Stopmouth had promised, reluctant and sad.

The rest of the men, like himself, had been hiding for days in buildings across the road from the mouth of the alleyway. He knew they were tired of waiting. Some of them openly doubted him. Yama's young followers in particular seemed eager to prove their dubious manhood and sooner or later he'd have to let them hunt, regardless of the consequences. Yama was still angry with Stopmouth too. He and his friends had agreed to take part in the plan, but insisted on forming their own hunting party. When Stopmouth had disagreed, Yama laughed at him in front of everybody.

'What are you going to do about it, *Chief*? Volunteer me? We haven't got to volunteer even one person since you took charge. Not one! Things will be done properly when I'm in charge, I promise you that.'

Sudden thumps and squeals shook Stopmouth from his reverie. The Slimer came running back up the stairs, trailing a spear. It waved its long tongue about in what might have been a scream for its kind. Stopmouth cursed under his breath. When he found the fool responsible for this, he'd have him working on water duty for a thousand days! He was about to finish the Slimer off himself when a white beast head popped up through the skylight. The human froze in his hiding place.

The Slimer sent its tongue flickering in the Skeleton's direction, but the humanoid dodged easily and pinned the tongue to the roof with a bone knife. The Skeleton held it there while two more of its kind ran onto the roof and speared their victim through the chest. Stopmouth winced in sympathy, something he'd never done before the arrival of the infant Fourlegger among the humans. Now he couldn't even eat without thinking of the pain that had brought food to his lips. Even so, his mouth watered.

The victors didn't butcher the body immediately. Instead, like the Slimer before them, they gazed across the road at Headquarters.

Stopmouth could hear more of them downstairs. It sounded like a large hunting party. One of the Skeletons leaned over the parapet and waved one of its four arms towards something Stopmouth couldn't see. A signal! His heart thudded in his chest as he realized the long-sought-after battle might begin that very day.

The Skeletons waited. The tallest wore elaborately decorated hides and the other two kept switching their glances between it and the Slimer's corpse, drool beading the sides of their narrow mouths. Stopmouth just wanted them gone. They were keeping him from his hunters and he dreaded what would happen to his plans if somebody like Yama took over the lead.

The tall beast with the decorated hides leaned over the

Slimer and dribbled onto it. Drool sank into the skin, changing its colour. The Skeleton chief (if that's what it was) touched the end of its arm to the wet spot. The flesh had become soft and the creature scooped a handful of it into its narrow mouth. Only then did the others feel free to jostle over the meat, spattering their strange drool everywhere.

Stopmouth's stomach continued to rumble. He hadn't moved in a long time and had wet himself where he lay. Moss juice covered every part of his skin, and sometimes its vapours stung the back of his throat. Not for the first time he wished he'd brought a blanket of the pounded stuff with him.

He didn't even realize darkness had fallen until the skin of his enemies began glowing. As one, they stood and descended the stairs. The old building seemed to shake with their movement. A short time later he heard them passing into the street.

Stopmouth restrained himself a little longer. When he could stand it no more, he grabbed a chunk of Slimer flesh and sneaked out through the back of the house. He was very nearly caught: glowing Skeletons were moving in from all directions. There seemed to be tens of them, maybe even a few hundred. What species could spare so many hunters? His old Tribe, certainly, had twice that number, but had never been able to marshal them. Men couldn't be forced to join a hunt. They preferred to attach themselves in small numbers to leaders who promised them meat.

His plan was looking shakier by the moment, but it was way too late to change things now.

The Skeletons pulled themselves into a large group on a street that ran at right angles to the puny barrier protecting Headquarters. More of their kind were arriving all the time. Most carried spears and knives, although a few had brought strange, flat pieces of wood.

They won't hurt us with bits of wood, thought Stopmouth, but he felt uneasy, especially when another group moved towards the front of the mob with the trunk of an uprooted tree. At least they'd be attacking in the right place – at the deliberately weakened barrier. And a creature with glowing skin that hunted by night couldn't be that smart!

Stopmouth ran hard until he reached the end of a meandering street where it opened onto the river. His feet made absolutely no sound against the thick moss of this area. Even his breathing felt muffled, as though the plant had grown over his face and eyes instead of nearby walls and roads. At night it lost its colour, becoming a black emptiness that only the tracklights above could relieve. Yama was already waiting for him along with a few of the others. Humans kept arriving in dribs and drabs – Varaha, the holy man, Kubar, and many more – until perhaps fifty men and a pair of women had gathered together.

Everyone carried slings and knew how to use them. But only Stopmouth and the two women Indrani had found, Sodasi and Kamala, could hit a target the size of a Skeleton with any accuracy.

The young hunter gave no speeches and knew none of his audience would have understood him anyway. He'd made a decision not to risk the Talker outside Headquarters. Never mind: the hunt had begun. If he needed them to do anything, he'd use the signals he'd taught them. It would be enough.

As agreed, the ex-gang members stayed with Yama while Stopmouth led the rest over to the river and down a couple of side streets. He wanted to circle around Headquarters and stake out a spot on the far side of the enemy. But the group circled too fast and came within heartbeats of dying. Behind Headquarters, at the base of the U, where the roof was lowest, a party of ten Skeletons was coming in the opposite direction. Stopmouth signalled everyone to stay down. In a fair fight the beasts would wipe them out. Even if the humans escaped such an encounter, the plan would be ruined and the Tribe doomed.

They hid as best they could, waiting for the beasts to join the main assault. But they never did. The glowing creatures had come up with a better idea. They weren't stupid, after all. Tree trunks were brought forward and placed quietly against the walls. Some of the Skeletons crowded around the base to steady the trunks, while the rest began a dangerous climb to the top. Stopmouth cursed. There'd be a fight now, whether he wanted one or not.

The nearest Skeletons were no more than a dozen steps away. Stopmouth signalled to his followers: 'sling' followed by 'spear'. They shifted nervously behind him. He could see their fear building. It wouldn't have time to grow. 'Shoot!' Twenty men and the two women twirled their slings, each releasing within a heartbeat of the others. Twenty-two stones flew towards the enemy, and before they reached their targets, Stopmouth and the others were running with levelled spears.

The men couldn't shoot straight, but with the Skeletons all clumped together, it didn't matter. Two of the beasts went down. Others clutched at various injuries and in their panic released their hold on the trunk. It fell sideways, sending all but one of the unfortunate climbers crashing back to earth.

The humans were among the beasts with plunging spears before they even knew they were under attack. Most died without lifting a weapon. One of them had the presence of mind to get its back to the wall, each of its four arms waving a different weapon. But Stopmouth had learned lessons from his own first encounter with the creatures and his men knew what to do. They surrounded it and struck at its weak arms with the butts of their spears. Finally one of the men moved in close enough to grapple with it. He fell back screaming. 'Sling!' Stopmouth signalled. 'Sling!' Urging them to finish it.

By now all the Skeletons in the small party had been killed except for one that hung desperately to the parapet of the roof. Stopmouth imagined its terror, alone, surrounded by enemies. Then he ordered Sodasi and Kamala to bring it down. The skirmish was over.

Men grinned and slapped each other on the back. Stopmouth knew how they felt. But the joy died in their hearts when they heard groans and found two of their comrades mortally wounded. One of them clutched his belly while blood and guts pushed through his fingers. The other lay back against the wall, the top of his face glistening and somehow blurred, as if it had been melted.

Kubar pointed at a dead Skeleton and mimed spitting, then pointed at the man. Stopmouth shuddered. Even though he'd seen the creatures eat, he'd never expected they could rot a man's face just by spitting at him.

Stopmouth remembered something Rockface had done once on a trip into Hairbeast long ago. He took his dagger and stabbed each of the dying hunters in the eye before they knew what was happening.

The others reacted in shock. Stopmouth pushed their angry bodies away and began walking towards the main assault so that they had no choice but to follow. He knew they didn't understand. By morning it would be different.

He could already hear sounds of battle beyond – tens of rocks crashing to earth, and another noise: the irregular pounding of the tree trunk against the first barrier. He saw this when they arrived at their position.

Rocks rained down on the Skeletons from above. They suffered less than Stopmouth had expected: many held flat pieces of wood like little roofs above their heads and rarely did the missiles break through. The ingenuity of it worried him more than he dared show his hunters.

'*Wait!*' he signalled. But they knew not to advance yet. According to the plan, they were to hold back until the first barrier had fallen and all the beasts had passed into the alley. Then, it was hoped, an assault from the rear coupled with a rain of stone from above would leave the attackers helpless. But Stopmouth could see there were just too many Skeletons. He doubted the alley could hold them all.

The pounding continued for a hundred heartbeats more. The centre of the wall gave way and the men and women who'd made a show of guarding it ran for their lives. Some of these – more than could be spared – fell under thrown knives and spears. The Skeletons pushed through the gap. Above the din Stopmouth could hear Indrani shouting orders. She seemed used to command. He marvelled how she was able to keep her people from pushing rocks into the alley too soon. They concentrated their fire on the enemy by the barricade, although the temptation offered by those in the alley must have been very great. But Indrani, hated and feared for reasons he could never understand, held them easily. He hoped Yama could command his group so well.

The first rocks fell when about half the beasts had passed inside. It meant they'd reached the second barrier, the one that was supposed to hold out for a while. Stopmouth and his men watched anxiously as more and more of the attackers pushed into the alleyway. He could see they'd already learned to keep to the centre and away from hurtling rocks. But so many of them were packed into the small space that a few were still crushed.

'Good,' he muttered. It was working better than he'd feared, although a large number of the beasts had yet to pass inside the wall.

Then he saw something strange. A few Skeletons outside the barrier fell down. Some were clutching at various parts of their bodies, others simply keeled over. Stopmouth didn't understand what was happening at first, until a very large group of attackers detached itself from the main body and charged off towards the place where Yama's men were supposed to be waiting quietly.

Stopmouth gasped. He'd told them not to attack! And now they were going to pay. He saw the other human group jumping up and running away, pursued by an equal number of Skeletons. The plan was in tatters. The enemy would hunt down Yama's band and annihilate them. Worse, a dozen Skeletons who had yet to enter the alley were organizing themselves into a rearguard that Stopmouth's group would be very lucky to overcome. Even if they did, all hope of a surprise attack was lost.

Stopmouth's hunters covered their eyes and muttered what may have been prayers or curses. The Skeletons were now passing the tree trunk through the gap it had made in the barrier. Human and beast corpses moved back the other way, out of human control.

Stopmouth needed to concentrate. Where would Yama lead his gang of doomed boys? Where could he take them that they'd be safe?

Here! he thought. He'll think I'll know what to do. Or maybe he's counting on the fact that our two groups together will outnumber the chasers. He'll think that means we can beat them. Wrong. Very wrong. But Stopmouth had to try.

He led his group at a run back the way they'd come. They needed to get far enough away from the site of the siege so as not to be heard, but not so far that the two groups of human hunters would run into each other.

They'd reached a spot around the side of Headquarters when the first of the fleeing humans came into view. Stopmouth shoved his men into doorways on either side of a wide street and signalled '*Silence!*' Then he signalled '*Sling*' and smiled grimly as they placed stones carefully into strips of Slimer hide. Only Kubar disobeyed. He grabbed the first fleeing hunter as he passed and hissed instructions that Stopmouth couldn't understand. Though exhausted, the boy nodded and ran on. Stopmouth glared at Kubar. The priest should have made the man wait to fight with them.

More humans ran past, sweating heavily. Most had abandoned their spears. Kubar didn't try to stop these, but Stopmouth guessed by now that the first man had been detailed to gather them up further along the way.

In the distance a great pounding noise started up. The second barrier, thought Stopmouth. At that moment he and his men were supposed to be closing the trap on the alleyway. Instead, they were here, too far away to intervene now. A chill settled on him.

A dozen more humans had passed before Stopmouth saw the first Skeletons. They jogged along together as a good hunting party should, heads high and pace even, driving terrified men before them. Yama was at the back, shouting at a plump-faced boy who looked ready to drop.

Come on! thought Stopmouth. Come on! He signalled frantically to those men who could see him that they should hold their fire. He hoped the signal was being passed down the line and that his hunters would have learned from the earlier disaster.

The last of the fleeing humans passed Stopmouth's hiding place. Only Yama and his friend remained.

Come on!

The friend, a boaster and a favourite with the girls, tripped.

Yama looked behind him and, seeing that the nearest Skeleton was barely a spear's length distant, cried out once and picked up speed. The other boy died screaming behind him.

The Skeletons increased their pace, their legs bent backwards, seeming to imbue every step with extra spring. Many had drool running down their chins, their narrow mouths working beneath a quartet of colourless eyes. Stopmouth waited until the main body had passed him. Then he screamed, '*Attack!*' in the only language he knew and began launching slingstones into the packed mass of beasts. For a heartbeat he was alone, but then stones were flying in from all directions.

The Skeletons had barely a moment to absorb this shock before men poured out of doorways with spears and knives. Many of the beasts managed to bring their own weapons to bear, and they might have slaughtered their inexperienced attackers if Yama's group hadn't come charging back into the fray at just the right time. They screamed as they advanced and the enemy, packed in together and caught on all sides, could do little to defend themselves.

The victors cheered and licked their weapons.

Stopmouth smiled so as not to dishearten them. Many men lay dead or volunteered, their faces melted away. Maybe twenty since the day had begun. Too high a price. In the distance the tree trunk was still pounding against the second barrier. Yama indicated they should go back towards it. 'There's no point,' said Stopmouth, knowing the boy couldn't understand him. 'They're expecting us.' He desperately needed time to think.

And then the pounding stopped.

His men, who were still celebrating their little victory, froze. They all realized what it meant. Stopmouth gripped the shaft of his spear like he meant to throttle it. He had nothing to say to them, nothing at all. The Skeletons would soon be inside the complex on their way to the women and children. He couldn't save them now. But perhaps . . . perhaps there was a way to be with them at the end.

'Let's go!' he shouted. 'Come on! Move!'

He led the men back to where the Skeletons had been trying to climb onto the roof of Headquarters earlier in the night. Corpses surrounded the fallen tree trunks.

He indicated to his hunters that they should help him raise one of the beams against the wall. Many were arguing, pointing back in the direction of the barrier. So Stopmouth began heaving at the wood by himself until the others joined in. The Skeletons had carved handholds into the trunk, and while the spacing wasn't right for human limbs, they were definitely helpful.

Stopmouth pointed at Yama and then the roof.

'*Go!*' he signalled.

For once the boy didn't try to contradict him. He climbed as well as any Flim while other men kept the trunk steady. When Yama reached the top, he stared around for a few heartbeats and then turned back and shouted something. Suddenly everyone was grabbing at the handholds, all of them trying to climb at once. Stopmouth and Kubar made them raise the other trunk and fought them into a rough queue. Then Stopmouth flung his spear over the parapet and followed it up.

Yama heaved him over the edge into chaos.

The roof he'd climbed onto was the lowest of the three that made up Headquarters. The others lay perpendicular to it and looked down on it by less than the height of a child. Defences were concentrated around the long flat roofs of the two buildings which lay to either side of the U's mouth. Defenders were streaming away from one of these now, while people on the other side jumped up and down in anxiety. Stopmouth could make out the figure of Indrani standing among the second group, urging them to stop staring, to keep throwing rocks. He could hear Rockface yelling in rage at the fools around him.

Stopmouth still couldn't see any Skeletons. But he

guessed that one of the ground-floor doors or windows had been breached and the enemy were now on their way up the stairs to the rooftop. And so the defenders were running away, seeking to preserve their lives a little longer when they could have sold them dearly at the skylight. Men and women pushed past Stopmouth and Yama at the base of the U. A few of the braver ones halted long enough to help hunters over the parapet. In this way Stopmouth had gathered most of his men together when the first Skeletons arrived through the skylight onto the recently abandoned building.

The beasts took their time. They had no need to rush now. They spread out to allow others of their kind to climb up unmolested.

Stopmouth brought his men over to join Indrani on the far side of the U from where the enemy had entered. Everybody here looked tired and afraid. Old women had bloody hands from pushing rocks and throwing stones. Men wept; some rolled into balls, their arms wrapped around their knees. The whole Tribe knew it was the end, that tonight the Skeletons would feast on their flesh.

Stopmouth looked at his woman. The tree-trunk ladders still leaned against the wall. If they ran now, the two of them could make another desperate try for the Roof. And yet not everyone had given up hope. Yama had gathered his boys together and he whispered to them fiercely. Kubar and others were picking up slingstones.

Meanwhile the handsome Varaha had finally lost his composure. He scanned the Roof, muttering to himself, fidgeting with his necklace. But he also held a spear in his white-knuckled hand and it was clear he intended to use it.

'We'll kill them all, hey?' Rockface stood right at his ear, a grin on his face. His belt bristled with spare weapons. The dullness of before had completely disappeared. 'They won't be getting my flesh!'

'I thought you w-wanted to v-v-volunteer.'

Rockface growled. 'Do I look like a volunteer to you? You asked me to guard the children. And I am.'

Indrani was busy too, dragging women to their feet, hissing at tired old men till they armed themselves. Stopmouth knew then that even if it meant his death, he couldn't abandon his people to this. They were Tribe and only the Tribe could give life its meaning.

'Everybody listen to me!' he shouted. As always, it amazed him the way they stopped and turned to him. 'We can still beat them!' he said. 'They're the ones who've suffered all the losses getting here! We're far more numerous now!' It wouldn't matter, of course. Women, children and weaklings against real hunters. 'But they'll beat us if we cower back here. We need to meet them just before the base of the U, where we'll have the advantage.' The enemy would have to climb half the height of a man to reach the defenders.

They followed him there and he marshalled them into a line with spearmen at the front and everybody else gathering up handfuls of stones. He took a deep breath. The Skeletons would pay dearly for their genocide.

'Hunters! Slings first.' The enemy would be exposed for several heartbeats as they jumped down on the other side.

He felt somebody move into the line beside him. 'Indrani?' Sweat and grime covered her from head to foot. She was magnificent, beautiful, and seemed utterly unafraid. 'Don't worry, Stopmouth. They brought the spirit-lovers here for a reason. They won't let me die. You'll see.'

'What do you mean? Who won't let you die?'

She didn't answer the question. She took his face in her hands and kissed him. 'I'm glad I found you,' she said. 'Now, we must be ready. Look!'

She turned to face the enemy.

Fifty or sixty Skeletons had made it onto the roof. It had been an expensive night for them. They must have lost tens under rocks plus those that Stopmouth and his men had already killed outside. It was more than any Tribe could afford and Stopmouth knew they'd never have been willing to pay the cost had they known it in advance. Now they came forward at a jog, crossing from one roof to the next on their arm of the U.

The humans waited for them in a mass of bristling spears and stakes without points. Many of the people there couldn't even hold a weapon the right way round. But the beasts didn't know that and stopped in their tracks just out of sling range.

Everybody waited, spears weighing on tired muscles, while the Skeletons seemed to confer amongst themselves. The beasts were in no rush. Stopmouth could hear children crying and mothers hushing them. Otherwise the humans were silent as the enemy made plans to kill them.

'We should attack them,' said Yama. 'They look confused.'

Nobody paid him any attention. Stopmouth sighed, his fear ebbing away. Maybe the enemy would call it a day now. It's what he'd have done. If the Skeletons made an orderly retreat and took all their dead with them, the humans were finished. Thirty days of hunger and attrition would guarantee it.

Then people around him cried out in dismay. Ten more Skeletons had climbed up through the skylight. They must have come from the rearguard at the barrier. One of these was the tall creature with the decorated hides that Stopmouth had seen at the beginning of the night. It gestured once with its spear, and all the others fell in around it. Then it pointed its weapon across the U at the humans. The beasts surged forward, leaping down onto the lower roof that separated them from their quarry.

'Stone them!' shouted Stopmouth. He needn't have bothered. Every human, from the smallest child capable of lifting a rock to the woman with the greyest hair, flung stones for all they were worth. Stopmouth's hunters used their slings, a few of them getting in two shots before the Skeletons had crossed half the roof. Most of the stones were ineffectual – some didn't even reach the enemy. But others struck home, and here and there a beast stumbled, fatally slowing the charge of its comrades and giving the defenders yet more chances to attack.

'Got one!' Rockface shouted. 'Got one!'

Stopmouth himself slung like a madman, matched stone for stone by Sodasi and Kamala.

Then the Skeletons were flinging knives before them. Women and children screamed as they were struck. Hunters fell. They were dragged away and replaced as the first of the enemy came close enough to fight. Men stabbed into the glowing mass of beasts. Sometimes the target of their attacks would grab a thrusting spear in tentacle-like hands, pulling humans down amongst slashing knives.

Stopmouth felt like he was watching himself fight, watching a stranger. Fear had left his body entirely and his Armourback-shell weapon worked in a blur before him. He was aware of Indrani nearby, backing him up, making sure he never had more than two to deal with at a time.

Behind the line of hunters, women and older children lobbed a continual rain of fist-sized rocks over the men's heads. Meanwhile the sisters, Sodasi and Kamala, were still managing to fire obliquely into the mass of the enemy. This close, they couldn't miss.

It all worked as Stopmouth had dreamed. Every weak link of the human body moved as one until the whole was stronger than the sum of its parts. Yet it wasn't enough. Yama screamed, his leg bubbling with beast spit. A pair of knives flashed through the air to take another man in the stomach. The defence began to buckle.

'I'm jumping!' shouted Indrani. 'I'm jumping now!'

And she did. One moment Stopmouth felt her beside him, the next she was gone, in amongst the enemy.

'Indrani!' he screamed.

He saw her fall to the ground just in front of him. A beast was reaching down for her with a knife. Stopmouth's vision turned red. He all but decapitated Indrani's attacker with a swing of his Armourback-shell spear. But two more of the enemy were already reaching for her and the rest of the humans were being driven from the edge of the roof. He felt a cut on his leg and found the Skeleton chief before him, pushing him back, away from Indrani. He screamed.

It was then that the Globe descended on them, a streak of shining, roaring silver. The sky flashed.

The whole world seemed to shake. A wave of heat washed over the combatants, followed by smoke. The fighting paused as human and beast took in what had happened. Half the lower building of the U was missing. Blackened Skeleton corpses covered the rest of it, some of them smoking, some in small pieces, as though torn asunder and flung in random directions. Only the rank of beasts nearest the humans had survived.

The pause was ended by the translated words of the Skeleton leader. 'Over the wall!' it shouted. 'We are finished! Over the wall!'

As the Skeletons turned to flee, Stopmouth picked up his Armourback-shell spear and flung it as hard as he could. The shaft flew true and plunged through the enemy chief's body. Then he was leaping down to the next level. His injured leg gave way under him. He forced himself up, pulling charred and smoking bodies from the spot where he'd seen Indrani go down.

'I'm unhurt,' she said when he found her, although her whole body shook. 'I told you. They wouldn't let me die.'

He wanted to ask her how she'd known the Globes would intervene – they'd never tried to save her before – but she seemed to be looking straight past him. He turned to find Varaha standing behind him. The man hadn't even suffered a scratch.

'I'm glad you're all right,' said the teacher. 'Whoever did this' – his eyes flickered to Stopmouth and then back to Indrani – 'will want something in exchange.'

She nodded once and the man turned away.

'Indrani . . . ?'

'I'm fine, Stopmouth.' She avoided his eyes. 'Your people need you now. They have no experience of this. Help them.'

It was true. The wounded were everywhere, crying out in pain or fear. Some people were tending them, others were finding Skeletons in a similar condition and taking revenge. Stopmouth glanced upwards. The attacking Globe had returned to its usual harmless floating.

He almost tripped over Kubar, tending the injured Yama.

'Staring's not going to help!' said the elder.

Bubbles of flesh and blood covered Yama's left ankle. His face was distorted in pain, the scars on his cheek darker than ever. He looked up at Stopmouth.

'We should have charged them when I said!' he raged. 'This would never have happened to me.'

A lot of people nearby turned at the sound of his raised voice.

'I see,' said Stopmouth. He nodded. He raised his own voice too, but kept it as calm as he could. 'You also said, I remember, that we should do things properly around here. That we should have volunteers from now on.'

'What do you mean?'

Stopmouth turned to Kubar. 'How long do you think it will take him to heal?'

'Well, how would I know? We've never even seen that kind of injury before!'

'Maybe not soon enough,' said Stopmouth.

'I'll heal!' said Yama. 'Oh, gods! I'll heal.' He started to cry, not like a man would, but like the boy he was, snivelling, blubbing. 'Please, Stopmouth. Please, not me.'

Stopmouth did not alter his expression. 'I trained you and these others, Yama. I wanted us to act like one body, to *be* one body. And that body can only have one head. Do you hear me?'

'Yes.' He had snot running down his upper lip.

Stopmouth felt wretched, lower than the worst bully. He kept his face impassive. All the survivors were watching. 'Who is the chief?'

'You are. You are, Stopmouth.'

'You will never disobey me again.' He limped away as quickly as he could. His own injured leg was about to give way. He didn't want anybody watching when that happened.

22.
WHO WILL LOOK AFTER THEM?

The orphans were supposed to be sleeping now that dark had fallen. Stopmouth listened to the echoes of their whispers and giggles as they rolled about the floor with the infant Fourlegger. He'd heard it could understand a few human words, but couldn't reproduce them. He wondered again at the wisdom of letting it live. How would such children grow to hunt Fourleggers now? How could *he* hunt them? He never used to have nightmares about killing beasts, but these days . . . He didn't know whether to blame the change on his woman or the Talker, but he wasn't sure he could survive without either.

'Leave the children,' he said to Indrani. 'Lie down with me.'

'I don't know who's going to look after them.' She held her hands across her belly in a gesture he'd seen before but couldn't place.

'You'll look after them,' he said.

She bit her lower lip and came to the bed of pounded moss they shared. As usual, these days, she lay down far enough away that he couldn't encircle her with his arms.

'It's been a long time – two tens, Indrani,' said Stopmouth. 'At least two. Why won't you move closer? Ever since the battle on the roofs it's like you . . .' *Like you died.* He'd said it before and didn't want to repeat it now.

Not too far away, through one of the many doorways that honeycombed the top floor of Headquarters, a woman was singing. Something lovely maybe, but distorted by echoes and frequently interrupted by the *slap slap* of small running feet and the pointless scolding of an adult voice.

Then all was quiet again. Stopmouth and Indrani were alone but for a charcoal figure somebody had drawn on the wall – a long-nosed beast, supposedly a god. It flickered in the light of a dying fire, its great mouth grinning at the chief's discomfort.

'What have I done to you?' Stopmouth said to Indrani.

He really wanted to ask her about Varaha. She'd seemed to dislike the man before, but was spending more and more time with him now.

'It's nothing *you've* done,' she said. And she turned away so he wouldn't see the usual look of guilt that crossed her face when he confronted her.

* * *

Stopmouth sighed and regarded the circle of hunters. Eight men and two women hung on his every word, looking at him as they might have looked at their gods, back before they'd abandoned them. Sometimes he felt like shouting: 'That's not me!' But Indrani wasn't the only one acting strangely since the battle. Stopmouth wasn't his usual self any more either; the tongue-tied boy, the lesser brother. The hunters obeyed him without question, but were too respectful to be his friends.

'Tonight we need three corpses.' He took the time to look each hunter in the eye. 'If those corpses are human, so be it. And don't think three'll be enough for even one meal for the Tribe! It won't. But I'll be taking another group out tomorrow night, and another one the night after that. In four nights' time you all get to go again.'

The chief hoped it would be enough. These were the best he had left. Sodasi and Kamala, the slingers; Sanjay, who could catch Stopmouth in a sprint and had uncanny accuracy when throwing the warped spear he'd made for himself; Vishwakarma, a brute of a man by these people's standards, who ignored pain to defeat skilled opponents; Kubar, the ex-priest, oldest of the group, but smart enough to stay alive in a fight . . . and then there was Varaha. He still wore the little wooden necklace he'd come with and the same knowing grin. It turned Stopmouth's stomach now. Varaha alone was unafraid of the chief – or indeed anything, as far as Stopmouth could tell. Except maybe marriage. He was the only unmarried adult man left in the Tribe, in spite of what he'd said once before about choosing a wife.

Only Rockface was missing, and perhaps that was for the best: even if he'd been able to run, this would be a hunt such as the big man had never seen and probably wouldn't want to see. None of this group would be charging into danger. The chief couldn't afford to lose them.

Stopmouth glanced up at the Roof, seeing how the panels darkened. It was time to leave. Nobody was there to wish them well and he missed the comfort of flicking a drop of blood at a loved one as a promise to return.

The hunters moved off as he'd taught them, passing through the double line of posts topped with beast skulls that now surrounded Headquarters. He winced at every clumsy noise.

Each hunter carried spear and knife and sling – the customary weapons of humans since the time of the Traveller. Oh, these people couldn't hunt in the traditional way – it took a lifetime to acquire that skill! But they'd used the time won in the battle to learn to fight as one being, to co-operate as no humans ever had. Still, they weren't ready. Not even these, his best and brightest. But time was short and people were going hungry.

Down the streets they moved, never too fast for the weaker ones. Each member of the group took up a position in the formation he'd worked out with Kubar: the best slingers ran at the sides; spearmen took the front, with knife men just behind, ready at a moment's notice to duck inside and gut the enemy. Their footsteps were silent over the bright patches of moss.

As they advanced, the streets narrowed, becoming twisty and unpredictable. Small, mean houses crowded the roadside. The few roofs that hadn't collapsed sloped upwards into little points that no one could possibly sleep on. A vision came to Stopmouth of this place in the time of the ancestors. Humans lived in every building. Women chatted across the width of the alleys from those little windows while their children ran in the streets. Everywhere was thronged like Centre Square on the day of a flesh meeting, and the scent of people and cook fires perfumed the air. Nobody watched the shadows for attack. Nobody had to.

How did they die? he wondered. Certainly Indrani knew, but he'd sworn not to ask about it. The temptation, however, tore at him constantly.

Suddenly Sodasi yelped and fell out of position. She had the presence of mind to call 'Tongue!'

The formation reacted instantly. The closest knife man ducked in to cut the tongue while spearmen held the charging Slimer at bay. Its weight knocked Kubar backwards to where more tongues emerged from windows to ensnare him. Like a swarm, the other humans turned on the owners of these

405

tongues, slashing and stabbing. One of the Slimers called out: 'Save me, brothers! Come to me, brothers! Oh, the pain!'

Shut up! thought Stopmouth. He opened his mouth to call off the attack, but luckily Varaha ended the creature's pleas with a thrust straight through its chest.

'We have to eat,' Stopmouth told himself. He knew he'd have to make a proper effort to learn the language of his Tribe, because he'd never be able to take the Talker hunting again.

The humans suffered a few casualties of their own: one slinger with a sprained ankle and a bad case of nerves; Kubar unconscious through lack of air; one of Yama's friends bruised and limping from a human slingshot to the back of the leg. Stopmouth himself had felt a stone whistle past his ear during the attack. 'We still have a lot to learn,' he commented. But he cheered along with the others, for they'd come less than a thousand paces from Headquarters and already they'd filled their quota.

'I'll show you how we celebrate,' he said. He slit open a steaming corpse and removed the first internal organ he could find. He had no idea what it was and didn't care. He sliced it into little squares for the others to share.

'These bits are always for the hunters,' he said.

They chewed, beaming. Only Varaha refused.

'Not after all that action!' he said.

'You're not even panting,' said Stopmouth. 'Go on, you've earned your share.'

'I'm not hungry.'

'That's not the point!'

Kamala intervened. 'He's just private, Chief,' she said. 'A lot of people are still ashamed at the way we eat here.'

She ducked her head at Varaha's beaming approval.

Stopmouth thought about ordering the man to eat, but hated acting the bully, whatever personal animosity he might have felt. Besides, what Kamala had said was true.

'Let's butcher these and get them home,' he said.

Back at Headquarters he made great show of cutting up the flesh and sharing it out. People listened with rapt attention while his hunters told their stories. They laughed as Varaha described Kubar's knock on the head as 'falling asleep on the job'. He continued loudly, 'Nor was this the first time. Just ask his wife!'

They pretended to be scandalized and maybe, in the Roof, they would have been. But Varaha had read them correctly and bathed in their laughter.

The crowd began to disperse and the teacher turned to leave. Stopmouth caught him by the arm.

'Chief?'

'Are you still not hungry, Varaha? You forgot your share of the meat.'

The man smiled his handsome smile. 'So kind of you to remember.'

'Varaha . . . what are you doing with my wife? Ever since the battle, you've been . . . you and her—'

Varaha surprised him by laughing in his face. 'Oh, I've seen this before! This is how your brother started with you, isn't it? He couldn't hold onto his wives and the next thing he was sending you and that buffoon, Rockface, off by yourselves to take on the Armourbacks.'

'How . . . how could you know that?'

'The Roof sees everything. Surely your woman told you as much?' Varaha's voice turned hard and his eyes glittered. It was a side of him that he'd never revealed before but must have been there all along. 'Now, listen to me, *Chief*. If you're falling asleep on the job like Kubar, that's none of my doing. My advice to you is to wait.' The scorn left his voice, to be replaced by what Stopmouth now recognized as false friendship. 'A few more days, Chief, and the problem will just go away. I promise you.'

The teacher left and Stopmouth found himself alone with Varaha's share of the flesh still in his hands. What had he meant by 'the problem going away'? What? Stopmouth leaned against a wall, fighting some of the most horrific thoughts of his life. He hadn't felt so lonely since his mother died.

As if to mock that memory, laughter erupted from a nearby annexe. 'Who's there?' he asked. He stepped under an arch to find that it was only some children, playing at hunting. Somebody had fashioned a little bag of Slimer hide and stuffed it with moss. Five or six boys and a pair of girls ran with it here and there, stabbing with little spears while Rockface shouted encouragement to them in Human. Everyone was screaming with mirth, Rockface most of all. A pair of infants too small for the game poked at the tattoos on his skin, while another rested in the crook of one massive arm.

'Do you see, Stopmouth?' he boomed. 'These ones are already better than the adults! These are worth my time!'

Stopmouth wanted to ask who'd made the spears, but then he remembered the perfect set of miniature weapons Rockface had created for his lost son, Littleknife. The chief realized his friend would be an ancestor after all, for his teaching would pass through these children and into every generation that followed them.

Stopmouth handed over the flesh. 'Varaha didn't want this.'

'He never does,' said Rockface, helping himself to an eyeball. 'Mmmm. Better than Armourback, hey?' Then he was shouting, 'No, Shankar! No! Use the point! Ah! Good boy!' To Stopmouth: 'He's a strange man, hey? That Varaha. Do you think your Indrani likes him? Is that it? You shouldn't let her spend so much time with him. It's not good for the chief. Remember Wallbreaker.'

Stopmouth did. All the time. It was like his brother sat

at his shoulder, watching everything he did. And more than that: he'd had a growing feeling, a certainty, that one day he'd meet his brother again, although that was impossible.

'You shouldn't let him get away with it either,' said Rockface. 'You know he leaves Headquarters every day by himself around this time? Down the ladder at the river window. That's probably when he meets her.'

Stopmouth felt sick. What if it was true? What would the chief do about it? He couldn't be sure, but for his own sanity he had to know what was going on. He had to.

Without another word, he left Rockface and ran full tilt for the river side of the building. Sure enough, when he looked out of the window there, he saw a human figure in the distance, disappearing in among the houses. It was against his own rules, but without a second thought he plunged down the ladder and ran after Varaha.

Soon he caught up, but kept a careful distance, tracking his quarry through the streets next to the river. Varaha never looked behind him, causing Stopmouth to scold himself for being such a bad teacher. How could an otherwise good hunter be so stupid? Did he think himself an ancestor who could just ignore all possible threats? Still, the chief was glad of the advantage it gave him.

The streets narrowed further and most of the buildings had surviving balconies, shielding both men from the Roof.

Stopmouth checked behind to make sure he wasn't being stalked in turn. When he looked back, he saw Varaha had disappeared.

He froze, wondering if he'd been spotted after all, if the other man now lay in wait for him round a corner. He stepped forward, eyes flicking onto the ground for clues, and up again. A strange window appeared in the wall, so low it was at street level. The moss in front of it had been scraped away in a few places.

Stopmouth crouched down, wincing at the little twinge in his leg left over from the battle. He made the elemental mistake of blocking some of the light cast into the window with his head, but he needn't have worried. Varaha was too busy to see anything. He stood with his back to the chief in a small room, with stairs leading up into the rest of the house. He was crouching in front of a massive chunk of masonry, easily as large as a man. Varaha grunted and heaved once. The chief stifled a gasp as the stone left the floor and was thrown to one side. How could one man do such a thing? And yet he remembered now how Varaha never seemed to tire like the others, never broke sweat, was never afraid. The man pulled handfuls of white wafers from a previously hidden niche in the wall. Stopmouth had seen their like somewhere. He couldn't quite remember where until Varaha started stuffing them into his mouth. Of course! The rations he'd found in the wrecked Globe. He'd tried eating them, but had thought them too powdery, too sweet to be food.

Stopmouth felt revulsion rising in his chest. Varaha seemed to have stacks and stacks of the stuff. He was *hoarding* it. He would have to answer for this crime, no matter how strong he was. Stopmouth was about to squeeze through the window after the teacher when the man spoke.

'You want some?'

Indrani was standing halfway down the stairs, her hands again over her belly. Stopmouth froze. He felt as if he were floating out of his body, like when his legs were broken and his world was all pain and nightmare. If she kissed Varaha . . . If she looked at him the way she'd looked at Stopmouth only thirty nights previously . . . Stopmouth gripped the shaft of his spear, but was saved from murder by the bitterness in Indrani's voice.

'You persist in this hypocrisy, Varaha.'

'What are you talking about, woman?'

'I hear you made a kill today and yet you still refuse to eat flesh.'

'You think I'm a savage? After saving your lives? You and all your precious spirit-lovers?'

Indrani sat down on the stairs glaring at him. 'Yes, I think you're a savage. Oh, I was one back then too—'

'Indeed,' he drawled, 'the chairman's daughter. The face of the Committee!'

'I believed in it,' insisted Indrani. 'In everything I did then. I can't deny that, much as it shames me . . .' She shook her head. 'It doesn't matter. It hasn't mattered since the day you shot my Globe out of the sky.'

'Oh, stop whining about that. I let you live when it would have been so easy to finish you off. I got into a lot of trouble for it. And now, lucky you, they want you back.'

'Shall I tell you why?' she asked.

Varaha looked at her in sudden fear. 'I don't want to know.'

'Maybe I should tell you anyway.'

'You do, and I swear I'll make sure your pet savage dies before I do! Look! See this?' He indicated a section of concrete wall. 'That's his head.' A rapid punch. A cloud of dust round a new hole.

Indrani struggled for control. Eventually she said, 'You promised not to touch him, remember? I could have revealed your identity to the Tribe at any time.'

He sneered. 'But you wanted to keep your options open. Lucky for you during that battle that you did.' He placed the rest of his food packets in a hole in the floor. Then he began hiding the crumbs and other evidence. Blood dripped from his knuckles where he'd punched the wall. 'This whole operation was my idea, you know. I thought I'd enjoy watching these snivelling pacifists die. But believe me, it's nothing compared to the pleasure of seeing them betray their ideals first and *then* dying. I never expected that.'

'You were always the cruellest of us. You belong here.'

'No, my sweet. I belong up there. Where I can watch. And yet . . . there is something in what you say. Seeing them so close, smelling their blood and shit as some beast grabs them in its teeth . . . Oh, hide your disgust. And you called me a hypocrite! You sicken me.'

'We need to change this place,' said Indrani. 'It's wrong, all wrong.'

'Are you saying the Deserters didn't get what they deserved? You're joking.'

'Oh, by all the gods, Varaha, the last of the Deserters died lifetimes ago! Are we religious that we believe they keep being reborn here as their own descendants? We're the guilty ones now, as bad as they ever were. We're killing them and all the beast prisoners as surely as if we lifted the spears ourselves!'

'Well, little miss chairman's daughter' – Varaha's grin was fierce – 'we'll just close it all down, shall we? Deny the masses their entertainment right when we need to keep them quiet? Strange coming from you when thousands are here by your say-so.'

Stopmouth's jaw dropped. He knew the Roof people watched his world, but never before realized they did so for entertainment. They'd sentenced the Deserters to die, and instead of honourably volunteering them, they'd amused themselves – *amused!* – with the deaths, the sufferings, the unending fear and hunger of generations. His heart sped up, a furious thumping in his chest. Not even the wasting of food could be so obscene. Stopmouth could think of nothing worse, nothing! Except that Indrani had played a part in the whole thing. How could he lie beside her again? She and those like her had caused the deaths of his mother, his father and everybody he'd ever held dear.

Now he watched her hang her head, and strained to hear as her voice became a whisper. 'I told you, I want to put it right. I've changed.'

'Sure! And you'll change back tonight.'

'T-tonight?'

'Or never. It's your choice. I have it all arranged. As we agreed. It's tonight or you can stay here and rot. And I swear, if you let me down, I will kill him.'

Indrani bowed her head. 'Tonight then,' she said meekly. 'We leave tonight.'

And the chief bit his own knuckles to stop himself crying out.

Stopmouth sent the orphans off to another chamber in Headquarters and was waiting for her when she got back, arms folded; clasped tight to hide the swarm of emotions tearing at him. When Indrani finally walked in, no words would come to him. She belonged to a group that sent creatures here to die or to kill in entertaining ways. He imagined the eyes that had watched him his entire life; he heard sniggers as he'd cried over Mossheart and scorn at the generations of *savages* who gave their flesh so that other *savages* might keep the game alive. He knew he should hate her, that he should punish her in some way.

But the sight of her sad, beautiful face made that impossible. She looked much older than when he'd first seen her; so tired about the eyes, so drained by all that had happened to her. He remembered then how she'd saved his legs and the way Wallbreaker had paid her back. How much she'd suffered in the care of his Tribe!

Indrani had already been punished and there was no doubting her sincerity when she'd told Varaha she'd changed.

'You ought to be more careful,' she told him quietly.

'*Me?*'

'Your head,' she said. 'You didn't pull it back far enough from the window.'

She sat down on the moss with her face in trembling hands. 'I wanted to tell you, Stopmouth, but wasn't sure how. I'm glad you saw. Now that you know what I've done, it'll make it easier . . .'

The chief felt drained of emotion. When he spoke, his own voice sounded empty to him. 'What was Varaha saying to you. What's happening tonight?'

Tears peeped between her fingers. Still she didn't look at him. 'He can get a Globe to take me out. They've already interfered too much here, so they'll have to make sure the other Globes are elsewhere when they do it.'

'But, Indrani, I thought I'd found a home for you, for us. I thought—'

She took her hands away and looked up at him, eyes swollen. 'You thought wrong! So wrong. And you should have known better. Have you forgotten the Diggers? I'm sure they haven't forgotten you. Nor have they stopped spreading. None of my orphans will be old enough to hunt by the time those creatures get here. A thousand days, or two thousand. Nothing we've built will matter then. But up there, Stopmouth, that's where I'll find a way to make up for my crimes and keep you all safe. Up there!'

'Why should the Roof people help you?' He didn't know what else to say. He felt completely numb.

'Something was lost during the war. Something or somebody. A secret. Apparently I know what it is. Not consciously, but I may have it stored in the part of my memory that's kept in the Roof. No one could access that but me. It's probably why they wanted me dead in the first place, why they sent me here.'

'But now they need it again?' She was still the most beautiful woman he'd ever seen. 'Indrani . . . what's to keep them from . . . from killing you when they have what they want?'

Red-rimmed eyes rose to meet his. 'They promised to stop the Diggers. To give you a chance, Stopmouth.' She lowered her face again. 'But I don't believe them. I don't believe anything they say now. I'm not . . . I won't go meekly to the slaughter. I won't let them hurt me and my . . . I won't go. I know how to fight. If I time it right, I might be able to capture the Globe. Some of the rebels must have survived the war and they'll want me and my secret, whatever it is. They'll give me the weapons we need to save ourselves.'

'I could go with you . . .' he said.

The relief on her face was too sudden, too strong to be faked and he realized she'd hoped for this all along, but for some reason had thought it impossible. 'Oh, Stopmouth! Stopmouth!' She pulled him close and tight for the first time in thirty days and both of them wept together.

A few of the orphans ran in and found them that way, pestering the adults with the usual hail of questions and complaints over who had pulled whose hair. Even as he dried his eyes so as not to upset the children, Stopmouth remembered Indrani's question from the previous night.

'Who will look after them?' she'd asked. And he didn't know the answer.

23.
THE WEAKER HAND

Varaha was waiting for them in an alleyway where no guard from Headquarters would see him. Roofsweat trickled down his forehead and onto the muscles of his upper body. They weren't that impressive – little larger than Stopmouth's. Rockface would have dwarfed the man. But then, Rockface could never have moved the boulder Varaha used to hide his food, let alone lift it off the ground! The man scowled when Stopmouth and Indrani arrived together.

'Are you mad, woman? You know there's not enough room in the Globe for him!'

'I had to tell him, he—'

'And besides, things are bad enough up there without bringing in a savage.'

'You needn't concern yourself, spy,' said Stopmouth, his eyes cold. 'My place is here.' He didn't like telling lies, but this one came out like he meant it. Earlier he'd asked

Indrani why Varaha needed to know she wasn't alone. 'I could shadow the two of you until you—'

'No, Stopmouth. You can't sneak up on a Globe. Its machines will spot you straight away and the pilot will stay clear. We'd be stuck here for ever.'

Varaha led them back past the room where he kept his food. His voice oozed the false cheer he'd worn throughout his mission. 'Sad to be losing your best hunter, are you, *Chief?*'

'A good hunter remembers to look behind him.'

'Behind or in front, Stopmouth, it doesn't matter. Your kind are no threat to me.'

The chief was curious in spite of himself. 'Would the Globes protect you as they did Indrani?'

Varaha snorted. 'I can look after myself. And no, they wouldn't come, not for me. She forced them to intervene when she knew everyone would be watching.' He cast a glance of pure hatred in Indrani's direction and Stopmouth wondered that he'd ever considered Varaha a rival. It suddenly dawned on him that the spy must have realized Stopmouth's fears all along, must have amused himself by encouraging them. All that talk of marriage could mean nothing else.

Stopmouth grabbed him by the shoulder. 'You've been playing with us the whole time!'

'Stopmouth!' said Indrani. Her eyes were pleading with

him. *Remember the plan*, she seemed to be saying. She'd warned him not to fight Varaha. And of course she was right. Anybody who could punch holes in a solid wall shouldn't be taken lightly.

Carefully he removed his hand from the other man's shoulder.

'I'd kill you now, Stopmouth, if you weren't so popular. But I warn you, tonight is the one night I'd get away with it.' He pointed upwards to where a single Globe hung against the Roof. 'That's ours. The others have all been sent to watch the Diggers put an end to the Longtongues. Do not provoke me further.'

The Globe shadowed them as they came into an open triangular area between three tall buildings overgrown with stringy moss.

'Will it land here?' asked Stopmouth.

Varaha snorted, but Indrani answered the question, her voice and face tense. 'Globes are deliberately made so that they can't land on the surface. The closer you get to it the harder they are to control. I presume we'll have to climb one of these buildings. It would be easier for the pilot that way.'

Varaha turned back to Stopmouth, his tone mild. 'I'll be interested in seeing how long you can keep those fools alive. There are too few of them, you know that, don't you?'

'We have the Talker.'

Varaha nodded, scanning the sky again. 'It won't do you

much good when the Diggers come. They don't negotiate with food. Their minds just couldn't cope.'

The three of them ducked into the door of a tower and headed up the stairs. It was utterly dark inside. A shame, thought the hunter, that they couldn't take advantage of it to attack Varaha. The man needed to be conscious for the arrival of the Globe and maybe for a little while after that.

The stairs seemed endless and pulled at the twinge in his leg. He kept seeing the faces of the orphans. Indrani was worried about them, he knew that, terrified of what would happen to them in her absence. And yet they were doomed anyway if she didn't go. The battle must have convinced her of that. It seemed to be the turning point.

Every step brought Stopmouth new worries. He wondered how long he'd be gone after stealing the Globe. Rockface would never run again and none of his other hunters were fit to go hunting without him. They were too few. Stopmouth knew they couldn't afford all the mistakes they'd make in his absence. Even if he found a weapon to combat the Diggers, what would he come back to in the end? Nothing, probably. Nobody. It was a bitter thought.

A square of pale light signalled the end of the climb. They emerged to an amazing sight. Normally Globes floated right next to the Roof, so far away a hunter could cover them with his hand. Stopmouth had only ever seen them up close in the form of wreckage. This one hung no more than the height of two men above the roof of the building. It seemed massive, as big as a house in its own right, its metal skin covered in protrusions and lights. It hummed, not loudly, but with a deep, deep sound that Stopmouth could feel in the cracked stone of the tower around him. And there was a smell too: like something smouldering and poisonous.

The Globe didn't land, of course. Stopmouth imagined it trying, collapsing the building or rolling off it altogether. He jumped when the shell opened up, like an eyelid.

A man stuck his head out. He had hair across the top of his lip and a sharp voice accentuated by his hanging upside down.

'Any trouble?' asked Varaha.

The man shook his head. 'There are Fourleggers in the area, but they never saw you. Ha! You must be glad to get out of this place. I nearly wet myself laughing when the savage tried to get you to eat this morning.'

'You saw that?'

'Everybody saw that!'

Varaha turned to Stopmouth with a vicious look on his face. The chief got ready to defend himself. He had brought a full stock of weapons, while his opponent, though incredibly strong, was unarmed.

'No, Varaha!' Indrani shouted. 'I won't go with you if you hurt him.'

Stopmouth stood his ground, refusing to show any fear. He'd been raised to hunt, had faced creatures that were weaker but much more fierce than this man, much more desperate.

'You're coming now, anyway, Indrani. Whether you like it or not.'

'Yes, Varaha, you could force me aboard. But you know damn well you can't use duress to get at my memories. The Roof would never allow it.'

Varaha said nothing, but he backed up a step. Then he signalled the pilot, who nodded and disappeared inside. A clever contraption rolled out of the hatch: two ropes joined together by smaller cross pieces, perfectly spaced for easy climbing.

'You're going up first,' said Varaha to Indrani.

She nodded. So far, things were working out exactly as she'd promised. She looked towards the ropes and back to her lover.

'I want to say goodbye to Stopmouth,' she said.

'So say it.'

'In private.'

He laughed. 'Don't be ridiculous: you know the Globe is recording everything. Say goodbye now or watch him bleed. You decide.' But he didn't object when she led Stopmouth over to the far side of the roof, following their every step with his sneer. 'I wonder,' said the spy, 'how you could let one of those savages even touch you, let alone get you—'

'Shut up, or I'm not coming! All right? Shut up!'

And he did, shrugging and turning away. Indrani put her arms around Stopmouth and pulled him close. 'Listen carefully. You'll only get one chance to knock him out. Remember what I told you – he's been altered. He's at least as strong as Crunchfist.'

Stopmouth stiffened. 'I know, I—'

'No stupid risks! Promise me.'

He sighed. 'I'll hit him just as soon as you've got the pilot. Then I'll climb up after you.'

'Good,' she said.

He followed her back to the ropes. Their damp palms felt like they were stuck together. Varaha waved her up. She pulled away from her man and climbed onto the first rung while the body of the Globe rocked gently under her weight. Stopmouth hefted the Talker pouch. He'd hoped the spy would present the back of his head while watching Indrani ascend, but he seemed more interested in Stopmouth's reaction.

'You'll never see her again,' whispered Varaha. He was no taller than Stopmouth, really. 'But she'll see you. We'll watch you die together.'

Stopmouth kept his face expressionless. His woman's legs had almost disappeared inside the craft.

'Remember,' Varaha continued, 'it was me who sent her to you, and now I'm taking her away.'

'Why didn't you just kill her at the time?'

'Nobody humiliates me, Stopmouth. That's why. She deserved everything she got down here. And you – you deserve this.'

Stopmouth had been waiting so carefully for an opportunity to attack, he hadn't realized that Varaha was doing the same. The spy's fist caught him hard in the face, driving him to the ground.

'How do you like that? That was just a tap.'

Stopmouth couldn't answer. He tried to pick himself up, but his head rang and his vision seemed blurred. Vaguely he was aware that Varaha was still looking at him, saying, 'Nobody humiliates me . . .'

Then Indrani's head popped out of the hatch. Varaha saw her too. 'What are you doing?' he shouted. 'Get back in there! I didn't kill him, all right? I just gave him something to remember me by. Hey! Hey!'

For some reason Varaha had jumped onto the ropes and was rushing to climb them. Then he and the severed ropes were falling, the height of two men, onto the roof of the tower.

'Hang on, Stopmouth!' Indrani called. 'I just need to—'

But she had troubles of her own. The Globe suddenly

took off, nearly throwing her out after Varaha. The craft sped straight up into the air and then flew erratically off in the direction of old Man-Ways.

Stopmouth staggered to his feet, head throbbing, and made his way over to pick up his spear. In spite of his promise, he'd underestimated Varaha and ruined everything.

'Think you'll be able to use that sticker on me, savage?' The spy's voice trembled with anger. 'You have a lot to learn.' He stood up, gripping the severed ropes. Scratches covered him along one side of his body and his face was scraped raw.

He's not so pretty now, thought Stopmouth. But he didn't let it distract him from what he had to do. He got himself into the correct stance and stepped forward, snapping the spear towards his opponent's belly. Varaha leaped aside. He swung his nest of ropes, forcing Stopmouth to duck. He swung again, and this time he snared the spear.

Stopmouth held onto it with all the strength of a lifetime of danger. He dug his heels against the rough surface of the rooftop and heaved. It didn't matter – Varaha grinned savagely, not even breathing hard as he reeled the hunter in.

The chief stopped resisting the pull and flung himself forward instead, his weight now behind the spear. The point cut a ragged line across Varaha's chest before he could knock it aside. Both men went down in a heap, the ropes and spear between them. Stopmouth reached back for his knife, but Varaha roared and threw the chief off him as though he weighed no more than an empty skull. Then he surged to his feet and bent the thick spear-shaft in his hands until it snapped.

'Your back is next,' he hissed.

Stopmouth knew the man could do it. He jumped into the skylight and didn't let an awkward landing keep him from running down the dark stairs as fast as he could go. Curses and footsteps followed him all the way. He didn't know what to do. Indrani was lost to him, kidnapped perhaps by the pilot of the Globe, taken somewhere he couldn't follow. And yet, as far as he knew, she still lived and might find a way to come back to him. Even if she couldn't and ended her days as a prisoner on the Roof, she'd want to know he was all right. She wouldn't want Varaha crowing about how he'd killed her lover.

He was already pulling out his sling as he reached the ground floor. He ran across the street and had a stone spinning back towards the doorway as Varaha emerged blinking. The shot missed anything vital. However, it did take part of an ear for its troubles and elicited a roar of pain. Varaha grabbed at his wooden necklace, but Stopmouth didn't wait to see why. He ran on.

Almost immediately he realized he was going in the

wrong direction. He had allowed his enemy to come between him and Headquarters, where help might be found. At least he still had his sling. He tucked it into his belt for later, knowing he could—

There was an intense flash of green light. The wall above Stopmouth's head exploded, stones raining down to either side of him. He felt an impact, a burst of terrible pain in his shoulder. He cried out, but managed to keep his balance. He staggered on another few steps before falling into a doorway. Stones half blocked the alley he'd run through and a giant had taken a bite out of one of the buildings. His right arm, his hunting arm, brushed against the doorway. 'By the ancestors!' Agony ripped through him, blurring his vision. He couldn't bend the arm at all, couldn't bear to touch it. Pain throbbed deep inside it with every heartbeat.

'I hope you're not dead,' called a voice. Somebody was scrambling over the stones in the alley. 'I want to finish you with my bare hands.'

The hunter stumbled into the back of the house, looking for a way out. The design was unfamiliar to him and he found himself in the wrong room even as he heard footsteps at the front door. His only escape was a waist-high window – awkward for a one-armed hunter in great pain. He had to back up to it and lever himself onto the sill with his good hand. However, his panic and the breathing he could hear in the corridor caused him to lose his balance. He tried to catch himself. His right arm refused to move and he tumbled backwards, landing on his injury with a scream, while the Talker rolled out of its pouch and came to rest against his bad shoulder. He knew he ought to pick it up, pick himself up and run. But suffering clouded his thoughts.

'Well, well,' said Varaha from the window. 'I wonder – should I twist your head off straight away or play with that arm of yours first?'

A memory came to Stopmouth then of the last time he'd thrown himself out a window this way, many tens ago in Blood-Ways.

'Brighter,' he whispered.

'What did you say?'

'Brighter than the Roof.'

The Talker flared suddenly and so sharply that even with his head turned and eyes closed, Stopmouth still got spots in his vision. He didn't wait to see what effect this had on Varaha. Weeping with pain, he rolled onto his good side and managed to make it to his knees and then his feet. He staggered towards a warren of alleys and narrow lanes that he didn't recognize. But he could hear the river far to his left and realized that this time, at least, he was going in the right direction.

A shout of rage and anger came from behind him. The green light flashed and a spray of stone erupted from the side of a building in front of Stopmouth. More explosions followed, but none came close to him. Varaha would need longer than that to recover his sight!

That was when Stopmouth realized he'd left the Talker behind him, giving his Tribe even less chance of survival. And him too, for how could he explain the threat that followed him if he reached home before his enemy?

He wandered for another tenth, down an endless maze of bone-filled alleys. Varaha would be moving far faster than he was and was bound to catch him soon. That's if exhaustion didn't pull him down first. Stopmouth had just reached the intersection of two twisty roads when he heard voices in conversation. He approached cautiously, checking above and behind, making sure he wasn't walking into a trap – a child could have bested him in his present condition.

Three Fourleggers crouched down at the entrance to an alleyway, their pointy faces all pressed together, one against the other.

'Home,' said one. 'The green light brings terror to this mind.'

'Hunger needs flesh,' objected the second.

'Flesh,' said the third.

Stopmouth tried to understand what was happening despite the constant distraction of pain. He'd left the Talker behind him under the window. Either the Fourleggers themselves had found it or else . . . or else Varaha had picked it up and was now nearby. Stopmouth scanned the mossy buildings and saw nobody. Wherever he was, the spy was certain to be listening to the beasts too.

'Why hasn't he killed them?' wondered Stopmouth. Varaha had no need of the flesh and yet the killing would be easy for him, maybe even enjoyable. But then the hunter realized that while the creatures couldn't be much of a challenge to Varaha's strange green weapon and unnatural strength, to Stopmouth they would be deadly; a barrier to force him back or funnel him in a direction he didn't want to go. Praying that Varaha hadn't spotted him and that the Fourleggers with their excellent hearing wouldn't notice, he took a curvy lane that ran in the general direction of the alley the beasts were blocking. He was exhausted by now. His heart beat fast, speeding up the throb of pain in his arm. He needed to get home soon or he'd collapse.

The lane ended in an open area with several exits. At one of these, crouching in wait, lay Varaha. Stopmouth mightn't have seen him if he hadn't been expecting to. As it was, most of the roads nearby seemed to meet at this place, and it might be morning before he could find a way around it. His strength wouldn't hold out that long.

He pulled back a step or two, wondering if his enemy could hear his ragged breathing. How could he escape? His injury wouldn't let him crawl through the shadows, and while some of the alleys were narrow enough for a hunter to jump from roof to roof, he'd never be able to take the impact of a landing. He checked himself for weapons. The fight on the tower had cost him his spear and he hadn't seen his knife since then either. Only the sling remained. He cursed. It might have been enough if he wasn't such a terrible shot with his left hand. He knew he'd be lucky to come within a body-length of his enemy and would never strike the head. Even so, Varaha mightn't know that. And perhaps an ancestor would smile on Stopmouth even now.

He crouched, out of sight of the open space, and laid the sling on the ground. He placed a stone on top, larger than those he normally used.

So much the better, he thought. It certainly couldn't make his left-handed accuracy any worse. He found it hard to rise afterwards. The twinge in his recovering left leg joined in with the chorus of suffering from other parts of his body.

'Why move?' sang the pain. 'You're dead anyway. Why move?'

'For the Tribe,' he gasped. 'For Indrani.'

A moment to recover. Then he spun the sling and stepped into the open. Varaha must have spotted him or caught a glimpse of the whirling motion for he ducked just as Stopmouth released. The rock flew through the darkness, missing the spy by at least ten arm-lengths and crashing into the alley behind him.

Varaha leaped forward, ready for action. And then stopped. His eyes took in the chief's helpless condition and the now harmless sling hanging from his fingers. A broad smile crossed his face: arrogant, superior, triumphant. Why hadn't Stopmouth seen through him from the beginning?

'You missed,' said Varaha. He held his wooden necklace in one hand and Stopmouth realized the delicate object must be the green light weapon.

The chief's voice cracked with weariness and pain. 'I didn't miss. You're such a fool, Varaha. I tried to teach you to hunt along with the others, but you never took me seriously.'

The man's eyes narrowed. 'What are you talking about?' He must have heard something just then, for he turned to look behind him. But the starving Fourleggers, attracted by the noise, were already upon him. He yelled in fear. The green light flashed once and two of the beasts exploded backwards in a shower of blood. The third, however, rose onto its back legs and shoved sharp claws deep into his belly.

Varaha's eyes widened in disbelief and horror. The beast twisted its claws in the wound. Its victim managed a single high-pitched scream before the creature's other paw punctured his throat.

Stopmouth stepped closer to where Varaha had fallen. He couldn't leave the beast in possession of the Talker, not to mention the strange weapon – it might make all the difference in the short-term survival of the Tribe. 'Hey,' he said to the Fourlegger, pointing his sling at it. 'Leave this place or I will use my green light on you.'

It paused, staring at him. Maybe it was wondering how he could speak its language. Or perhaps it was weighing up the risks – death by starvation against death by green light.

'You may take one limb of your kill,' said Stopmouth. 'The rest belongs to me.' The effort of holding up the sling was becoming too much and his hand began to shake. The Fourlegger stared at him, daring him to shoot if he could. Then it roared at him. It tore a leg from its victim and ran back the way it had come.

Stopmouth sank to the ground, careful of his various agonies. Not least of them was the fear that Indrani was in trouble – already under the control of those who'd kill her as soon as she told them what they wanted to know. He daydreamed about going after her. Long ago she'd told him how to get to the Roof: thirty days' travel from here perhaps. Down the river to the giant Wetlane thing called 'sea', and then along the banks of 'sea' to a hill so tall it touched the sky. 'Stopmouth!' Was he still dreaming? He raised his head and saw her, directly above him, leaning out of the hatch of a jittery Globe, too near to the surface.

She had blood on her face. 'The pilot hit me,' she explained. 'He was more of a handful than he looked.'

They smiled at each other, too far apart to embrace, even if Stopmouth could have made it to his feet to do so.

'Wait,' she said. 'I don't want the pilot here when he wakes up.' She ducked back into the swaying craft and presently she slipped out the body of the hairy-lipped man. He fell twice his own height to land, little damaged, on the Fourlegger corpses. Indrani reappeared.

'I saw the weapon flash,' she said. 'I thought . . . I thought . . .'

'I'm all right,' he lied.

She smiled. 'I can't land here, can't even get close to you. You'll have to climb a building, the taller the better. But you need to hurry. They may already know what I've done. They'll be sending for the other Globes.'

Stopmouth looked at her, taking in the emotions running across her face: fear, excitement, love. Each made her beautiful in a different way. Each was uniquely Indrani.

'I can't come with you.'

'W-what?' A droplet of blood ran down her cheek to hang on her chin.

Her face blurred and he wiped his eyes. 'I'd be useless to you in the Roof, Indrani. You know that. I'd slow you down. But the people here . . . They wouldn't be alive by the time we came back. They need me.'

'Oh, Stopmouth.' And now she was crying too. He could see she wanted him to come with her, but must have known that he was right, that he had no choice in the matter.

'Promise me you'll come back,' he said.

'I have no Tribe, Stopmouth,' she said. 'No Tribe but you. Of course I'll come back. I'll find seeds for us to grow so nobody ever has to volunteer again. I'll find weapons to fight the Diggers. And I'll never leave you after.' Her voice broke into a sob. 'Never.'

A raucous sound came from inside the craft. Her eyes widened. 'They're – they're coming!'

'Go!' he said. 'Go and come back to me!'

She nodded, but stayed looking at him a few precious heartbeats more. Then she ducked back behind the closing hatch and the Globe rose straight into the air at great speed.

Stopmouth heard a groan from nearby. The pilot seemed to be waking up. He glanced in horror at the hunter beside him.

'By the gods!' he cried. He scrambled backwards through the guts of one of the Fourlegger corpses, then threw up at the sight of his gore-spattered clothes.

'Welcome to the Tribe,' said Stopmouth. Really, the man should be grateful to be alive.

The chief felt a wetness on his head, too warm to be Roofsweat. He touched his fingers to it and frowned when they came away red and sticky. He didn't remember getting a scalp wound. 'Indrani's!' he realized with a smile. This was the best of all possible omens.

'Your blood has come back to me,' he whispered, 'and so will you.'

He looked off in the direction she had flown. Her Globe had already become a dot. Another heartbeat, and it disappeared.

Acknowledgements

I need to thank the following people in order to avoid them killing me. They've worked hard to help me out of the many dead-ends I encountered on my way here. They know it and I know it. I grovel before them. I grovel even lower before those whose help I have selfishly forgotten.

David Fickling, who fell off a chair. Ben Sharpe, eagle-eyed and cruel. Tiffany, deliverer of soup and sushi. Patrick Walsh, agent of all he surveys. Sue 'the suggestor' Armstrong and Jake of the many contracts.

My readers were many and filled with helpful advice, such as, 'you should stick to the day job.' First among all comes Tracylea Byford, Mama of the Critterlitter writers group and instigator of extraordinary plots. Other early readers were Nathan D English, Alan Ennis, Peter Lee, Derek Cramer, Carlos Mendoza, Roberto Basavilbaso and Patrick Moran.

Those whose help was less concrete include my

long-suffering family: one very supportive mother; an equal number of sisters and my nephew, Luke, who always needs to know what's going on. Others include Alan Dee, who supplied the music, and web wizards like Manix McPhillips and DjTaz.

Last of all, I would especially like to thank Corky, who dances down the stairs in red shoes.

Read an excerpt from

THE
DESERTER

by PEADAR Ó GUILÍN

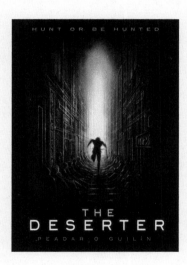

Available from David Fickling Books

Excerpt from *The Deserter* by Peadar Ó Guilín

Copyright © 2011 by Peadar Ó Guilín

Published in the United States by David Fickling Books, an imprint of Random House Children's Books, a division of Random House, Inc., New York. Originally published in Great Britain by David Fickling Books, an imprint of Random House Children's Books, a division of the Random House Group Ltd., London.

PROLOGUE

They're hunting for Indrani, combing the Roof, projecting her picture everywhere. Squads burst into apartments. They wave weapons, shine torches in women's faces. 'Is this her, do you think? Man, for a reward like that . . .'

But Indrani is hunting too. Everything she has seen in her short life has been recorded at ninety frames per second. Almost three billion images per year, and that's just the visual information! Smells too have been digitized and stored away; every odour encountered since the age of four, immaculately preserved on the tiny chance that she might want it again some day.

She can choose to play back the scent of her father's skin from the first fight she had with a rival toddler in the care group.

'Bad girl!' he'd said, but whenever she accesses that recording (one of her favourites), she can hear the pride he'd been trying to suppress over her victory. He was training her even then, whether he'd meant to or not; moulding her into 'the girl who never loses'. Until she lost *him*, murdered by Religious rebels.

What she especially likes about that scene is the slightly damp feel of her father's skin against hers. He'd been sweating, genuinely worried. Proof that he'd loved her, although he used to keep that kind of thing to himself.

But Indrani can't afford to wallow in childish triumphs. These days she spends far more time poring over the events leading up to the moment when she was shot down over the surface of the world. Somebody – *Say it, Indrani, say it*: the Commission, the rulers of the Roof, her supposed friends and allies – somebody had tried to have her killed. She can't understand that, but even stranger is the fact that they later changed their minds and went to enormous lengths to rescue her instead. 'We'll take you back,' they had promised. 'We'll allow your savage to live. Just come home . . .'

The answers to that riddle lie hidden deep amongst the 42,601,850,100 images that make up her life, or in the terabytes of sounds and smells, or the recordings of everything she has ever felt . . . All she has to do to save herself and those she loves is to dig it out.

Impossible, of course. More chance of a blind woman tracking down a single grain of rice on the surface of the world. Indrani cries sometimes at the thought of it. She never cried before leaving the Roof, but she's not 'the girl who never loses' any more. She has killed intelligent beings and eaten their flesh. She has suffered enough horror to realize how fragile happiness is, how eager the universe is to take it away.

So she keeps searching, always searching. And meanwhile the Commission, her pursuers, draw ever closer.

1. THE DESERTER

The Globe hovered no more than two man-heights above the injured Stopmouth. Indrani hung out of the door, blood on her chin, one hand stretching down towards him.

'Promise me you'll come back,' he said.

'Of course I'll come back. I'll find seeds for us to grow so nobody ever has to volunteer again. I'll find weapons to fight the Diggers. And I'll never leave you after.' Her voice broke into a sob. 'Never.'

Stopmouth woke with a groan. *I'm dreaming.* And he was. The usual awful dream.

Sweat drenched his body, and all the wounds he'd suffered the day Indrani left ached as though fresh. He missed her. He missed her *so* much. But in his sleep he never got to relive the great times they'd spent together. He only ever saw her leaving. Night after night.

A fire hissed and popped beside him. All around were the moans and whimpers of his poor little tribe, still trapped in sleep. Stopmouth paused. Were they usually this noisy?

He shook his head and grabbed a handful of pounded moss to mop away the chill of his sweat. As he raised his neck to wipe it clean, he chanced to look out of the window, and froze.

I'm still dreaming.

Stopmouth's heart began to pound in his chest. Beyond the circle of firelight lay only darkness. *Wake up, fool! Wake up!* The sky was completely black, with no lights where the camps of the dead should be. None at all. As though the Roof itself had disappeared and taken his Indrani with it.

He stumbled over to where the window should be, heart racing, his lips moving to childhood prayers. But even as he reached it, the grid of tracklights came on all at once for as far as the eye could see.

He waited for something more.

'Oh, go to sleep,' somebody groaned at him. It sounded like Kubar, his voice rough at the best of times. 'We've a big day tomorrow.'

Of course. The dream was always more vivid on nights like this.

A single big risk might win his vulnerable tribe a bit of breathing space, might even guarantee survival for generations to come. He'd need his rest. They all would.

He listened. Perhaps it was his imagination, but the fearful sounds of nightmare seemed to have died down already.

* * *

'Liven up, Stopmouth!' An elbow nudged him in the ribs and Rockface's foul breath exploded over his face in a cloud.

'Pay attention, hey?'

'Sorry, Rockface.' Stopmouth blinked. High above him the panels of the Roof glared with intense blue light. Once he'd believed the dead lived there – his ancestors and those of his enemies. 'I was just—'

'I know where you were, boy. The whole tribe knows.' Near them, in the shadows, other hunters pretended to be watching the streets, not listening as the big man scolded their young chief. The sisters Sodasi and Kamala whispered to each other, casting sidelong glances at them. Big, twitchy Vishwakarma struggled to keep still.

'Indrani's been gone a hundred and fifty days, but we're still here, hey? And we need you, especially for the next tenth.'

'Of course, of course.' Stopmouth gripped the Talker in his hand, a piece of magic from the Roof that hid his stutter from the others. He could feel himself doing it, though. It happened most when he was nervous or simply ashamed. Before he could pinpoint the cause, something moved in the shadows and everybody jumped.

Stopmouth hissed, 'Vishwakarma, no!'

Just in time.

'Sorry, Chief.' The man's warped spear pulled back from

the throat of a scout, a boy barely tall enough to reach Stopmouth's shoulder and too young to realize how close he'd come to death.

'They're on their way!' said the boy, panting hard.

'Fourleggers?' asked Stopmouth.

'Yes, yes! A trio of them.' The boy gestured into the alley behind him. 'Just one trio.'

Everybody smiled. These beasts always hunted in multiples of three. Had the ancestors wished the tribe ill, as many as nine might have been out there at once.

'Yama's leading them here now.'

Stopmouth nodded and signalled *Silence* to the others. Everybody knew what he meant. Fourleggers had hearing so good they'd be able to tell that Yama was alone and limping. From now on, anybody talking could spoil the plan and jeopardize the future of the struggling human tribe. There weren't enough of them to survive. Stopmouth had always known it. Sooner or later, one too many of his people would be hunted and eaten, or die in an accident, and their numbers would just collapse in a matter of days. It was always the way, always.

This lot would have been extinct already had it not been for the arrival of Stopmouth, Rockface and Indrani. The little group had saved the bigger and had, in return, been granted a home. If only Indrani had stayed. If only he could see her lovely face just one more time . . .

Rockface nudged him. Drifting again. Not allowed, not today. He had to get control of himself. He bit his lower lip hard enough to bleed, then stepped out carefully to where he could see the plaza, glaring in the unforgiving light of the Roof.

A moment later, he spotted the hobbling figure of Yama, moving as fast as his recovering injury would allow him. The boy was arrogant, but there had never been any doubting his bravery – he'd volunteered for this job. 'What if their ears are good enough to hear if someone's only *faking* a limp? They'll be looking out for trickery, but there's no hiding my scars, is there?'

As he ran, Yama never once glanced towards any of the places where his comrades hid. *Good man*, thought Stopmouth. The boy was learning at last, praise the ancestors.

Mere heartbeats later, the shadows stirred in the alleyway that Yama had just fled. A voice the human ear should never have been able to detect said, 'Hunting needs silence to listen.'

'No,' said another 'voice' translated by the Talker, 'hunting needs speed! It flees alone.'

'This one heard two of them,' insisted the first.

'Two, yes, but one strong enough to escape. Another is abandoned to us and waits only for our claws. We must not refuse it by delay.'

Stopmouth's eyes had adapted well enough now to see three Fourleggers, snouts pressed together in the shadow of a wall. They made no sound at all, but the Talker brought him what might have been their thoughts, or a language all of smells. Who knew? His hated brother, Wallbreaker, might have figured it out, but Stopmouth had escaped him long ago and hoped never to see him again.

From the alley through which Yama had run, a rock crashed to earth, and somebody cried out as though in pain and fear. The Fourleggers immediately separated and surged towards the source of the sound, all claws on the ancient road, spraying dirt and moss with each step. Vishwakarma stood up too soon, but the beasts scattered enough rubble to mask the sound. Stopmouth waited for the last of them to disappear into the alley. Then he shouted, 'Now!'

Humans emerged from hiding in every part of the plaza. Almost half the able-bodied men and women of the tribe were out today – a terrible, terrible risk. But this was to be no ordinary hunt; no mere search for food. They had bigger plans than that.

With the help of the ancestors, the Fourleggers would find that their limping prey had reached a dead end. He had climbed a rope ladder and pulled it up after himself.

'In,' shouted Stopmouth. 'Everybody into the nets! Use your clubs, not the spears! Clubs!'

And that was when everything went wrong.

A great *crack* rang through the air, followed by screams of terror from the people he'd placed on the roofs surrounding the alley. One whole house slowly curved itself over, like an injured man bending down. Then it fell in an explosion of dust and flying splinters.

Stopmouth saw the three beasts coming straight at him out of the cloud, running on all fours. Or trying to. One of them held a forelimb clear of the ground, and blood from a scalp wound dribbled over its eyes. Stopmouth knew it would have to dodge him to get away. He took aim with his club, but the wounded creature chose to smash into him instead, knocking him flying and tumbling with him to the ground.

'The pain!' it howled. But it scrambled to its feet before any of the humans could react, and only slingstones caught up with it after that. None struck home.

'Help me,' somebody said from the caved-in alley. Other groans were audible now as the stone settled down.

'I'm cut,' said Vishwakarma, blood streaming down his face. 'I think . . . I think . . . Oh, by the gods, by the gods, don't eat me, please don't . . .'

'Where are you, Vishwakarma, lad?' Rockface's breath was so bad, Stopmouth could actually smell him walking past. He reached the stricken Vishwakarma, a knife held behind his back. But he wouldn't have to use it. Even from the ground, Stopmouth could see that the wound was little more than a scratch. Others might not be so lucky. At least two had fallen from the roofs where they'd been stationed.

Rockface left Vishwakarma and walked back to the plaza, his back hunched over a little so as not to aggravate some of his old injuries.

'Ha!' he shouted.

'Get everyone together,' Stopmouth told Kubar. 'Find out if anybody's missing.'

Rockface was peering at something on the ground, one hand resting on a pile of rubble, the other pressed against his back, as if he feared his spine were about to force its way out into the air. His face showed only triumph, however.

Stopmouth crouched beside him and saw a small pile of rust-coloured scales smeared with sticky black blood.

'You want a live one, hey, Chief? Just able to talk?'

Stopmouth had a bad feeling about this. The big man was calmer since the injuries that had nearly stopped him hunting. Several times, in despair he'd volunteered the flesh of his body to feed the tribe, but small numbers and the battle for survival against the Skeletons had made food plentiful enough, so no such sacrifice had yet been necessary. Now he was almost back to his old cheerful self. A guarantee of trouble.

Stopmouth reached a calming hand towards the man's shoulder, but it was already too late.

'Come on,' said the grinning Rockface. 'We can still catch it, hey? Come on!'

'Rockface! Wait! We have to—'

But the big hunter had lost his hearing and was loping off after the trail of blood. Had it been anybody else, anybody at all, Stopmouth would have let him go, never expecting to see him again. The adults of the tribe had grown up in the Roof and knew little of survival before they'd met him. He'd drummed it into their heads again and again that a lone hunter was little better than a free meal for the first pack of beasts to pick up his scent.

He turned to the others. 'Vishwakarma! There's nothing wrong with you. Now, get up. Sodasi, Kamala, Kubar – you know what to do. You're the scouts. Get everybody home in one piece. No hunting, no trouble of any kind.'

He didn't wait for an answer. Rockface had already disappeared from the far side of the plaza. Stopmouth took off after him. As he ran, he checked his knife and sling. Apart from these, all he had was a club. There was no time to fetch a spear.

He heard his friend shouting from only a few streets away and picked up the pace. His leg hurt a little, and the shoulder he'd dislocated the day Indrani left would probably trouble him for the rest of his life. Yet it felt good to run by himself again, with no pack of inexperienced and clumsy hunters to slow him up. Buildings whipped past and his feet slapped over stone or sank into moss with a scatter of insects.

But then he ran round a corner to find the three beasts, one injured, two unscathed, standing over a fallen Rockface. Humans weren't the only ones capable of ambush.

He knew his friend was finished. In the old days, before the dozen injuries that plagued him and with his Armourback-shell spear in his hand, Stopmouth might have dared this fight with a slim, slim chance of success.

The best he could do now would be to flee, because the moment Rockface was dead, the two healthy Fourleggers would come after him. They were strong enough and hungry enough to drag a pair of full-grown humans home to feed their people.

'Go!' shouted Rockface, his voice hoarse. 'Go!'

'I can't,' said Stopmouth. He knew he had to run – he was the chief. He was *supposed* to run. Nothing else made sense.

One of the creatures looming above Rockface pulled back its arm, the claws aimed right at the fallen hunter's neck. Stopmouth would never get there in time. He swung the club above his head, thinking it might put the Fourlegger off long enough for him to make one final suicidal charge. The two other beasts had gone back onto all fours in preparation for just such a move. Their jaws were working as though they could already taste his flesh.